EAST END DIAMOND

Dani Oakley and D. S. Butler

If you would like to be informed when the new Dani Oakley book is released, sign up for the newsletter:

http://www.danioakleybooks.com/newsletter/

http://www.danioakleybooks.com

For My Family x

1

MARY DIAMOND GROANED AND COVERED her eyes. Bright sunlight poured in through the open curtains. Her head was pounding, and her mouth was so dry that her tongue stuck to the roof of her mouth.

Not again.

She'd fallen asleep in the armchair for the second night running. An empty bottle of gin was wedged between her body and the cushions. Her cheeks burned in shame. She knew little Jimmy was already up because he'd opened the curtains, and he'd tried to lay a fire in the grate.

He hadn't done a very good job, and the flames had already burned down to glowing embers, but the poor lad was only ten years old. He shouldn't have to do it in the first place. That was her job.

Her lip wobbled. She only hoped Jimmy hadn't spotted the bottle of gin.

Mary's fingers nervously tugged at the knitted blanket tucked around her legs. Jimmy must've covered her with it last night. She smothered a sob. The poor little sod. She knew he was worried about her, and that made her feel even worse.

He had started to watch her in the evenings. His big, dark blue eyes followed her every move. He didn't like her drinking, and who could blame him?

Mary rubbed her bleary eyes. This had to stop. She couldn't

carry on like this. She'd started drinking after Kathleen, Jimmy's mother, had died. At first, she just had a couple to help her sleep at night. After two or three gins, Mary found she wasn't plagued by the nightmares and night terrors that had haunted her previously.

These days, the trouble was she didn't stop at two or three. Her drinking started earlier and earlier, and yesterday… Well, yesterday was a complete blur. She couldn't even remember if she had cooked Jimmy any supper.

Mary leaned forward in the armchair, determined that today was the day she turned her life around. Little Jimmy deserved so much better. He hadn't had the best start in life, the poor little bleeder.

He was a sweet little boy. And thankfully he hadn't turned out anything like his father, the gangland boss, Martin Morton, who had ordered the death of Mary's precious daughter.

Of course, Mary couldn't prove that. The bastard was too clever for that.

She thanked her lucky stars Jimmy had turned out the way he had. There was no sign of Martin Morton's evil nature about him, and as much as she loved her daughter Kathleen, Mary was well aware that Kathleen used to be a little self-centred at times. Jimmy was a little angel in comparison.

Of course, he got into scrapes now and again just like any boy his age, but he was always polite and respectful.

Mary was determined to do right by him. When she'd brought him back to the East End, she had planned to reveal everything to the little boy.

She'd been so caught up with grief over her daughter, she hadn't thought about how delivering such news would affect Jimmy.

But Mary had come to her senses just in time and realised the innocent young boy shouldn't suffer the sins of his parents.

Mary struggled to stand up and then clasped a hand to her stomach as her belly churned.

Her gaze flickered back down to the gin bottle, but then she straightened her shoulders. No. She wouldn't have a drink. Not at this time of day. What she needed was a nice cup of Rosie. That would sort her out.

She shuffled across to the front door and opened it, shivering as the cold autumn breeze rushed in. She reached down for one of the milk bottles on the step, and as she did so, she lost her balance, cursing loudly and tumbling down the front step.

The bottle of milk smashed, and milk splattered everywhere. Mary shouted out a string of expletives before realising she was being watched.

Across the road, the Mackenzie family, a young couple and their small daughter, stared at Mary in horror.

She knew she must look a right state this morning, and they'd seen her stumbling about all over the place as though she were still drunk. But instead of dropping her head and scurrying back inside, Mary glared at them angrily.

"What the bleeding hell are you looking at?" she yelled across the street.

Laura Mackenzie gasped in shock, put her hands over her little girl's ears and ushered her inside as Mary stooped down to pick up the other bottle of milk that thankfully was still in one piece.

She trudged back inside, unable to face clearing up the mess just yet. She would tackle that after she'd had a cup of tea.

She made her way back to the kitchen and put the kettle on to boil before carefully spooning tea leaves into her teapot.

She walked through into the larder and saw she had some potatoes and a couple of carrots. She frowned and tried to remember the last time she'd been to the shops.

She decided she'd go to the butcher's and get a little bit of beef and make a stew for Jimmy's supper.

He loved stew, and heaven knew he deserved a treat after the last few days.

Perhaps, she thought as she poured the hot water onto the tea leaves, they could go down and visit Bev in Romford this weekend. Jimmy loved going to Bev's little bungalow, and she couldn't blame him. It was a lovely little place, and the garden backed onto a nice children's play area. Mary often wondered if she had done the right thing by bringing Jimmy back to the East End.

She put off telling Jimmy everything she knew about his mother's death, but she couldn't delay the inevitable. As he got older, he was bound to hear gossip. Mary sighed. For all she knew, the poor lad had already been teased about it at school.

Jimmy loved to hear stories about his mother, and Mary would tell him how beautiful and clever she was. He would listen to Mary talk about Kathleen with a soft, dreamy smile on his face, but he'd stopped asking questions about how she'd died a few years ago.

Mary lifted her cup of tea with shaking hands and took a sip.

She only had a few hours before Jimmy would be home from school, and the butcher would be out of the best cuts of meat by now anyway. Maybe she should do the stew tomorrow. She could always nip down to Maureen's and pick up some pie and mash for supper.

Mary lowered her cup of tea and put it down on the kitchen table and then slowly walked back to the front room.

She looked at the bottle of gin that was still propped up in the corner of the armchair. There was only a dribble left in the bottom, but Mary had another couple of bottles stashed away upstairs.

Perhaps she could have one quick sip... The hair of the dog would do the trick and get the day started. After all, the way she felt right now, she wasn't going to get a lot done. Surely one small drink wouldn't hurt.

***

When Jimmy Diamond arrived home from school, the first thing he saw was the smashed bottle of milk on the doorstep. Thinking something terrible might have happened to his grandmother, Jimmy pushed open the front door and quickly ran inside.

He breathed a sigh of relief when he saw his grandmother dozing in her favourite armchair but scowled when he saw the bottle of gin. He was sure that was a new one. It had a white label and the label on the bottle he had seen that morning had been red.

He reached over and gently pulled the knitted blanket up to his nan's chin as she let out a loud snore.

He screwed the bottle cap back on the gin, so it didn't spill, and then headed into the kitchen.

He was absolutely starving.

He'd found a lump of stale bread in the larder this morning and had eaten it for breakfast with the last of the margarine.

He knew his nan would be out for the count for the rest of the evening, so he had two choices: find himself some food or go without.

He stepped into the small larder just off the kitchen and gazed at the shelves.

They didn't look any different to when he looked this morning.

There were a couple of potatoes and a single carrot. Jimmy reached for the carrot and took a bite out of it without bothering to peel it.

Jimmy's stomach rumbled as he thought of the last meal his grandmother had prepared him. Beef hash… his mouth watered. Although he'd settle for bread and beef dripping right now, anything to fill the emptiness in his stomach.

He supposed he could go to his mate's and try to scrounge

dinner at his house. But Jimmy knew if he did that too often people would start talking. The last time he'd had dinner at Bobby's house, Bobby's mother had launched into a round of questions, asking him how often his nan cooked his tea and asking when was the last time he'd had a bath.

Jimmy didn't mind missing baths so much, but the food...he missed that like mad.

His stomach growled loudly as he polished off the last of the carrot. It wouldn't keep him going for long. He didn't want to get his nan in trouble, or cause people to gossip about her, but he was starving. He had to do something. Maybe he could ask Bobby to sneak him out some bread. He rubbed his stomach as he walked out of the kitchen and tiptoed past his nan, who was still snoring in the chair.

When he opened the front door, he saw the smashed milk bottle still scattered on the front step. He carefully picked up the broken pieces of glass, put them in the dustbin and ducked back inside to grab a cloth. After tidying it up the best he could, he headed off towards Bobby Green's house. He chose the route that would take him past the chip shop. When he turned the corner, the delicious smell of vinegar on hot chips wafted past him. Jimmy breathed in deeply, and looked enviously at a man, leaving the shop, carrying his fish supper wrapped in newspaper.

Jimmy hadn't gone much further when he saw Linda, who was heading home from work. He'd been so focused on the chip shop, he hadn't noticed her until she was almost beside him.

Jimmy liked Linda. She'd been a friend of his mother's, and he liked hearing her talk about the old days. Nan said Linda and Jimmy's mother had been ever so close, and since Jimmy was never going to get to know his mother, talking to Linda about her seemed to be the next best thing.

She smiled widely as she approached him. "Hello, Jimmy. How are you and your nan doing?"

"We are fine, thank you," Jimmy said politely.

Linda frowned as she looked down at Jimmy's skinny legs poking out of his school shorts. "Shouldn't you be home by now?" Linda asked. "I'm sure your nan's got dinner on the table."

Jimmy looked down at the floor. He didn't want to lie to Linda. But he didn't want to cause his nan any grief. His nan was a very private person, and she'd hate it if anybody saw her in the state she was in now. Just last week, she'd broken down in tears, apologising to Jimmy, promising him that soon things would get better, and she'd sworn to stop her drinking for good.

She hadn't stopped drinking yet, but Jimmy was positive she would soon.

He thought, just this once, a little white lie wouldn't hurt. "Actually, we are having chips tonight. She's just sent me out to get them."

Linda looked quite surprised and then she glanced over her shoulder at the chip shop two doors along. "They do smell nice."

Jimmy nodded. "Yes, I like them best with lots of vinegar."

"Me too. Don't let me hold you up," Linda said, nodding towards the shop entrance.

Jimmy's eyes widened. Now he was going to be caught out in his lie. Nan hadn't sent him for chips, and he didn't have any bleeding money anyway. He shoved his hands into the pockets of his shorts and pretended to search for a coin.

"Oh, no!" he said. "I forgot to pick up the money."

Linda wasn't stupid, and Jimmy was sure she hadn't fallen for his lie. As Linda looked at him with pity-filled eyes, Jimmy felt his cheeks burn. He didn't like people feeling sorry for him, but he'd feel even worse if Linda knew he was a liar.

He considered telling Linda the truth and then quickly gave up on that idea. If Linda went back and told his nan about this, there would be hell to pay. His nan always said loyalty to family came first, and if she found out he'd told anybody their personal business, she'd have his guts for garters.

Jimmy turned on his heel. "I'd better get back home and pick up the money then," he said.

Linda shook her head, and her long, brown, glossy hair swung around her shoulders. "No, don't bother going all the way back home, Jimmy. Here, take this." She rummaged around in her bag and then pulled out her purse and extracted a shilling. "Get the chips with this."

Jimmy could have hugged her. Chips! Oh, he couldn't wait! His mouth watered at the prospect, and he reached out to take the coin from Linda before she changed her mind.

"Thank you very much," Jimmy said, beaming at her. "It's very nice of you. If you wait here, I'll go in and then give you your change."

Linda smiled and ruffled Jimmy's hair. "Nonsense," she said. "You get your chips and keep the change. Maybe you can get yourself a little treat tomorrow?"

Jimmy rubbed the shilling between his finger and thumb, grinning, unable to believe his luck.

"It's the least I can do for my best friend's little boy," Linda said, smiling fondly at him.

Jimmy imagined his mother would be a lot like Linda, kind and sweet, and at times like this, Jimmy missed her badly, even though he'd never really known her.

Jimmy ducked inside the chip shop and asked for two portions of chips. He doubted his nan would wake up this evening, but if she didn't, it didn't matter. Jimmy was so hungry, he was quite sure he could polish off two portions.

Linda waved goodbye and then crossed the road, continuing her journey home.

He'd overheard a conversation between his nan and her friend, Phyllis, talking about Linda. They'd talked about the fact Linda had been married for a while now, but she didn't have any children of her own. Jimmy wondered if that was why she was so nice to him. Maybe she liked the idea of him being around.

As he walked home, eating his chips and licking the salt and vinegar from his fingers, Jimmy Diamond grinned. He thought his life was pretty good all things considered.

2

BABS MORTON FORCED HERSELF TO smile as she tapped a long, painted fingernail on the kitchen table impatiently. She was trying to talk some sense into her husband's brother, Tony.

Since Martin had been banged up, Tony had been the face of Martin's outfit. Behind-the-scenes, though, Babs ran the show. Of course, it wouldn't do to let Tony believe that. Babs was careful to flatter him and present her ideas and strategies very subtly, so that nine times out of ten, Tony believed he came up with the ideas himself.

It had worked brilliantly up until now. As the years had passed, Babs carefully guided Tony through various conflicts and troubles.

They played the long game, making sure they were earning enough to keep them all afloat but not getting greedy. The last thing they wanted was any trouble. Without Martin Morton's physical presence, they were vulnerable. Martin's reputation still counted for a lot in the area, but they couldn't risk encroaching on the territory belonging to other faces in the East End. Babs had been especially careful not to get on the bad side of Dave Carter.

But now it was time for a change.

They needed to expand, and they needed to be clever about it.

Right now, they were just treading water, and people were starting to realise that. Once word got out that the Morton group were weakening, especially with Martin behind bars, they'd lose respect, and in this game, respect was everything.

But trying to explain that to Tony was like trying to explain it to a brick wall.

Tony was far better looking than Martin. He was suave and appeared sophisticated, and he certainly knew how to charm the ladies. Unfortunately, his good looks were the only thing he had going for him. Babs was convinced he had nothing between the ears except cotton-wool.

"Of course, you know far more about these things than I do, Tony," Babs began. Flattering Tony, was a necessary evil. "But I've been hearing whispers lately, and red-haired Freddie told me the landlord at the Queen Victoria was a little reluctant to hand over the money he owed us."

Tony gave her an easy smile. Nothing seemed to bother him much to Babs' irritation.

"It's nothing for you to worry about, love," he said. "You know you can leave the business to me. Everything is in good hands."

Babs smiled again, this time through gritted teeth. The stupid man really didn't realise that she'd been the one keeping the business afloat all these years. Without her, Tony would have run the whole thing into the ground long before now.

"Oh, you're doing a fine job, Tony. I know that, but on my last visit, Martin mentioned he wasn't happy that takings were down. I really do think he'd like things to be ticking over nicely when he comes out."

Tony's ears pricked up at the mention of his brother's name. Tony was eager to please Martin. All his adult life, Tony had played second fiddle to his gangster brother, Martin.

Babs expected entering the real world had come as a shock

to Tony. As a child, he'd been spoiled rotten. He was his mother's favourite, and as a boy, he'd never had to work hard for anything, so it wasn't really surprising he didn't have the same grit and determination as Martin.

But his brother's opinion meant a lot to him, so Babs was counting on this as a way to persuade him.

"What did Martin say exactly?" Tony frowned.

Babs shrugged her shoulders. "Oh, you know me, Tony. All that business stuff goes right over my head, but he did say it was important to try and take on new business and go after our competitors aggressively. Otherwise, he reckons people will start to think we are weak."

Tony's frown deepened. "Weak?"

A flash of anger played over Tony's handsome features, and Babs wondered whether she'd gone too far. "That's only what Martin said. Of course, I don't think you are weak."

Tony nodded and was quiet for a moment as he thought over Babs' words. You could almost hear the wheels turning in his brain, Babs thought. It was becoming harder and harder to manipulate Tony these days. Overseeing Martin's business interests had filled him with confidence and the silly man had let the success go to his head. He really believed he was responsible.

Martin hadn't really said anything about changing their strategy the last time she went to visit him. But if that little white lie aided her progress, Babs didn't see anything wrong with it.

To be honest, she'd been a little bit worried about Martin the last time she'd seen him.

For the first few years, he'd been banged up, Martin was ever so keen to hear all about how the business was running on the outside, and he was obsessed with ensuring no one tried to muscle in on his patch — especially Dave Carter.

But over the last six months, Martin really seemed to be drifting away from the real world. Every time she went to visit him, he only wanted to talk about prison life, and enjoyed telling her how he was throwing his weight around, making sure everybody knew he was the boss.

Babs couldn't see the point. It wasn't like he could earn much in prison. So what if a bunch of criminals let him boss them around? Martin had a small black market ring organised, and he was blackmailing a couple of prison guards, but that was small potatoes compared to the money the real business brought in.

They still had the club, of course, and although they'd had to cut back on the protection racket that still brought in a fair few pennies every week. They'd ramped up the sale of the black market booze and cigarettes, and that definitely helped.

But there were so many opportunities out there for the taking, and Babs wanted to exploit them if only she could make Tony see sense.

Just when she thought she might be finally making some headway, the front door opened, and she heard her children making a racket as they made their way inside.

Babs got up from her seat at the kitchen table and went to see her children. Ruby and Derek were now teenagers, and they were both sour, moody individuals.

As soon as Martin had been locked up, Babs had quickly sold their house in Essex and moved back to Poplar. She'd never really liked living out in the country anyway. She was definitely a city girl. London was her heart and soul.

Unfortunately, the children had started to settle and make friends in Essex, so they resented her for making them move back. Babs simply hadn't been able to cope. A few months after Martin got sent down, their youngest had died. Little Emily hadn't lived to see her second birthday. The child's death had devastated Babs, and she hadn't been able to cope. Frieda Longbottom, an old family friend, had saved Babs in that dark, tragic time. She took care of Ruby and Derek when Babs couldn't look at them without bursting into tears.

Over the past few years, she'd tried to make it up to Ruby and Derek but ended up just spoiling the kids with material possessions, giving them anything they asked for. Sadly, that didn't make the children any happier. Instead, they both developed surly attitudes and miserable scowling demeanours. They could be rude little sods at times, too, especially when they spoke to Babs. She was at the end of her tether.

"Hello, sweethearts. Shall I put the kettle on and we can all have a cup of tea together? Frieda brought round a fruit cake earlier."

"No. I'm going out with my mates," Derek grunted as he dumped his school bag on the floor and nipped back out the front door before Babs could say anything.

Babs smothered her frustration and turned to her daughter. "What about you, Ruby? Uncle Tony is in the kitchen. Why don't you come and say hello?"

Ruby lost her scowl as soon as Babs mentioned Uncle Tony. For some reason, both of her children thought the sun shone out of their uncle's backside. Babs couldn't figure it out.

Babs set about making the tea as Ruby told Tony all about her day at school. To his credit, Tony at least appeared to look interested.

But Babs wasn't really listening to her daughter's inane chatter as she put the tea leaves in the teapot. She was still thinking about the best way to persuade Tony to expand their business interests. So she was surprised when Ruby said, "Mum, are you even listening to us?"

Babs turned around. "Sorry, what was that, love?"

"Uncle Tony was saying Grandma Violet wants us to go around hers tonight for our tea."

Babs suppressed a shudder. She couldn't bloody stand Violet Morton, and the feeling was mutual. Martin's mother had disliked Babs since the first day she'd met her. She was constantly criticising Martin and that included his choice of wife. She'd remained disappointed with Babs ever since.

She quickly tried to think of a way to get out of it. They'd sprung this on her on purpose. Over the last few months, she'd managed to avoid visiting Violet by making up some excuse or another every time she was invited.

"It will save you cooking, Babs," Tony said, trying to be encouraging.

Babs felt her shoulders slump. It was pointless trying to resist. She couldn't get out of it this time.

"All right," she said and then turned to Ruby. "You'd better go and find your brother. He needs to have a wash before he goes to his grandmother's."

Ruby got to her feet and trudged out of the kitchen towards the front door.

How both of her kids had turned into such sulky little bleeders was beyond Babs. She sighed and patted her platinum blonde hair. She needed to look good for her face off with Violet. The woman had eyes like an eagle, and God forbid she saw Babs or her children with so much as a hair out of place. The last family dinner a few months back had been derailed after Violet had spotted a smudge of dirt on Derek's cheek.

She gritted her teeth. The last thing Babs needed was a blooming family dinner at Violet's, but it didn't look like she was going to get out of it.

3

"I'D LIKE A WORD, MALCOLM," Martin Morton said with a broad smile as he looked at the prison screw.

The man flushed and shiftily looked from side to side to make sure they were unobserved before following Martin along the corridor.

Martin had been in prison a long time, certainly long enough to know the ropes. Most of the screws were on the take here and there, and Martin knew how to play the game to his advantage.

If he had to be locked up, then Martin was going to make the best of it. That meant enjoying little luxuries that weren't usually afforded to prisoners. It also meant exercising his sadistic streak when he fancied it.

He wasn't wearing plimsolls. Instead, he had some very comfortable handmade leather shoes someone had smuggled in for him and the prison guards were smart enough to turn a blind eye. Last week someone had given him a pair of Chinese-style slippers and a pure silk dressing gown. It looked fancy, and Martin got a kick out of wearing it as he knew it irritated the screws.

Martin led the way into his cell and gestured for Malcolm to follow him as if he was welcoming him into his home. Well, Martin supposed it was his home, at least for now, and an Englishman's home was his castle.

He'd been allowed many comforts that were usually banned, which made his time in prison a little more tolerable than it might have been otherwise. He had an elegantly carved antique bookshelf with framed photographs of his children set on top. Babs had brought him in some special shaving soap, although the screws had drawn the line at allowing Martin his own razor.

Stopping at the end of the cell, Martin turned to Malcolm and fixed him with a hard stare. Malcolm had turned up at Wandsworth two years ago, and much to Martin's disgust, he refused to be bought. Right from the start, he was out to cause Martin trouble.

Martin never had a problem with other prisoners — they could always be dealt with using violence, and he was good at that. But the screws required gentle handling. It hadn't taken long for most of them to come around to Martin's way of thinking.

It was amazing how a few quid bunged in the right direction had eased Martin's life in prison. But Malcolm had remained stubbornly indifferent to Martin's bribes.

The last straw had been two months ago when Malcolm had taken it upon himself to confiscate Martin's bag of toiletries.

It had started off as a normal inspection. The screws carried them out half-heartedly every week or so. Usually Martin, along with all the other inmates, stood outside the cells and one of the guards would come in and take a token look around, pretend he couldn't see anything contraband and leave again.

But six weeks ago, Malcolm had been part of the inspection team.

He'd grabbed Martin's wash bag and smirked as he made a tut-tutting sound.

Martin had let his temper get the better of him.

Unable to restrain himself, he'd swung for Malcolm,

bruising his cheekbone, and knocking him to the floor before the other guards had rushed into the cell to hold him back.

That had earned him some time in solitary. Apparently, there was a limit to what even Martin Morton could get away with.

The entire time he'd been in solitary, Martin had plotted his revenge. Sure he could slit Malcolm's throat before one of the guards got to him, but that wasn't what Martin wanted.

He wanted Malcolm to submit to him and become one of his lackeys. That would be the ultimate win in Martin's opinion.

Luckily, after a week in solitary confinement, Martin had been pleased to see all his belongings had been returned to his cell in his absence.

He'd had a good long talk with the governor over cigars in his office. Although the governor, had apologised for the incident, he'd explained tactfully Martin couldn't go around hitting prison guards and expect to get away with it.

Martin nodded and agreed with the stupid bastard, all the while seething and planning Malcolm's downfall.

Today, the big day had finally arrived. Malcolm would soon understand who held the power in this prison.

"Would you like to take a seat?" Martin asked grandly, even though there was only one chair in the room.

It was a hardback, wooden chair, but his mother had brought him in a nice, plump cushion which made it far more comfortable.

Resentment burned in Malcolm's eyes, and Martin knew he didn't want to be here. That just made it even more gratifying.

Malcolm perched his arse on the edge of the chair. "Let's get on with this, Morton. I've got things to do."

Martin gave him a tight smile, but other than that, he didn't show how Malcolm's disrespect bothered him. Instead, he turned around and lifted the bottom of the mattress, extracting a large brown envelope.

With a grin, he held it under Malcolm's nose. "Have a gander at that, mate."

Malcolm's eyes widened a little as he looked at it. Then he looked back up at Martin, but he didn't take the envelope straight away.

Martin shoved it in his hands. "Go on. Take a look inside."

"Not so tough now, are you?" Martin murmured as he watched the man's hands tremble as he opened it.

Malcolm's cheeks paled as he pulled the contents from the envelope. Inside, were four, large, glossy black-and-white prints.

By the time he completely extracted the photographs from the envelope, Malcolm was sweating profusely.

He clutched them to his chest in horror as if he could stop anybody else seeing the contents.

It didn't matter. Martin had already seen the photographs, and he'd paid the man who took them.

"Of course, it's none of my business what you screws get up to in your personal life. But I think the governor might be a bit put out if he saw those, not to mention your wife."

At the mention of his wife, Malcolm's cheeks flamed red. "How dare you! You bastard!" Spittle gathered at the corner of his mouth as he shouted at Martin.

The plonker had overstepped the mark. Martin took two steps across the small cell and wrapped his hands around Malcolm's throat. As he squeezed, Malcolm's eyes bulged, and his cheeks turned purple. Martin felt a rush of pure joy. There really was nothing like holding someone's life in your hands…literally.

The photographs Malcolm had been clutching to his chest fell to the floor, but Martin didn't bother to look.

He knew there were various shots of Malcolm dressed up in women's clothing. Apparently, Malcolm liked to go to a club in Soho called Claudette's, which catered largely to transvestites.

Martin also knew Malcolm was having a relationship with a man called Brian, despite the fact he had a wife and two kids at home.

Everyone has secrets, and therein lies their weakness, Martin thought as he tightened his grip. It was just a matter of finding a secret and exploiting it to your advantage. That was the real path to power.

As Malcolm's struggles grew weaker and weaker, Martin forced himself to let go. He didn't want to. He wanted to strangle the life out of the little sod, but that would only add more years to his sentence. If they sent him to solitary for punching a guard, what would they do if he killed one?

No blasted solicitor would take him on for an appeal, and the last thing Martin wanted was more years inside.

When he let go, Malcolm collapsed onto the floor in a heap, wheezing.

He clawed at the collar of his shirt. "You crazy bastard. You nearly killed me."

Martin looked down at the man in disgust. "Get up off the floor, you flaming streak of piss. Pick up those photographs and take them out of my sight. You can burn them if you like. It doesn't matter. I've got copies. From now on, I'm the boss of you, and you will do everything I say. Do you understand me?"

Malcolm nodded, but he was still breathing too heavily to reply.

It didn't matter.

Martin's victory was sweet. He could see the despair in Malcolm's eyes. The man knew he had been beaten, and he'd accepted his fate.

***

Jimmy had finished the first bag of chips in no time, but he carried the other newspaper-wrapped parcel of chips under the crook of his arm.

He'd returned home just to check whether his nan was awake and hungry, but she was still asleep in her armchair, snoring loudly. So Jimmy decided to eat the second portion later.

He now wished he hadn't gobbled down the first lot of chips so fast because his stomach had been empty for so long it had given him a bellyache.

But he hadn't been able to stop himself. The chips had been the most delicious thing he'd ever tasted.

He didn't want to stay indoors and listen to his nan snoring for the rest of the evening, so he decided to take a walk past the old bomb site to see if any of his mates were hanging about.

None of Jimmy's friends were there, but he recognised a group of boys, who were a couple of years above him at school, hanging around beside a row of terraced houses that were soon to be demolished.

Jimmy contemplated joining them, but it didn't look like they were doing anything interesting. It seemed like they were kicking about a bundle of rags.

Jimmy tightened his grip on his parcel of chips and turned around, preparing to go home, when he heard a shout.

It sounded like somebody in pain.

When he turned back, he saw the bundle of rags they were kicking was, in fact, a little boy.

Jimmy didn't recognise the lad. He couldn't see him properly from where he stood. Jimmy dropped his chips. There were five of those big lads, and the boy on the floor looked even younger than Jimmy.

"That ain't fair," Jimmy muttered under his breath. He stashed his bag of chips beside a pile of rubble and strode across to them, shouting out as he went. "Oi!"

His shout attracted the older boys' attention, and they turned around to face him, momentarily leaving the little boy on the ground alone.

The looks they gave him made Jimmy's stomach twist nervously. But he didn't regret intervening. Jimmy Diamond wasn't afraid of a fight. He'd seen plenty of them.

The fact that his mother had been murdered was common knowledge, as was the fact he'd been born out of wedlock, so he'd experienced plenty of fights after kids had teased him about being an orphan and a bastard.

He pulled himself up to his full height, which was still head and shoulders below the tallest boy of the group.

"Leave him alone," Jimmy said, trying to sound stern as he came to a stop just a couple of feet from the group of boys.

The tallest boy stepped forward in front of Jimmy. "And what are you going to do about it if we don't?"

In the past being hotheaded hadn't got Jimmy very far, so he tried a different tactic. "Look. He's only a little'un."

Jimmy pointed at the little boy on the floor, who had sat up and was looking at Jimmy with wide tearstained eyes.

Now he was closer, Jimmy recognised him as Georgie Carter. He was in the same year as Jimmy at school, but everybody knew Georgie was a little bit slow, and that just made Jimmy angrier. What kind of person picked on somebody like that?

Georgie had only been at Jimmy's school for a few months. Before that, he'd been in a special school. When he'd arrived, Jimmy's favourite teacher, Miss Muswell, had told them all they needed to make Georgie feel very welcome.

"What do you know about it, bastard?" one of the boys taunted.

He had a spotty face and greasy hair, and Jimmy knew he was what his nan would describe as all mouth and no trousers. Although he shouted out his comments, he hung back behind his friends. If it came down to a one-on-one with him, Jimmy knew he could beat that kid no problem.

The trouble was it wasn't one-on-one. Right now, it was five against one because it didn't look like little Georgie was putting up much of a fight.

"Come on," Jimmy said. "You've had your fun. Let the poor little bleeder go home."

The tallest one, the one Jimmy had now recognised as the ringleader, took a menacing step forward.

"And who's gonna make me?"

Jimmy gave a cocky smile. "Me," he said simply.

Perhaps most people would have held back and not thrown the first punch, but Jimmy had spent the last several years learning how to fight.

There was no honour in a street fight, no rules, and he knew now that a fight was inevitable. The time for talking was over. His survival instinct kicked in, and he knew that he had to go in first and go in hard.

With a roar of outrage, Jimmy rushed forward and grabbed the tall boy's school shirt. He yanked it down hard, giving him the chance to bring his head down hard on the bridge of the boy's nose.

It took a moment for the other boys to realise what had happened.

The tall ringleader took a couple of steps backwards, staggered a little before falling down on his arse, dazed from the head-butt. Blood poured from his nose, and his eyes watered so hard it looked as if he was crying.

Before Jimmy could congratulate himself, the other boys charged him.

This time, he didn't have the element of surprise on his side, and he only got a couple of blows in before he realised the best use of his hands was trying to defend his head and ribs from their punches and kicks.

As they continued to rain blows down on him, Jimmy thought it would never end until finally he heard the sound of a deep, male voice.

Suddenly all the blows stopped, and when Jimmy dared to look up, he saw a huge man towering above him, holding one of the boys by the scruff of the neck and shaking him as if he was a rag doll.

Jimmy held his breath.

Was this man a policeman? Was he going to get into trouble?

Surely his nan would understand if Jimmy explained he was only trying to stick up for poor little Georgie Carter.

The man flung the boy to the ground, and within seconds, it was all over. All the boys had scarpered.

Jimmy was too scared to move. The man glaring down at him looked so furious. All Jimmy could do was gaze up at him mesmerised.

He was so caught up in this new arrival, he didn't even notice little Georgie coming over and putting a hand on his shoulder.

"Thanks for s…sticking up for me," Georgie said with a lisp. He handed him a handkerchief.

When Jimmy took it, but didn't do anything with it, Georgie stuttered, "You've got some b…blood on your nose."

Jimmy managed to mumble thanks and then clamped the handkerchief to his nose to try and stem the blood.

The tall man standing beside them kneeled down and put his face close to Jimmy's. His eyes were sharp and unflinching, and Jimmy felt like the man could see inside his head and read his mind. "What's your name, son?"

Jimmy gulped. He was a policeman. Oh no. Now he would get in trouble and those bullies would get off scot-free.

But little Georgie didn't seem to be afraid of this huge man. To Jimmy's amazement, he put his arm around his shoulder and hugged him.

"His name is Jimmy, Dad. He goes to the same school as me."

Dad? Jimmy's mind scrambled to make sense of the situation. Georgie Carter…did that mean this man was Dave Carter? Even Jimmy had heard of him, mainly from his nan telling him to steer well clear of the Carters. But Carter was a common enough name and Jimmy would never have suspected little Georgie was related to the notorious gangster.

Jimmy felt a wave of relief. At least he wasn't a copper. Maybe he wouldn't get into trouble, after all. He could nip back over to the other side of the bomb site, collect his chips and be on the way home. With any luck, he'd be able to see to his cuts and bruises before his nan noticed them.

"What was going on here?" the man demanded.

"Jimmy was sticking up for me. Those boys were bullying me again."

The man turned back to Jimmy. "My name is Dave Carter."

He held out his hand, and Jimmy looked at it in amazement. It took him a moment to realise he was supposed to shake it.

When he did, he felt a bit silly. His tiny hand was dwarfed against Dave Carter's huge fingers.

"Thank you for sticking up for my boy."

Jimmy managed to speak finally. "I like Georgie. Those other kids are older than us. They shouldn't be picking on him."

Dave Carter stood up and then turned his head, looking off into the distance. The bullies had run off in that direction but there was no sign of them now.

"I couldn't agree more, Jimmy. And I can promise you something. Their families are going to regret what happened today."

Jimmy looked up at him in awe and shivered. He suddenly felt very glad that he wasn't one of those boys.

4

DAVE CARTER LIKED TO THINK he was a man in control of his emotions, but when he'd seen little Georgie bruised and battered, he'd been filled with fury. It was all he could do to restrain himself from wringing those little bastard's necks.

He'd taken Georgie straight home, carrying the boy in his arms as though he were a baby again. Every time he looked at Georgie's tear-streaked face, he felt another wave of fury flood his body.

Georgie seemed to sense his father's dark mood and didn't ask any questions or talk at all on the way home.

After Dave stepped through the front door of their terraced house, he sat Georgie down on his feet.

"Let's get you cleaned up." Dave tried to keep his voice gentle, but it sounded gruff.

Only now he had brought Georgie safely home did he allow himself to focus on what he was going to do next.

Dave could always keep a level head when dealing with business, but this wasn't business. It was personal. He couldn't get over the fact that those boys had taken such liberty. Did they not know who Georgie's father was? Or did they not care?

Dave was going to make Georgie tell him the names of every one of those boys, so he could pay their parents a special visit. They would soon learn not to mess with Dave

Carter's family.

Dave pulled off Georgie's coat and hung it on the peg along with his own, and all the while, Georgie kept his big blue eyes fixed on his father.

"Are you angry with me, Dad?" Georgie asked.

Dave shook his head. "Of course, I'm not. I'm angry with those horrible boys. Now go upstairs and wash your face."

Georgie nodded and then slowly turned and started plodding his way upstairs.

Dave walked into the kitchen. He was still shaking with anger. He hated feeling like this. He was used to being in control.

Sandra was sitting at the kitchen table, looking dazed. She hadn't even looked up when Dave entered the kitchen. It wasn't surprising really. She was drugged up to the bleeding eyeballs again.

Dave ran a hand through his hair in frustration.

Sandra had started popping the pills straight after Georgie was born.

He'd understood at first. After all, anything that helped her through that awful time when they lost Lillian had to be a good thing.

Dave had expected it to be a temporary stopgap. The trouble was Sandra never stopped taking the pills.

She blinked up at him now, finally realising he was in the kitchen.

"Oh, hello, love. I didn't realise the time. I'll get dinner on."

She got up from the chair and wobbled, leaning heavily on the kitchen table to support herself.

"Don't worry," Dave said. "I'll fix something for us."

The boys would both have to put up with bread and cheese tonight. There was no way Dave could risk letting Sandra loose in the kitchen. The last time she'd cooked when she'd been this drugged up she'd managed to set the chip pan on fire. He wasn't chancing that again.

He looked at his wife and wondered whether it was possible for them to go back to how it had been before they'd lost Lillian. Dave knew he had changed as well. He was colder now and less emotional.

For the first six months after Georgie's birth, he could barely stand to hold the poor little sod. It wasn't Georgie's fault he was born on the same day as his sister's funeral.

In his heart, he knew it was wrong, but he'd resented Georgie. Nobody could replace Lillian in his affections, but as Georgie got older, Dave couldn't help but grow to love him. He had such a good heart, and he was the sweetest little boy. It wasn't his fault he was a bit slow. The doctor had said it was because he was born too early.

"Sit down, love," he said to Sandra, trying to keep his voice soft.

She had started moving about the kitchen, picking things up and putting them down again, and right now, she was standing there with a knife, looking bewildered as though she couldn't remember where it went.

Sandra licked her lips, nodded slowly and then sat back down at the kitchen table.

Dave sat opposite her and reached for her hand.

"I found some boys bullying little Georgie," Dave said. "But you're not to worry. I'm going to sort it."

Sandra's forehead wrinkled with a frown as though she struggled to understand him.

Dave removed his hand from Sandra's and sat back from the table, pulling away from her. What chance did his boys have when their mother was acting like this?

He wanted to shake some sense into her, but Dave had never laid a finger on a woman in his life and wasn't about to start now.

He turned as he heard the front door open. It was Trevor, their eldest boy. He slammed the door behind him, which irritated Dave.

"And where have you been?" Dave asked, fixing Trevor with a glare the moment he stepped into the kitchen.

Trevor narrowed his eyes and gave his father a surly look. "With my mates."

Dave had to bite his tongue. He wanted to lay into the boy and get him to show some respect. Trevor was always moody, and Dave found it impossible to have a proper conversation with him. Of course, he'd improved vastly over the past few years. For the six months following Lillian's death, Trevor hadn't spoken a word to anyone, but eventually, he started to talk at school and then at home.

Dave tried to be understanding, but it wasn't easy.

He'd spent his childhood looking after his younger brother, Gary. He'd always felt protective of Gary, so he didn't understand why Trevor just didn't care about little Georgie.

"While you were with your mates, poor little Georgie was getting set upon by a gang of boys at least three years older than him."

Dave waited for Trevor's response. If he asked how his brother was, or even showed the least bit of concern for him, Dave was prepared to forgive him.

But Trevor scowled. "It's not my job to look after him."

"Of course, it is," Dave said, rapidly losing patience. "You're his older brother. You're supposed to make sure he's all right. Why weren't you looking out for him?"

Trevor looked down at the floor, but it wasn't in shame. He was just having a sulk.

Dave shook his head. "Luckily, there was another boy who intervened on Georgie's behalf. He stuck up for him."

Dave paused to see whether Trevor would ask who this boy had been, but Trevor continued his moody silence.

"The boy was called Jimmy. Do you know who that is?"

Trevor shrugged. "No."

"Go and check on your brother," Dave said, giving up. "And then wash your hands and come down for supper."

"What have we got?" Trevor asked looking round the kitchen and noticing there was nothing cooking on the stove.

"Cheese sandwiches," Dave said. "You don't deserve anything else."

Through the whole conversation, Sandra said nothing. She just stared blankly into space.

***

Trevor stomped upstairs. It wasn't fair. He always got the blame when Georgie got hurt. He shouldn't have to look after his little brother. None of Trevor's mates had to look after their brothers and sisters. If Georgie couldn't look after himself, he should just stay at home.

Trevor knew his father liked to blame him for everything. If he hadn't been scolded for not looking after Georgie, his father would have found another reason to tear strips off him. His father had always hated him. He wished Trevor had died instead of Lillian.

Georgie opened the bathroom door and stepped out onto the landing in front of Trevor. The collar of his shirt all wet from where he'd splashed water on his face.

"What have you been up to?" Trevor asked, petulantly.

Georgie blinked in surprise. "I just had a wash," he said.

"No, dummy. I mean what did you do this afternoon that's made Dad so upset. He just had a right go at me. Practically chewed my ear off."

"Oh, that wasn't my fault. Some bad boys were calling me names, and then they started to hit me."

"Who were they?"

"It was Ronnie Patterson who started it, the boy in the year above you."

Trevor nodded slowly. Patterson was a well-known bully at school. It was also well-known that his father laid into him practically every night, and he was always turning up at school with bruises covering his body.

Still, Trevor couldn't let him get away with beating up his

little brother. His dad was right about that. Georgie was an annoying little brat at times, but he was still Trevor's brother.

"Dad's going to want their names. I think he'll probably talk to their parents."

Georgie nodded slowly then smiled at his big brother, showing off the gap in his front teeth. "Can I walk to school with you tomorrow?"

Trevor was on the verge of refusing when he thought better of it. The last thing he wanted was his brother hanging beside him on the way to school like a little limpet. His mates would laugh at him. But on the other hand, Dad would throttle him if anything else happened to Georgie, so he would have to put up with it.

"All right," Trevor said, grumpily. "But you have to keep quiet and not chatter on like you normally do."

The smile disappeared from Georgie's face as he nodded solemnly.

Trevor nipped into the bathroom and quickly washed his hands when he heard their father calling them down for supper.

He couldn't wait to finish his sandwich and then sneak back off to his room. The less time he spent with his family, the better as far as Trevor was concerned.

5

BABS MORTON SAT RIGIDLY IN her chair. She had just sat through one of the most tedious dinners of her life, and considering how many dinners she'd shared with Violet Morton, that was really saying something.

Violet had been waltzing around like usual, putting on all her fake airs and graces. She'd served up steak and kidney pudding, and went on and on about how long it took her to cook it.

Personally, Babs thought the suet pastry was a little soggy for her tastes, and she'd only managed to take a few bites before pushing the rest of it around her plate and trying to hide it under a mountain of carrots.

Tony had wolfed his down, of course. Babs thought he must have an iron stomach.

Violet smiled fondly at her youngest son as he asked for a second serving.

Both Ruby and Derek had made good headway in getting through the mounds of steak and kidney pudding, boiled potatoes, carrots and cabbage, but even that wasn't enough to appease Violet.

"What on earth is wrong with you?" Violet said sharply, looking at Ruby. "That's good wholesome food. I suppose your mother doesn't make you things like this at home, but while you're under my roof, you will clear your plate."

Violet looked at Babs as though she was daring her to respond.

But what Violet had said was true enough. Babs couldn't remember the last time she'd spent all afternoon in the kitchen preparing dinner. The children didn't appreciate it anyway. It was easier to fry up a bit of steak or bacon.

Even when she made a stew, she just bunged it all into a pot and stuck it in the oven for a couple of hours, and she didn't have to do any more work the rest of the day.

Sod making bloody pastry. There were more important things in life, especially now that she had Martin's business to run.

Of course, Violet Morton would never appreciate that. She couldn't understand why Babs wanted to be involved in the family business anyway. She firmly believed that a woman's place was in the home, and Babs shouldn't be interfering in men's affairs.

Violet Morton was an idiot.

"They get plenty of wholesome food, thank you very much," Babs said sharply. "But they're not used to having their plates piled high like that."

"The pudding was absolutely gorgeous, Mum," Tony said, interrupting and trying to head off a potential argument between Violet and Babs.

It worked well enough. Violet turned back to her son and beamed. "I'm glad you liked it. It's nothing really. You know how much I enjoy cooking for you."

Babs' eyes flickered to the clock. They'd been here for an hour and a half already. Surely they could be making their excuses and getting home soon. But Violet hadn't finished goading her daughter-in-law yet. The old cow's sharp voice interrupted Babs' thoughts. "When was the last time you visited Martin, Babs?"

Babs didn't much enjoy visiting Martin. She found the whole thing tedious, but she did it out of duty. She had been to see him just a fortnight ago and told Violet so, although she would have preferred to tell the interfering old witch to mind her own business.

Violet's eyes narrowed as she looked at Ruby and Derek. "And when was the last time the children went to see him?"

Babs sighed. They'd been through this already. But it seemed as if Violet still wasn't bored of raking over the same old ground.

The children hadn't been to visit Martin for over six months.

Martin changed his mind constantly. When he was first inside, he hadn't wanted the children to visit at all, insisting they were too young. Then he'd decided he missed them and asked Babs to bring them along. They'd been visiting him regularly for the past five years, but six months ago, Martin decided he couldn't stand it any longer.

He told Babs he couldn't bear to see the pity in his children's eyes, so Babs had obeyed his wishes and had not taken the children to visit him since.

Personally, Babs thought it was likely that Martin would change his mind again soon.

She knew Martin well enough by now and was sure it was only a matter of time before he demanded to see his children again. The worst thing she could do in this situation was try to pressure him into it. If she did that, he would just dig his heels in.

"As you know, Violet, they've not been to see him for a few months. Martin doesn't want them to visit him and see him locked up. It upsets him."

Violet snorted. "He doesn't have much of a choice, does he? He's still got a few years on his sentence. If he was so worried about his children, he shouldn't have got himself arrested in the first place."

Tony sensed the change of atmosphere as Babs glared at her mother-in-law. He leaned forward, pressing his palms flat against the table. "Now, come on, Mum. Martin didn't exactly get arrested on purpose."

But Violet was on a roll now, and there was no stopping her. "He's never been much of a father to them. I don't know what I ever did to deserve such a family. When I think of all the years I worked my fingers to the bone for you lot."

Babs closed her eyes and took a deep breath. She longed to tell the silly old trout to give it a rest. Both Ruby and Derek had been sitting in silence throughout the meal, looking absolutely miserable. Babs supposed she should thank her lucky stars they didn't give their grandmother as much cheek as they did Babs. Otherwise, Babs would truly never hear the end of it.

Violet reached out and put a hand on Tony's arm. "If it wasn't for my Anthony, I would have given up long ago."

Here we go, Babs thought. You could set your watch by her. The next thing out of her mouth would be a sob story about how fragile her health was, even though she was as strong as an ox, the crafty old bird.

But before Violet reached that part of her rant, her eyes focused on Derek. "Heavens, boy, don't eat with your mouth open like that. Did you not teach them table manners, Babs?"

That was it. Babs had had enough of this. She gritted her teeth and turned to snarl at Violet. "That's it. Come on, children, we are going home."

Babs would be the first to admit Ruby and Derek were little sods, but they were her little sods, and she wasn't going to sit around and let Violet pick holes in them like that.

It wasn't as if Violet had been a perfect mother anyway. Martin and Tony were proof of that. The old cow had some nerve criticising her children.

Babs got to her feet and glared at her mother-in-law. "Thank you for dinner, Violet. We'll see ourselves out."

***

The following morning, Linda was rushing about in a hurry

to get ready. She'd overslept, and she was due at Bevels in less than half an hour. Her husband, Geoff, had come home roaring drunk last night, and it had taken ages for her to get back to sleep.

She rubbed a hand over her tired eyes and then smothered a yawn. She hadn't expected to still be an employee at Bevels after all this time. She had married Geoff over seven years ago, and she'd expected to have a baby on the way in no time, but it hadn't happened yet. Seven long years of marriage and no sign of a baby.

The first couple of years of their marriage hadn't been too bad. At least Geoff had managed to hold down steady work at the docks, and they'd had two wages coming in. But when Geoff had been laid off, things got much worse.

Linda looked at her good-for-nothing husband as he snored loudly and slept off his hangover. With a sigh, she picked up his dirty washing from the floor and then grimaced as Geoff gave a loud belch and turned over in bed.

Linda hurried out of the bedroom, shutting the door behind her.

She couldn't be late. They only had one wage coming in now, so she had to keep her job.

A short while ago, she had managed to get a promotion, and she now oversaw all the machinists.

The new role came with a pay rise, and Mr. Bevel himself had told her a year ago how pleased he was with her work. Linda had been pleased as punch, and when she came home, she couldn't wait to tell Geoff the news. She'd thought he might be proud of her, or at least grateful for the extra money coming in, but Geoff just laughed and then said she was stupid for not asking for even more money. In his opinion, Mr. Bevel was just taking advantage of her.

Linda trudged down the stairs. She considered making Geoff a cup of tea before she left, but she was so irritated by the way he'd woken her up last night, she decided not to. He didn't deserve it.

She'd given up hope of Geoff ever getting another job. After he'd first been laid off, he was forever telling Linda he had a job lined up just around the corner, but it never seemed to quite materialise, and now Linda listened to his stories with a smile and a nod but didn't expect anything to come of them.

Linda stopped by the hall mirror and applied some lipstick. It was her little act of defiance. Geoff said she shouldn't wear makeup for work because it made her look like a trollop. But that was silly. All the girls wore a little bit of makeup, and Linda felt more confident wearing lipstick and a little powder. It made her feel smart and properly dressed for work.

She heard the sound of some schoolboys passing by and realised it was almost time for her to leave the house. The sound of their youthful voices reminded her of Jimmy, and Linda paused, thinking about the poor little lad and hoping he was okay.

She wondered whether she should have made more of an effort to be part of Jimmy's life. After all, Kathleen, his mother, had been Linda's best friend, and she probably knew more about Kathleen than anybody else in the world.

The last time Linda had seen Mary Diamond, she'd been taken aback. She looked so much older. Her hair was now completely grey, and her face was heavily lined. The thing that worried Linda the most, though, was Mary's heavily bloodshot eyes and shaking hands. Most people liked to think of Linda as naive, but she knew the signs of someone with an alcohol problem when she saw them.

Of course, she felt terrible for Mary, and she understood why the woman had turned to drink after the loss of her only daughter, but she couldn't help thinking it was just another blow to poor Jimmy.

Pressing the lid back onto her lipstick and slipping it into her bag, Linda made a decision. She was going to make more of an effort to look after little Jimmy for Kathleen's sake.

***

Babs woke up with a start.

What on earth was that noise?

As if in answer to her question, she heard it again. Derek's roar of frustration, followed by Ruby's high-pitched screaming.

"Those bleeding kids," Babs muttered under her breath and threw back the covers.

She shivered as the cool air hit her body, but determined to give the little sods a piece of her mind, she stood up and stomped out of the bedroom.

By the time she got downstairs and into the hall, she saw both Ruby and Derek glaring at each other angrily, and they were still shouting.

Babs pinched the bridge of her nose with her thumb and forefinger and gritted her teeth. She'd only been asleep a few hours. After dinner last night, she'd gone by to check the club. And what she'd seen there had worried her. It wasn't that the club wasn't busy. On the contrary, Mortons was jam packed and doing great business, and that's what had thrown Babs for a loop.

According to Tony, they hadn't been doing very well, and takings were down, but Babs couldn't see how that could possibly be true.

She doubted it was Tony himself who was cheating the club. He didn't have the smarts for that, but something dodgy was going on, and it was down to Babs to get to the bottom of it.

So the last thing she needed this morning was her children going at it like hammer and tongs.

"Keep your noise down," Babs yelled over the children. "Now, what the hell is the matter with you both?"

She glared at the children as they began to talk over each other.

Babs groaned. Ruby and Derek were both teenagers now,

and there was no reason why they weren't perfectly capable of getting themselves up in the morning and making themselves breakfast. Babs didn't think she was asking much. She just wanted them to pull their weight.

Sometimes it seemed like everybody was out to make Babs' life more difficult. Why couldn't they just get ready for school without kicking off for once? Was it really so much to ask?

"He stole my hairbrush," Ruby yelled, pointing at her brother.

Babs jerked her head to look at Derek and saw the offending hairbrush in his hand. "Well? What are you doing with your sister's hairbrush?"

"Well, I wasn't going to use it to play the flute, was I? I was going to brush my hair," Derek said sarcastically, earning himself a clip round the ear from Babs.

"You cheeky little bastard. You keep a civil tongue in your head when you're talking to me, do you hear?"

Babs shook her head in disbelief. All this bleeding noise over a hairbrush!

"For goodness sake, Ruby. Does it really matter if your brother uses your hairbrush? From the noise you pair were making I thought someone was being murdered."

Ruby looked horrified at the very idea of Derek using her hairbrush. She pointed at Derek's hair again. "No. I don't want him to use it. He uses that Brylcreem, and it will make my hairbrush all sticky."

Before Babs could reply, Derek turned and snarled at his sister. "Fine. Keep the stupid brush!" And as he said those words, he flung the hairbrush back at Ruby, but she wasn't prepared and didn't catch it in time, and the hairbrush struck the mirror behind her shoulder.

The mirror hanging in the hallway was one of Babs' most prized possessions. She'd inherited it from her late mother.

At the sound of smashing glass, Babs felt sick. Her lower lip wobbled as she turned to survey the damage.

Derek's face paled, and Ruby's eyes grew wide in shock.

"I'm sorry, Mum. I didn't mean to break it," Derek said.

Babs had never felt more like crying than she did right at that moment. But instead, she straightened her shoulders, turned to glare at her son and gave him a sharp slap around the side of the head.

"Seven years bad luck you'll have now! And you deserve it! Go on, the pair of you, get to school. I'm sick of the sight of you."

After the children had gone, Babs sat down at the foot of the stairs and looked up at the broken mirror. It had shattered, but the glass had remained within the mirror's frame, thankfully. It seemed like a symbol, reflecting the state of her life right now. Everything was broken.

She tried to make the house look nice and prepare meals for the children while keeping the business running like clockwork. And this was the thanks she got for it.

Everyone took her for granted. If she wasn't careful, she was going to have a pair of monsters on her hands. Ruby and Derek were spoilt little gits, and she was going to have to decide what she was going to do about it.

If she didn't act soon, it would be too late. Already the selfish little brats didn't listen to her half the time.

As Babs got to her feet, preparing to go back upstairs and get ready for the day, there was a knock at the door.

Babs groaned. Who on earth could that be at this time? If it was one of the children, she would throttle them. She was not in the mood to see their faces again this morning.

She opened the front door a crack, remembering she was still wearing a nightgown, and there on the front step was Frieda Longbottom, an old friend of her late mother's.

"Oh, Frieda, it's you, love. I'm sorry I was out late at the club last night. I'm still in my nightie. Why don't you come in? I'll go upstairs and get my dressing gown on, and we can have a brew."

"Right you are, love. I only stopped by to see if you were all right. I heard an almighty racket coming from your place as I was passing. I was heading to the club to start the cleaning. If you're busy, don't let me get in your way."

"I'll be honest with you, Frieda. I could do with a chat. I'm sure the club can wait ten minutes."

Frieda came in the front door, and then shut it behind her as Babs hurried upstairs to get her dressing gown.

By the time Babs got back downstairs, Frieda had started making a pot of tea and set two cups down on the kitchen table.

"Now," Frieda said. "Why don't you tell me all about it?"

Babs sat down, and as Frieda suggested, she told all about her worries with the club and how the children had been playing up. It felt good to get it off her chest.

"I'm at my wits' end, Frieda. Really I am. I need to sort those little sods out one way or another. But it's not easy. I've had to bring them up single-handed with their father inside. And God knows Violet Morton hasn't been much help."

Frieda grunted in agreement. She'd never had much time for Violet Morton, and in her eyes, Babs could do no wrong. She adored Babs as if she was her own daughter and she'd watched her grow up into a lovely young lady. Personally, Frieda believed Babs was wasted on Martin Morton. A woman with her looks and brains could have done so much better.

They chatted a little while longer over their tea, and Babs thanked her lucky stars she had a friend like Frieda she could turn to. She felt she could tell Frieda anything... Well, almost anything. Babs had a secret she'd never told anyone.

And as much as she loved and trusted Frieda, she wasn't prepared to share that secret.

Babs' marriage to Martin had never gone smoothly since the early days, and after he'd had an affair with Kathleen Diamond, Babs had been thirsty for revenge, so when Dave

Carter had approached her, asking for a little information on Martin, Babs had been more than happy to oblige.

She'd given him little details here and there but had never really imagined quite how the information she provided could damage Martin. She certainly hadn't expected to be part of the reason her husband had been banged up.

But she couldn't say she was disappointed. In fact, she was rather pleased. The only thing that terrified her was the chance that Martin might find out. For the entire first year Martin had been locked up, Babs had been on tenterhooks, positive that Martin was about to find out at any time, but Dave kept his word and hadn't told anybody about Babs' involvement, at least as far as she knew.

It seemed her secret was safe for the time being.

6

WHEN TREVOR CARTER ARRIVED AT school, he walked away from Georgie, leaving his brother on his own as soon as they passed through the school gates. He knew he would be safe enough in the playground. Trevor might have a duty to look after his little brother, but there were limits.

"Do you want to play Bulldog?" Georgie called out as Trevor turned his back.

"No," Trevor snapped. "Sometimes you're such a baby, Georgie. Nobody plays that anymore. And besides how are we supposed to play British Bulldog with only two of us?"

Trevor walked away, shaking his head. He had business to attend to.

Over on the other side of the playground, nearest the railings, was Ronnie Patterson. Patterson had been the ringleader for the attack on Georgie, and though he knew his father would be dealing with things in his own way, Trevor was going to make sure his presence was felt.

Patterson was in the top class, and a whole year older than Trevor. But Trevor was tall for his age, and had filled out well, and he was confident he could take Patterson in a fight if it came to it.

But like most bullies, Patterson would probably back down as soon as he was confronted.

Patterson had his little group of friends gathered around

him. They were mostly younger kids, Trevor noted, apart from the boy in Patterson's year who walked with a limp.

Trevor didn't pay the other boys any attention. His eyes were fixed on Patterson.

Trevor was nearly on top of them before Patterson realised he was approaching, and for a moment the boy looked flustered, and then tried to regain his poise by jutting his chin out and looking at Trevor through narrowed eyes.

"What do you want, Carter?"

Trevor stood still and put his hands in his pockets as he looked at Patterson with a smirk on his face. "So, you do know my name. I take it you know who my father is, too?"

Trevor was gratified to see the blood flood Patterson's cheeks.

Trevor jabbed a thumb in the direction of Georgie. "And he's my little brother. Did you know that?"

By the way Patterson started stammering and looking around for his friends, Trevor guessed he was now regretting messing with the Carter family.

Trevor took a menacing step forward and enjoyed the fact that Patterson flinched and seemed to shrink back against the railings.

He shook his head. "I didn't know he was your brother. I would have never touched him otherwise."

Lying bastard, thought Trevor. Patterson had known exactly who Georgie was and tried to impress his friends by beating up a Carter. Trevor jerked forward, and Patterson let out a little yelp as his friends scattered.

"It doesn't look like your pals are going to stick around and help you out, does it?"

Patterson put his hands up. "Sorry. I really am sorry."

As Trevor raised his fists, ready to plant a punch straight in the middle of Patterson's face, he heard a sharp cry and turned around.

Well, wasn't that typical?

There was never usually a teacher in sight at break time. They were all too busy inside, drinking tea and keeping warm while the poor kids shivered outside. But there was Mr. Barnet, standing a few feet away, watching Trevor closely.

Patterson breathed out in relief.

"Don't get too comfortable, Patterson. There's always after-school," Trevor said.

Patterson looked down at the ground, and his lower lip wobbled just like a baby. Trevor thought it was pathetic.

He turned around and grinned at Mr. Barnet. "Morning, sir," he said cheekily.

He started to walk towards the school building as the bell rang out for lessons and noticed little Georgie was over on the other side of the playground, and he was no longer standing on his own. Georgie had a habit of playing on his own and making up imaginary friends. Whatever made him happy, Trevor supposed. He didn't feel much of a bond with Georgie. Not the sort of bond his father wanted him to have anyway, but Trevor supposed deep down he loved the little sod. He probably loved him more than anybody else in his life.

Georgie was standing next to a tall boy with scruffy dark hair and skinny legs.

"Oi, Patterson," Trevor jerked his head in the direction of Georgie. "Do you know who that is with my brother?"

Patterson looked over Trevor's shoulder and then gave a nod. "Yes, that's that stupid pillock, Jimmy Diamond."

In response to Trevor's blank expression, Patterson continued, "You know. He is the orphan. The one whose mother was murdered and dumped in the canal."

Trevor nodded slowly.

He looked at Jimmy with dislike.

His father had raved about Jimmy intervening and saving poor Georgie from a beating, but Trevor didn't see it like that. In his opinion, Jimmy had just done it to make him look bad.

And Trevor didn't like that at all.

He walked swiftly over to Georgie, tugged on the little boy's jumper and glared at Jimmy Diamond. "Come on, Georgie. Don't be late for your lesson. And be careful who you're mixing with."

Trevor gave Jimmy a look that would have made anyone else take a few steps back. Anyone with half a brain would have got the message pretty sharpish, Trevor thought. But Jimmy seemed oblivious.

He smiled at Trevor and held out his hand. "I'm Jimmy," he said.

Trevor sneered and looked down at Jimmy's outstretched hand. Who the bleeding hell did this kid think he was? Some kind of old-fashioned country gentleman? Whoever heard of boys shaking hands?

Trevor ignored him, turned his back and escorted Georgie into school.

***

At lunchtime, Babs was sitting at her kitchen table staring at Tony and listening to yet more excuses as to why the club profits were down.

She shook her head in frustration. "I'm sorry, Tony. But something isn't right. When I went in there yesterday, the place was heaving. Profits should be rising not falling. I need you to show me the books."

Tony leaned back in his chair and interlaced his fingers behind his head as he stretched out his legs in front of him. He looked like he didn't have a care in the world much to Babs' annoyance. "You don't need to worry about that, Babs," Tony said. "Old Mo deals with all the finances."

Babs scoffed at the mention of Martin's old accountant. She had long suspected the man was a crook. She didn't understand why Tony was so oblivious to the possibility. Was he really that stupid?

Babs took a deep breath. "I'm sorry, Tony, but I'm going to

have to insist on seeing the books."

"But Old Mo has been with us for years. Surely you don't suspect he's on the fiddle?"

"I'm not accusing anybody," Babs said slowly, feeling her patience evaporate. "But Martin is not going to be happy if I tell him profits are down yet again."

Tony sighed.

"I'm going to see him next week, Tony, and if he asks me why the profits are down, I can't tell him without seeing the books, can I?"

With some reluctance, Tony nodded. "I suppose you're right. But sometimes it's better not to rock the boat, Babs."

Rock the bleeding boat? If somebody was stealing from the Mortons, Babs was going to do more than rock the boat. She was going to bloody sink it.

She opened her mouth to snap at Tony, but she was saved from her own temper by a knock at the door.

Babs slapped her hand on the table in frustration, making the teacups rattle. "I'll be back in a minute," she said and walked off to answer the door, leaving Tony at the kitchen table.

She opened the door and saw a middle-aged man standing on her front step, blinking up at her expectantly.

Babs folded her arms over her chest. "Yes?" she prompted when the man didn't say anything.

She didn't have time for this. She had a business to save.

"Mrs. Morton?"

"Yes, that's right," Babs snapped, eager for the man to get on with it.

"Ah, sorry. I wasn't expecting Derek and Ruby's mother to be quite so young."

Babs found herself warming to the gentleman, and she chuckled. "All right. There's no need for you to try and charm me. What is it you want?"

"My name is Mr. Barnet," he said, and Babs did her best to

smother a smirk.

That was a most unfortunate name because he didn't have much of a barnet to speak of. The man was as bald as an egg.

"And what can I do for you, Mr. Barnet?" Babs asked, trying not to laugh.

"I've brought some school work for Ruby to complete," he said, and for the first time, Babs noticed the man was clutching a collection of papers.

"I'm the English teacher at St. George's. I'm concerned she's going to fall behind."

"Why on earth would she fall behind? She is a bright girl. Don't let her pull the wool over your eyes." Babs wouldn't put it past the little madam to be trying to get out of her school work.

Mr. Barnet blinked in surprise. "Well, because Ruby hasn't been at school this week."

Babs' jaw dropped open. The sneaky, conniving little cow. She was going to throttle that girl when she got her hands on her. Babs felt her cheeks flush crimson.

"Right," she said and reached out to snatch the papers from Mr. Barnet's hands.

"Perhaps I could see Ruby and explain some of the lessons?"

Babs felt her cheeks flame an even deeper red with shame. She was not about to admit to this teacher that Ruby wasn't at home, and she had absolutely no idea where her daughter was.

"I'm afraid that won't be possible, Mr. Barnet. Ruby is sleeping at the moment, but I will give her the work, and she'll be back in school tomorrow."

"Ah, I see." Mr. Barnet pushed his spectacles back on his nose and then said, "Actually, there was one more matter… I don't seem to have received a reply from the letter I sent last week."

Oh, for goodness sake. What was this man talking about

now? What letter?

Babs' forehead creased in confusion. "Letter? I'm sorry. You'll have to jog my memory."

"About the fight Derek got into last week. I'm afraid-"

"Fight?" Babs practically roared the word, and her response caused Tony to rush out into the hall to see what was going on.

"Is everything all right, Babs?" Tony asked, putting a hand on her shoulder and glaring at the man for upsetting her.

Babs put a hand to her forehead. "This is Mr. Barnet. He is the English teacher at St. George's. Apparently, Derek's been in a fight."

Mr. Barnet nodded gravely. "I'm afraid it wasn't just the one fight. That's why I wrote the letter. I needed to talk to you about Derek's suspension from school."

Babs let out a little cry of shock. "Suspension? You can't suspend him!"

Mr. Barnet gave a smug smile that made Babs want to give him a slap. Any warmth she'd felt toward Mr. Barnet earlier had quickly evaporated. Now she couldn't wait to get the horrible little man off her doorstep, and she certainly wasn't about to invite him in.

"I'm afraid we can suspend him, and we will. Derek is disrupting the other pupils to the detriment of their education. It really isn't fair on them. I'm sure you understand."

"No, I bleeding don't understand. You come here to have a go at me for Ruby not being in school, and my Derek wants to go to school, and you won't let him!"

Mr. Barnet frowned. "I thought Ruby was sick?"

"Never mind all that now," Babs said. "Look, I'm busy. I'll talk to my children, and they will both be in school tomorrow."

Mr. Barnet shook his head urgently. "No, Mrs. Morton, Derek is not permitted to come back to school. His suspension starts today."

But Mr. Barnet ended up talking to the front door as Babs had slammed it hard in his face.

"Well, I never," Mr. Barnet said to himself as he straightened his jacket, lifted his chin and walked away from the house.

Inside the house, Tony was trying to persuade Babs that it was all just a bit of spirited fun. "Boys get into fights all the time. Besides Derek hasn't got long left at school. He'll be part of the family business in no time at all."

Babs sank into the wooden chair beside the kitchen table. She shook her head in disbelief. Her children had been getting up to all sorts right under her nose, and she hadn't had a clue. It was the last straw. She was going to straighten out those little bleeders even if it killed her.

There was no way in hell she would allow Derek to come into the family business next year. The boy was a liability, and she clearly couldn't trust him as far as she could throw him.

No, Babs had a much better idea in store for her children. They weren't going to like it, but the little sods would just have to lump it.

7

WHEN JIMMY LET HIMSELF IN after school, he stopped dead in the hallway. What was that smell? He sniffed the air and then grinned. If he wasn't mistaken, that was stew and dumplings. His stomach rumbled as he hurried through along the passage towards the kitchen.

His nan was quietly whistling away a cheerful tune, and Jimmy felt happier than he had done for ages. It was good to see his nan back to normal.

"Hello, Jimmy, love. I thought we'd have an early tea, and I've made an apple dumpling for afters."

Jimmy nodded eagerly and rushed upstairs to wash his hands ready for dinner.

When he'd stepped close to nan, he'd still been able to smell the gin, but it wasn't so bad. At least she was cooking again, and he hadn't found her asleep in the armchair.

Dinner was lovely, and it was just like old times.

Jimmy loved his nan desperately, and he hated it when she was drunk. Although she'd always been partial to a drink while he was growing up, she'd never gotten as bad as she had over the past few months, but now Jimmy hoped she'd put it behind her, and things could get back to how they used to be.

Jimmy told her all about his day at school as his nan served him a second portion of the beef stew and dumplings.

She barely touched the food on her own plate, though, and Jimmy tried not to flinch when he saw her reach for a bottle of sherry.

"I think I deserve this today," she said. "I've been working hard in the kitchen."

He found it hard to swallow his next mouthful of stew past the lump that had suddenly formed in his throat. But he tried to ignore it. It was just one sherry.

The alcohol made his nan maudlin, and when she was in that sort of mood, she liked to talk about his mum, Kathleen.

Jimmy didn't mind that at all. He loved hearing her memories of his mother. They hadn't had any photographs, and the only way he felt he could get to know his mother was through his nan and people like Linda, who had known his mum before she gave birth to him.

"I saw Linda the other day, Nan," Jimmy said as he polished off his final mouthful of stew. "It was when you'd fallen asleep in the armchair," he added awkwardly. "She gave me some money for chips."

The benign expression left his nan's face in an instant, and she pursed her lips together, looking furious as her cheeks flooded with colour.

"Did I do the wrong thing? She was really nice, and I was hungry."

His nan's hand tightened around her sherry glass, and she closed her eyes for a moment before shaking her head.

"No, you didn't do the wrong thing. I know I've been a little under the weather lately, but that's changed now. We don't need anybody's charity, and after dinner, you are to go straight round to Linda's and give her back the money. How much did she give you?"

His nan stood up, walked to the small cupboard beneath the stairs and pulled out her handbag.

Jimmy told his nan what Linda had given him, and his nan took the appropriate coin out of her purse and set it on the table.

"Linda is a lovely girl," his nan said, sitting down at the table again. "She used to be a bit in your mother's shadow, but that was only to be expected. Kathleen was such a beauty."

Jimmy rested his chin on his hands and leaned forward, eager for more information. He liked it when his nan was in a talkative mood.

"What was she like, Nan?"

"She was a beauty. Everyone thought so. She had lovely dark hair, and she had the same dark blue eyes, almost violet, just like yours."

His nan sat back in her chair as if lost in her own memories. "Of course, she wasn't perfect, and she gave me the runaround from time to time. She definitely had a bit of mischief in her, but she adored you, Jimmy. After she had you, it was as if she blossomed. She would have made such a lovely mum."

His nan's eyes filled with sadness as she looked down at the table, and Jimmy felt guilty. He didn't want to upset her.

From Mary's descriptions of his mother, Jimmy thought Kathleen must be practically an angel. He imagined she must have been very like Linda, only even prettier.

He'd only asked his nan a couple of times about how his mother had died.

Growing up around here, Jimmy couldn't escape the whispers. He knew she had been murdered but no one knew who had killed her.

He'd been teased at school, but it wasn't only children who talked about it. Sometimes he overheard adults, who cruelly spoke about him as if he wasn't there.

Every time he thought about the body of his beautiful mother being dumped in the cold water of the canal, Jimmy shivered.

He was only a boy now, but he had already made up his

mind he would one day track down the person who had killed his mother and get revenge.

"I know somebody killed her, Nan. And when I'm older, I'm going to find out who it was."

His nan's eyes widened in shock, and she shook her head. "Let's not talk about that now, Jimmy. You know I find it very difficult to talk about Kathleen."

Jimmy nodded sadly as his nan slid the money across the table to him.

"Go on then, Jimmy. You go off to Linda's and give her back the money with my thanks."

***

Tony had left long before the kids were due home from school. So Babs had taken the time to give the downstairs of the house a quick once-over and sweep out the kitchen.

When she'd finished, she sat down at the kitchen table, glared angrily at her cup of tea that had dared to get cold and lit up a fag.

She bloody hated housework. She thought she might ask Frieda to pop in a couple of times a week and give her a hand. Especially if she was going to be pouring over the books for the next couple of weeks.

Tony had finally agreed to let Babs look at them, and she would need to go through them with a fine-tooth comb to make sure that Old Mo wasn't cheating them.

She took a deep drag on a cigarette and then blew out the smoke, mentally preparing herself for the challenge that lay ahead.

As soon as the children came home, she would tell them and get it over with. They wouldn't be happy, but so what? Babs was sick and tired of being taken for a mug.

After everything she'd done for those kids, they could have shown a little more gratitude. With Martin inside, it had only been her taking care of them, and they repaid her by lying and giving her cheek when she dared to confront them about it.

A small smile played on Babs' lips. She couldn't wait to hear the inventive lies the pair of them would come up with to try and get out of their latest little escapade.

The truth was Babs was too busy to keep an eye on them all the time. So she needed somebody who could.

There was a rattle as the front door opened, and Babs turned around to see Ruby and Derek both trudging through the front door, bickering as usual.

Babs stubbed out her cigarette in the ashtray and then said, "Both of you come into the kitchen."

She kept her voice steady so the children wouldn't suspect anything.

Reluctantly they both entered the kitchen and gave their mother matching sulky stares.

Babs turned to Ruby first "How was school?"

Ruby shrugged. "It was all right."

"What lessons did you study today?"

Ruby looked at her mother, startled. She knew something was going on. Babs didn't normally pay this much attention to Ruby's schooling. She wasn't normally interested.

"The usual subjects," Ruby said, but she shot her brother a panicked look.

"Your cheeks look a little flushed, Ruby. Maybe you're coming down with something. You're not sick, are you?" Babs added, glaring at her daughter.

Ruby's cheeks flushed. Now she knew her mother had caught her in a lie.

Babs wasn't finished yet. She turned to Derek next. "Anything you want to tell me, Derek?"

Derek looked towards his sister and then back at Babs, blinking rapidly. She could tell he was trying to work out just how much his mother knew. But she wasn't going to make it easy for him.

Derek shook his head.

"Are you sure about that? No letters you want to hand over?" Babs arched an eyebrow.

"It's not as bad as you think… Mum… Honestly. It wasn't my fault…" Derek stammered as he flinched under his mother's angry glare.

"I had a visitor at lunchtime. Your English teacher. He informed me that Ruby was off sick today and that you had been fighting at school. So well done, Derek, you've got yourself suspended, and Ruby, you should be ashamed of yourself, young lady. Can you imagine the embarrassment I felt with that man on my doorstep asking to come in and visit you at your sickbed, so he could give you a bit of extra work to do at home?"

Both children started to talk at once, but Babs put her hands up. "Enough," she roared, furious with both of the little bastards.

"I have had it up to here with your behaviour. I'm not standing for it any longer."

"But Mum, I'm almost old enough to leave school now anyway," Derek said. "Uncle Tony said it was about time I started working for the family business."

Babs' nostrils flared as she laid into her son. "No, it is not time for you to start working. Over my dead body. I'm not having you working for the business when you can't even stay out of trouble at school. You need a cool head for this business." She jabbed a finger into Derek's chest and then turned and did the same to Ruby. "Both of you are going to boarding school in Surrey. If that doesn't sort you out, nothing will."

With that little declaration, Babs fell back into her seat beside the kitchen table, feeling exhausted from the confrontation.

Both children gaped, looking at each other in horror, and then looked back at their mother as if they couldn't quite believe she was serious.

"But Mum," Ruby said, "I don't want to go to boarding school."

"Well, you should have thought about that before you started giving me the runaround," Babs said unsympathetically as Ruby began to cry.

She could turn on the waterworks for as long as she liked as far as Babs was concerned, but it wasn't going to move her. She had made her decision, and boarding school would hopefully instil some sense into her children.

She hadn't made the decision lightly. It wasn't exactly the done thing around the East End to send your kids to boarding school, or even to pay for education, but they had the money, and Babs knew that if she didn't do something now, she'd look back on this in ten years, see the mess her children had made of their lives and she would blame herself.

Next, Derek tried appealing to his mother, desperate to change her mind, but Babs wouldn't budge an inch.

Derek stormed out of the house, slamming the door behind him, and Ruby spent the rest of the evening wailing in her bedroom.

Neither child ate the dinner Babs had prepared, but it didn't make her feel sorry for them. If anything, it reinforced her decision and made her certain that she'd made the right choice.

Her kids had somehow turned into spoilt brats, and it was time they woke up and learned to live in the real world. They needed to learn some life lessons, and Babs was too busy to teach them herself. So she just had to hope that boarding school would shake some common sense into the pair of them.

8

WHEN LINDA GOT HOME FROM work, the house was dark and deserted. Geoff must be down at the pub, she thought with a sigh, as she hung up her coat on the hook by the front door.

She carried her bag of shopping into the kitchen and began to unpack it. She'd popped out at lunchtime to the grocer's and the baker's, which were just round the corner from Bevels.

She'd made a stew yesterday and that would do for dinner again tonight with some bread and butter on the side.

She often made stews or meals that wouldn't be ruined if they had to be kept warm, because Geoff was often down at the pub, and Linda never knew when he would return.

She lit the gas beneath the pot to warm the stew and then began to butter the bread.

She usually tried to wait until Geoff got home to have her dinner, but today her stomach was rumbling, so she fixed herself a slice of bread and butter as a stopgap.

But the fluttering in her stomach had nothing to do with hunger. Her stomach was churning because she was nervous.

Lost in thought, she munched on the bread as she leaned against the kitchen windowsill and looked out of the window at the small backyard.

She had made an appointment with the doctor for

tomorrow and now she was starting to panic.

Geoff had strictly forbidden her to go to the doctors, but she needed to know what was wrong with her. She should have fallen pregnant by now, so there had to be something wrong.

Every time she brought the matter up in the past, Geoff had flown off the handle, but this time, she had decided to take a different approach and hoped he would understand.

When the front door slammed, Linda jumped.

She put the piece of bread she'd been eating on the breadboard and quickly washed her hands.

"Hello, love," Linda said to Geoff as he walked into the kitchen.

He stank of booze. Linda suspected he'd been in the pub all afternoon.

Geoff walked across to the stove and peered into the pot.

"Stew again. I'm sick of bleeding stew," Geoff grumbled.

Linda nodded. "I know, but I've been at work all day, and I didn't –"

Geoff cut her off. "I've got a good mind to stop you going in to work. That Mr. Bevel treats you like dirt and only pays you a pittance while you don't even have time to cook me a proper evening meal."

Linda shook her head. She knew that she often cooked stew, but there was a reason for that. It was because she never knew what time Geoff would be home!

She was about to tell him so when she stopped herself. She didn't want to get into an argument. Not when she had to broach the subject of the doctor. That was a sensitive enough issue on its own.

Instead, she said brightly," I thought I'd pick us up some lamb chops tomorrow, and I'll cook some potatoes and garden peas to go with it."

Geoff grunted in what Linda took to be approval.

She turned back to the stove so he wouldn't see how

annoyed she was. Honestly, that man! He was going to stop her from going to work, was he? And how exactly would they afford to put any food on the table then? Geoff hadn't brought any money into the home for over a year.

If Linda hadn't managed to get her pay rise and promotion, they wouldn't even be able to afford the rent on this place, let alone buy meat every week.

Linda kept quiet and laid the table as Geoff took his shoes off and got comfortable.

They always ate in the kitchen because it was quite a large size, and they never had visitors or any reason to use the little folding dining table in the front room.

Linda put down a bowl of stew and plate of bread and butter in front of Geoff and stood beside him, waiting.

Eventually, with his mouth still full of stew, he looked up at her and said, "Well, what is it? You're as jumpy as a rabbit."

Linda smoothed her hand down her skirt, licked her lips, took a deep breath and then said. "I've made an appointment with the doctor tomorrow."

Geoff stopped eating and looked up at her through narrowed eyes. "What for? Are you ill?"

"Not exactly. It's just I wanted to see the doctor and find out why we've been having so much trouble… you know…" She gestured to her stomach area.

Geoff slammed his fist on the table so hard the cutlery rattled, and Linda jumped.

"Not this again," he growled. "I've told you. You are not to go to the doctors for that. Do you hear me?"

Linda nodded. "Yes, but I don't see what harm it can do to just ask him if…"

Geoff slammed his fist again on the table and then stood up, leaning intimidatingly over Linda. "You are my wife, and you will do what you are bleeding well told. You will cancel that appointment first thing tomorrow."

Linda tried to blink away the tears in her eyes and put a

hand over her mouth to stifle her sobs.

Geoff straightened up and looked down at her in disgust. "I've had enough of this. I'm going back to the pub."

"But what about your dinner?" Linda asked, pointing at Geoff's bowl.

"Stick your bleeding stew," Geoff said, and with one hand, he flicked the bowl over, sending it spinning onto the floor.

It cracked in two, and the meat and gravy spilled onto the tiles.

He stormed out, leaving Linda crying behind him.

***

Jimmy Diamond whistled as he strolled along Narrow Street. He was heading towards Linda's house to return the money she'd given him for the chips the other night.

He was sure Linda wouldn't mind if he kept the money, but his nan was proud and wouldn't hear of him taking handouts.

It was just beginning to get dark, and Jimmy suspected his nan had wanted him out of the house so she could have a quick mouthful of the gin she'd stashed in the kitchen cupboard behind the tinned fruit.

He'd just turned the corner when he saw the door to Linda's house open and Linda's husband storm out, slamming the door behind him.

Jimmy paused where he was. He didn't like Linda's husband very much. He had big ears, big hands, and Jimmy had never seen him smile.

Jimmy didn't trust people who never smiled.

It was like his nan had always said: There was always something to smile about if you looked hard enough.

He leaned against the brick wall and watched Geoff stalk off in the opposite direction.

When the coast was clear, Jimmy continued to Linda's house and knocked on the door.

He could hear footsteps, but Linda didn't open the door

straightaway.

He saw the curtains twitch in the front room and then his cheeks flushed. Perhaps Linda had seen it was him and decided she didn't want to speak to him.

Jimmy turned on the step, preparing to go back home. He would have to tell his nan that Linda hadn't been home.

But before he could make his getaway, the door opened.

Linda didn't have the lights on, so it was difficult to see her clearly as she stood in the doorway.

Jimmy dug his hand in his pocket for the money and then held it out to Linda.

"Nan said I should give you the money back."

As he moved closer, he saw that Linda had been crying. Her eyes and nose were red and she had tear stains on her cheeks.

Jimmy clenched his teeth. He bet Geoff had made her cry.

"Are you all right?"

"Yes," Linda said wiping her eyes. "I've just been cooking and the smoke got in my eyes."

Jimmy didn't think she was telling the truth. He thrust his hand forward again, waiting for her to take the money.

Linda poked her head out of the door and looked down the road in the direction her husband had just walked off.

Seeing there was no sign of Geoff, she said, "Do you want to come in for a minute, Jimmy, and have a glass of orange squash?"

Jimmy thought about it for a moment. His nan hadn't specifically told him to get straight back home after he delivered the money, and he was pretty sure she'd be asleep in the armchair by now and wouldn't miss him, so he nodded. "Yes, please."

He followed Linda through into the kitchen. Linda's house was very much like his nan's home. The furniture was a little more modern, and she didn't have so many knickknacks and ornaments, but all the rooms were the same size and layout.

Jimmy sat down at the kitchen table as Linda poured him a glass of orange squash and then set it on the table in front of him.

"How is your nan, Jimmy?"

"She's very well, thank you," Jimmy said politely and took a sip of his orange squash.

The sad look on Linda's face made Jimmy feel bad. He couldn't help thinking that Linda had been very good friends with his mother, so he should look out for her.

Sometimes, Jimmy wished he was older. He'd like to wallop that horrible Geoff for making Linda cry.

He answered Linda's questions about school and general things for a little while, and then he edged forward on his chair and asked a question about his mum.

He almost didn't do it. It always made Linda look sad to talk about Jimmy's mother, and she was already sad enough today.

But the only way Jimmy could understand what his mother had been like was by talking to people like Linda, who had known her. Other than his nan and Linda, he didn't know who else he could ask.

"What did she look like?" Jimmy asked, even though he'd asked the very same question just a few months ago when they'd had a similar conversation.

Linda smiled sadly. "She was very beautiful, Jimmy. Everybody thought so. And she liked to wear nice clothes in the latest fashions."

Jimmy nodded eagerly, waiting for Linda to continue.

"It didn't matter what she wore, though. She always looked stunning. She would help me with my hair and pick out clothes for me to wear."

"How long did you know her?"

"A long time. First at school, and then we worked together at Bevels."

Jimmy nodded, taking all the information on board. The

more he knew about his mother, the better chance he would have of finding her killer when he was older.

He stared down at his orange squash, trying to gather the courage to ask his next question.

He didn't dare look at Linda when he asked, "Do you know who killed her?"

Linda gave a muffled exclamation as she slapped a hand over her mouth. Then after a shocked pause, she reached out and clutched both of Jimmy's hands. "I know it's horrible, Jimmy. But the police never found out who did it.

Jimmy wasn't daft, and he knew Linda was hiding something. For some reason, she didn't want to tell him the whole truth. Maybe she didn't think he was old enough yet. He got the same impression from his nan as well… as if they knew more than they were letting on.

It wasn't really fair. Kathleen Diamond had been Jimmy's mother, after all, and he deserved to know the truth.

"I know the police didn't find out who did it, but I thought you might have some idea? Maybe she said something to you before… you know…"

Linda's grip on Jimmy's hands tightened, and her face paled.

"It's a complicated business, Jimmy, and I don't know much more than you. You're better off talking this through with your nan. But maybe you should wait until you're a little bit older."

Jimmy pulled his hands away. He didn't want to wait until he was older. He was plenty old enough right now.

He'd thought that Linda might understand, and as he drained his orange squash and said goodbye, he felt let down.

9

WHEN ARTHUR PATTERSON GOT HOME from the boxing club where he worked, his wife, Barbara, met him at the door.

"Thank goodness you are home," she said in an urgent whisper as she took Arthur's coat from him.

Arthur frowned. "Why? What is it? What has happened?"

He was more than a little concerned. His wife was a sensible woman and dealt with the problems in the home without much fuss.

Arthur was a real man's man. He'd enjoyed a short career as a boxer when he was younger, but he was past all that now. These days, he spent his time cleaning the club. But that was hard graft, and all he wanted to do when he got home was eat his tea and then sit with his feet up in front of the fire in his favourite armchair.

Studying his wife's worried face, it occurred to Arthur that his son may have got himself in trouble again. It was becoming a frequent occurrence, and despite the fact Arthur had given him the belt three times this week already, it seemed like the boy's spirit couldn't be broken.

"I had a visitor this afternoon," his wife said. Then she lowered her voice and moved even closer, whispering in Arthur's ear, "From Dave Carter."

Arthur's eyes widened, and he felt the blood drain from his face as he stared at his wife. "Dave Carter?" Even to his own ears, Arthur's voice sounded panicked.

His wife nodded, and her eyes darted from the hallway to the front room, where Arthur guessed their son was hiding. If the boy had gotten them into trouble with Dave Carter, hiding wasn't going to help him.

Arthur was positive he had done nothing to upset Dave Carter. He had lived in the East End all of his life, and despite the rumours the police put out, Arthur had never considered the major players in the area to be a problem. In his opinion, they kept the toe-rags in line. An honest, hard-working person didn't have to concern himself with the likes of Dave Carter. A normal law-abiding family didn't have anything to worry about as long as they were careful not to tread on any toes.

Arthur scratched his head, puzzled. For the life of him, he couldn't think why Dave Carter would want to speak to him. It had to be a mistake.

Yes, that was it. It must be some kind of misunderstanding, Arthur thought, and then he narrowed his eyes as the penny dropped.

If he hadn't done anything to anger Dave Carter, and he was sure that his wife wouldn't have either, that only left his son, Ronnie.

Arthur tried to swallow the bitter taste in his mouth.

Ronnie better not have done anything stupid. Arthur would bleeding kill him.

"Did he tell you what it was about?" Arthur demanded as he strode into the front room and glared down at his son, who was sitting on the floor, pretending to do his homework.

The boy looked up as his father entered the room. He looked like butter wouldn't melt, but Arthur knew different.

His wife had followed him into the front room, but she was clearly uncomfortable discussing the matter in front of their son. The daft cow still thought the sun shone out of his backside. Unfortunately, she was about to get rudely awakened.

"Well?" Arthur demanded, turning away from his son and looking at his wife. "What did Dave Carter say?"

His wife swallowed nervously, her gaze darting between Arthur and her son. Finally, she said, "He told me he would like to talk to us both about a problem concerning his son."

Oh, no. Arthur clapped a hand to his forehead. He'd been right. Ronnie must have somehow gotten himself mixed up with the Carters.

His fingers itched to lay into the boy, but instead, he said, "What did you do, Ronnie?"

His son was still sitting on the floor, cross-legged, and as he looked up at his parents, he looked the picture of innocence. Pah, that was a joke, Arthur thought.

"I don't know what you're talking about. I haven't done anything."

"Something to do with Dave Carter's son. Does that ring any bells?" Arthur asked, studying his son carefully for his reaction.

The boy's cheeks flushed and immediately Arthur knew they were in deep trouble. Whatever Ronnie had done, it was going to take a lot of grovelling on Arthur's part to make it up to Dave Carter.

"Do you realise what you have done? You have brought Dave bleeding Carter to my door."

Ronnie got to his feet and shrugged. He was trying to act tough and look unaffected, but his hands were trembling and his knees were practically knocking together.

"Dave Carter isn't a big deal, Dad. They call him the greengrocer gangster, and with all your boxing experience–"

Ronnie's words tipped Arthur over the edge. With a loud yell, he reached forward and swiped the boy around the ear. "You stupid little boy! They call him the greengrocer because he doesn't look like your typical gangster, but he is the most dangerous one of the lot! Any fool could tell you that."

Ronnie ducked as he tried to avoid another wallop from his father, and his mother rushed forward, trying to separate the pair of them. "No, Arthur. Keep calm. Mr. Carter could be here at any moment."

As soon as the words left his wife's mouth, there was an ominous knock at the front door, and Arthur felt his stomach drop down to his boots. How the hell was he going to manage to get out of this one?

***

Dave Carter stood outside the front door of the Patterson's house and waited for them to answer. He'd let some time pass between the bullying incident and his visits to each of the parents. If he'd learned one thing in his life, it was to not take revenge in the heat of the moment. Revenge was always so much more effective when you acted with a cool head.

Dave had been so furious after finding poor little Georgie in that state, he'd wanted to tear the boys limb from limb. It wasn't easy, but he had forced himself to wait.

The front door opened, and he saw a short man with broad shoulders and long arms. His cheeks were flushed, and his wide eyes stared up at Dave.

Dave didn't even have to say anything. The man was terrified already.

Dave had carried out meticulous research on this family after finding out Ronnie Patterson was the ringleader of the gang who'd bullied Georgie.

"Aren't you going to invite me in, Arthur?"

Arthur nodded quickly and stood aside, opening the door wide so Dave could enter.

"Cat got your tongue?" Dave said with a smirk as he stepped into the narrow hall.

Arthur still didn't speak as he continued to stare at Dave, with his mouth opening and closing like a fish.

After a moment, Arthur's wife rushed forward. "Well, don't just stand there, Arthur. Invite Mr. Carter into the front room.

Please, Mr. Carter, let me take your coat."

"Thank you." Dave shrugged off his overcoat and held it out and then he followed Arthur into the front room.

Dave felt his chest tighten as he clapped eyes on the little bastard who had been tormenting Georgie. He looked much smaller now as he cowered up against the fireplace.

Dave stared at him until the boy broke eye contact and stared down at the floor.

"I'll just make us a nice cup of tea," Arthur's wife said, wringing her hands anxiously, and then she disappeared off into the kitchen.

Dave didn't bother to sit down. He walked across to the fire and put a hand on the old mantelpiece, which caused young Ronnie Patterson to flee to his father's side.

"There seems to have been some sort of misunderstanding, Mr. Carter," Arthur said, licking his lips nervously.

Dave chuckled and shook his head. "Oh, no, there's been no misunderstanding, Arthur."

Arthur's face paled even further, and then he smacked his son on the side of the head.

"He's sorry, aren't you? Tell Mr. Carter how sorry you are."

The boy's eyes filled with tears, and his lower lip wobbled. Like most bullies, he didn't enjoy it when the shoe was on the other foot.

He lowered his head and then said quietly, "I'm very sorry, Mr. Carter. It won't happen again."

And then the boy turned and ran from the room, and Dave could hear him crying in the kitchen as his mother tried to console him.

With a cold smile, he turned back to Arthur.

"W…What are you going to do to him, Mr. Carter? He's a little tyke, but deep down, he's not a bad kid. I know he did wrong but–"

"Arthur, I'm not a monster. I don't beat up children." Dave took a step towards Arthur, who was now shaking and trembling. "Don't look so frightened. I'm sure your boy is genuinely sorry, and he will never touch my son again, will he?"

Arthur shook his head frantically. "Absolutely not. I can guarantee you he will never even look at your son in the wrong way again."

Dave smiled. "Well, there we go then. It's nice to have that matter sorted, isn't it?"

Arthur nodded and swallowed hard. He had a confused look on his face as if he couldn't understand why Dave Carter was letting him off quite so easily.

"Unfortunately, though, we can't just leave it at that. As much as I would like to. You see, I can't just let him get away with it, can I? Somebody has to pay for what he did, and as I don't hurt children, I'm afraid it's going to be you that has to pay, Arthur."

Arthur's legs gave way under him, and he flopped back into his armchair unable to stay upright.

He gave a petrified low moan as Dave cracked his knuckles.

"Although…" Dave cocked his head to one side and looked at Arthur as if he was considering something. "Perhaps we could come to some arrangement."

Arthur leapt upon those words as though they were a lifeline. "An arrangement? Yes! Whatever you say. An arrangement is a great idea."

Dave smiled and then walked over to the armchair opposite the one Arthur was sitting in.

He sat down, turned to Arthur with a smile and said, "Your brother owns the boxing club on Victoria Street, doesn't he?"

Arthur blinked a couple of times. That was a change in direction he hadn't been expecting. Why would Dave Carter be interested in the boxing club? Unless he had discovered their secret. He gulped.

Although Arthur couldn't understand how Dave's mind

worked, he had a terrible feeling he'd just jumped from the frying pan into the fire.

10

GARY CARTER WAS FEELING ON top of the world as he sat at the centre of a group of admiring punters. He was perched on a barstool in The Lamb public house and was drinking heavily. Having an audience, helped boost Gary's ego no end. With a brother like Dave, sometimes Gary felt a little trapped in the big man's shadow. He loved his brother, absolutely adored him, but sometimes it wasn't easy being the younger, less successful Carter brother.

The people gathered around him were listening to his stories avidly. They couldn't get enough of him and argued over who would be next to buy him a drink.

It had been a struggle, but Gary had managed to stay away from the cocaine for the last month or so. To fill the void in his life left by the addictive drug, he had turned more heavily to alcohol. He had always been a social drinker, and never drunk by himself during the day, but at night, alcohol made him the life and soul of the party.

"You never did!" A middle-aged woman called Denise said in response to Gary's latest tale.

All right, so Gary had exaggerated just a little bit. But it was what his audience wanted. They loved to live vicariously through his stories, and Gary was happy to oblige.

"I did, and that's not all. You should have seen his face when he saw the bucket of fish!" Garry said, delivering the punchline to his adoring audience.

The people surrounding him exploded with laughter, and Denise was forced to wipe away the tears streaming down her cheeks as she leaned on her husband's shoulder.

Gary beamed happily until a reedy voice piped up, "I hope your brother is all right, Gary. I heard his business is on the downturn."

"Who said that?" Gary demanded, twisting around on the barstool.

A short man with a thatch of dark, curly hair stepped forward. "I didn't mean any offence. I think the world of your brother."

Gary tried to focus on the man. He didn't recognise him, but the sheer quantity of beer he had consumed that night made it hard to think clearly.

"I'll have you know my brother is doing fantastically. He is going from strength to strength."

The curly haired man seemed to sway in front of Gary, but Gary put that down to the booze.

"I heard Martin Morton might be getting out soon. That will cause him some problems."

Gary's lip curled up in disgust. "That won't bother Dave. He's a much better man than Martin Morton will ever be."

The rest of the crowd quietened down a little and took steps back, as they sensed the atmosphere change between the two men.

Gary jerked forward, trying to get off the barstool, but he was so drunk, he stumbled a little. "I think you need to be taught a lesson," Gary said.

The dark-haired man laughed and slipped away before Gary, who was far too inebriated to follow through on his threat, could do anything.

He turned to Bob, who was propping up the bar next to him, "Who was that cheeky bastard?"

"Oh, he's no one to worry about, Gary. He was just trying

to wind you up."

Gary nodded at the barmaid and ordered another beer. "He doesn't know what he's talking about."

"Of course, he doesn't," Old Bob agreed as he took another sip of his pint.

"Dave is a bloody genius when it comes to running his firm. He's got plans for another little project. Patterson's boxing club. Have you heard of it?"

Old Bob turned slightly on his barstool, so he was fully facing Gary. "What does Dave want with a boxing club?"

Gary grinned and then tapped the side of his nose. "That's why Dave is so clever. He spots the opportunities that pass everybody else by."

Old Bob frowned and looked a little confused, but he didn't bother to press Gary. He'd spent his whole life in the East End and had learned the less he knew about certain matters, the better.

But Gary couldn't keep it to himself. He leaned forward, resting his elbows heavily on the polished surface of the bar. "It isn't just a boxing club."

Old Bob cocked his head to one side. "It isn't?"

Gary shook his head and grinned again. "It's just the front. They're moving stolen goods through it, and Dave is going to get in on the action. Smart, eh?"

Old Bob looked suitably impressed, and Gary happily went back to drinking his fresh pint. Unfortunately for Gary, Old Bob wasn't the only one listening.

***

Henry the Hand, so-called because he had lost a couple of fingers in a factory accident years ago, picked up his pint and smiled. It was fascinating the things you could hear in a boozer once alcohol had loosened people's tongues.

What Gary Carter had just disclosed was interesting. Very interesting. And if Henry wasn't mistaken, he was sure the Mortons would be able to use it to their advantage.

Henry finished off his pint and stood to leave. He could have left the bar without anyone noticing, but he couldn't resist letting Gary know he had overheard.

He paused by the bar and said, "Hello, Gary."

As soon as Gary clapped eyes on him, his mouth dropped open, and he grew pale. He immediately knew he had screwed up. That much was obvious from the expression on his face.

Henry grinned. He wished he could be a fly on the wall when Dave Carter found out his brother had been blabbing his mouth off.

***

Babs drummed her long, red fingernails impatiently on the table as she waited for Martin in the prison waiting room.

As the prisoners were led in by a prison guard, Babs looked out for Martin. He'd sent another visiting order and said he needed to see her urgently.

She would have preferred to have waited to visit him until after she'd seen the books. Tony had finally agreed to let her have a look at them, and he was going to deliver them tonight, so she could look through the club's figures and try to work out what was going on.

She'd hoped to unmask whoever had been cheating them and then present her evidence to Martin. She figured that if she managed to break the news at the same time as telling him she was sending the children to boarding school, Martin might be a little distracted and less likely to blow his top.

But when she got the summons from Martin, Babs didn't have any choice but to show up. Even in here, the bastard held all the real power. Tony was like a limp fish in comparison. Babs couldn't motivate him to do anything unless she threatened to go running to Martin.

Not for the first time, Babs thought the world would be a better place if it were run by women.

Martin sauntered up to the table, and Babs struggled to

raise a smile.

"Hello, darling," Martin said easily, kissing Babs on the cheek. "You're looking smashing."

Babs inclined her head at the compliment. She'd always thought it was important to make the best of herself. She still kept her hair dyed a bright shade of blonde, almost platinum, and kept it in curlers all night, even though the blasted things dug into her scalp and made it hard to sleep. And she never left the house without a full face of make-up. Today she was wearing three of the rings Martin had given her, along with some sapphire earrings and a large gold chain. She also wore her fur coat, which was her pride and joy although it was nearly ten years old now.

It was hot in the prison waiting room, but Babs was damned if she was going to take her coat off. When she visited Martin, she was determined to look the part of his glamorous wife.

"What was so urgent?" Babs asked. "I was only here last week."

"I missed you, didn't I?" Martin said smoothly, and Babs knew he was lying. She'd been married to the man for nearly twenty years. And she was nobody's fool.

"Cigarette?" Martin asked, and Babs delved into her bag and pulled out a packet of fags, pushing them across the table to Martin.

After Martin lit up and had taken his first drag, he said, "I wanted to ask you if you had seen Big Tim lately?"

Irritated at being dragged all across London to talk about Big Tim again, Babs snapped, "No. I haven't seen him. Not for ages anyway."

Why was Martin so worried about Tim? He never asked about any of the other men. After Martin had been sent away, most of the crew had stuck by them and started working for Tony as if it was business as usual. Red-haired Freddie was his right-hand man, and Henry the Hand was as faithful as ever.

But Tim, who'd probably been Martin's most trusted man, had gone off the rails. He'd turned to drink.

It was sad really to see such a powerful, strong man like that be reduced to a gibbering wreck who drank himself stupid every day. Still, it wasn't any of Babs' business, and so long as he didn't cross her, she didn't see why he was a problem.

"He's a drunk Martin. He's lost it. I don't know why you're so worried about him."

Martin narrowed his eyes as he took another draw on the cigarette. "He was one of my men. I'm always concerned when one of my men goes off the rails."

Babs shrugged. She thought Martin was probably concerned that Tim would mouth off when he was drunk and spill some of his secrets. "Look, he's not causing us any problems, and I can't see how he would be a danger to us. The man is just a waster these days."

Martin nodded slowly and seemed a little distracted, so Babs decided this was the perfect moment to tell him about Ruby and Derek.

"I've enrolled the children in a boarding school."

Martin jerked to attention, and his head snapped back towards Babs. "You what?"

Here we go, Babs thought. He hadn't wanted to see the children for the past few months, but now he pretended to be the perfect father.

"They were going off the rails, Martin. They need discipline, and I think this is the best way."

"And you didn't even bother to tell me before you enrolled them?"

"I'm telling you now, aren't I?"

Martin snarled. "I can't bloody believe it. You are going to ship off your own kids to a boarding school. What sort of mother are you?"

Babs bristled. "You don't know what it's like, Martin. They don't listen to me anymore, and they cause me no end of trouble. It's only for another year or two until they're old enough to leave school."

Martin glared hard at Babs as he smoked his cigarette.

Babs had expected this attitude, but it still pissed her off. It was all right for him in here acting like the master of all he surveyed, while she was stuck out there, having to deal with two little brats who seemed to hate her.

"Fine. Do what you like," Martin said irritably. "How's Tony doing? He was blabbering on about the club's takings being down on his last visit."

Babs fumed but tried not to let it show. Bloody Tony. She'd told him not to bother Martin with it yet, not until they at least had some proof. She had been intending to handle this and show Martin exactly how useful she could be to the business.

Right now, it seemed to Babs that she was doing all the hard work and yet getting none of the credit.

She met Martin's glare and folded her arms over her chest. Well, things were about to change. It was about time Babs got the recognition she deserved.

11

LATER THAT EVENING, BIG TIM was walking home. He'd had a skinful as usual at the Blind Beggar and was swaying from side to side on the pavement. It was still early in the evening and only just getting dark, but he'd been propping up the bar since opening time.

He didn't drink for enjoyment any longer. He'd just drunk enough to get to sleep and keep the night horrors away.

Now that he no longer worked for Martin Morton and only did jobs here and there when he was sober enough, he had a lot more free time, and that meant more afternoons in the pub.

God knows what he would have done if Martin hadn't been arrested.

He couldn't have stood looking at that man every day and remembering how he had ordered Tim to kill Kathleen Diamond. So Martin's arrest was a blessing in disguise for Tim, and he had taken the opportunity to walk away.

It wasn't as if he was worried about what Tony Morton would do. The lily-livered Lothario was hardly going to punish him for walking away. He was just interested in having a good time and living it up.

Big Tim stumbled a little on the pavement and reached out to steady himself, placing a big hand on the brick wall.

He didn't have far to go. He had digs just around the corner in Chances Lane.

Which was a good job because the bloody pavement had started to spin.

At least he wouldn't be thinking about Kathleen tonight. He would drift off into a deep, dreamless, alcohol-induced sleep with any luck.

Feeling a little steadier on his feet, Tim let go of the wall and began to walk again, but as he raised his head and looked towards the end of the street, he saw a young boy walking towards him.

At first, he didn't pay any attention, but as the boy got closer and didn't move out of the way, Tim glared at him and prepared to shout at the cheeky little sod. And that's when he saw his face.

Tim stopped walking abruptly. His eyes widened, and he gaped at the boy in front of him.

He looked so like…

His hand reached up to his chest of its own accord, and he crossed himself as he looked down in horror at those familiar dark blue eyes staring up at him.

Big Tim blinked rapidly, telling himself this was just a dream. He must have drunk even more than he'd thought. Maybe he had passed out somewhere and now he was dreaming.

He shook his head, trying to clear it of this horrible apparition.

"Are you all right, mister?"

Big Tim's jaw worked up and down, but no sound came out of his mouth. The boy looked just like her.

The little boy pushed back his dark hair, and his forehead wrinkled in confusion as Big Tim lurched against the wall and crumpled down on his hands and knees before throwing up in the gutter.

That scared the little boy, and he flinched.

As Tim felt a cold sweat envelop him, he slumped in a

wretched heap on the pavement and managed to gasp out, "What is your name?"

"Jimmy."

"Last name?"

The little boy took a step back, wary of this huge giant of a man asking too many questions. He cocked his head to one side and then said, "Diamond. I'm Jimmy Diamond."

***

The following morning, Red-haired Freddie turned up in his gleaming maroon Jaguar. He pulled up outside the Morton house in Poplar, got out of his motor and polished a smudge on the bonnet of the car with his shirtsleeve. It was his pride and joy.

Before he'd even knocked on the door, he could hear Ruby's high-pitched voice protesting.

He had brought his daughter Jemima along for the day, and as Freddie caught her eye and rolled his eyes, Jemima giggled.

He rapped on the door and before long, Babs, looking frazzled, yanked it open.

Freddie gestured grandly and said, "Madam, your carriage awaits."

Babs barely raised a smile as she stepped out of the doorway and yelled at Derek to get a bloody move on.

Then she turned to Freddie and said, "Thanks so much for this, Fred. I know Martin will appreciate it."

"It's no bother at all, Babs." He jerked his thumb at the car. "I've brought my daughter along. You remember Jemima, don't you? I hope you don't mind her coming with us."

Babs noticed Jemima for the first time and narrowed her eyes. Jemima had inherited Freddie's flaming red hair, and she was a knockout. It cascaded down her back in loose curls, and her smooth pale skin seemed to glow with health.

Babs scowled. She didn't like hanging around with younger women. It just made her feel past her sell by date.

"I didn't think you'd mind, Babs. Of course, she'll sit in the back with the kids, and you'll sit up front with me."

Babs nodded. She could hardly protest when Freddie was doing them a favour. So she turned her attention back to the children and gave them a clip round the ear as they finally emerged from the house.

Freddie put their cases into the boot of the car, and after another five minutes moaning from Ruby and Derek, they were on their way to Surrey.

Babs already had a bloody headache. They'd gone on and on last night and then started up again as soon as they got out of bed this morning.

They really thought they were going to change her mind. Well, Babs had news for them. If she hadn't already been convinced, their bellyaching would have tipped her over the edge.

After spending the first half an hour in the car sulking, Ruby couldn't resist talking to the glamorous Jemima. She wanted to know where Jemima had bought her lipstick.

Babs closed her eyes and tried to ignore the inane chatter.

When they'd moved out to Essex, Babs had been thoroughly miserable, but that didn't mean she couldn't appreciate the countryside in small doses. As they got further and further from London, she enjoyed the sight of the greenery rushing past them and smiled as she saw horses galloping in a field they drove past. No, she didn't mind the country. She just didn't want to live there.

Luckily, she had found both Ruby and Derek places in schools very close to each other. They were managed by the same education board, but both schools were single sex, and Babs thought that was for the best.

They dropped Ruby off first.

"Look at that," Babs said. "See, Ruby, it's not so bad. Just think of all the rich kids you'll be mingling with."

Ruby didn't answer and instead muffled a sob.

The outside of the school was very grand. It had a long gravel driveway, and Freddie parked beside an ornate fountain at the main entrance. Babs stalked out of the car, snatching the case from Freddie before he could offer to carry it inside for them.

She grabbed hold of Ruby's arm and practically dragged the girl towards the school.

The outside of the building was made of a type of old stone, and it had some plant growing up the side of it that Babs didn't recognise. It looked very old and crumbly, though. She'd expected something a little more modern and exclusive, considering how much they charged per term.

Babs gave Ruby a prod in the back to hurry her along, and they entered through the large oak doors. They stepped into the cool of the reception area and were met by the school secretary, who asked them to take a seat while she went and fetched Sister Claire and Miss Bunce.

Babs shot a glance at her daughter and actually felt quite guilty. Ruby looked absolutely terrified. But Babs reassured herself she was doing this for Ruby's benefit, and the girl would soon settle in.

When Miss Bunce and Sister Claire arrived, Babs could scarcely believe her eyes. Miss Bunce was short and as round as a ball, and Sister Claire was tall and skinny. They made a funny pair.

The women walked towards Babs in a synchronised fashion.

She'd half expected them to talk as one. But the skinny one spoke first. "Mrs. Morton, I am Sister Claire, and I teach English and deportment. From the information you provided, I think I shall be spending a lot of time with your daughter."

Her pale, watery, blue eyes settled on Ruby, who had bowed her head and was looking miserably at her lap.

Babs awkwardly got to her feet. "Right," she said, feeling very self-conscious about her accent and the amount of makeup she was wearing. "Well, I'd better be off. You be good, Ruby."

She hesitated for a moment and then leaned over and gave her daughter a quick kiss on the cheek. "Don't forget to write."

Babs walked towards the door, and the round Miss Bunce waddled along following her while Sister Claire stayed beside Ruby.

"Would you like to have a look around the school before you go, Mrs. Morton? Most parents like to see their child settled before they leave."

"Well, under normal circumstances, of course, I would love to do that," Babs said, carefully pronouncing each word in what she thought was a posh accent. "But I have got my son in the car, and we're dropping him off at school also."

Miss Bunce looked taken aback at the sudden change in Babs' voice.

She nodded her head once and then said. "Of course, Mrs. Morton. As you wish."

Babs scurried out of there as if her heels were on fire.

She hated feeling like people were looking down on her, and she started to feel a little guilty about leaving poor Ruby there.

But she quickly shook that feeling off. This was what Ruby deserved. Hopefully, it would be the making of the girl.

Babs was unusually quiet in the passenger seat as they drove to Derek's school. It was so close, Freddie had pulled up outside less than two minutes later.

It was larger than the girls' school and appeared more austere. There was no fountain in the driveway for one thing. There were funny little ghoulish animals dotted all around, carved into the stonework, which gave Babs the creeps. She shivered as Freddie opened the car door.

"Come on, Derek," she said, getting out of the car.

This time, Freddie picked up the case and carried it inside.

A young man with glasses had spotted their arrival and asked them to wait until he went and got Mr. Stockingham.

Babs put a hand to her chest. She was getting indigestion. She hadn't expected the whole experience to be so stressful.

She looked at her son and felt the familiar stirring of guilt. He looked so sad.

"Cheer up," Babs snapped. "It is not the end of the world. You're only here for one term before the summer holidays."

Derek shot his mother a look that told her exactly how much he appreciated her comments.

He stayed sulkily silent, which irritated Babs no end.

Shortly after that exchange, they were joined by Mr. Stockingham. He was a very tall man and very slim, and he carried a cane.

When Babs saw that, her eyes widened. She hoped he didn't use that on the children.

But then she noticed he was walking with a slight limp and breathed a sigh of relief. That explained the cane.

Mr. Stockingham gave a small, formal bow, and Babs felt unsure of what to do in response. Blimey. This place was posh. Did he expect her to curtsy, or what?

But she was saved from embarrassing herself when Mr. Stockingham suggested they go into his office.

As they walked along the wood-panelled corridor, they passed a group of boys. They were all wearing blazers and ties and looked ever so smart. No shirts were untucked, and all their shoes were polished to a high shine. But the thing that stood out most for Babs was the fact they were all silent.

There was no laughter or hijinks. There was no shouting out. No boyish behaviour at all, really.

It made Babs feel a little uneasy at first, but then she thought maybe it was a good thing. They looked like little gentlemen. She wouldn't mind if Derek came home and acted a little more civilised.

Inside Mr. Stockingham's office, Derek and Babs sat down,

and Mr. Stockingham sat behind his desk.

"Welcome to Trumpleton, Derek," the schoolmaster said in a deep voice. "We run a very tight ship here, but as long as you play by the rules, I'm sure you'll fit in without any problems."

Derek didn't answer but looked up sulkily through his long dark eyelashes at Mr. Stockingham.

Babs leaned over and nudged him hard with her elbow. "Well, what do you say?"

"Thank you, sir," Derek mumbled as Babs glared at him.

Before anyone could say anything else, there was a knock at the office door, and when Babs turned, she saw a short, stout boy with freckles, who had perfectly combed hair.

"Ah, Rogers," Mr. Stockingham said. "This is Derek Morton. Please show him to the dorm rooms, and he will be joining you for maths this afternoon. Make him feel at home, Rogers."

Rogers' eyes flitted to Derek for a second as if he was weighing the boy up and then returned to Mr. Stockingham.

"Of course, sir," Rogers said in a cut glass accent.

Babs bit her lower lip. Blimey. Was there anyone who didn't speak like the Queen of England around here?

She hadn't expected the schools to be quite so posh. She started to worry about how Derek and Ruby would fit in.

All of a sudden it seemed that Derek was whisked off with Rogers to his dorm room, and Babs hadn't even had a proper chance to say goodbye.

She felt shell shocked as she looked at Mr. Stockingham.

The schoolmaster sat back in his chair, stretching out his long frame as he looked at Babs.

"Now, Mrs. Morton. I know it's worrying when you send your children away to school for the first time. But I will personally keep an eye on Derek and make sure he gets settled."

Babs nodded. "Thank you," she said, trying to put on a

posh accent again and failing miserably. "I'll be off now then."

"Jolly good."

Mr. Stockingham showed her out, and as she left the dark school corridor and stepped out into the bright summer sunlight, her eyes watered.

She told herself it was just because the sun was so bright, and blinked furiously, determined not to let Freddie and Jemima see her crying.

She quickly got into the car, shut the door and stared straight ahead, ignoring Jemima in the back seat and Freddie at the steering wheel.

"Did everything go all right, Babs?" Freddie asked, looking concerned.

"Absolutely fine," Babs said as her voice broke and tears rolled down her cheeks. "Just drive, Freddie. Just get us home."

12

ARTHUR PATTERSON DRAGGED HIS FEET as he made his way to his brother's boxing club. He was dreading this. How had his stupid son got him into this mess? It was only a quarrel between two schoolboys, that's all it was. A fair man would have let it go, Arthur thought moodily. Everyone liked to harp on about how fair Dave Carter was. And they called him the greengrocer gangster! Well, that was a laugh.

Dave Carter was the worst of the lot. And now if Arthur didn't do what Dave Carter had ordered, he would be in deep trouble.

As the large, square building that housed his brother's boxing club came into view, Arthur felt his stomach churn. His brother was going to bloody kill him when he knew Dave Carter had found out about their little enterprise.

Arthur sighed as he pushed open the door. He didn't have a choice, so he may as well get it over and done with.

Inside the boxing club, it was warm and smelled of rubber mats mixed with the tang of old perspiration.

Usually, Arthur would have arrived and gotten straight on with the cleaning. He did the changing rooms first followed by the main gym area. Today, though, he needed to talk to his brother first.

His brother, Gregory, was standing on the side of the ring, leaning on the ropes and shouting out encouragement at two of the lads sparring off.

There were only a few lads gathered beside the ring. The rest of them were using the punch bags at the far end of the gym.

Arthur watched the boxing for a moment in silence. The bigger boy should have had the advantage, but it was the younger one, who was faster with his feet and hands, who was getting in the best blows.

When Gregory barked at the two lads to take a break, Arthur chose that opportunity to approach him.

When Gregory noticed his brother, he frowned. "All right, Arthur. Have you made a start on the changing rooms yet?"

Arthur shook his head, and Gregory's frown deepened.

Sometimes, Arthur really hated working for his brother. He used to work at a warehouse, packing and moving boxes, but he had been laid off two years ago and had to come cap in hand to Gregory asking for a job. Which really ate away at his pride.

To his credit, Gregory had given him a job without a murmur, but every time Gregory looked at him, Arthur thought he was stifling his irritation.

He hated to be thought of as the less successful brother. Everyone loved Gregory. With his fair good looks and sparkling blue eyes, he'd had the ladies chasing after him since he was a teenager. Arthur was always in the golden boy's shadow, and he resented it. Then Gregory had taken over the boxing club and turned it around into something special. He'd managed to get a couple of prize-winning fighters training in the gym after he took it over, and since then he'd gone from success to success.

Boxing could be a lucrative business, with the right promotion and money for fights, not to mention a little gambling on the side, but Gregory's wealth didn't simply come from boxing, although it was a nice legitimate front.

"Why the long face, Arthur?"

Arthur swallowed nervously then said, "We need to talk."

"We are talking."

"No, I mean we need to talk in private."

That familiar look of irritation flashed across Gregory's face and then he jerked his chin in the direction of the small room at the back of the gym he used as an office.

Arthur followed his brother over to the office and then shut the door behind them.

"Right. Come on then, spit it out."

Arthur's legs felt a bit shaky, and he wanted to sit down, but as Gregory remained standing, he did so too.

He knew the best way was to just come straight out with it. There was no point trying to butter him up first. Gregory didn't like that, and he would see through Arthur immediately.

"Dave Carter was round my house last night. He wants a cut." Arthur held his breath as he waited for his brother's reaction.

Gregory was dangerously silent. He cocked his head to one side and narrowed his eyes as he looked at his brother. "And how the hell would Dave Carter know about our little side business?"

Arthur put up his hands and shook his head frantically. "I didn't tell him. I swear I didn't. But somehow he has found out, and he wants a cut in exchange for protection."

Gregory gritted his teeth and then leaned heavily on the desk, cursing loudly.

He'd had it far too good for too long. Arthur wanted to remind him how lucky he was that nobody had got wind of it before now. He'd been skating on thin ice for a long time. If Dave Carter had got wind of their stolen goods racket, then it wouldn't be long before others did, too.

"What exactly does he know?"

Arthur licked his lips. "I'm not sure. He came round to mine because of some bust up between my boy and his. I thought he was going to bleeding kill me, but then he told me he needed my help. He asked me to persuade you, but he left me in no doubt that if I couldn't, he would turn to more aggressive tactics."

Gregory slammed a fist on the desk. Arthur hadn't seen his brother lose his cool like this before and a small part of him actually felt pleased.

Gregory snapped his head around to face his brother. "You really are a fool, Arthur. Did Carter only mention the stolen goods…or was he referring to something else?"

Arthur shook his head, feeling confused. "Something else? What else could it be?"

Gregory clenched his fists. "This is all I need. We've been so careful. I didn't even trust my own brother, and I'm glad of that now," he muttered.

Arthur was about to ask his brother what he was going on about when he saw the fury in Gregory's eyes and decided to bite his tongue.

Arthur kept quiet as Gregory ranted and raved about Dave Carter.

Finally, after his brother ran out of steam, Arthur asked, "What are we going to do?"

Gregory's head jerked up as he glared at his brother. "What are we going to do? We aren't going to do anything, are we? You're gonna get out there and clean the sodding bogs, and I will have to sort this out on my own. Go on, get out of my sight."

Arthur felt his cheeks burn in response to his brother's treatment. He really could be a git at times.

Arthur stalked out of the room, wishing he had another job he could go to, so he could tell his brother where to stick this one.

***

That afternoon, after Freddie had driven her back from Surrey, Babs sat in the front room, nursing a sherry and feeling very sorry for herself. She had an absolutely blinding headache and still felt tearful. Her throat ached from all the tears she had shed earlier.

She'd almost polished off her first sherry when there was a loud hammering at the door.

Babs stood up and glanced out of the front room window so she could see out onto the street, and she caught sight of her visitor's navy blue, wool coat and curly grey hair.

Oh, Christ. A visit from Martin's mother was all she needed.

Babs set down her sherry glass on the coffee table and marched up to the front door.

She yanked open the door, and before she could even say hello to Violet, the old woman launched into a vitriol-filled tirade.

"You've really blown it this time, my girl! What kind of woman sends her own children away?"

Babs was in no mood for this. She had been just about to invite Violet in, but now there was no way she was going to allow that woman to step foot inside her house. She crossed her arms over her chest and blocked the doorway, preventing Violet from entering.

"Get out of my way," Violet ordered, trying to push past Babs.

But Babs stood firm. She was sick and tired of being pushed around by Violet.

"I've got a headache, Violet. It's not a good time," Babs said as she prepared to shut the front door.

"Don't you bleeding shut that door on me!" Violet screeched.

Babs noticed some curtain twitching going on over the road as Violet caused a scene. Usually, Babs would have ushered her mother-in-law inside and tried to calm her down, but today she really didn't care what the neighbours thought.

"No."

"No? What do you mean no?" Violet's face was a picture.

She looked up, horrified. Babs had never refused her entry in the past, and as her sons both bowed down to their mother, she was used to getting her own way.

"You heard me," Babs said. "The children are in school. It's the best place for them."

"I always knew you were a rubbish mother. But if you are having trouble, you're supposed to turn to family. You should have come to me and told me you couldn't cope."

Babs' cheeks flamed red, and her palms itched to reach out and slap Violet Morton's face.

There was no way she would ever go to Violet for help with her children, especially seeing how Martin and Tony had turned out.

"They're my children, and I'll do what I see fit," Babs hissed.

Violet shook her head. "I told Martin you'd be a terrible wife. He should have listened to me. Look how those poor little kids have turned out."

"There's nothing wrong with my kids," Babs roared, forgetting that just this morning she was despairing of the pair of them. "And I don't see how you have the nerve to come around here spouting off advice after the way your two boys have turned out!"

"What are you talking about, you silly tart? My boys are both perfect gentlemen."

"One of your boys has been in prison for the last ten years, and the other one is only happy when he is surrounded by women and booze. He can't even manage the family business without my direction."

Violet's tiny figure shook with rage, and she raised her handbag and jerked forward to whack Babs with it.

Babs easily ducked out of the way and cackled with laughter. "The truth hurts, doesn't it, Violet?"

As Babs laughed on and on and tried to wipe the tears from

her eyes, Violet's face was getting redder and redder until it almost looked purple.

Just then, an older woman and a young lad walked past on the other side of the street.

The lad asked the woman what was happening. He was clearly engrossed in the argument between Babs and Violet. But the woman hurried him along and then she turned to him and said in a very loud voice, "Don't you mind about that one, Jimmy. She is all fur coat and no knickers."

Babs stop laughing abruptly, and both she and Violet turned to look at the woman. Babs opened her mouth to shout some insults back at the old trout who had dared to insult her when the words froze in her throat.

She recognised the woman. Mary bloody Diamond. And that meant… The boy with her was Jimmy Diamond.

Babs felt sick. Suddenly her argument with Violet was no longer fun.

That boy was Martin's son. Seeing him felt like a kick in the stomach, a reminder of the child Babs had lost. Her precious Emily had been taken while that bastard boy had thrived.

Babs furiously slammed the door in Violet's face and stormed back inside.

For a full ten minutes, Violet shouted at her, hammering on the front door and even leaning over to rap on the window with her knuckles, but Babs ignored her.

Seeing that little boy had brought back all the memories of the betrayal she'd felt when Martin had had an affair with Kathleen Diamond, and she felt her heart ache from the loss of her little one. How was it fair that Martin's bastard had survived while her poor baby hardly had a chance to live?

Martin told her he'd arranged for Kathleen and the child to be taken off somewhere safe, but when Kathleen's body was found floating in the canal, Babs had put two and two together. It was an uncomfortable thought. She knew Martin could be an evil bastard, but to murder the mother of his child... Babs shivered. He really was a monster.

Since Mary Diamond only lived a couple of streets away, she couldn't really avoid seeing them. Every time she saw Jimmy, it was like a slap in the face.

Babs had been so angry at Martin when she discovered what he had done, so she hadn't been thinking straight when Dave Carter approached her. If she'd have been in her right mind, she would never have betrayed Martin. Not because she loved him, but because she was afraid of him.

Martin was banged up, but Babs would never be safe. She would have to live with fear for the rest of her life. It was inevitable. One day, Martin would find out how she'd betrayed him.

13

WILLIAM MOSS WAS HAVING ONE of the worst days of his life. He'd thought he'd sunk as low as he could go when he'd been sentenced to five years for fraud a few months ago. As a solicitor, that pretty much meant an end to his career. So not only was he banged up for five years, he also had no job or career to return to at the end of it.

But if he thought he'd hit bottom when he was sentenced, he was gravely mistaken.

William realised that now as two heavyset men loomed over him in the exercise yard.

He'd been glad of the fresh air and the chance to see the sky when he'd first stepped out on the bright summer's morning, but now he wished he was safely back in his cell.

He didn't recognise the men and had no idea what he'd done to upset them. But sadly, he had already learned that prison was a place where people would attack you for no reason at all.

William was a weedy man. There was no way he could match up to these men physically. The only things he had to his advantage were his brains and his quick wits.

"Hang on, fellows, surely we can just talk things over like gentlemen."

The taller of the two men bellowed out a booming laugh and turned to his friend. "Did you hear that, Michael? He thinks we're gentlemen."

Michael cackled with laughter, showing a mouthful of rotten teeth that made William feel sick.

Michael leaned closer to him, breathing his stinky breath all over William's face as he said, "We are not gentlemen."

William shook his head. "If I've done something to upset you, I apologise."

"We don't want your apology," Michael said and spat on the floor. "We want payment."

William swallowed and dug around in his pockets until he pulled out a bar of chocolate, he thrust it towards Michael. He hoped that would do. That was all he had. "Here, you can have it with my compliments."

Michael pocketed the goods and then looked at his friend. "His compliments. Did you hear that?"

And just as William was hoping the matter was all settled, Michael made one swift movement, bringing his arm around and hitting William on the side of the face. It was an open-handed slap and didn't have much force behind it, but it was still hard enough to make William's ears ring as he gaped in surprise.

William felt horrified as he realised he was close to tears.

It was so unfair. He'd given the men what they wanted, and now they were going to beat him up anyway.

He raised his arms to try and ward off some of the blows, but before Michael got a chance to hit him again, he heard a low voice quietly murmur, "That's enough lads."

There was a change in the atmosphere immediately. William heard Michael's sharp intake of breath, and when he dared to look up through his fingers, he saw a tall, slim figure standing over him.

He might have had no idea who the two men who accosted him were, but even William Moss knew who Martin Morton was.

William began to tremble. This day was going from bad to

worse.

With a few muttered apologies, Michael and his crony quickly left the scene.

Martin stared down at William, and it was a moment before William realised he was still crouched on the floor with his arms up over his head. Feeling a little bit daft, he quickly straightened up, nodded once at Martin Morton and then made to walk away.

If he just kept his head down and kept on walking then maybe he'd get out of this alive…

"Not so fast."

William's stomach churned with nerves as he slowly turned back around to face Martin Morton.

"Mr. Morton. It's a pleasure to meet you." William held out his hand formally.

A smirk twitched on Martin's mouth, but eventually he reached out and took William's hand in a vice-like grip, shaking it firmly.

William stood there, transfixed. He was shaking, and while he tried to tell himself it was due to the cold nip in the air, he knew it was really because he was standing in front of Martin Morton, the gangster, who was well known to rule the roost in prison.

"Can I help you with something… sir?"

William added sir to his question as an afterthought. It didn't hurt to show as much respect as he could.

"I've heard you are a solicitor."

William nodded slowly as the penny began to drop. "I used to be."

"What are you doing in here then?"

"Fraud," William said. There didn't seem to be any point in lying.

"Something concerns me, William."

William picked up on Martin's use of his first name. He hadn't thought Martin would know who he was.

"Are you really any good at your job? I mean, if you are a good solicitor, one would hope you'd manage to keep yourself out of prison."

Although it was foolish, William couldn't help bristling from the insult. He'd been an excellent solicitor. The trouble was, William's boss was a conniving bastard, and had set William up to take the fall for his fraudulent activities. William had been sewn up like a kipper.

"I was very good at my job," William said. "Unfortunately, I trusted the wrong people."

Martin nodded slowly as if he was considering William's words carefully. "You'd be wise to trust no one, William. I hope you've learned that lesson now." William nodded. He had. Now that he'd lost his job, and he had nothing to do with his days, he spent most of his time plotting revenge against the people who had put him in here. Never again would he fall for such a dirty trick.

"I appreciate you intervening just then," William said, feeling a little more confident now that Martin was talking to him like a normal person. Perhaps he wasn't so bad, after all. "I'm not sure what I did to upset them. But they seem to have it in for me."

"Prison life isn't much different from life on the outside, William," Martin said. "You need to operate in much the same way, and that means making the right connections. Do you understand?"

William nodded. "I do. That makes sense."

William did understand, and it was all very well to say make the right connections, but William had always been on the right side of the law. He didn't know how to operate in the underworld, and honestly, he wasn't keen on finding out how either.

But it seemed like he didn't have much choice.

"Now, if you stick with me. I'll make sure those lads don't bother you again."

William exhaled a long breath in relief. He didn't know why Martin Morton was being nice to him, but he wasn't about to look a gift horse in the mouth. "That's really very kind of you, Mr. Morton."

Martin smiled then, a cruel grin full of menace, which sent a shiver up William's spine. "Kind has got nothing to do with it, William. I just think we could have a mutually beneficial arrangement."

William gulped, but he managed to croak out. "I'm sure we could, Mr. Morton. What did you have in mind?"

***

Linda tried to smother another yawn and hoped that Mr. Bevel didn't catch sight of her. He got extremely annoyed if he thought his staff weren't bright-eyed and bushy-tailed, and he was fond of telling Linda that every morning.

She got up from her desk and began to wander along between the rows of sewing stations — making sure each machinist was putting out good work and at a satisfactory speed. She had tried to encourage Mr. Bevel to move with the times and produce some more fashionable items. After all, they were now in the sixties. But Mr. Bevel didn't listen and continued to stick with his less contemporary lines, insisting that was what his buyers wanted.

Linda hadn't slept well last night, tossing and turning and worrying about the future. She had cancelled the doctor's appointment as Geoff had ordered, but she couldn't help thinking she'd done the wrong thing. She was at her wits' end and had no idea how to get Geoff around to her way of thinking.

Linda was lost in her own thoughts as she walked along the next row of sewing stations. So when Mr. Bevel called her name, she jumped and then scurried over to him quickly.

His bushy eyebrows were knitted together, and he didn't look like he was in a good mood.

He jerked his thumb at Linda, indicating she should go to

his office, and she trotted along behind him.

He had piles of paperwork all over his desk, and he pointed to one of the stacks.

"We're behind, Linda. And that's not good."

They'd been through a period a couple of years ago when commissions had dried up, but fortunately, Mr. Bevel had managed to get a couple of big contracts. The downside was they demanded a very quick turnaround time, which put everyone under stress.

"And I've just been asked to complete this job by next Wednesday, too." He handed Linda another piece of paper, and her eyes widened. Two hundred pairs of knickers! When on earth were they supposed to fit this work in?

"Could we hire some temporary machinists, Mr. Bevel? Just until we've got this job out of the way."

Mr. Bevel shook his head. "There's no money for that," he snapped. "You'll just have to get the girls to work faster. We will cut the lunch break by ten minutes, and nobody, I mean absolutely nobody, is allowed outside for a cigarette break during work hours."

Linda set her mouth in a firm line. The truth was since Linda had been in charge, none of the girls had been nipping out for cigarette breaks, but she truly believed that each girl should have a whole half an hour for lunch. She was pretty sure that Mr. Bevel wasn't going to be paying them for that extra ten minutes.

Linda hesitated for a moment, wondering whether to speak up on behalf of the girls. She hated to think Mr. Bevel was taking advantage of them, and the fact he'd bought a brand-new motor last year hadn't gone unnoticed by Linda, so money couldn't be that hard up surely.

Linda opened her mouth to voice her concerns, but Mr. Bevel raised a hand and made a flicking motion, dismissing her.

What a cheek, Linda thought. She turned around and

stalked back into the machinists' area.

Her eyes scanned the stations, and she noticed that one was empty.

She walked up and asked the woman at the next desk, "Where's Valerie gone?"

"She's gone to the lav, Linda."

Linda shook her head. Again. Valerie had already visited the outdoor lavatory three times this morning. Linda started to suspect she was sneaking off for a cheeky fag break.

"I'll be back in a minute," Linda said and strolled out of the room.

She was going to have to have a word. Valerie was really taking liberties.

All the girls knew they were supposed to ask when they needed a break to use the lav. Linda didn't exactly agree with that, but it was company policy, and the girls had to stick by the rules if they expected to keep their jobs. It wasn't fair if all the other girls followed the rules and Valerie didn't.

Linda quickly crossed the backyard, heading towards the outdoor lavatory. Mr. Bevel kept promising to fit an indoor toilet, but he had been saying that for years and one had never materialised. Linda wrinkled her nose as she heard Valerie retching in the small outhouse.

"Valerie, it's Linda. If you're not feeling well, you can go home. I'm sure Mr. Bevel will understand."

There was no answer, so Linda waited, and after a moment, the door of the toilet stall opened, and Valerie's pale face appeared. Her eyes were rimmed with red, and she looked a mess.

"You look terrible, Valerie," Linda said sympathetically. "You get yourself off home and get into bed. I'll clear everything with Mr. Bevel."

At Linda's kind words, Valerie burst into tears.

Linda patted her on the shoulder. "There, there, you'll feel better when you get home and get into a nice warm bed."

Valerie shook her head, and through sobs, she said, "It isn't going to get better."

"Of course, it will," Linda said. "You've just picked up a tummy bug. You'll be right as rain in no time."

Valerie hiccuped and tried to dry her eyes. "You don't understand, Linda. I'm not sick. I'm pregnant."

Linda let her hand drop from Valerie's shoulder and felt her body tense.

Valerie mistook her reaction for shock, and so she babbled on, trying to explain, "I know it seems terrible. But me and Barry are getting married. I told him last week. Only he has gone away on the boat, and we can't get married until he gets back. I'm sure he will marry me, though."

Linda felt sick herself. How was it fair that a girl like Valerie got pregnant at the drop of a hat, and she wasn't even married, and yet Linda, who'd been married for years, was unable to have a baby?

Valerie sniffed. "You won't tell Mr. Bevel will you? I just need a bit of time until Barry gets back from sea."

Linda closed her eyes. Although she felt sorry for Valerie, she couldn't help but feel jealous. It also brought back floods of memories from the time when Kathleen had fallen pregnant with Jimmy. Kathleen had been unmarried and Mr. Bevel had sacked her. They weren't in the fifties anymore, but she wasn't sure Mr. Bevel would be any more lenient with Valerie.

Everyone at Bevel's had turned their back on Kathleen, and that had been cruel. Linda still felt a little guilty for not offering her friend more support.

She sighed and put her hand back on Valerie's shoulder, giving it a gentle rub. "Your secret is safe with me, Valerie. Now try to tidy yourself up before Mr. Bevel notices you're missing."

14

BABS WAS SITTING DOWN AT the kitchen table with a cigarette in one hand and the accounting books for the club in front of her. She took a long, thoughtful drag on her cigarette and then blew out the smoke slowly.

She'd left school at twelve, but she'd always been pretty good with numbers. And if Babs wasn't mistaken, there was a serious problem with these books. She'd made an appointment with another accountant, whom she'd found in the phone book, for a second opinion. Of course, that was a risk, but she had copied out some numbers on a sheet of paper ready to show him. She'd given a false name when booking the appointment and felt quite confident that even if the accountant did find something fishy, he wouldn't be able to trace her or report her to the police.

She rubbed her eyes, which were stinging. She'd been looking through the bloody books for hours.

Seeing Jimmy Diamond again had knocked her for six. Of course, she'd known that Mary and her grandson only lived a few streets away. But somehow, she'd managed to cope by pushing it all to the back of her mind. They didn't mix in the same social circles, and that was good enough for Babs as long as they kept their distance.

Babs took another drag on her cigarette and tried to block the memory of finding baby Emily dead in her crib. Even now, the pain of remembering that day took her breath away.

She didn't even want to contemplate how Kathleen had met her end. Although she was loath to admit it, deep down, Babs was very scared she could end up the same way as Kathleen.

She stubbed out her cigarette viciously in the ashtray, annoyed she was allowing her mind to wander again, and tried to concentrate on the figures.

She put a finger on the page and trailed it down the column of numbers, adding up the figures. She had done it three times already, and each time, she was coming up about fifty pounds short every month. She had all of the order receipts, but they didn't match up with what was written down in the book.

Babs rubbed a weary hand over her face, thinking perhaps she'd better take a break before her eyes went boss-eyed, when there was a knock at the door.

She stood up, stretched and tried to release the crick in her neck by rolling her shoulders as she walked towards the front door.

When she opened it, she saw Frieda Longbottom smiling at her.

"Ah, Babs, sweetheart, I thought I would come round and see how you are doing. You must be in bits."

Babs stepped back, surprised, and arched her eyebrows as Frieda marched into her house and walked along the passage towards the kitchen.

She had no idea what Frieda was talking about. Why would Babs be in bits? What had happened?

As the two women entered the kitchen, Babs asked Frieda, "What's the matter? What am I supposed to be upset about?"

Frieda looked taken aback. "The children, of course. I only just heard you had to send them away."

"Oh, that," Babs said, waving a hand dismissively as she walked over to the stove and picked up the kettle. "It was the best thing for them, Frieda. I must say it's strange not having them around, but the peace and quiet is welcome."

Frieda looked shocked.

"I'm not saying I'm not going to miss them," Babs added hurriedly. "But sometimes we have to do things for our children that are difficult to benefit them in the long run."

Frieda nodded doubtfully, and Babs could tell she wasn't completely convinced.

"Have you spoken to either of them today?"

Babs filled the kettle and laid it down heavily on top of the stove.

"I need to give them a little while to settle in. I'm sure the other parents aren't calling every minute of the day."

Frieda made a humph sound and looked at Babs with disapproval.

She didn't know why but Babs yearned for Frieda's approval. Probably because Frieda had been like a mother to her, and she'd been Babs' rock after she lost Emily.

Babs had never been particularly maternal. She certainly wasn't the type to coo over babies, but she did love her own children, and she didn't want people thinking she didn't care.

"I know people will think me harsh, Frieda. But I'm only doing this for Ruby and Derek because it's for the best. I spoiled them rotten after I lost Emily, and it turned them into a pair of horrors. I want them to make a success of their lives, and we can afford it. They are getting the best education money can buy."

"They are so far away from family and everything they know, but I suppose you know best. What's the school like?"

Babs leaned back against the kitchen worktop as she waited for the kettle to boil. "They're attending two connected schools, one for girls and one for boys, so each school is single sex, which is for the best. They are ever so upmarket. Both schools are in old country houses, and they are huge. You wouldn't believe the size of them." Babs smiled dreamily, picturing her children hobnobbing with the toast of English society. "They'll make friends soon enough."

Frieda nodded although she still looked doubtful, but Babs didn't notice as she was busy preparing the tea.

When she set two steaming cups down on the table and sat down opposite Frieda, she was about to launch into a long-winded explanation of why the children needed to be at boarding school, but before she could, there was another knock at the door.

"Excuse me, Frieda. I won't be a moment, love."

Babs got up from the table and bustled towards the front door.

When she opened it, she was surprised to see a young lad she didn't recognise. His cheeks were pockmarked with acne, and his hair was too long and tucked behind his ears.

"Yes," Babs snapped.

"Are you Babs Morton?"

"Yes. Who's asking?"

"I've got a note for you. It's from Dave Carter."

Babs snatched the note from the boy's hand, and he turned and scarpered up the street. She stared down at the piece of paper as if it might spontaneously explode.

Why on earth would Dave Carter be writing her a note? Surely it couldn't be about Martin after all this time?

She put her hand to her throat and could feel her pulse racing.

She hadn't had anything to do with Dave Carter, not since before Martin got sent down. She had purposely avoided him.

Babs was so distracted she didn't notice Frieda had got up from the table until she was by her side.

"Did he just say a note from Dave Carter?" Frieda said, trying to look over Babs' shoulder.

Babs mentally cursed Frieda's sharp hearing. She crushed the note in her fist and shook her head.

"Yes, but I'm sure it's nothing important. Now, Frieda, I'm

really sorry, but I had better get on with the books. I don't have much longer to go through them."

Frieda glanced back towards the kitchen at her untouched cup of tea. "But I haven't even finished my brew."

"I know. I'm sorry, but it's really not a good time."

Frieda pursed her lips, clearly put out by the fact Babs didn't want to confide in her.

As she stepped outside the front door, Frieda couldn't resist turning around and asking, "What does the note say?"

But Babs didn't answer. "Bye, Frieda. Thanks for coming round." And with that, she shut the door.

With Frieda safely out of the way, Babs rushed to the kitchen and then stared down at the crumpled note in her hand.

She could hardly bear to read it.

What if Dave had changed his mind and was going to tell Martin all about their little collusion? Christ. Martin would do his nut if he ever found out.

Slowly, Babs took a deep breath to calm her nerves and opened up the folded note.

She quickly scanned it and saw that Dave was asking for a meeting in Victoria Park this afternoon.

Babs bit down on her lip. She didn't like the sound of that. It had to be bad news. She'd gotten away with it for so long, but what if Dave had been merely biding his time? Was he now going to use what he knew against her?

If he told Martin about the role Babs had played in his downfall, she knew Martin would kill her. Babs put the note down on the table with a shaking hand. She was a dead woman walking.

15

BABS CHANGED HER OUTFIT FOUR times before finally settling on a smart, dark red dress. She touched up her powder and applied a fresh coat of lipstick. Finally, she pulled on her fur coat and patted her hair down while checking in the mirror to make sure she looked presentable, and then at three p.m. she set out for Victoria Park.

She was as nervous as hell about the meeting, and for the entire walk, she fretted about what Dave was going to say. At one point when she was halfway along Camberwell Road, she put a hand to her churning stomach, positive she was going to be sick.

She knew one thing for sure, she couldn't let her nerves show. If Dave sensed any weakness, he would exploit it. He was famous for that.

It was a long walk, and when Babs finally approached the miniature boating lake, she scanned the area for Dave and saw he had already arrived. It didn't take long for her to spot him standing beside the water. Suddenly, her mouth felt dry.

Dave wore a long dark overcoat, as the weather had turned chilly for summer, and Babs was glad of her fur coat. Not just for the warmth. She felt it made her look important and intimidating.

As Dave walked slowly over to her, Babs' body froze, and she had to will herself to move her feet and continue walking towards him.

Despite telling herself over and over again to be relaxed when she spoke to him, as soon as he was within hearing distance, she blurted out, "I thought you said you were going to let sleeping dogs lie?"

Dave frowned at her outburst. "Hello, Babs. You're looking lovely as usual."

Babs was impatient. Her life was on the line, and she didn't have time to listen to his flattery. She wanted to know what business he had calling her all the way over here and whether or not he was going to spill the beans to Martin.

"I'm a busy woman, Dave. If you've got something to say, please go ahead."

A smile played across Dave's face as if he found her amusing, and Babs felt herself bristle.

He was well out of order. The very fact that she was married to Martin Morton afforded her at least a little respect. And Babs didn't like the thought of Dave Carter laughing at her.

"What are you laughing at?" she snapped.

The smile slipped from Dave's face, and his expression was dangerously calm.

"You seem upset, Babs."

"Upset? Of course, I'm bleeding well upset. You've dragged me out here, though goodness only knows why. You told me the matter was finished."

Dave shook his head. "You've misunderstood, Babs. You don't have to worry. I'm a man of my word. That little matter is over and forgotten."

Babs felt relief wash over her, and she put her hand to her forehead as she felt a little dizzy.

Dave put an arm around her waist to steady her.

"Are you all right?"

He stood so close, Babs could smell his aftershave, and as she looked up into his eyes, she realised for the first time what a good-looking man Dave Carter was. And all at once, she wondered how her life would have turned out if she'd married someone like Dave rather than Martin.

"That's good to hear. I'm fine," Babs said.

"I asked you to meet me here so we could have a little privacy. I wanted to ask you something."

Babs licked her lips and nodded. She noticed that Dave's hand was still cupping her elbow.

She nodded. "What did you want to ask?"

"I don't want to step on anyone's toes, Babs. Least of all yours. I've got a lot of respect for you. The fact you are running Martin's business hasn't gone unnoticed. Nobody believes it's Tony behind the wheel."

Babs gave a little giggle and put her hand over Dave's. "Well, it's true. Tony does need a little bit of guidance."

Babs felt much more relaxed now in Dave's company. She was more than a little flattered by his compliments and was more willing to hear what he wanted to ask her now.

"The fact of the matter is, Big Tim has approached me for a job. I know he's not been working for the Mortons for some time, but I won't employ him if it upsets you."

Babs blinked a couple of times. She hadn't been expecting that. As far as she knew, Big Tim had spent the last decade drunk out of his skull.

"He's got a booze problem," Babs said, thinking it was only fair to warn Dave.

Dave nodded. "I'm aware of that, but I still think I can find some use for him. As long as you have no objection to that."

Babs didn't see the point in objecting. It wasn't as if she wanted Big Tim to work for them. She shrugged. "I don't have a problem with it."

"And do you think Tony will be amenable?"

Babs gave Dave a saucy smile and squeezed his arm. "Just leave Tony to me. I know how to handle him."

When Dave returned her smile, Babs felt butterflies in her

stomach.

Dave suggested they take a walk around the boating lake and discuss a bit more business, and Babs didn't see the harm in it, so she linked her arm through Dave's.

He really was rather charming, and Babs found herself being swept off her feet as he escorted her around the park.

It had been so long since she'd been interested in a man.

Once she'd been smitten with Martin, but she'd soon come down to earth with a bump when she realised what he was really like. But until this moment, she'd never really missed having a man around. In Babs' opinion, they usually turned out to be more trouble than they were worth.

With her arm linked with Dave's, she could feel the strong muscles beneath his coat and started to think it might be nice to have a little male company now and again.

They sat down on a bench and watched a couple of small children playing with their sailboats.

As they chatted, Babs felt more and more relaxed until finally she put her hand on Dave's knee and gave it a squeeze.

But Dave reached down and clasped her hand, taking it off his knee and putting it on her lap.

"I'm a married man, Babs."

Babs recoiled as if he'd slapped her. The embarrassment rolled through her body like a tidal wave. Her cheeks flushed, but immediately after the first wave of embarrassment passed, it was replaced with anger.

Dave had been toying with her. She knew a flirt when she saw one.

She glared at him angrily. "And I am a married woman, Dave. I don't know what you think I am. I was just being friendly."

Dave gave her a knowing look and said, "Of course, you were, Babs."

Babs gave a little growl of outrage and got to her feet. "I

think we're done here," she said and then turned around and stalked off, clutching her fur coat tightly around her body.

How could she have been so stupid? So what if he was a good-looking man? She didn't need any men in her life. Especially not ones like Dave Carter, who was practically a carbon copy of her monster of a husband.

She was almost out of the park when all of a sudden, Babs let out a peal of laughter, drawing shocked and disapproving looks from two mothers wheeling their prams. She'd just imagined how outraged Martin would be if he found out his wife had slept with Dave Carter.

It was a shame Dave hadn't been up for it. It would have been worth it just to see the look on Martin's face.

16

THAT EVENING, BABS WAS STILL smarting from Dave Carter's rejection as she sat in the flat upstairs over the club.

Since Martin had been locked up, his brother, Tony, had taken over the flat, and Babs looked around in distaste at the mess.

The fact that there were used plates and glasses lying on the kitchen counters only served to put Babs in more of a temper. He could have at least treated it with a little more respect. Tony Morton really didn't understand how easy he'd had it.

Everything Martin and Babs had worked for had just fallen into Tony's lap.

He hadn't gone through the years of graft that Martin had. And Babs was peeved that he got to live here and enjoy the benefits of their hard work without putting in the effort.

Usually, she tried to be tactful when dealing with Tony, especially if other men were around. Male pride was a fragile thing.

There were four of them gathered in the flat tonight for a meeting. Babs and Tony along with Henry the Hand and Red-haired Freddie. The men met once or twice a week to talk about business matters, but usually, Babs wasn't invited. This time, she had taken it upon herself to wangle an invite. She really hadn't given Tony much choice.

Babs shot him a scornful look. He was sitting at the table,

opposite her, and looking like a cowed little schoolboy. All the men looked uncomfortable, which pissed Babs off no end.

She knew more about the business, after living with Martin for so long, than any of them did. But they thought she wasn't worth listening to because she was a woman.

She longed to impress them by revealing she'd discovered who had been cheating the club out of money and fiddling the books, but until she was a hundred percent sure, Babs had to keep quiet.

They had just spent the last ten minutes discussing something completely irrelevant, in Babs' opinion, and she was now getting bored.

She drummed her fingernails on the table distractedly as the men droned on. But her ears pricked up when Henry the Hand said he'd found something out that might make them a bit of extra money.

Babs had been on at them for the last few weeks, telling them they needed to knuckle down and work harder. They'd been coasting for the past few years. All right, Martin's incarceration had been a shock to everybody, and for a while, it was all they could do to try and steer the boat through those choppy waters, but now they had established their little stranglehold on the local boozers, they needed to look for more ways to bring in money.

"There's a boxing club on Victoria Street, it backs onto the docks, and I've got it on good authority it's being used as a halfway house for stolen goods." Henry the Hand paused and waited for the news to register.

Red-haired Freddie's eagerness was obvious. She could practically see the pound signs appear in his eyes. Tony looked reluctant, though. Tony never liked to upset the status quo. As long as enough money was coming in to keep him in girls and booze, he was happy. He had no ambition.

Babs ignored him and turned to address Henry.

"And why is this of interest to us?" Babs asked somewhat

snappily.

"Well," Henry began, talking slowly as if he was explaining to a child and not an intelligent woman who had lived with Martin Morton all these years. "We might take a piece of the action. They are operating on the edge of our turf, and as such, I reckon we should get a cut."

"I don't know," Tony said. "Is it really worth the bother? You said it was just a load of old antique stuff."

Henry nodded. "That's what I heard. But it's attracted a bit of interest, and the chap in charge, Gregory Patterson, has been throwing his money around a bit recently, so he must be doing all right out of it."

Babs watched as the three men discussed the matter in front of her, not once asking her opinion. They had no idea how much power she really held.

Tony was a wimp. He kept saying it wasn't worth the risk.

Freddie was more interested. According to him, the Pattersons weren't a big deal. Security was light, and he believed they could get a cut of Gregory's profits in exchange for protection. If they'd heard about it, it wouldn't be long before other people did, too. He believed they should take a cut before someone else got in on the action.

Round and round they went, arguing left, right and centre. And all the time, Babs remained quiet. After another ten minutes, she said, "Listen up, boys, I've made a decision."

Her gaze clashed with Tony's as she dared him to contradict her, and she had to stifle a smile at the shocked look on Tony's face.

"Yes, I don't see why we shouldn't get a piece of the pie for ourselves, Henry. As Freddie said, we can offer them protection, so it's not as if we are looking to get something for nothing. Besides, they are operating on our turf, so they need to pay our taxes. Isn't that right, Tony?"

Tony blinked a couple of times and looked at the other men, obviously wanting one of them to contradict Babs.

But Henry and Freddie stayed quiet. They understood their places in the firm.

"Babs," Tony began, his voice dripping with charm. "It's not quite as simple as just walking in there and demanding some money."

"Of course, it is," Babs said.

The charming smile slid from Tony's face. "I think this would be a mistake. Yes, we're doing all right at the moment, but we don't have the same power we had when Martin was still around. We don't want to start any wars."

"We are not as powerful as we were when Martin was around because nobody is showing any balls, Tony. It looks like none of you men are going to step up, so it will have to be me."

Red-haired Freddie stifled a laugh, and Tony turned pale.

"That ain't fair, Babs."

"Life ain't fair. You had your chance, Tony, but we are losing money left, right and centre, and I am not going to stand by and let that happen. For a start, Henry and Freddie can approach Patterson's boxing club and find out more about this little stolen goods racket he has running, and then we can turn this firm around, so that when Martin does come out, he has a thriving enterprise waiting for him."

The men seemed too shocked to reply, so Babs stood up and gave them all a cool smile.

She picked up her handbag. "If that's all, gentlemen, it's late, so I'll take my leave. See you all tomorrow."

She stalked out of the flat as the men murmured their goodbyes.

She'd certainly set the cat among the pigeons tonight. Maybe she played her hand too soon, but Dave Carter's behaviour this afternoon had triggered something in Babs. She didn't appreciate being treated like a fool, and she was determined to show the East End exactly what she was made of.

17

BRIGHT AND EARLY ON SATURDAY morning, Mary took Jimmy on the bus and headed out to Romford.

Jimmy was full of beans. He couldn't wait to see his Auntie Bev again. Though she wasn't his real auntie, Jimmy didn't know any better and loved her as if she was.

After Jimmy had been born, Mary had faced a very difficult decision. With her daughter murdered in cold blood and dumped in the canal, Mary thought she would be left to bring up her grandson alone, but when she had a visit from Big Tim, one of Martin Morton's scariest henchmen, she'd realised that Jimmy wasn't safe, and so she'd shipped him off to Bev, one of her oldest friends, who now lived in Romford.

Bev had a charming little bungalow with roses round the door and a winding path that led up to the front door. The back garden was at least ten times as big as Mary's backyard, and Jimmy was in his element when he was allowed to play out there.

It looked like it was going to be a lovely sunny day, and Mary expected Jimmy to spend most of the day in the garden, allowing her time to catch up with Bev.

She enjoyed a natter about the good old days.

When they arrived at Bev's bungalow, she was overjoyed to see them. She smiled and scooped Jimmy up in a big hug.

When she raised her eyes and looked at Mary, she

smothered a gasp and put a hand against her mouth.

"Good grief, Mary. Have you been ill?"

Mary felt a spark of outrage. She knew she didn't look her best at the moment, and that was probably down to the booze, but like any woman, she didn't appreciate being told she looked rough.

She opened her mouth to make a sharp retort but then swallowed the nasty words on the tip of her tongue. Bev was only concerned about her after all. She was a dear friend.

"I'm all right, love. It's just been a difficult couple of months."

Mary noticed that Jimmy was watching this conversation with avid interest. He was too sharp for his own good. Those big, blue eyes of his never missed a trick.

Bev followed Mary's gaze and realised she didn't want to talk in front of Jimmy, so she waved them inside and began to tell Jimmy all about the cakes she'd bought for their tea.

When they'd sent Jimmy off to play in the garden, Mary eased herself down into one of Bev's comfortable armchairs and sighed.

She looked around the pretty little bungalow and felt a pang of envy.

Bev had really done well for herself. They'd been brought up in the same neighbourhood and even raised their children together, but after Bev's daughter died, Bev and her husband had decided to make the move to Essex, and poor old Fred had died not long afterwards leaving everything to Bev.

It was hard not to compare Mary's pokey little terraced house to this beautiful bungalow.

She wished she had made the move years ago, but now she couldn't bring herself to leave the East End as that would mean leaving behind all the memories of her daughter.

As the two women chatted away, Mary felt herself relax. It felt good to be in the company of an old friend.

***

Outside, Jimmy had already climbed to the top of his favourite tree — an old gnarled apple tree. He'd inspected some of the fruit, but it would take another couple of months before it was properly ripe.

He took a peek behind the hawthorn hedge and saw a small bird's nest. He crept around the side of the house, pretending he was a soldier in the jungle, creeping up on the enemy. As he got closer to the bungalow, he heard the voices of his nan and auntie drifting out of the open sitting room window.

He didn't mean to eavesdrop, and he would have walked away but for the fact he heard them mention his mother.

He moved closer to the house until he was crouching directly below the window.

***

Inside, Bev asked, "Have you told Jimmy about Kathleen?"

She asked Mary the same question on every visit. Mary sighed. When she'd come to collect Jimmy from Bev, five years ago, she'd informed her friend she was going to tell Jimmy everything and rely on him to get revenge for his mother.

Bev thought that was a terrible idea, and she never missed an opportunity to tell Mary so.

Although Mary's grief hadn't lessened over the years, she had been able to see a little more clearly, and she understood that Jimmy had his own life to live. If there was one thing she could do for her daughter now, it was to make sure her little boy didn't have a bitter, unhappy childhood.

Mary shook her head. "He knows his mother was murdered. I couldn't exactly hide that from him. He's ten years old now, Bev. At school, everybody knows, so there was no point trying to keep it from him."

Bev nodded. "That's why I thought it was better for him to stay in Romford. It's a fresh start, and he doesn't have the past hanging over his head."

Those words got Mary's back up. Bev was a kind woman. She had been there for Mary and Jimmy in a very difficult time, but Jimmy was Mary's grandson, and he was her responsibility.

"You know how I feel about that, Bev," Mary said, her voice sharp.

Bev got up to pour more tea into each of their cups. "I know he's your grandson, Mary, and you should be the one to bring him up. But hear me out. Why don't you and Jimmy move down here together? I've got a three-bedroom bungalow. It will be a bit of a squeeze, but we could make it work."

Mary pursed her lips and shook her head. She'd explained to Bev before how she couldn't even consider leaving the East End. "I can't move away, Bev. I do appreciate the offer, though."

Bev nodded as if she'd expected that answer. "Fair enough, love. But the offer is still open if you change your mind."

***

Outside in the garden, Jimmy was thinking about what he had just overheard. He knew his mother had been murdered, but he didn't know the whole story. That much was obvious. What had Bev been referring to? Perhaps she was talking about Jimmy's father.

He'd asked his nan about his father before, and when he was younger, she'd told him he had been killed in an accident at work before he and Jimmy's mother could get married.

He asked more questions as he got older, but his nan would get irritated and snap at him every time he brought the subject of his father up. In the end, Jimmy had stopped trying. But if Bev had known his father, maybe he could find out more from her.

18

SPENDING SATURDAY EVENING HAVING DINNER at her parents' house wasn't exactly Linda's idea of fun. It had taken her over an hour of nagging to persuade Geoff to come along as well.

Usually, Linda turned down her parent's dinner invitations, but she hadn't been able to get out of this one. Her brother was getting married next month, and her mother had insisted on a family dinner to discuss the arrangements.

When Linda and Geoff had turned up and found out that Linda's brother and his fiancée were not coming, after all, Geoff looked like he was about to do a runner off to the pub.

So Linda clutched hold of his sleeve and gave him a stern warning look.

When Linda had plucked up the courage to ask her mother where her brother and his fiancée were, Linda's mother said, "They've gone to the cinema. There was a film they really wanted to see, and I didn't have the heart to ask them to miss it."

"So we're having a dinner to discuss a wedding without the future bride and groom?" Geoff's voice was a dangerous rumble.

Linda felt her stomach churn, and she mumbled a prayer under her breath. Please don't let him kick off.

Linda's mother glared disapprovingly at Geoff, but she

didn't respond. Instead, she turned to her daughter, "Linda, please hand your father the potatoes."

Linda did as she was told, handing the large china bowl to her father.

When they'd eaten at home as a family, Linda's mother would always serve up the dinner directly onto their plates and then bring the plates to the table. She wouldn't use extra bowls because she couldn't abide making more washing-up than was necessary. But for some reason, whenever she and Geoff came to dinner now, her mother treated it as if it was a great event and brought out the best china and serving dishes.

Linda miserably helped herself to a spoonful of peas and then added some gravy to her plate.

She could practically feel the anger rolling off Geoff as he sat beside her.

He almost looked smart this evening, and it reminded Linda of the first time she'd met him. His hair was carefully combed, and she'd pressed his shirt before they'd left the house. It was odd to recall those first few months of their relationship when she had been so smitten.

Her mother and father had been against Geoff from the start. They'd quickly picked up on the fact that Geoff had never managed to hold down a steady job, but Linda had been too infatuated to notice such small details. She was convinced she and Geoff were going to live happily ever after.

If she was honest, one of the reasons she hated coming to her parents' house with Geoff was the look her mother would give her from time to time — a look that said I told you so.

But it was too late for regrets. For better or worse, Linda was now stuck with him, and she had to make the best of it.

He drank away a good portion of her wages down at the pub every week, but it could be worse. Some men were addicted to gambling and got into debt. At least Geoff had never done that! A friend of Linda's from school called

Bernadette had married an awful man who got into debt and then ran off, leaving the bailiffs to come and claim all of Bernadette's furniture.

Because Linda was the one earning, she controlled the purse strings, which Geoff hated, but he couldn't do much about it.

Linda's mother chatted on, trying to make conversation about the forthcoming wedding.

Linda didn't see much point discussing the bride's dress since she wasn't even here, but for her mother's sake, she nodded her head at the right moments and muttered her approval at her mother's idea of holding an engagement party next Saturday night for the happy couple.

Lost in her own miserable musings, Linda almost missed her mother's barbed comment.

"What was that?" she asked as she noticed that Geoff had tensed beside her.

"I said it's a good job your brother is getting married soon because it doesn't look like you two are going to give us any grandchildren."

Linda swallowed her mouthful of mashed potato and peas and felt tears form in her eyes.

She knew she would have to laugh off the comment and pretend that it didn't bother her, but she felt like running away from the table and never coming back.

She put down her knife and fork, but before she could respond, she felt Geoff's hand on her forearm, and he said, "These things can take time. And besides, Linda and I are happy as we are, aren't we, sweetheart?"

Linda could have kissed him. But all she managed to do was nod and smile gratefully at Geoff.

It meant the world to Linda that he would stick up for her, and she began to think perhaps she'd been judging him too harshly. After all, he'd stuck by her through all of this.

So what if he enjoyed a drink now and again. A man had to

have some pleasures in life.

Linda's mother looked perturbed. She didn't like being put in her place.

As her mother served up a suet sponge pudding with custard, Linda glanced at Geoff and squeezed his hand.

The pudding was delicious, but Linda couldn't stomach more than a few mouthfuls. Her mother's comments were still weighing heavily on her mind. It was so unfair.

She had spent yesterday at Bevels rushing around trying to cover for Valerie, who kept darting off from her workstation in the factory to be sick. It felt like everywhere she turned there was someone else to rub her nose in it and remind her that she and Geoff didn't yet have any children.

After she'd taken her second bite of sponge pudding, Linda's father leaned over to whisper in his daughter's ear. "Are you okay, Linda? You're not working too hard, are you, girl?"

Linda shook her head and smiled at her father. "No. I'm fine, and the job is going well."

Her father smiled. "I'm ever so proud of you, you know? It's not many women who get promoted to supervisor," he added with a wink.

When they'd finished eating, and Linda had helped her mother with the dishes, Geoff was courteous and acted like a perfect gentleman as he helped Linda on with her coat.

They said goodnight to her parents and then stepped out of the front door. Linda turned to the left, in the direction of their house, but Geoff, who had been holding her arm, turned in the other direction.

Linda looked back at him, surprised.

"I thought I'd go for a quick one before closing time. Have you got any money on you?"

Linda tried to not look too disappointed. He'd actually made an effort tonight and had made the evening bearable. It could have been so much worse, so instead of objecting,

Linda simply nodded and gave him some money from her purse.

"I've got some good news, love. I've landed a job. Soon we won't have to watch the pennies quite so closely."

"Oh, that's brilliant, Geoff. When do you start?"

"Well, it isn't really a full-time gig. I'll be working for Dave Carter as and when he needs me."

Linda's face fell. "Dave Carter? Are you sure that is a good idea?"

Geoff scowled and shoved the money she gave him in his pocket. "You're never happy, are you? Nothing I do is ever good enough."

"I didn't mean that. It's just…" But Linda took a deep breath instead of continuing her sentence. It wasn't worth having an argument in the street over. She smiled, apologised and told him she'd see him later.

She turned away, pulled up the collar of her coat as the air had turned chilly, even though it was the beginning of summer.

She turned back, deciding to thank Geoff for this evening and tell him how much she appreciated him sticking up for her tonight.

But when she turned around, he'd already gone, and the street was dark and empty.

19

ON MONDAY AFTERNOON, AFTER SCHOOL, Jimmy was walking home with his friend, Bobby Green, when he heard a voice behind him. It was little Georgie running after him, trying to catch up.

Jimmy stopped and waited, wondering what Georgie could want. His brother Trevor had made it very clear that he didn't approve of Georgie talking to someone like Jimmy.

Although Jimmy had been intrigued by the fact Dave Carter was Georgie's father, he had enough common sense to know he was better off not getting involved with a family like that.

Beside him, Bobby Green grew restless. He had a coin burning a hole in his pocket, and he wanted to go and spend it on sweets. "What are you talking to him for?" Bobby asked sulkily.

"Go on ahead," Jimmy told him. "I'll catch you up."

Bobby shrugged and ran off.

"Everything all right, Georgie? Nobody has been bullying you again, have they?"

Georgie shook his head. He was a slight boy and a good few inches shorter than Jimmy. "No, nobody has picked on me since. I think my dad must have had a word."

Jimmy nodded. "Right. Well, I'd better get on. Bobby is waiting for me."

Jimmy almost felt guilty as a look of disappointment passed across Georgie's face.

"Did you know my dad's got a workshop?"

Jimmy turned back. "A workshop? What for?"

"Motors. They fix cars and coaches. Do you want to see?"

Jimmy hesitated and considered his options. On the one hand, Bobby would probably share his sweets with Jimmy, but on the other, Jimmy loved motors of any sort, and it would be interesting to have a gander.

The eager look on Georgie's face swung it. The poor kid didn't have any friends at school, and Jimmy felt sorry for him.

"Go on then. Lead the way."

As they walked along in the early summer sunshine, Georgie chatted away about his dad's workshop and all the business he did. Although Jimmy was interested, he was cautious, and so he didn't ask the question playing on his mind: was Georgie's father really a gangster?

When they got to the workshop, Jimmy was quite taken aback. It was much bigger than he'd expected, with a large ceiling and different types of tools everywhere. The place smelled of grease and engine oil.

There was a large coach at the back of the workshop, and towards the front, there was a red and white car above a pit. A brown-haired man with a round face was standing in the inspection pit beneath the car, holding a spanner.

The man obviously recognised Georgie because he gave him a wave.

Georgie led the way inside proudly. "My dad's got an important contract for the coaches." He jerked his thumb at the small bus at the back of the workshop, but it was the car that had attracted Jimmy's attention.

It looked flash. A Ford Zodiac in two-tone metallic blue with whitewall tyres. Jimmy could just picture himself driving it around London. He made up his mind on the spot that whatever job he ended up doing he would definitely have a fancy car like that.

Jimmy walked a little closer to the car and crouched down to admire the bodywork, completely unaware he was being watched.

***

Big Tim had recognised Jimmy Diamond straightaway. Since the other night, he hadn't been able to get the boy out of his head. He'd told himself it must've been a hallucination, and the drink had made him conjure up the image of a boy who looked just like Kathleen Diamond.

It was strange he hadn't seen the boy around before. But he'd been lost in a drunken haze for the past few years just trying to get through each day as best he could.

But after running into Jimmy Diamond on the way home from the pub the other night, even alcohol couldn't wipe the boy's face from his mind.

For the past couple of days, he'd hung around near Mary Diamond's house, waiting for another look at the boy.

He'd seen him again a few times now but had been careful to keep his distance.

But when he'd seen him walking down the road with Dave Carter's son, Big Tim hadn't been able to stay away. The boy was the spitting image of his mother, with his dark hair and dark blue eyes that seemed to look right into Tim's soul accusingly.

It was hard to see much of Martin about the boy at all, except the slight dimple in his chin.

Tim had followed the two boys to the workshop and now stood across the street, watching.

He knew it was a mistake. The sheer size of him made it impossible for Tim to blend into the background. And just a minute later, Brian Moore clambered out of the inspection pit, wiping his hands on a piece of rag and narrowed his eyes as he spotted Tim on the opposite side of the road.

Brian said something over his shoulder to someone in the workshop. Tim couldn't see who else was in there. The rest of the room was in shadow. He hesitated, leaning on the balls of his feet, ready to make a quick getaway. Not that it mattered now he had been spotted.

Big Tim had worked for Martin Morton for years, and everyone around these parts knew it. After Martin had been put away, Tim had spent most of his days half cut, and Tony had been quick to get rid of him, bunging him a few quid every now and again, but not relying on him to do any of the big jobs. Not that Tim minded.

He knew he needed to turn his life around and get away from the Mortons once and for all, and that was why he had approached Dave Carter. Tim could not have faced working for Martin Morton again, but his skills were hardly in high demand anywhere else. Dave had been his last shot at a steady job.

***

Inside the workshop, Jimmy was focused on the car.

"You like the look of that one, son, do you?"

Jimmy turned at the sound of a man's voice. A tall, dapper man grinned at him. He was young and thin and wore a three-piece suit. Jimmy thought he looked very smart and then he caught a glimpse of the gold pocket watch, and his jaw dropped.

Jimmy was impressed. This was exactly the kind of man he wanted to be when he grew up.

"It's brilliant," Jimmy said, smiling widely.

"Do you want to have a look inside?" the man asked.

Behind them, little Georgie spoke up, "I don't know, Charlie. My dad doesn't like me to get in the way."

"You're not in the way, Georgie. Anyway, your dad isn't here, and what he doesn't know won't hurt him." Charlie tapped the edge of his nose and grinned at the boys.

Jimmy was in his absolute element as Charlie opened the

door and allowed both boys to explore the car. They were so busy pretending to drive, neither boy noticed Dave Carter entering the warehouse.

"What's going on here?"

Both boys froze as if they'd been caught with their hand in the biscuit tin.

Dave let out a loud laugh that echoed around the workshop.

Charlie strolled across to Dave and spoke to him in a low voice. "We noticed Big Tim hanging around a few minutes ago."

Dave frowned. "Where?"

"Just out there." Charlie nodded to the opposite side of the road where Big Tim had been standing. "He's not there anymore. But I thought it would be a good idea to keep little Georgie here until he'd gone."

"Tim is nothing to worry about. As a matter of fact, he'll be working with us soon."

Charlie spluttered. "Are you serious?"

Dave didn't answer. He had noticed Jimmy staring at him and listening to their conversation. He patted Charlie on the shoulder and walked towards the car.

Feeling guilty, as if he'd been caught doing something he shouldn't, Jimmy let his hands slip from the steering wheel. "I'm sorry, Mr. Carter. We were just having some fun."

Dave leaned on the car and smiled at Jimmy as he ruffled little Georgie's hair. "There's nothing wrong with having a bit of fun. Do you like cars?"

Jimmy beamed. "I love them."

"I tell you what then. How about I give you two boys a job?"

Jimmy chewed his lower lip. A job? He wasn't sure his nan would approve of that.

"What kind of job?"

"Washing the cars. If you come by for an hour every day

after school, I'll pay you wages at the end of the week. How does that sound?"

That sounded great to Jimmy. He didn't think his nan would object if he was just washing cars.

"What about me, Dad?" Georgie asked. "Do I get a job, too?"

"Of course, you do," Dave Carter said, smiling fondly at his son. "I expect to see you both here tomorrow after school."

***

Dave smiled as he looked on at the two boys playing inside the car. He couldn't remember the last time he'd seen Georgie playing with a lad his own age.

Dave had been concerned about removing Georgie from his special private lessons. Since he'd been a baby, Dave and Sandra had been protective of the boy, probably too protective, and Georgie's childhood had suffered. Dave loved the boy to the moon and back, but that wasn't enough. He needed friends if he was to ever have much of a life.

Putting him into the main school a few months ago had been nerve-wracking, to say the least. But Dave had thought his reputation would go a long way towards protecting Georgie. He hadn't considered the fact it might make the boy a target.

Charlie Williams stepped up beside Dave and began to give him a run down on the problems they'd had with one of the coaches. Dave was keen to keep the customer sweet because this was his legitimate side of the business, and it was important to him to make it a success. If he could have relied on his brother Gary, Dave would have gladly handed over the rest of the business to him. But he couldn't. He would have felt more confident putting his business in the hands of Charlie.

The only thing Dave could rely on Gary for was spilling his secrets. Dave had learned that lesson long ago and now only told Gary things he wanted his rivals to know. Gary had once been Dave's weakness, but now he'd turned that into a strength.

If Dave divulged information to Gary, he could be assured his brother would soon be boasting about it after a few drinks. Dave loved his brother, but he wasn't above exploiting his unreliable nature to his benefit.

Charlie Williams was a different story.

He'd taken him on as a young lad, and Charlie had more than proved himself over and over again.

He'd filled out a little now but was still a lanky lad, and his arms and legs looked too big for his body, but he had a charming smile that the ladies seemed to love, although he had skilfully avoided going up the aisle so far. The fact that he still lived at home with his overbearing mother probably had something to do with that.

Charlie lowered his voice when he said, "You do know who that boy is, don't you?"

Dave frowned.

Charlie continued, "Jimmy Diamond. Kathleen Diamond's son. The woman who was murdered and dumped in the canal ten years ago. Jimmy is being brought up by his nan."

Dave nodded. He remembered that murder well. The whole community had been shocked at the death of such a young woman. Dave had kept his ear to the ground, and he'd heard the rumours along with everyone else. The gossip-mongers whispered that Kathleen had been Martin's mistress, and he'd gotten her pregnant, which meant as Jimmy was the same age as Georgie, there was a good chance Jimmy was Martin Morton's son.

Dave cocked his head to one side and studied the boy carefully as he watched him through the windscreen of the car.

He couldn't see any particular similarities — maybe the slight dimple on the boy's chin — but other than that he couldn't see any resemblance that might suggest Martin was his father.

"You heard the rumours about Martin and Kathleen?" Dave muttered.

Charlie nodded. "Yes, that's why I mentioned it. There was some talk about the fact Martin was behind her death… But I don't know whether that is true."

Dave nodded. Martin was a nasty bastard, and Dave would not have been surprised to learn he was responsible.

He wondered how much Jimmy Diamond knew about his mother and whether he had any idea who his father was.

As Dave watched the two boys, he tried to work out what to do. If Jimmy had suddenly befriended Trevor, Dave could have easily told Trevor to stay away from him, but Georgie had never had a real friend.

Dave smiled. Jimmy seemed a nice enough kid. He would let Georgie keep seeing him for now and do a little bit of digging to find out whether Martin kept any tabs on his son.

Gary chose that moment to walk into the workshop. He was suited and booted and reeked of aftershave. His hair was carefully Brylcreemed into a slicked back style, and he had a smug grin on his face as he walked up to Dave.

Gary had never done a proper day's work in his life. Dave loved his younger brother, but he knew his faults. He was a lazy sod, who enjoyed the finer things in life, like booze, women and drugs. They were supposed to have had a meeting with a new supplier this morning, but Gary hadn't bothered to turn up. Most days he didn't get out of bed before noon.

Charlie Williams noticed Dave's change in mood and tactfully walked away, leaving the brothers to talk.

Gary walked up and slapped Dave on the back. "Hello, bruv."

"You're a few hours late, Gary," Dave said.

"Oh, I know. Sorry. Running late today. I had a million and one things to do."

Dave shook his head but said nothing. It wasn't worth it. Gary could never see the error of his ways. In his mind, he was a major player, but Dave paid his wages and most of the time, Gary did absolutely nothing to earn them.

That would have to change soon. They were going to have to shake things up around here, and Gary would need to pull his weight. Martin Morton was getting closer to the end of his sentence, and Dave needed to be prepared for when he got out.

The Carters had had it easy for the past few years with no real challenges on their turf. Dave had crushed a couple of young upstarts wanting to chance their luck, stamping out that rebellion as if they were ants beneath his heel.

Martin Morton would be another story, though, and if Dave wanted to keep his powerful position in the East End, he would have to act now before Martin got out of prison.

He had nothing against Martin's wife or his brother. Neither of them were a real threat to Dave, so he had been more than happy to let them ply their trade in their little corner of the East End, but you didn't get far in this game by being soft. It was time for Dave to show them exactly how hard he could be.

20

OLD MO WAS A WEALTHY man. He'd been working for the Mortons in one way or another for almost fifteen years. He had trained as an accountant and made it his business to know every trick in the book when it came to hiding money. He specialised in helping the Mortons hide their profits and channel them through legitimate enterprises like the club that Old Mo was now sitting in.

He was having a grand time tonight. He loved the lifestyle. It was a world away from the old days when he'd had a pokey little office in the West End and a dried-up old secretary.

These days, he owned a nice house out in Essex and kept a little flat off St Paul's way for business in the week.

Old Mo was sitting between two pretty young ladies wearing skirts so short his eyes nearly bulged out of his head each time he looked at them.

He took a puff on his cigar and grinned at the girl sitting to his right. "What's your name again, darling?"

The girl tittered out a little laugh and said, "It's Doreen. You already asked me that."

"Oh, that's right, I remember now." He wrapped his arm around her shoulders and let his fat fingers drift down her back so he could squeeze her body tight against him.

Doreen pulled a face and shifted back in the seat as far as

she could. "Are you sure you really know Tony Morton and can introduce us?"

Old Mo took another mouthful of his Scotch and then smacked his lips together. "Of course, I can, darling," he lied.

These young girls were so predictable. They were lining up to hop into bed with Tony Morton. If only they knew what old Mo did. Tony was a fool. Nothing like his brother.

Old Mo had been terrified when he'd started working for Martin Morton. He was forever looking over his shoulder, and he would never have dared to do any creative accounting if Martin was still around. But after Martin got locked up, it wasn't long before Mo realised that Tony hadn't got a bleeding clue what was going on. He never even bothered to look at the books or get anyone to check Mo's work.

Of course, it helped that Mo was an intelligent businessman. Unlike these thugs who extorted money from other criminals, Mo didn't use violence. He didn't think what he was doing was wrong. In his opinion, the Mortons didn't deserve the money, so pilfering a little bit off the top hurt no one as far as he was concerned.

But despite Tony's stupidity, the young girls around here worshipped the ground he walked on.

"Are we going to meet him tonight?" Doreen asked putting a hand on Mo's forearm.

He grumpily shook her off. He was getting fed up with her whining about Tony.

"Go up to the bar and get yourself another drink," he said waving his fat, stubby fingers in her direction.

Then he turned to the young girl on his left. Maybe he would have a little more luck with her.

She seemed ever so enamoured with his gold rings.

"Are they all real gold?" the girl asked, flicking her long, brown hair back from her face.

Old Mo couldn't remember what she was called, but she was pretty enough.

He took his cigar out of his mouth, so he could give her a big smile. "Of course, they are, darling."

Old Mo put his meaty hand on the girl's knee and was just about to lean in for a kiss when the girl squealed and sat up straight in her chair.

"Oh my goodness," she said. "It's Tony Morton. It's really him."

Old Mo grunted and looked up.

Sure enough, Tony had just walked into the club. It was like he was a celebrity — one of those fancy singers on the radio. He walked in with a swagger and was immediately surrounded by ten young women. Lucky bastard, Mo thought, but his jealousy was eased by the fact he knew he was slowly bleeding Tony dry, and the stupid prick didn't have any idea.

Mo remembered this was why he didn't come to the club anymore. When he splashed his money around like this, he expected to be the centre of attention. He didn't want to be upstaged by anyone, especially not a dimwit like Tony Morton. He'd only come tonight because red-haired Freddie had passed on a message that they wanted to see him. He'd heard on the grapevine that they were planning to take a cut from a shipment of stolen goods coming in from the docks and being stored at Patterson's boxing club.

He had to hand it to the Mortons. They were certainly opportunists. Mo smothered a yawn as Tony walked over to him.

If it had been Martin, Mo would have scrambled out of his seat and practically bowed in front of him, but as it was only Tony, Mo stayed sitting where he was, sprawled out against the red velvet chair as the girl beside him bounced up and down in excitement.

"Hello, Mo." Tony delivered a blinding smile. The smile the girls said made him look like a film star.

The girl beside Mo giggled uncontrollably, and it was all

Mo could do to resist giving her a backhander.

"Hello, Tony, I hear you wanted to see me."

Tony looked over his shoulder and then looked back at Mo. "It's not me, Mo. Babs wanted to have a word. She will be in shortly."

Mo only just managed to resist curling his lip in disgust. He hadn't thought much of Tony previously, but now Mo realised he was letting a woman get involved in his business… well, that just said it all, didn't it?

"I'll wait here for her then," Mo said, starting to get to his feet because he fancied another whiskey. He was going to need a drink to get the bitter taste out of his mouth. He scowled when he saw the brown-haired girl, who had been by his side, had now joined the gaggle of women around Tony.

Well, sod them all, Mo thought. The stupid cows didn't appreciate a good man when they saw one.

***

Babs had gone over the books time and time again, and now she was absolutely convinced that Old Mo had been cheating them.

She felt a mixture of trepidation and excitement as she made her way to the club. It was a lovely summer's evening, and the air was warm as she strode confidently along the street.

She'd asked Tony to make sure old Mo was there tonight. It wasn't strictly necessary for Babs herself to speak to him, but she wanted to. She wanted to look the man in the eye. She wanted to see if he was able to lie to her face without remorse.

She tried to talk to Tony about it and had even shown him the books, but it was no good. Tony didn't want to hear it. He swore to her old Mo was loyal. But Babs knew different, and now she had to show that she could be just as ruthless as Martin when it came to dealing with a betrayal.

She knew both red-haired Freddie and Henry the Hand would back her up.

They knew she was really the one with the intelligence to run Martin's business. They'd worked closely with Tony over the years and saw his weakness for what it was.

Babs nodded to the bouncers on the door and walked straight past the queue into the club. It was heaving. She pursed her lips. Mo must have thought they were absolute idiots to believe takings could be down when business was this good. That's what hurt most of all. It wasn't that he'd just taken off a little bit here and there. He'd stolen from them as if they were idiots and would never realise.

Babs tugged the hem of her dress self-consciously, which was at least six inches longer than most of the skirts the other women in the club were wearing.

She felt shocked. How could they call this fashion? She narrowed her eyes as a slim young girl waltz past, wearing a skirt that ended halfway up her thighs. Babs shook her head, scandalised. The sixties had a lot to answer for.

How did their mothers let them out at night? Babs would definitely put her foot down if Ruby tried to go out in a getup like that, she thought, looking at another girl with her skirt well above her knees.

Babs' excitement and anticipation faded, and she felt old surrounded by these pretty young girls. On the other side of the club, she recognised Jemima, red-haired Freddie's girl. She was a stunner. Her long, red hair cascaded down her back, and she looked absolutely beautiful. The bloke she was with couldn't tear his eyes away from her. Babs remembered a time when she'd attracted attention like that.

She stifled a sigh and then scanned the club for Freddie and Henry.

There was no sign of Henry, but she saw Freddie over by the bar and walked over to join him. He was chatting with a couple of men Babs recognised, but as soon as Babs approached, Freddie made his excuses and turned his back on them.

He got her a drink and then they walked over to the side of the bar, where it was a little quieter, to talk.

She caught sight of Tony, surrounded by his usual collection of floozies, but ignored him. Babs was better off handling this on her own.

"Is Mo here?" Babs asked.

Freddie nodded. "Yeah. He's sitting at that table over there." Freddie jerked his thumb over his shoulder, and then Babs saw Old Mo.

He looked fatter than ever. Babs scowled. He was getting fat on her money, the bastard. And what did he look like with all those bloody gold rings on? She never trusted a man who wore too much jewellery.

"Have you made a decision, Babs?"

Babs nodded. She was going to speak to Mo first, but it didn't really matter what he said. She had made up her mind. Old Mo needed to be punished.

"Yes. We'll do it first thing in the morning. We have to act quickly."

Freddie was an old hand at this game, and he didn't look shocked and didn't try to change Babs' mind, despite the fact he'd worked side-by-side with Old Mo for the past fifteen years. Freddie's loyalty was to the Mortons and no one else.

"Of course, Babs. Have you talked about this with Martin?"

Babs licked her lips and took a sip of a drink as she decided how to answer. She could tell Freddie the truth because she was quite sure he would be loyal to her, but she didn't want to take the chance. Especially not if Tony found out. As far as Tony knew, they were just talking to Mo about the accounts.

Babs nodded. "Yes, Martin has given it the green light."

Red-haired Freddie grinned. "Right then. Where do you want to do it?"

Babs swallowed. It was all starting to feel real now. She

hadn't done anything like this before. So she had to rely on Freddie's advice. "Where do you suggest?"

Freddie shrugged. "The warehouses behind the wharf would be good." He gave her a devilish smile. "No one will hear his screams there."

His words made Babs feel a little dizzy, but she didn't intend to show it. She gave him a firm nod and then said, "Right. Have him there by nine o'clock tomorrow morning."

Then she said goodnight to Freddie and made her way over to Mo's table.

***

By the time Babs finally arrived, Mo was a little worse for wear. He'd said hello to some of the faces he recognised, but mainly it was youngsters hanging out at the club these days, and he felt well out of place.

He was getting on for fifty now, and he couldn't abide all this fast music, although he had to admit he appreciated the shorter hemlines. He licked his lips as he took a lecherous look at a girl who leaned over the bar to reach her drink, causing her skirt to rise up.

He puffed on his cigar moodily and had downed another two scotches before Babs slid into the seat next to him. She'd been quiet and because of the noise of the music in the club, Mo hadn't noticed her approach.

He embarrassed himself by jumping in surprise.

"Babs," he said, quickly recovering his poise. "What a pleasure, darling. I haven't seen you in a while."

Babs didn't return his smile. She gave him a sharp nod in greeting and then launched right into business.

Babs Morton had once been a looker. Mo could remember how beautiful she'd been when she was younger. But now those elegant, fine features that had made her such a stunner had turned hard. The lines on her face betrayed a difficult life. Her platinum blonde hair had now been dyed so many times it practically looked like straw. She had it smoothed back from her face in a trendy style, but it didn't help. Compared to all the young women in the club, Babs was looking old.

"You're looking as gorgeous as ever," Mo said, trying one of Tony's lines on Babs.

It didn't work. Babs' hard features didn't soften as she glared at Mo.

"I've been taking a look through the books, Mo. Tony told me takings were down."

For the first time in years, Mo felt a pang of nerves. The way Babs was looking at him, he could almost believe she was on to him. But she couldn't be. What the hell did she know about the business?

"That's true, Babs. Takings have been down, and the price of booze has been going up. It's a difficult time to run a business. Not like back in the fifties. Things were easier then."

"What I don't understand," Babs said as she tapped a long, red, painted fingernail on the table in front of them, "is why this place is packed to the rafters every night and yet takings are down? Sorry, Mo. That doesn't make any sense."

Jesus Christ, thought Mo, breaking out into a cold sweat. She knows. The canny bitch had worked it out. He'd been getting greedy. At first, he'd only taken a few quid here and there, gently skimming off the top, and nobody would have noticed if he'd stuck to that.

Beneath the table, he clenched his fists, desperately trying to think of a way to get out of this mess.

"It looks busy, Babs, but the kids don't drink as much these days. If you look around, you'll see they are all youngsters in here. They're not your old-fashioned, heavy drinkers, are they? The clientele has changed."

Babs gave him a cold smile, and that's when Mo knew he really had been rumbled.

Crap. He had to get out of there. Thank God Martin was still locked up.

"I don't think that is the case at all, Mo."

"No?" Mo said, trying to sound innocent, but the sweat pouring off his forehead told a different story.

"I think somebody has been dipping their hand into our pockets."

Mo swallowed hard and shook his head frantically. "I hope you're not suggesting…" he began to say haughtily, but then the words faded in his mouth as he saw the look on Babs' face.

Maybe Mo had been wrong. He'd been keeping his eye on Tony all this time, but maybe he should have been watching Babs. He could only hope Martin's wife didn't have the same taste in revenge as her husband.

21

SHORTLY BEFORE MIDNIGHT, RUBY MORTON slipped out of bed and quietly put on the skirt and blouse that she'd stashed on the chair beside her nightstand before lights out.

No one else in the dormitory was awake. Ruby had to share a room with six other girls. The school was run like a prison, and the dormitories were inspected twice a day.

Ruby absolutely hated it there, and she hated her mother for making her stay.

Tonight she was sneaking off to meet her brother, Derek, and his new friend, Stuart. It was something they'd done a few times since their mother had dumped them out in the sticks. Ruby liked to feel like she was getting one over on her mother.

Stuart was a total dreamboat, and as Ruby thought of his handsome face and sandy hair, she couldn't help smiling.

She winced as she opened the cupboard to retrieve her shoes and the door gave a squeak. She held her breath for a moment, but nobody stirred.

Sighing with relief, she quickly slid her feet into her shoes and grabbed her cardigan. She was almost at the door when Clara Tottingham let out a small snore and turned over in bed.

Ruby froze by the doorway. Clara was a complete snob, and Ruby didn't like the stuck up, toffee-nosed girl at all. Clara had attempted to bully Ruby when she arrived but had had no idea who she was dealing with. She soon realised she had picked on the wrong girl.

Ruby gave a self-satisfied smirk. She bet Clara now wished she had never started their feud. In the short time she'd been there, Ruby had played some delightful pranks. At least, that part of her school life was entertaining.

The best trick she'd played was pouring a bowlful of water on Clara's bed at night, and convincing all the other girls that Clara had wet herself. Now she was known as Clara Leaky Drawers.

Confident that none of the other girls had woken up, Ruby left the dormitory and strode down the corridor. It was dark, but she had made this trip a few times now. It was easy enough to escape for an hour or so, and Derek's school was only a short walk away.

He hated it as much as Ruby did — or at least he said so. He'd made friends and managed to settle in. The boys in his classes weren't quite as snobby and nasty as the girls at her school.

Trust her mother to send her to a school run by bleeding nuns! Ruby shook her head. The head of the nuns was a dried up old prune called Sister Bernadette. She was supposed to be religious, forgiving and kind, but Ruby saw none of those qualities in her. Instead, she thought the woman was vindictive and enjoyed punishing her students. If she found one of the girls out of bed, Ruby was sure she would be able to think up a very imaginative punishment. Ruby shivered as she got to the large oak front doors. There was no chance she would get out that way without being seen, so she quickly walked past the front door and headed to the laundry room.

The laundry room door backed out onto a small courtyard and it was always locked, but they left the old window above the sink open a crack as the latch was broken.

Young and agile, Ruby climbed on top of the counter,

stepped over the sink, opened the window and slipped outside, pushing the window shut behind her.

The courtyard garden was where the nuns grew vegetables and roped the girls into helping with the weeding, which Ruby felt was practically slave labour.

On the far wall of the courtyard, there was a trellis supporting a low-growing apple tree, and Ruby nimbly climbed up the trellis and swung her leg over the wall. The other side was a little trickier — but because the wall was old and crumbling, there were little holes she could use for her feet, and she managed to grip onto the old stone.

Smiling and feeling pleased with herself, she turned ready to dash off, but then she heard a rustling in the bushes on her right. She pressed back against the wall in fright before she heard the sound of giggling. Bloody Derek! She'd murder him!

Derek and Stuart had obviously decided to play a trick after getting bored waiting for her.

As both boys sheepishly climbed out of the bush, Derek pulled a twig from his hair and said, "I thought you would never get here. What took you so long?"

"It isn't quite as easy for me!" Ruby said indignantly.

At the boy's school, they had a porter who was supposed to monitor the boys at night, but fortunately for Derek and Stuart, the porter enjoyed a tipple and was always fast asleep in his chair by eleven o'clock every night. The boys were then able to exit the school via the gym. They didn't have to navigate any high walls or climb out of windows.

Stuart held up a chocolate bar. "Peace offering."

Ruby's mouth watered.

There was no chocolate at her school. It was all home-cooked and home-grown food. She had no idea where Stuart got the chocolate from, but she was more than happy to share.

The three of them walked far enough away from the school so they wouldn't be spotted and strolled along the wide country lane until they reached a small copse of sycamore trees.

Under the cover of the trees, Ruby sat down on an upturned tree trunk, and the boys joined her.

"That school is driving me mad," Ruby complained, taking the piece of chocolate Stuart offered her.

"We've only got another few weeks until the summer holiday," Derek said, speaking through a mouthful of chocolate.

That was easy for him to say, he didn't have to put up with the nuns.

"I'm going to make her pay for this," Ruby said glaring down angrily at the floor and kicking a pile of leaves with her foot.

"She doesn't care about us," Derek said philosophically. "She just wants us out of the way."

Ruby scowled. "Yes, she does. But Dad will be out of prison soon, and then she won't be able to send us away anymore."

Derek shrugged.

"What will it be like having your dad around again?" Stuart asked. "I can't imagine what it's like to live with a criminal."

Both Ruby and Derek shot Stuart a scornful look. He had been born with a silver spoon in his mouth. There was no doubt about that.

At the moment, Ruby hated her mother with a passion because she was the one who was around and seemed to be trying to ruin Ruby's life, whereas she believed her father was a hero, who'd been hard done by and wrongly persecuted.

"Our father is innocent," Ruby said. "He was fitted up. He'll be out soon, and everything will go back to how it should be."

Derek looked dubious, but he didn't say anything.

Ruby noticed her brother didn't seem particularly supportive of their father and she glared at him. "You do tell people that Dad is innocent, don't you?"

Derek shrugged. "No. I quite like them thinking my father's a gangster. Everyone wants to ask me questions about it. I've had three boys invite me to their houses over the summer!"

Stuart grinned. "I'd invite you to mine, but I've already told my mother about your father, and she'd have kittens if you showed up at our house. She has already threatened to disinherit me unless I stay away from you. Apparently, you are a bad influence."

Derek found that exceedingly funny and laughed loudly. "That's me, a bad influence through and through."

Irritated with the pair of them, Ruby put a finger to her lips. "Keep quiet. Anyone would think you wanted someone to hear us."

Derek stood up and stretched. "You worry too much, Ruby. And you shouldn't scowl like that. You look just like our mother when you pull that face."

Ruby sprung to her feet and launched herself at her brother.

Stuart was so shocked, he scooted back on the log they'd been sitting on and ended up falling arse over elbow into the ferns and stinging nettles.

Stuart's cries of pain drew Derek and Ruby's attention, and they stopped their fighting only to fall about laughing.

Stuart got to his feet, grumbling about the lack of sympathy, and Ruby gave her brother one last shove. "Take it back."

Derek grinned. "Don't worry. I'm only teasing you. You look nothing like Mum."

Ruby nodded, mollified, and then blushed furiously when Derek added, "Stuart thinks you look pretty, don't you Stuart?"

Stuart looked horrified at his friend's betrayal and couldn't look Ruby in the eye.

"I think it's time for us to get back," he muttered.

They walked back to Ruby's school first, and Derek got

down on his hands and knees, so Ruby could climb onto his back and get a bunk up over the wall.

Although he was less than gentle, and Ruby managed to graze her hands on the other side of the wall, she couldn't help smiling.

So, Stuart thought she looked nice. She grinned again as she imagined the shock on her mother's face if she came back home with a boyfriend.

It would serve the old cow right.

***

While her children were messing about in the woods, Babs was tossing and turning in her bed. She couldn't sleep. The moonlight was streaming in through her bedroom window.

The house felt so empty without the children. Since she had dropped them off at school, she had received only one letter from Ruby and had heard absolutely nothing at all from Derek.

Not for the first time, she wondered whether she'd done the right thing.

Before she had packed them off to school, she was sure both children would eventually get over their temper tantrums and realise she had done this for their own good, but now she was second guessing herself.

It was hard not knowing what her children were doing every day. Babs was certain they'd be getting up to mischief, but she reassured herself they couldn't get into too much trouble at boarding school, especially not the ones Babs had picked out.

She particularly liked the idea of Ruby being taught by nuns and being out of the way of any boys.

She remembered what she'd been like at Ruby's age.

Babs sat up in bed and rearranged her pillows. She remembered giving her mother hell when she'd been a teenager, and then her mother had died not much later. She'd give anything to have that time over again and to let her mother know how much she appreciated her. But it was too late for that. There was no going back.

Ruby was old enough to leave school now, and Babs knew she was in for a struggle if she wanted to persuade Ruby to go back for another year in September.

But the girl wasn't ready for real life yet. It would chew her up and spit her out. Babs couldn't imagine any job Ruby would want to do after leaving school, and there was no way she would agree to let Ruby marry at a young age and ruin her life like she had with Martin.

It might make Ruby hate her, but Babs thought it would be best if she stayed at the boarding school for another year.

With a sigh, Babs adjusted her rollers. Maybe she should have told Tony about her plans for Old Mo. It was a big step to take on her own.

But if she changed her mind now, she would look weak. She'd already issued orders to red-haired Freddie, and if she didn't see it through, Martin's men would lose respect for her.

She glanced outside at the large moon and then tried to get comfortable by rearranging her pillows yet again. She needed to get to sleep because she had a huge day ahead of her tomorrow.

22

BABS HAD BAGS UNDER HER eyes the size of suitcases. She had had a terrible night's sleep and felt like she'd only just managed to drift off when suddenly it was time to get up. Her stomach churned, and she had been forced to skip breakfast, making do with an extra strong cup of tea.

Just before nine a.m., Babs approached one of the abandoned warehouses on the docks that was owned by Martin. The surrounding area was deserted, and Babs' heels clicked loudly across the cobbled road. She was wearing her fur coat, as usual, but it was already starting to warm up, and the sun overhead was promising a hot day to come. She was sweating but didn't know whether that was due to the sun on her back or fear.

Old Mo had to be dealt with. There were no two ways about it. Babs had been married to Martin long enough to know these things went on, but somehow, being the one behind the order wasn't all it was cracked up to be. It was easy enough, to tell the boys to get rid of Old Mo and wash her hands of it, but if she wanted to gain their respect, she needed to be there when it happened.

Babs pressed her lips together. Her mouth felt dry, and she would have killed for another cup of tea.

When she reached the third warehouse along Wharf Road, Babs paused outside. This was it. There was no turning back now. But still she hesitated.

Why was she having all these doubts? Old Mo had clearly been cheating the Mortons and laughing at them as he did it. He deserved to be punished. He didn't deserve Babs' pity.

Despite that, Babs had an overwhelming desire to turn on her heels and run back home. Before she could, the big, old door at the front of the warehouse creaked open, and Henry the Hand poked his head out.

"All right, Babs? I thought I heard someone out here. He's inside." Henry gave an evil chuckle. "We've warmed him up for you."

Babs nodded and followed Henry inside the warehouse. Compared to the bright sunshine outside, the warehouse was dim, and Babs' eyes struggled to adjust to the light.

Babs blinked. She could just about make out a couple of figures in the centre of the huge building. They were at least fifteen yards away. As she walked towards them, she recognised Freddie's bright red hair and saw the fat figure of Old Mo tied up in a chair. When she got closer still, she saw the blood.

Babs' knees almost gave way from under her and she reached out to grab onto Henry's arm. "Christ, what have you done to him?"

Henry looked confused. "The usual. We've been trying to find out if anyone else was involved in his little scam before we get rid of him."

Old Mo looked a terrible state. Babs recognised him from his fat figure and old-fashioned brown suit. He still wore the gold rings on his chubby fingers. But his face had been pummelled to a pulp, and Babs thought his own mother wouldn't recognise him now.

His eyes were swollen shut, and he had red marks all over his face, which would never have time to develop into bruises if Henry and Freddie followed her orders.

Jesus Christ. What had she gotten herself into? This wasn't

right.

Old Mo had heard Babs' voice, and he turned his head, even though he couldn't see her through his bruised and battered eyes. "Babs? Is that you? Tell them to stop. Please, Babs."

Babs' mouth opened in horror. She didn't know what to say to him. There was no pleasure in seeing a man broken like this.

Old Mo took Babs' silence as weakness and tried again to beg for his life. "I'll repay the money and move out of the area. Please, Babs. Please."

Horrified, Babs held a shaking hand to her mouth. She wanted to scream and rush over to untie him.

"It doesn't seem like anyone else was involved, Babs," Freddie said.

She turned to look at him and realised as he wiped the sweat away from his forehead with the back of his arm that he had blood on his knuckles. Old Mo's blood.

Babs shook her head.

Henry walked over to the side of the warehouse and crouched beside an old, brown sack on the floor. No one spoke, and it was silent apart from Mo's quiet sobs and the sound of Henry's shoes hitting the stone floor as he walked.

When he walked back towards them, he was carrying a long knife. Babs felt dizzy and clasped a hand to her forehead.

"We'll finish him off now," Freddie said as if he were merely discussing plans to slaughter a pig. He took the knife Henry handed to him.

It was no good. Babs couldn't let it happen. "No. I've changed my mind."

Both Henry and Freddie looked at her with puzzled frowns on their faces, but they didn't get to question her motives because all of a sudden the doors to the warehouse burst open.

Everyone turned to see who it was, even old Mo, although he wouldn't be able to see properly. Babs guessed he was doing it on instinct.

"What was that? Who's there?" Old Mo asked with a tremor in his voice.

It was Tony Morton. "What the hell is going on here?"

Red-haired Freddie still held the knife in his hand but let it drop to his side as he answered, "We are dealing with Old Mo as ordered, boss."

Tony's gaze rested on Old Mo. "Whose orders?" he demanded.

Babs had never seen Tony look so angry. He'd never looked more like Martin than he did at that moment.

Freddie and Henry exchanged glances. They didn't want to get caught in the middle of a power battle that much was obvious.

But Henry didn't dare not answer Tony's question. "Babs' orders. She found out Old Mo was cheating and wanted him dealt with."

Babs was positive she was going to be sick as Tony turned his eyes on her. He gave her a cold hard stare and then took two menacing steps towards her. "What the hell have you done, Babs?"

Babs shook her head and stammered, "It was a mistake, Tony. I didn't think it would be like this."

She wrenched her eyes away from Tony's and looked back at Old Mo, who was now pulling against his restraints.

"Tony? Tony, is that you? Oh, thank God. Get me out of here, please, mate."

Tony's whole body was tense, and his fists were clenched at his sides.

He growled at Babs through gritted teeth. "Get out of here. Now."

Babs didn't need telling twice. She turned and hightailed it out of the warehouse, only stopping when she was safely out in the sunshine. She wanted to go home and get out of there as quickly as she could, but something compelled her to stay. She needed to know what Tony was going to do. She slipped down the side of the warehouse and placed two discarded crates on top of each other, so she could stand on them and peer into one of the dusty windows. It was dark, but she could see them all crowded around Old Mo. They hadn't untied him yet.

What happened next shocked Babs to the core.

Tony held his hand out, and Freddie gave him the knife. Tony clutched a handful of Old Mo's hair and yanked back his head, exposing his neck. With one brutal slash of the knife, he slit Old Mo's throat.

The fat man jerked for a moment and then stilled. It was over.

Babs tumbled down from the crates, and on her hands and knees, she vomited over the cobbles.

23

IT WAS AN IMPORTANT DAY for Big Tim. He had done a couple of jobs for Dave Carter here and there, but today was the day he met the other lads for the first time. Of course, he'd met them before, but he hadn't been one of Dave Carter's men at that point. Things were different now. It wouldn't be easy getting the other men to accept him. He'd worked for Martin Morton for years, and people didn't switch allegiances easily in the East End. They would be suspicious and rightly so. Tim wouldn't blame them for that. In fact, he'd think less of them if they accepted him with open arms.

He was meeting Dave at the workshop, the front for the legitimate side of Carter's business.

It was only just after nine a.m. and as he approached he could already hear the sounds of men working inside. When Big Tim stopped outside the workshop, he watched them unobserved for a moment. The workshop was large and had an industrial-sized metal door, which was rolled up, making it easy to get vehicles in and out of the yard. There were two cars in there at the moment, and Tim recognised Brian Moore and Charlie Williams working on the Ford Cortina. Charlie murmured a joke that Tim didn't quite catch, and Brian spluttered out a laugh. It was clear that the two men got along well.

Tim cleared his throat and stepped forward into the

workshop. He knew Dave Carter would have told his men to expect him this morning, but that didn't mean they were going to be happy about it. By the scowl on Brian's face, Tim guessed he was very put out.

"Is Dave here yet?" Tim asked.

Brian picked up a rag and wiped his hands on it as he walked towards Tim. "Look who it is, Charlie. We're going to have to start calling you two-faced Tim from now on."

Brian smirked, and Tim immediately knew the man was going to cause him trouble. Brian was almost a foot shorter than Tim, but the man was almost as wide as he was tall. He was all muscle, the type of man who had to turn sideways to get through a door because of the width of his shoulders. Tim knew he had the edge, though. He always did. There weren't many people in the East End who could challenge Tim one-on-one.

He could start by showing Charlie and Brian he meant business. He could wrap his hands around Brian's wide neck and hold him a foot above the ground, but that wouldn't solve his problem. Brian would only resent him even more.

Still, he couldn't let Brian's little dig pass. "You'll start calling me sir if you know what's good for you."

The smirk on Brian's face disappeared. He opened his mouth to give him more grief when he spotted someone over Tim's shoulder and abruptly shut his mouth.

"Good. You're here early on your first day," Dave Carter said as he walked into the workshop. "I see you've already met Brian and Charlie."

Tim nodded and waited to see whether Brian would complain to his boss about Tim working at the workshop. But Brian said nothing.

"I've got a few things to do today, but I'll leave you in Charlie's capable hands," Dave said.

"Thanks, boss," Tim said.

Brian screwed up his face and went back to working on the

car. The crisis had been averted for now, but Tim knew Brian wasn't about to make his life easy. He would need to be on his guard.

After Dave picked up a few pieces of paperwork and left the workshop, leaving the men alone again, Charlie Williams approached him.

He held out his hand and smiled. It was easy to like Charlie. He had the sort of face that seemed friendly and honest, but it was misleading. Charlie was probably one of the men Dave Carter trusted most in the world, and that made him dangerous. He was well known for wearing his three-piece suits, and always had his grandfather's gold pocket watch tucked into his waistcoat pocket.

Tim took his hand and shook it firmly. "I know we have history. But this is a new start for me. I hope you won't hold my past against me."

Charlie's smile widened and Brian snorted from under the bonnet of the car.

"Don't mind him. He'll get used to you in time."

Tim heard Brian mutter, "Not bloody likely."

Tim spent the rest of the morning helping Charlie on the other motor and avoiding Brian as best he could. He couldn't help warming to Charlie, who was friendly and talkative. Tim wasn't much of a talker, so Charlie's chatter took the pressure off him.

It had been a long time since Tim had spent a whole day at work, and he was surprised to find himself absolutely shattered by three o'clock in the afternoon. Charlie said they tended to shut up the workshop between four and five o'clock unless they had an important job on. Today, Charlie had to go and pick up some parts, so he left the workshop at three thirty, leaving Tim alone with Brian.

Tim didn't want any aggro and figured Brian didn't want him looking over his shoulder, so instead of helping Brian on the motor, Tim sat down in the corner of the workshop on a creaky old chair, intending to rest for a few minutes.

But he hadn't realised how tired he was, and within seconds of closing his eyes, he was out for the count.

***

Tim quickly drifted off into a dream. It was a cold night, and the moon was glinting on the surface of the canal. He knew there was something in the water — something waiting for him, and as he inched forward, he felt icy cold fingers of dread creep up his spine.

"I'm sorry," Tim muttered.

He realised this was his punishment. He had been brought back to the site where he had murdered Kathleen Diamond.

There was something just beneath the water, but it was too dark to make out what it was, so Tim leaned further forward, straining to see.

Suddenly the surface of the water broke, and Tim tried to backup, but he was too slow. Kathleen emerged from the water, her skin tinged blue, and she grabbed the collar of his shirt and shook him hard.

As he looked into those deep, blue eyes that he would never forget, he said desperately, "I'm sorry. I'm so sorry."

But Kathleen didn't release her grip on his shirt, and he knew it was only a matter of time before she pulled him down into that dark water with her.

She opened her mouth and said, "Wake up, Mister."

What a funny thing to say, Tim thought, as he slowly came back to reality. When he opened his eyes, he found himself looking into those same dark blue eyes. Tim jerked and stood up so quickly he knocked the chair over.

"Jesus Christ." Tim crossed himself as he stared wide-eyed at the boy in front of him.

Jimmy Diamond.

Jimmy looked at him as though he were mad. "You were asleep," he said accusingly. "Me and Georgie are nearly finished washing the motors. Charlie normally locks up, but he isn't back yet." Jimmy held out a keyring packed full of keys. "Charlie said you should lock up today."

Tim nodded, although his heart was still beating frantically. His eyes searched the boy's face, trying to work out what features came from Kathleen and what part of him came from Martin Morton.

"Are you going to take the keys?" Jimmy asked, exasperated.

Tim reached out and took the keyring. "Yes. It's fine. I'll lock up. I just drifted off for a moment."

"I noticed. You were shouting out all kinds of things. What were you dreaming about?"

Tim felt the blood drain from his face. He could confront most things in life without fear, but this young boy struck terror into his heart. He was a reminder of Tim's evil deeds.

"What did I say?"

Jimmy shrugged. "I couldn't make most of it out. It sounded like gibberish, but you did keep saying sorry over and over again."

Tim rubbed his hands over his face, trying to snap out of it. "It was just a dream, nothing important. Now, hurry up and finish those motors, so I can bring them back in the workshop. I don't want to be here all night."

Jimmy rushed off outside, picked up his polishing cloth and joined Georgie. Tim had to admit they'd done a good job for two youngsters.

He'd have to be more careful around here. There could be no more naps on the job. It was too dangerous. He should never have approached Dave Carter for a job, it was suicide. When Martin got out, he would be looking to punish Tim, and Tim knew better than anyone that Martin's punishment would be severe. But he hadn't been able to resist approaching Dave Carter when he knew Jimmy was working here.

He had no idea how, but Tim was determined to figure out

a way to help Jimmy. Tim would never be able to make amends for what he had done, but his conscience wouldn't rest until he'd at least tried to make Jimmy's life a little better. He hadn't worked out how he was going to do that yet, but in time, Tim would make sure he was there whenever Jimmy Diamond needed anything.

***

Ruby Morton was absolutely fed up to the back teeth of her stupid school. The nuns were driving her mad. The rules were ridiculous and far too strict, and Ruby had had enough. If her mother thought this experience would somehow mould Ruby into one of those stupid stuck-up girls in her class, she had a surprise in store.

This morning when she hadn't been able to answer a question when called on in Maths, Sister Teresa had slammed down the oversized ruler on Ruby's desk, narrowly missing Ruby's fingers. She had snatched her fingers away just in time, but she hadn't been able to stop herself letting out a curse. Ruby thought that was perfectly understandable given the circumstances. However, Sister Theresa didn't agree, and Ruby spent the rest of the lesson, in the corner of the classroom, facing the wall.

It had been the last straw. Instead of going to her next lesson, which was outdoor hockey, Ruby was going to get out of this place.

She thought it would be a while before they missed her. It might be more sensible to wait until tonight after lights out, but Ruby didn't much fancy trying to navigate the dark roads at night around the school, and she couldn't bear to be stuck in this place any longer.

She didn't bother to pack, but she wanted to take a cardigan rather than her navy blue school blazer. Otherwise, she would stick out like a sore thumb.

She didn't have any money either. That was yet another thing wrong with this place. Ruby knew full well her mother would have sent money both to her and Derek, but in her school, the nuns kept it locked up. Ruby thought that was a bloody cheek. It was her money. How dare they keep it from her?

But she would show them. She was going to get home with or without any money.

Sticking her arms through her cardigan and chucking her blazer down on the bed, Ruby rushed out of the dormitory. She intended to get as far away from the school as she could before they realised she was missing.

Unfortunately, at the door to the dormitory, Ruby ran into Clara. Of all the people who could have caught Ruby running off, it just had to be Clara, didn't it?

Ruby tried to push her way past, but Clara had already cottoned on to the fact Ruby was up to mischief.

"Where do you think you are going? You're supposed to be playing hockey."

Ruby pulled a face. "What business is it of yours? You need to keep that horrible big nose of yours out of it!"

Clara's cheeks flushed pink as she scowled. "You really think you're something special, don't you? Well, you are not. My mother says you are as common as muck."

"I'd rather be common than fat and ugly!" Ruby said spitefully and then pushed herself up against Clara, so the girl was pinned hard against the wall.

Ruby raised her forearm and pushed it firmly against the girl's neck. "If you tell anybody you saw me, I'll do far worse than make everyone think you wet the bed."

Clara attempted to push her off. "You don't scare me, Ruby Morton."

But Clara's face told a different story. She looked terrified.

Ruby jabbed an elbow hard into the girl's ribs. "I'm warning you. You don't want to make an enemy of me. So you're not going to tell anybody you saw me, right?"

Clara pouted and rubbed her bruised ribs. "All right. Just

get off me. I don't care what you do anyway."

Ruby let the girl go and rushed off towards the stairs. Stupid, interfering cow. Ruby had wasted precious minutes having to deal with her.

Ruby sped along the corridor. If she didn't get a move on, she was going to get caught. When she reached the large oak doors, Ruby put a hand on the brass, circular door handle and twisted it, but as she did so, she felt the weight of a hand on her shoulder.

"You should be in class, young lady."

Ruby's hopes sank at the sound of Sister Bernadette's voice. Sister Bernadette had made it her task in life to make Ruby's time at the school absolutely miserable. She enjoyed the power she held over all of the girls at the school and was a nasty, bitter, twisted individual in Ruby's opinion.

Ruby tried desperately to think of an excuse to tell Sister Bernadette, but when she turned to face the nun, she knew the woman wouldn't fall for any of her stories. Frustrated with her failure to escape the horrible place, Ruby lost her temper.

"It's none of your business, you horrible old bat."

Sister Bernadette's eyes widened in shock. None of the girls dared to talk back to her normally, let alone insult her. Her eyes sparked with fierce determination.

"You've got the devil in you, child. In my day, we would use the cane to thrash it out of you. But for some reason, the school board doesn't approve of that anymore, so for the next week, you will be copying passages out from the Bible in all your free time."

Ruby's shoulders slumped in defeat, and her eyes filled with tears. It was so unfair. If she hadn't run into Clara in the dormitory, she could have got past Sister Bernadette unnoticed.

But then Sister Bernadette said something to Ruby that made her mood change in an instant.

"I could see it in you as soon as your mother brought you that first day. You'll never get anywhere in life. You're just like your father."

Sister Bernadette had intended her comment to hurt Ruby, but in fact, it spurred her into action. She might have meant the comparison to her father in a derogatory way, but to Ruby, it was the perfect complement.

The nun was right. Ruby was like her father, so why was she allowing this bullying woman to ruin her life?

Sister Bernadette was marching Ruby down the corridor when she stopped abruptly.

"You can wait in here while I report your behaviour to Miss Bunce." Sister Bernadette pulled a large keyring from her belt, and Ruby realised with horror that she intended to lock her in a small room with no windows. It was scarcely bigger than a cupboard.

But when Sister Bernadette tried to push her inside the room, Ruby spun around, grabbing the nun by her habit and thrusting her inside the room. Sister Bernadette was taken by surprise and had no time to react before Ruby snatched the ring of keys from her hands and slammed the door shut, locking it.

The door was thick and made of solid wood, so Sister Bernadette's cries were muffled. Ruby grinned. Well, she had really blown it now. There was no going back from this.

She took the stairs two at a time and reached the main entrance hall, breathless. She needed to be quick as it wouldn't be long before someone heard Sister Bernadette's cries. She quickly scanned the area to make sure none of the nuns were present, and when she saw that she was alone, she made a rush for the main oak doors. There was no point trying to sneak out of the laundry window today. For one thing, it was probably in use, and she knew if she kept to the tree-line along the driveway, she would be out of sight from the main building anyway.

She ran along the gravel driveway and then skipped up onto the grass verge, weaving her way in between the trees. For the first time since she'd been admitted to the stupid school, Ruby felt happy. If she got out of here, maybe she could persuade her mother to let her stay at home. If not, she would have to turn to her grandmother, Violet Morton. That would be a last resort. Violet didn't look favourably on Ruby. She was too boisterous and too much of a tomboy in her grandmother's opinion.

But Ruby was clever enough to realise she could play her grandmother off against her mother. If Violet got wind of the fact Babs wanted to send Ruby back to school against her wishes, Ruby had no doubt that her grandmother would intervene on her behalf. If only to annoy her daughter-in-law.

She looked over her shoulder and saw that the coast was still clear. She grinned. Once she was out of the driveway and onto the main road, her plan was to hitch a lift. She realised she wouldn't get taken all the way home, but as long as she could get close to London that would be good enough.

A low hanging branch smacked her in the forehead as she ran past, and she bellowed out a curse, putting a hand to her head to make sure she wasn't bleeding. She hated the bloody countryside with all the trees and plants. It was a dangerous place to live.

Ruby couldn't wait for her dad to get out of prison. She adored him, and her memories of him being around when she was little were all good. Her mother said she had a selective memory, but then she would say that. For some reason, she didn't like her husband, probably for the same reason she had no time for Ruby and Derek. But Ruby knew everything would be all right when her father got out of prison. He would keep her mother in line.

Ruby liked to think he'd be proud of her. She hadn't seen him for a long time because he didn't want his children to see him in prison. She could understand that, but it still hurt. She missed him desperately.

The thought that one day soon they would all be back together again as a family kept Ruby going.

24

TREVOR CARTER COULDN'T BELIEVE HIS eyes when he got to his father's workshop. His mother had sent him down to ask his father to pick up her pills on the way home. But when Trevor got to the workshop, his father wasn't there. Instead, he saw his little brother, Georgie, messing about and splashing water at Jimmy Diamond.

Trevor had already told Georgie to stay away from the boy, and so he approached the pair of them, furious and ready to let rip.

"What are you playing at, Georgie? I told you not to have anything to do with him."

Both boys stopped messing about immediately, and Georgie dropped a wet sponge on the floor. "It's all right, Trevor. Jimmy is working here now."

What was the crazy boy talking about now? "That's ridiculous. Don't be stupid, Georgie."

Jimmy smiled cockily and annoyed Trevor further. He didn't like the way Jimmy Diamond acted. He was an orphan, and everybody knew his mother had been killed. It was also common knowledge that his nan was a drinker, so why did he think he was something special?

"Georgie is right. Your dad gave me a job after school, washing the motors," Jimmy said, keeping that infuriating smile on his face.

Trevor narrowed his eyes. "That's not true."

There was no way his father would give Jimmy a job here at the workshop. If he needed somebody to wash the motors, surely he would have asked Trevor. Why would he give a job to this orphan boy and ignore his own son? It didn't make sense. Jimmy Diamond had to be making it up.

"It is true! Georgie said stamping his foot and then picking up the wet sponge and throwing it at Trevor. "And I'm n... not stupid!"

Trevor's jaw dropped open. He couldn't believe it. Georgie had just thrown something at him. Georgie, who had always worshipped the ground he walked on, was now talking back to him. Trevor shook his head in disbelief.

"Watch yourself, Georgie. Pick that up," he said, pointing to the wet sponge that had narrowly missed him.

"Pick it up yourself," Georgie said, grinning, but Trevor noticed he took a step closer to Jimmy.

The little sod. After everything Trevor had done for him. Trevor reached down, picked up the wet sponge and threw it as hard as he could at Georgie. It hit his little brother right between the eyes, and Georgie let out a scream.

He was shocked rather than hurt. After all, it was only a wet sponge, but unfortunately for Trevor, his father picked that moment to return to the workshop.

"Trevor, leave your little brother alone," he roared.

Trevor turned to protest his innocence, but when he saw his father's angry face, he gave up before he'd even opened his mouth. There wasn't any point. His father never took Trevor's side in anything.

Hurt and confused, Trevor turned away, preparing to go home, but as he did so, he caught sight of the smirk on Jimmy Diamond's face, and it filled him with rage. "What's he doing here?"

"We've been washing the cars," little Georgie lisped.

Their father didn't contradict Georgie, and Trevor realised

his little brother had been telling the truth. Their father had chosen some horrible little orphan boy to work for him over Trevor.

Trevor bit down on the inside of his mouth so hard he tasted blood.

He hated his father, and he hated Jimmy Diamond.

He turned to go but then remembered the purpose of his visit. "Mum wanted you to pick up some more of her tablets."

His father didn't even bother to reply but shook his head in disgust.

As Trevor turned and walked away, he could hear little Georgie and Jimmy laughing as they picked up the buckets of water, and resentment burned deep within him. He had no idea what he had done to deserve a father that hated him so much, but he was determined not to care. He'd show him one day. He'd show all of them that Trevor Carter was worth more than all of them put together.

***

Dave Carter watched his eldest son walk away with a heavy heart. He found it so difficult to communicate with Trevor. Little Georgie was a different story. He was sweet and naive, and Dave couldn't help feeling protective of him. Trevor hadn't had it easy, though, and Dave would have liked to have had a better relationship with his son.

When he was younger, Trevor had gone through a phase where he refused to talk to anyone, and Dave had found it very hard. Although Trevor grew out of it, he was never a talkative boy, and Dave found it difficult to work out how he was really feeling.

It seemed like every time he spoke to Trevor these days, he was telling him off for something.

Dave was absolutely furious with Sandra for sending their son to ask him to get her more pills. They'd had a huge bust up last night over her constant pill popping. It had to stop. It had reached the point where Dave was doing most of the jobs around the house, including preparing all the family meals. He didn't have much time, and he had never been talented in the kitchen, so both Georgie and Trevor were suffering.

He'd employed old Betsy to come in and give Sandra a hand with the housework, but the main reason for giving her the job was so she could keep an eye on his wife. Dave was terrified he would one day come home and find Sandra had overdosed. According to Betsy, Sandra did nothing all day but sit at the kitchen table and stare into space.

Dave ran a weary hand through his hair and turned to watch Georgie and Jimmy packing up their cleaning gear. He couldn't help smiling in response to their happy laughter. He was very grateful that Jimmy Diamond had befriended Georgie, both boys hadn't had the best start in life.

"The motors are all inside now, boss. Shall I lock up?" Big Tim asked as he approached Dave holding the keys.

Dave held out his hand. "No, don't worry. I'll lock up today. How did you enjoy your first day at the workshop?"

Big Tim looked at him through bleary eyes and nodded. "It was good, boss."

He handed Dave the keys, said goodbye and then headed out of the yard. When Tim had approached him for a job, Dave had been in two minds about it. On the one hand, there was no doubt that Tim was past his best. Physically, he was still intimidating. But mentally, he had lost his edge. Dave had decided to take him on because of his past experience with Martin Morton. He was sure one day it would come in handy.

Martin had only a couple of years left on his sentence. If he was sensible, when he got out, he would keep a low profile. Dave was more than happy to let the Mortons run their small operation on the fringes of his turf. But Martin Morton had never been sensible. Dave knew he would have a battle on his hands when Martin was released. The man had a huge ego and prison wouldn't have changed that.

When Martin was out, Dave had no doubt he would try to reclaim this corner of the East End. But Dave was prepared and was building up his defences.

A key part of that was to sabotage the current Morton operation. It was a shame. They had stayed within their boundaries and hadn't caused him any aggro, but Dave had been at this business for a long time, and he knew the best defence was an early attack when the enemy were least expecting it.

***

Trevor left the workshop and stormed home. He was furious with his little brother and his father, but the person who had him really seeing red was Jimmy Diamond. Why was Jimmy hanging around their family anyway? He didn't have his own family, and now he was trying to steal Trevor's.

He let himself in through the front door and wandered through to the kitchen. He wanted to tell his mother everything that had happened and yearned for her to put her arms around him and tell him everything was all right. But when he walked into the kitchen, she was sitting beside the table with her head in her hands. Her hair was askew, and her face was red and blotchy because she never bothered to fix her face in the mornings anymore. When Trevor was younger, his mother used to be proud of her appearance and would never leave the house without applying some face powder and lipstick. These days she just didn't bother to leave the house. Sometimes if she remembered, she would send Trevor to the shops and would ask him to help fix dinner. Most of the time now, though, his father prepared the meals.

Trevor stomped up to the kitchen sink and made himself an orange squash. His mother didn't even look up.

Sometimes, he tried to convince himself he didn't care. It was nice not to have his mother nagging him all the time. He could pretty much do whatever he wanted after school as neither of his parents cared, but today it all felt a bit too much, and as Trevor looked at his haggard mother, he felt his eyes brimming with tears.

He rubbed his eyes furiously. He would not cry. He wasn't a baby.

He had a lump in his throat, which made it hard to swallow, so he poured the rest of his orange squash away and then walked out of the kitchen, hoping his mother might notice and say something to him. But she didn't.

All at once, Trevor felt he had to get out of the house. He didn't want to be reminded of how much his parents couldn't stand to look at him. It had to be because of Lillian. They blamed him for recovering when his poor sister had died.

He dashed out of the front door, slamming it behind him.

He hated feeling helpless, and tried desperately to think of something that would make him feel better. Then Trevor smiled. He knew exactly what would cheer him up. He would lie in wait for Jimmy Diamond and make the boy pay.

25

TREVOR QUICKLY MADE HIS WAY up along Narrow Street. He hoped he hadn't missed Jimmy. They'd been about to pack up when he left the workshop so Jimmy could be home already. Trevor's hands curled into fists, and his fingernails dug into his palm. He needed a release, somewhere to channel all his anger, and right now, his fist hitting Jimmy Diamond's face was the only thing that would make him feel better.

At the end of the street, he leaned back against the brick wall. There was no one else about apart from two little boys playing with some kind of home-made wagon attached to a piece of string.

He peered around the corner. There was no sign of Jimmy yet. Trevor chewed on a fingernail. If he didn't manage to sort it today, he would have to deal with him tomorrow. Jimmy needed to be put back in his place.

As Trevor remembered the cocky look on Jimmy's face, he gritted his teeth. He wanted to turn that cocky smirk into a look of fear.

He heard Jimmy coming before he saw him. He was chattering away, and so Trevor poked his head round the corner and saw to his annoyance that Jimmy was walking towards him with little Georgie.

Georgie should have gone straight home. Jimmy Diamond

was influencing everyone, and not in a good way as far as Trevor was concerned.

He kept himself hidden around the corner, so he could jump out and surprise Jimmy. He didn't really want to give Jimmy a battering in front of little Georgie, but it wasn't his fault. If Georgie wanted to hang around with Jimmy, he didn't deserve Trevor's protection anymore.

He held his breath as Jimmy and Georgie got closer, and finally when they were only a couple of yards away, he made his move. He stepped on the pavement in front of them, spread his legs and folded his arms across his chest as he stared down at the youngsters.

"Get home, Georgie. Now." Trevor didn't often shout at Georgie because he was a silly little baby and would cry when people raised their voices, but now Trevor was too annoyed to care.

Georgie's lower lip wobbled. "Why are you s…shouting at me?"

"Because you're a stupid little idiot. Go home!"

Georgie smothered a sob, and Jimmy Diamond put a hand on the little boy's shoulder. He was in the same year as Georgie at school, but Georgie was very small for his age. Seeing Jimmy trying to comfort his little brother when it wasn't his place to do so made Trevor furious.

"Don't call him stupid. He doesn't like it," Jimmy said.

That made Trevor see red. How dare this little upstart tell him how to speak to his own brother?

Trevor strode forward and shoved Jimmy firmly in the chest, making him stagger backwards. "Don't you dare tell me how to talk to my brother. I'll talk to him how I like."

"No, Trevor, don't!" Georgie wailed, watching his older brother grab a handful of Jimmy's shirt.

But Trevor barely heard him. All he could see was Jimmy's mocking, dark blue eyes. If he looked scared or remorseful, Trevor would have probably let him go, but he didn't.

Not flinching, Jimmy met Trevor's gaze as though he wasn't bothered in the slightest that the older boy was about to give him a beating.

"What's wrong with you?" Jimmy asked. "What have I done to make you so angry?"

Trevor had never been much of a talker, and he'd much rather let his fists do the talking. Jimmy questioning him added to his anger. Too many thoughts were rushing around in his head, and he couldn't think straight. All he knew was that his parents didn't like him, and now even his simple little brother was taking somebody else's side over Trevor's.

He raised his fist and brought it down hard on Jimmy's face. He'd been aiming for his nose, but Jimmy turned his head just in time, and Trevor's knuckles grazed his cheekbone.

Jimmy's dark blue eyes didn't look so cocky anymore. They blazed with anger. Instead of backing away from the fight, he pushed up close and brought his forehead down hard on the bridge of Trevor's nose.

Dazed, Trevor staggered, feeling very unsteady on his feet. The street seemed to swim before his eyes, and he could hear Georgie's voice echoing from far away.

He leaned back on the wall and sunk down until he was sitting on his backside.

Holding his hands to his nose, he realised he was bleeding. The sodding bastard had head-butted him. He blinked up at Jimmy through watery eyes. It was so unfair. He hadn't been expecting a dirty fight.

"What did you do that for?"

Georgie kneeled down beside his brother and tried to wipe some of the blood away with the corner of his shirt. "Oh, no, you're bleeding."

Trevor pushed his brother's hands away and glared up at Jimmy.

Jimmy stepped forward and held out his hand, offering to

help Trevor to his feet. "You did start it, Trevor."

"Piss off, you horrible little orphaned bastard," Trevor said spitefully.

Jimmy let Trevor's words roll off his back and shrugged. "Suit yourself," he said, withdrawing his hand and putting it in his pocket. "I'll see you tomorrow, Georgie."

Jimmy turned and left Trevor sitting on the pavement feeling very hard done by.

He glared at Jimmy Diamond's back as he walked away and swore he'd get his own back on the little bastard one day soon. He turned and realised that Georgie had stuck by him. His little brother's eyes were red and watery.

"Are you all right, Trevor? I'm sorry you g...got hurt."

Trevor felt a rush of warmth towards his little brother, at least the silly little sod had stuck by him. He reached out to put his arm around Georgie's shoulders and gave him a squeeze. "I'm fine. Let's get you home."

***

As Jimmy Diamond walked away, he rubbed his cheek. He would have one hell of a bruise tomorrow thanks to Trevor. He didn't understand what he had done to the boy to make him hate him so much, but he guessed Trevor was a little jealous of his new job at the workshop. He didn't think Trevor's blow had drawn blood, but just in case, he didn't want to go straight home. His nan would have kittens if she saw him in this state.

She had been trying to stay off the drink so hard over the last few days, and Jimmy didn't want to give her any reason to turn back to the bottle. He thought of popping to Bobby Green's house and asking his mother if she had any antiseptic, but word would probably get back to his nan if he did that.

As he turned into Whitethorn Street, he realised he wasn't far from Linda's house. He was still a little disappointed that Linda hadn't felt he was old enough to be trusted with whatever she knew about his mother, but he was sure Linda would have antiseptic cream, and she wouldn't go running to his nan.

He turned right, heading into the narrow alley behind the row of houses. He chose that route because he wouldn't run into anybody he knew. He counted the backyards as he walked past the individual houses. He knew Linda's was the seventeenth house in the row. As he got closer to her house, he heard the sound of a disturbance.

There was a lot of banging and what sounded like a woman screaming. Jimmy quickened his step.

When he realised the noise was coming from Linda's house, his chest tightened.

He didn't bother to call out. Instead, he unlatched the gate to the backyard and rushed across to Linda's back door. What he saw in the kitchen made him gasp in horror.

Linda was on her hands and knees, and in front of her, was a broken plate and what looked like the remains of dinner. Linda's brute of a husband kneeled over her, clutching her hair and forcing her head down into the food on the floor.

Neither of them had noticed Jimmy's arrival.

"Eat it, you silly bitch. When I come home, I expect a decent meal on the table, not this muck, and if you weren't gallivanting off all day, you'd have time to mop the bleeding floor."

Linda sobbed and tried to pull away from her husband, but he held her too tightly.

Jimmy couldn't stand it anymore. "Get off her!" he screeched and ran at Linda's husband with his fists held high.

With a roar, Linda's husband loosened his grip on Linda's hair and stood up. "Who the hell are you?"

"I'm Jimmy Diamond, and if you touch her again, I'll kill you."

As Geoff took a menacing step towards Jimmy, Linda scrambled to her knees and pushed herself in front of Jimmy, protecting him. "No, you leave him alone, do you hear me?"

Geoff gave a grunt of disgust. "Clean this place up. It looks like a pigsty."

He turned and stormed out of the kitchen, heading up the passage and opening the front door.

Jimmy watched him go with his heart in his mouth. When Geoff had left and slammed the door behind him, Jimmy helped Linda to her feet.

He felt like he had hundreds of words jammed at the back of his throat, things he wanted to say, but he wasn't sure what to say first. Linda's left eye was red and swollen, and she was going to have an even worse bruise than Jimmy tomorrow. Her hair was all messed up from where Geoff had pulled it, and her eyes were red from crying.

Linda wiped her tears away with the back of her hand and then smiled at Jimmy. "It looks like you've been in the wars as well. Let me get the antiseptic lotion."

Silent, Jimmy watched as Linda bent down and pulled out a little first-aid tin from underneath the sink. She placed it in on the kitchen table and pulled out the antiseptic lotion. She put the bright yellow iodine onto a piece of cotton wool and then gestured for Jimmy to come closer.

As he stood beside her, she gently applied the antiseptic to his grazed cheek.

When she'd finished, she said, "There you go. All done."

Jimmy thanked her, and when she moved to start clearing up the mess on the floor, he said, "Wait a minute."

He grabbed the bottle of iodine, put a few drops on a fresh piece of cotton wool and handed it to Linda so she could attend to her own injured skin.

Linda took it from him with a shaking hand, and her eyes filled with fresh tears. "Thank you, Jimmy."

Afterwards, Jimmy helped her to clean up the mess. Neither of them spoke about what had happened. It didn't take a genius to work out that Geoff was a wife-beater, and

Jimmy knew better than anyone that talking things through never helped anyone at the end of the day. Nothing changed. He could talk about his mother as much as he liked, but nothing would bring her back.

26

BABS MORTON WAS BESIDE HERSELF. One minute, she felt scared to death about what had happened to Old Mo, but the next, she was furious with herself for not seeing it through. Babs had always considered herself a tough old bird, but today had revealed her fears and insecurities. To make matters worse, her mini breakdown had been witnessed by Freddie, Henry and worst of all, Tony.

She had come home from the warehouse and gotten straight into bed. An hour spent crying and wailing into her pillow hadn't really made her feel much better. All it had done was smudge her eye makeup.

So she'd spent the rest of the day chain-smoking and drinking extra strong tea at the kitchen table.

When she heard a knock at the front door, Babs was tempted to ignore it. She didn't want to face anyone right now, but curiosity got the better of her, and she peeked through the front room window to see who it was.

Tony. The sight of him made Babs feel sick, but she couldn't ignore him. She'd have to deal with him eventually and now was as good a time as any. She would have to listen to him scold her like a schoolgirl and what made it worse was that Babs knew she deserved it. She had let everyone down.

She opened the front door and stood back so Tony could come in. She didn't say anything but blinked at him, feeling very sorry for herself.

Tony looked like a different person. There was none of the rage she had seen on his face earlier today. Instead, he looked at her with sympathy.

"Come on, Babs. Let's have a brew," he said kindly.

But Babs wasn't taken in. She was just waiting for Tony to rub her nose in it. For the past few years, Babs had been on at him to be a stronger leader, and when it came down to it, Babs was the coward, not Tony.

She led the way into the kitchen and filled the kettle. When she turned to talk to him, to her horror, she burst into tears.

Tony, who had been about to sit down at the kitchen table, opened his arms and walked across to her. "Don't cry, Babs. It's not that bad. It's all sorted out now."

Babs allowed him to gather her in his arms and stroke her hair. It felt nice to be held and comforted. Babs had tried to be strong for so long, she'd almost talked herself into the fact she didn't need anyone else.

The truth of the matter was she had vastly underestimated Tony.

"I'm sorry. I just didn't expect it to be so hard."

Tony continued to stroke her hair as he said, "Doing something like that is never easy, Babs. If you found it easy, I'd think there was something wrong with you."

Losing patience with herself more than Tony, Babs pushed him away. "That's easy for you to say. You weren't the one who bottled it, were you?"

She turned away and busied herself making the tea, trying to get her emotions back under control. Letting Tony see her like this was humiliating.

So, she hadn't handled things well and panicked. It was only to be expected. It was her first time, after all.

Tony gave her the space she needed and went to sit down at the kitchen table. He didn't speak again until Babs set the teapot down in front of him.

"Do you want to know what happened after you left?"

Babs felt her throat tighten, and for one horrible moment, she thought she might be about to be sick. She shook her head quickly. "No."

She could feel Tony's eyes on her, but she wouldn't make eye contact.

"Fair enough. I thought we should talk about what we are going to do next, though. We need to find a way to move forward."

Babs' hands shook as she poured the tea. "You are just trying to make me feel better. You don't really want me putting my twopenn'orth in, do you?"

"Of course, I do, Babs." He reached up and took her hand. "Come on. It was just a little setback. This isn't like you. Nothing normally stops you putting your oar in," he teased.

Babs' cheeks flushed pink, and she opened her mouth to give him a piece of her mind, and then realised what he was doing. She gave a small smile. "You cheeky blighter."

The truth was Babs wasn't sure. What had happened with Old Mo had shaken her to the core and made her doubt her ability. She'd been so full of confidence, but that had trickled away and had been replaced by anxiety.

"I'm sorry, Tony. I should have just let you run the business the way you saw fit. I shouldn't have interfered."

Tony gave her a wry smile. "Who the hell are you? And what have you done with my sister-in-law? That's not Babs Morton talking. Look, I've been thinking. Why don't you visit Patterson's boxing club tomorrow, eh?"

"I thought you were against that?"

Tony nodded. "I was, but I've decided you're right. We do need to expand."

"Are you just saying that to try and make me feel better?"

Tony grinned, but he shook his head. "No, Babs. I thought about what you said, and you're right. So will you do it?"

Babs sipped her cup of tea thoughtfully. She had been badly

shaken today, but she still believed that getting a cut of Patterson's side business was a good idea. If she could secure the Mortons a piece of that particular pie, it would show both Tony and Martin what she was capable of, and it would restore her own confidence.

After a moment, she smiled and nodded. She was fully aware that Tony was charming her. Everyone always said Tony could charm the birds out of the trees, but Babs didn't care. He had made her feel good about herself again and given her a challenge. Babs couldn't wait to get started.

***

Despite a horrific journey from Surrey back to the East End, Ruby Morton was feeling on top of the world. Her throat was parched, and her feet were killing her, but as she gazed around the streets of the East End, feeling the sun on her back, she couldn't help being cheerful. She was back home exactly where she belonged.

Her travels hadn't been a particularly pleasant experience, but thankfully, she had made it back in one piece. She hadn't expected hitchhiking to be so arduous. At first, no one had stopped for her, and it felt like she'd walked for miles. Then she'd been picked up by a lorry driver and soon wished she hadn't been. The dirty old pervert hadn't been able to keep his hands off her, but when they'd stopped at a petrol station, Ruby had made her escape. The dirty bastard had followed her into the rest area and demanded payment, but Ruby was having none of that. She'd kneed him between the legs and swiftly made her get away.

The next driver had taken her as far as Limehouse. That had been a much more pleasant experience. He was an old chap who kept warning Ruby about the dangers of hitchhiking. But it wasn't as if she'd had much choice. She had absolutely no money and no other way to get back to the East End.

As she got closer to her house, Ruby's good mood seemed

to desert her. She wasn't sure how her mother was going to react. Well, that wasn't strictly true. Her mother was guaranteed to fly off the handle.

She took a deep breath and pushed open the front door, preparing herself for her mother's sharp tongue and possibly some stinging slaps, but she heard voices in the kitchen. Her mother wasn't alone.

Uncle Tony! Ruby couldn't believe her luck. If one person was guaranteed to be on her side, it would be him. She thought the world of her uncle.

As Ruby strode into the kitchen, Babs' jaw dropped open. "What the bleeding hell…?"

Ruby grinned. "Hello, Mum."

***

Babs could barely believe her eyes. How on earth could Ruby be here in the kitchen when she was supposed to be in Surrey? She rubbed her eyes, bewildered, unable to process the fact that her daughter was standing right in front of her.

Then as it sunk in, Babs got to her feet. "If you have run away from that school, I swear to God…"

Ruby's smile was replaced by a scowl, but before Babs could lay into her daughter properly, Tony stood up.

"Hello, darling," he said, drawing his niece into his arms and kissing her on the forehead. "Long time, no see."

Babs was speechless. As Tony grinned and stroked his niece's hair, Babs could only think that those fingers had been clutching Old Mo's hair only a short while ago. It all flashed before her eyes again, and as she closed her eyes, she could visualise Tony drawing the knife across Mo's exposed throat.

She clapped a hand to her mouth and stifled a sob.

Tony frowned, concerned. "Are you all right, Babs?"

Babs finally found her voice again. "No, I am bleeding not all right, thanks to this little madam. You get upstairs! I'll deal with you in a minute."

Ruby put a hand on her hip and glared at her mother. "I'm

not going back there. I don't care what you say. That school is awful."

Babs sunk back down into a chair with a heavy sigh. This was all she needed today. Somehow she would have to find the time to beg and plead with Ruby's school to let her back again. Goodness only knew what they would say.

"You really are a selfish child," Babs said. "You don't know the hoops I had to jump through to get you into that school. You should be grateful. And you needn't look at me like that. You'll go back to school if you know what's good for you."

"They won't have me back anyway," Ruby said confidently.

Babs' eyes narrowed. "Why? What did you do?"

A wide smile spread across Ruby's face. "I locked Sister Bernadette in one of the unused rooms."

Babs gasped and crossed herself. "You little heathen!"

Tony turned away and tried to stifle his laughter, but didn't quite manage it.

"Don't encourage her, for goodness sake!" Babs said, clamping a hand to her forehead theatrically. "You are going to be the death of me, girl."

27

WILLIAM MOSS SAT ACROSS THE table from Martin Morton in the recreation area of the prison. He stretched himself back in the chair casually and interlinked his fingers behind his head as he surveyed the other inmates in the area. No one else had dared touch him since Martin Morton had taken him under his wing, and that had given William confidence.

When he'd been sentenced, William had been expecting to be eaten alive inside. He wasn't the type of man who typically thrived in prison. He had never done anything illegal in his life, and it had shocked him to the core that a legal system he believed in so fervently had let him down. William thought he knew himself very well but soon found prison revealed a side of his personality he'd previously kept hidden.

William had been the fall guy for his old boss's corruption, and their betrayal had eaten into him day after day until Martin had approached him.

Martin still had a couple of years left on his sentence, but he was determined to get out before then. He needed a better legal team for his appeal, but nobody would touch his case no matter how much money Martin had promised them.

William was overjoyed to give Martin the name of his old firm.

He grinned, imagining the face of old Mr. Forsyth when he realised William had stitched him up. He'd persuaded Martin that if he worked on his case inside, and Mr. Forsyth was the public face of their legal team, they had a good chance of getting Martin out early. Of course, Mr. Forsyth hadn't exactly been willing to go along with the plan at first, and who could blame him? A link to the criminal underworld was not something a solicitor took on lightly.

After his first request for legal representation was refused, Martin had arranged for some of his men to visit Mr. Forsyth, who miraculously changed his tune and was happy to come on board.

"Well, what do you think?" Martin Morton demanded.

William quickly straightened in his chair. He'd been daydreaming and hadn't been listening. It wasn't hard to guess what Martin had been talking about, though. It was all he ever talked about: How to get out of prison.

"I think you're going to be out of here before you know it. Although I don't know what I'll do when you leave."

Martin looked satisfied at his answer, and William breathed a sigh of relief.

"I told you, you need to toughen up. When I'm gone, hit the first bastard that tries it on. Hit him hard, and hit him first. Make sure he goes down and stays down. Show everyone you're not a victim."

William nodded, although, he couldn't really see that plan working. He'd never been one to use his fists. He preferred to use his brain.

"How long have you got left?" Martin asked.

"Another few years at least, even if I get time off for good behaviour."

"Well, when you do get out, look me up. I'll sort you out a job."

William grinned. "Really?" He could never have imagined feeling so excited at a job offer from someone like Martin

Morton, but the fact of the matter was when he left prison, William would be unemployable. All those years studying law would be wasted, but in Martin's organisation, a criminal record could be overlooked.

"Sure," Martin said. "You helped me out a lot in here. I pay my debts."

William's face fell. Martin probably meant his job offer was dependent on him getting out early. If William's work and scheming against Mr. Forsyth came to nothing, and Martin was forced to serve out the remainder of his sentence, William would be back where he started — unemployed and without a future.

"I don't see why they can't bump up the hearing date," Martin said.

This wasn't the first time William had heard Martin moaning about this, and more than once, he'd tried to explain that the law was its own mistress and wouldn't be hurried along, not even for Martin Morton.

But that answer didn't satisfy Martin, and William had learned to just nod and agree with him. It was the safest way.

"What are you most looking forward to when you get out?" Martin asked. "I've been in here so bleeding long I've probably forgotten how to live my old life."

William doubted that very much. A man like Martin Morton would slip into his old life like he was slipping on a pair of old, worn, comfortable shoes. Prison didn't work for someone like him. He wouldn't come out a changed man. When he was released, he would be angry, more determined and more dangerous than ever.

"I miss my Eloise most of all," William said.

"I didn't know you had a girl?"

Of course, he didn't, usually Martin Morton couldn't care less about William's personal life. He only cared what he could do for him. Which made this conversation very odd. Martin was in a strange mood, very reflective, and William couldn't help wondering whether something had happened.

"I don't anymore. She finished with me as soon as I was sentenced."

Martin laughed, and William looked up, shocked. All right, he hadn't exactly expected sympathy from Martin, but he didn't think the man would laugh at him.

"Don't look so miserable, son. I keep telling you. Everyone will let you down eventually. You can't trust anyone in this world. Keep your guard up at all times."

William wondered whether someone had recently betrayed Martin. He couldn't imagine anyone being so stupid, but he was intrigued enough to ask, "Did someone let you down?"

As soon as the words left his mouth, William regretted them. The number one rule when dealing with Martin Morton was to not ask questions.

Martin looked at him sharply, but then he relaxed and said, "I learnt someone had been cheating me. Someone who'd been close to me for a number of years."

William couldn't fathom it. Would anybody really dare to cross Martin Morton?

"I'm sorry about that," William said, unable to think of anything better to say.

"Not as sorry as the bastard who double-crossed me was." The look on Martin's face sent a shiver down William's spine.

"I take it he won't be doing it again."

"No. You know what they say, fool me once…"

William nodded. "Ah, yes, fool me once, shame on you, fool me twice, shame on me."

"I have a slightly different version of that saying."

"Really?"

Martin gave a cruel smile. "Yes, fool me once, and I'll fucking kill you."

28

THE FOLLOWING MORNING, BABS MORTON set off early, leaving her daughter Ruby sound asleep in bed, the lazy mare. They'd had a huge row last night, but the stubborn little cow refused to see sense. Right now, Babs had more important things to worry about. She'd have to deal with Ruby later, when she got back.

She was paying a visit this morning, dropping in unannounced to Patterson's boxing club. She was going alone. At first, she thought it might be better to take red-haired Freddie and Henry the Hand with her. Showing a little bit of muscle sometimes told these people you meant business, but Babs thought she would try the softly, softly approach first and see how she got on.

She was determined to make a success of this. She still felt like a fool after messing everything up with Old Mo.

She'd been absolutely terrified that it would get back to Martin because she'd taken a risk and decided to get rid of Mo without consulting Martin or his brother, Tony. But in the end, she just hadn't had the stomach for it. What she didn't know until last night was that Martin had already ordered Old Mo to be dispatched. So in the end, his death was inevitable. It really hadn't mattered what Babs did or said.

It didn't stop her feeling silly, though. She had made a hell of a fuss about Tony not having the balls to run the Morton enterprise, and then he'd shown up and finished the job she'd been too scared to do. Babs needed to show people she could still play an important role in the business, and getting a cut from the Pattersons was exactly what she needed. It would prove she was valuable.

Babs remembered the old boxing club, and as she stood outside the building, she was actually quite impressed with what Gerald Patterson had done to the place. He'd really spruced it up.

She didn't bother to knock and walked through the large double doors into a small reception area. She could hear the general noises of the gym coming from the second set of double doors in front of her and strode confidently through those doors as well.

She stopped to survey her surroundings and wrinkled her nose. It smelt a little bit like old socks. The room was large, and the ceiling was high. To the far right of the gym there were two boxing rings set up, and to Babs' left, there were a number of blue mats on the floor. There were a couple of lads going hammer and tongs on the punching bags, but no one currently in the boxing rings.

As Babs cast her eyes around the room, one by one the men fell silent. Women were not usually found in boxing clubs. Babs was a well-known figure in the East End, and most of them appeared to recognise her. That was good.

She didn't recognise any of the men, though. Irritated that she couldn't spot Gerald Patterson, the man in charge, she called out in a booming voice, "Where's your governor?"

At first, no one answered, and then an older man, who had been holding one of the boxing bags, stepped forward. There was something vaguely familiar about him. His eyes looked tired, and his hair was turning to grey.

Babs narrowed her eyes. She had definitely seen him before somewhere, but she couldn't quite put her finger on it.

The man smiled, "It's a pleasure, Mrs. Morton. Gerald is

out back. I'll take you to him."

As the man spoke, it dawned on Babs exactly who he was. Knuckles Bancroft. He was a blast from the past. He'd been the talk of the East End once upon a time, and people viewed him as potentially the greatest fighter to come out of the East End in a generation, but the accolades and fuss had soon died down after he'd broken his hand in a fight, and his promising career had faded into insignificance.

Babs decided not to mention it. She imagined it was a touchy subject.

She followed Knuckles Bancroft through the gym as the other men watched her in silence. When Babs stepped inside the small office, she clapped eyes on Gerald Patterson, and had to admit what Tony had said was true. He was certainly a good-looking man. Babs guessed he must be in his early thirties. He had his hair carefully styled, but his best feature was his sparkling green eyes surrounded by long, dark lashes. They wouldn't have looked out of place on a girl.

Babs reassured herself she was immune to his charms.

Gerald stood up as soon as she stepped into the room and held out his hand. He was quite clearly taken aback but hid it well. "Mrs. Morton, it's an honour."

Babs was pretty sure he wouldn't still think that when she'd got through with him.

"Thank you," Gerald said with a nod to Knuckles Bancroft to let him know he'd been dismissed.

"Please, take a seat," Gerald said, gesturing to the chair beside his desk as he sat down himself.

Babs sat down, carefully arranging her skirt and crossing her legs, purposely delaying telling Gerald why she was here. She knew his mind must be racing through the possibilities.

Eventually, he couldn't bear the suspense any longer and asked, "To what do I owe the pleasure?"

Babs smiled and didn't answer immediately, letting Gerald know who was the boss in this situation.

After gazing around the office and not seeing any sign that this place was anything other than a legitimate boxing club, Babs leaned forward and said, "It's your lucky day, Gerald. I've come with a business proposal."

The smile didn't leave Gerald's face, but his features tightened almost imperceptibly. "That sounds intriguing. Tell me more."

"It's come to our attention that boxing isn't your only business these days."

Gerald let out an easy laugh and leaned back in his seat. "I'm afraid I don't know what to tell you, Mrs. Morton. Patterson's is just a boxing club." He gestured around him, smiling confidently, and Babs immediately had him pegged as a player.

"Please, call me Babs. We are all friends here."

Gerald inclined his head slightly. "Babs, what is it you want from me?"

"The first thing I would like is a little honesty. Don't treat me like a fool, Gerald. My information is good, and I know you're handling illegal goods through this building."

"I don't know who has told you such a thing, Babs," Gerald began to bluster.

Babs raised an eyebrow. "Shall we take a look upstairs?"

Gerald's face flushed, and Babs knew she had caught him out. She imagined he had all sorts stashed up there.

Gerald took a deep breath and sighed. "We've got some stuff coming in now and again, but it's nothing major. We've got a couple of guys working on the docks who pass things on to us occasionally. We sell it on. The boxing business can be hard, and a little bit of money on the side helps things tick over."

"Of course. It sounds like smart business to me," Babs said, thinking now she was finally getting somewhere. At least, Gerald had admitted to handling the stolen goods.

They both knew where this conversation was heading next.

Babs was going to demand a cut, and Gerald would try to argue her down to a lower percentage. She wouldn't have expected anything less and was preparing herself for a good barter when suddenly Gerald's face creased with concern.

For some reason he'd cut the charming act and looked genuinely distraught.

"I know you are about to ask for a share of the profits in exchange for some protection, and I can't accommodate you, Babs."

Babs' eyes narrowed. Like hell he couldn't. She wasn't about to take no for an answer.

"I think you will find you don't have much choice in the matter, Gerald," she said coldly.

Gerald raised his eyes to the ceiling and let out yet another deep sigh. "Carter got here before you."

"Carter?" Babs demanded. "Dave Carter?"

Gerald nodded.

She couldn't believe it. The Patterson enterprise had been so hush-hush. And yet Dave Carter had managed to get here before them. The disappointment was bitter, and Babs' stomach twisted as she saw her opportunity falling away, everything she had worked so hard for. She needed this. She had to prove to her husband and to Tony she could bring in fresh business.

Bloody Dave Carter. He was the bane of her life. He was raking it in right now, so he didn't even need something small like this. The greedy bastard. Now he wouldn't even let the Mortons take the scraps from his table.

Babs clutched her handbag and was about to stand up when suddenly she felt a rush of anger. No. She wasn't going to stand for it. If Dave Carter wanted a cut of the Patterson's business, he would have to pry it from her cold dead hands. This was rightfully hers, and she was not going to give up her claim.

Gerald might take a little more convincing. Babs smiled.

She had the perfect method in mind.

29

GERALD WATCHED BABS MORTON LEAVE with a feeling of trepidation. He let out a shaky breath. He had no idea what Dave Carter was playing at, but Gerald had done exactly what he'd told him to.

Dave had ordered him to refuse Babs' deal at first, and then when she came back, Gerald was to accept her offer. Now, all Gerald had to do was wait for her to come back, but from the look on her face, Gerald was worried her next request wouldn't be quite so politely worded.

"You all right, bruv?"

Gerald turned and saw his brother standing in the doorway, looking nervous. He was surprised he was still here. He thought his brother would have scarpered as soon as he'd noticed Babs Morton's arrival.

"Of course, I'm not all right. Thanks to you I'm stuck in the middle of a standoff between Dave Carter and the Mortons."

Arthur had the decency to look ashamed. He looked down at the floor.

"I'm sorry, Gerald. It was my boy, Ronnie. The little sod got us involved in this."

Gerald sighed and shook his head. He'd heard all of Arthur's excuses before. They didn't help.

"Did you do what Dave asked you to?"

"Of course, I did! I haven't got a bleeding death wish."

Arthur nodded slowly. "What did Babs say?"

"Well, put it this way, she didn't leave the club with a smile on her face."

"So now you have to wait until she comes back and accept her offer next time?"

Gerald nodded miserably. He had a feeling next time Babs returned, she wouldn't be alone, and he only hoped he could accept before things went too far. He heard the Mortons' favourite trick was hanging people out of windows.

Gerald shivered and glared at his brother. It wasn't fair. Why should he be stuck in the middle of this because of his brother's dimwit of a son?

"I'm sorry, Gerald. I wish there was something I could do."

Gerald lost his temper and grabbed a paperweight off his desk and threw it at his brother. "Get out of my sight!"

His brother ran off, and Gerald put his head in his hands. This was not going to end well. He'd seen the look in Babs' eyes as she'd left him, and he knew she had something very nasty planned for him.

***

On her way home from the boxing club, Babs made a detour. She knocked on the front door of red-haired Freddie's house, and his daughter, Jemima, opened the door.

Once again, Jemima's youth and beauty struck Babs, and she tried to quash her jealousy. The girl obviously hadn't been expecting any visitors, and her long, wavy red hair spilled down over her shoulders.

Babs hated to admit it, but Jemima's youth was exactly what she needed.

"Hello, Mrs. Morton. I'm afraid my father is not in."

Babs gave the girl a beaming smile. "That's all right, sweetheart. It was you I wanted to talk to anyway."

Jemima looked surprised, but she stepped back so Babs could enter.

Babs walked past her into the hallway and shrugged off her

coat, handing it to Jemima. "Why don't you make us a nice cup of tea? We've got lots to talk about."

As Babs walked through into the front room, she had to admit she was surprised at how nice Jemima had kept the family home. It was just her and her father now. Red-haired Freddie had only had one child, and his wife had passed away five years ago.

As Jemima busied herself in the kitchen making the tea, Babs settled down in an armchair. She knew that red-haired Freddie thought his daughter was an angel. In his eyes, his daughter was a sweet, innocent young girl. Babs suspected Jemima was more like she had been at that age, and Freddie probably turned a blind eye because it suited him to do so.

Jemima brought the tea in on a tray and watched Babs warily as she began to pour the tea.

Babs waited until she was finished because she didn't want to broach the subject while Jemima had scalding hot tea in her hand. Babs thought her proposal might come as a shock.

Jemima settled herself in the armchair opposite Babs and then looked directly at the older woman and said, "What did you want to talk to me about, Mrs. Morton?"

Babs decided honesty was the best policy. "I need your help, Jemima. Your father thinks the sun shines out of your backside. He thinks you are a complete innocent, but do you want to know what I think?"

Jemima's teacup rattled slightly as she replaced her cup on the saucer. "What do you think, Mrs. Morton?" Her voice was guarded as she spoke.

"Call me Babs. I think you're old enough for that, Jemima, don't you? You're nineteen now, is that right?"

Jemima nodded. "I am. I have a feeling you want me to do something for you."

Babs had to hand it to the girl. She was a smart one.

"You're right. I did come here to ask you to help me out. I thought we might come to some sort of understanding. I imagine living with Freddie could be a little stifling for a girl like you. I remember being your age, and all I wanted was for someone to take me seriously."

Jemima watched her with sharp eyes, and Babs thought the girl could go far in life if she had the right guidance.

"It's a man's world out there, Jemima. But if you look closely, you'll see it's nearly always an intelligent woman who is pulling the strings. You're a very attractive girl, and you shouldn't let that go to waste."

Jemima arched an eyebrow, and Babs noticed there wasn't a single frown line or wrinkle on the girl's face. What Babs wouldn't give to have smooth, soft skin like that again.

"I'm not sure I understand what you're getting at, Babs."

"As women, we don't have many weapons at our disposal, and I think it's only right we use what God has given us. I've got a job for you, Jemima. I'll pay you well, and if things work out, it could be a regular thing."

Jemima looked confused, and then all of a sudden the confusion cleared, and she looked indignant. "I hope you're not suggesting…"

Babs waved her protests away. "Hear me out. There's a man called Gerald Patterson who is giving me a little trouble. He is rather partial to pretty girls, and I want you to get him to the flat above Mortons' club tomorrow night."

Seconds passed before Jemima replied. "How am I supposed to do that?"

"Use your imagination," Babs said, starting to lose patience.

"And that's all I have to do? You just want me to get him to Mortons' club?"

"Not just the club. You need to get him upstairs to the flat. I'll give you the key. You'll need to be there by nine o'clock tomorrow night. Do you think you can handle it?"

A small smile played on Jemima's lips, and Babs knew she'd been wise in her choice. She had gotten the impression that Jemima was bored with her life. She wasn't the type of girl who would be satisfied with settling down with some man, making his tea and keeping the home tidy. Babs saw a lot of herself in Jemima.

Jemima nodded. "I'll do it."

As they finished their tea, Babs told Jemima where she could find Gerald, and they worked out the details of the plan.

When Babs stood up and prepared to leave, she turned and looked over her shoulder at Jemima. "There is one more thing."

Jemima looked up. "Yes?"

"You'd be wise not to tell your father about this."

***

Later that day, Babs took Ruby to see her father in prison. The girl hadn't been to see him for ages, and she was as excitable as a puppy.

Babs wasn't happy. She would prefer Ruby to be shut up in her room, feeling miserable. And if Babs had anything to do with it, that's exactly where the girl would be as soon as they got home. Ruby had to learn she couldn't have everything her own way.

After they got off the bus and walked the short distance to the prison, Ruby didn't stop chattering. Despite her best intentions, Babs couldn't help smiling. It was like they'd gone back a few years, to the good old days when Ruby used to talk to her mum about everything.

"I forgot you could talk the hind legs off a donkey," Babs said as they signed in.

Ruby's face fell, and Babs felt bad. "I was only teasing. Don't be so sensitive."

"It's not that... What if he's angry with me?"

"If he is, you deserve it. You did run off from school, after all. You weren't expecting a welcome home parade, or for me to bake you a cake when you returned, were you?" Babs asked sarcastically.

Ruby didn't retaliate with her normal sulky reply. She really did look worried. "What if he's disappointed with the way I've turned out?"

Babs put down the pen she had used to sign them in and ushered Ruby away from the desk. She swallowed the lump in her throat as she looked at her daughter. "Don't be so daft. You know he loves you."

They didn't have any more time to talk before they were called through to the prison visiting room, where they sat down on one side of the table and waited for Martin to be brought in with the other prisoners.

Ruby couldn't stop fidgeting.

"Will you keep still?" Babs said. "You will wear a hole in that chair with your backside if you don't stop wriggling."

But Ruby wasn't listening. She was completely focused on the line of prisoners entering the room, and when she saw her father, her face broke out into a broad grin.

Martin swaggered over to them. "Babs," he said with a nod, and then he turned to his daughter. "Hello, sweetheart. Give your old dad a kiss."

Ruby leaned across the table, wrapped her arms around her father's shoulders and kissed him on the cheek.

"That's quite enough of that," one of the screws said from the corner of the room. "Sit down."

The three of them sat down, with Ruby gazing at her father adoringly.

"So, what's new?" Martin asked them.

Ruby cast a worried look at her mother, clearly panicking that she was going to tell her father about Ruby's latest escapade.

But Babs wasn't feeling particularly vindictive that morning.

"Same old thing," she said. "Old Mo has gone away for a long holiday." She gave Martin a meaningful look as she spoke in code.

Martin nodded. "Yes, Tony told me."

He didn't look bothered, Babs thought. It was like water off a duck's back to him.

"Well, I've got some news," Martin said, grinning at his daughter.

For some reason, that made Babs feel nervous. "What news?" she asked snappily.

"I could be getting out of here sooner than we thought."

"That's brilliant," Ruby said, looking as pleased as punch.

Babs wasn't quite so thrilled. "Why? What has happened?"

"It's the new legal team I've got working on my case. They've secured a date for the appeal."

As Ruby chatted on with her father happily, Babs let her mind drift. Life would be very different when Martin got out. She wasn't looking forward to it, at all. She'd gotten used to having the house to herself and being the one who made all the decisions at home. She hadn't had to play second fiddle to Martin for a long time, and she was quite sure she would hate returning to their old life.

"You don't look very happy, Babs," Martin said, and she picked up on the mocking tone in his voice. She realised he could tell what she was thinking.

"I'm fine," she said, and then she forced herself to add, "It's brilliant news."

Martin laughed and then asked Ruby to go off and get them some biscuits. When their daughter was safely on the other side of the room beside the large tea urn, Martin leaned forward and spoke to Babs in a whisper. "Tony told me what happened."

Babs stared down at the table. She should have guessed Tony wouldn't keep it to himself. But she wouldn't give Martin the satisfaction of rubbing her nose in it.

"It was nothing. It's all sorted now."

Martin nodded slowly. "Everything is sorted just as long as you remember your place, Babs."

Babs let out a laugh. "How could I forget, Martin? You and Tony remind me of it constantly."

Martin's features hardened, but before he could respond, Ruby was back with the biscuits, so they went back to playing happy families.

30

JEMIMA TUCKED HER RED HAIR behind her ears and licked her lips nervously. She was standing outside The Queen's Head in Poplar, debating whether or not to go inside. Babs Morton had told Jemima that Gerald Patterson drank at this pub. Jemima tried to peer through the window. The bar didn't look too busy. There were a few men propped up by the bar, but Jemima wouldn't know whether one of them was Gerald. She only had a brief description from Babs.

She looked up the street wondering whether she should run away. She didn't know whether or not she could trust Babs. Every time the older woman looked at her, Jemima felt as though Babs was judging her, and it made her feel nervous. She had followed Babs' advice and not told her father what she was planning to do tonight. In fact, she hadn't told anyone and was now starting to worry that had been a bad idea. What if things went south? Perhaps she should have asked one of her friends to come along, but they were all too immature and wouldn't understand why Jemima would want to do such a job for Babs Morton.

The truth was Jemima craved the excitement, at least she had earlier, but now she had her doubts.

She took a step backwards as a boozed up middle-aged man burst through the doors of the pub and staggered out onto the street.

"Hello, sweetheart. What's a lovely young girl like you doing out here all alone?"

Typical old letch, Jemima thought and turned her back on him. She knew she looked nice as she had taken her time over her appearance this evening. Her long red hair, her best feature, was piled on top of her head, and a few loose tendrils fell down framing her face.

"Stuck up bitch," the man muttered over his shoulder as he stalked off down the street.

Jemima ignored him, took a deep breath and pushed open the door to the pub. The smell of cigarette smoke and stale beer hit her immediately. It was still early so conversations were less boisterous than they would be later on. As Jemima stepped inside the main bar, it seemed to her like everybody stopped talking at the same time. Heads swivelled towards her.

Jemima tried to toss her hair, momentarily forgetting that she had pinned it back. Her cheeks flushed, but she tried to look confident as she strode across to the bar. It only took seconds before one of the punters sidled up to her. Jemima was pretty sure this wasn't Gerald Patterson. Babs had told her Gerald was a good-looking man, and the greasy haired man in front of her with a patchy beard certainly wasn't.

"Can I get you a drink, darling?" He asked as his eyes travelled up and down Jemima's body.

Jemima forced herself not to shudder. "I'll get my own drink, thank you," she said primly.

Unfortunately, the man didn't take the hint and instead of going away and leaving her alone moved even closer to her.

"Don't be like that. A drink will loosen you up a bit."

Fortunately at that moment, the man behind the bar asked Jemima what she would like to drink and so she turned to him and ignored the greasy haired man. "I would like a port and lemon."

The Barman nodded, and as he began to prepare Jemima's

drink, she said, "Is Gerald Patterson in tonight?"

The man on Jemima's right muttered, "Oh I should have guessed you would be one of Gerald's girls."

The Barman's eyes narrowed slightly as he looked up at Jemima suspiciously. He paused for a moment, and then seemed to decide she wasn't a threat and nodded in the direction of the window. "He's over there by the window, drinking alone. Perhaps you can cheer him up. I've never seen him look so miserable."

Jemima turned and saw a handsome man sitting at a table by the bay window, staring into his pint. Babs had been right. He was good-looking, so perhaps that would make this evening a little easier.

Jemima paid the Barman and took her drink across to Gerald Patterson.

"Do you mind if I join you?" Jemima asked, turning on her brightest smile.

She needn't have bothered. Gerald didn't even look up before saying, "I'm not in the mood for company tonight."

Jemima hadn't expected that. She had never been turned down by a man in her life, and didn't quite know how to react. For a few moments, she stood there dumbfounded, looking like a fool.

Her cheeks flushed with embarrassment. How humiliating. If she couldn't even manage to persuade Gerald to buy her a drink, how would she persuade him to traipse across Poplar to Martin Morton's club? Suddenly, she felt very much like a little girl playing an adult's game.

Jemima could feel the eyes of the other men in the bar on her and she felt like they were laughing at her.

She plonked a glass on the table and then sat down in the empty chair opposite Gerald. "Well, I'm going to sit down anyway. These heels are killing me."

As she spoke, Gerald's gaze focused on her feet and then travelled up her legs slowly before his eyes met hers. She saw the spark of interest in them, but she wasn't about to make it easy for him. He had turned her down once, so now he was going to have to grovel.

"I'm sorry. I've had a rough couple of days," he said and smiled.

Jemima didn't answer and simply took a sip of her port and lemon. She didn't return his smile. Instead, she reached inside her handbag for her cigarettes.

"Here let me," Gerald said, reaching over to light a cigarette and holding out a gold lighter.

Jemima leaned forward and allowed him to light the cigarette.

"Forgive me for being rude," Gerald said. "What's your name?"

Jemima pretended to hesitate before replying. "Jemima. I don't normally come into pubs like this, but I was supposed to be meeting a friend and they haven't turned up."

"Their loss is my gain," Gerald said smoothly.

Jemima smiled, hoping to encourage him. Afterwards, she wished she hadn't been quite so encouraging. Gerald proceeded to tell her how difficult things had been for him lately, and as the drinks kept coming, he moaned more and more and drank so much that Jemima wondered whether he would be able to walk.

As Gerald stood up, preparing to order another round, Jemima put a hand on his arm. "I've had enough here," she said and gestured around the pub which had now filled up quite considerably. "Let's go somewhere else."

Gerald grinned. "Where did you have in mind?"

"Um." Jemima pretended to think for a moment. "Let's go to Mortons. They have fantastic music there."

Gerald shook his head. "It's too noisy there for me."

Jemima pouted. "But it's my favourite club."

Gerald hesitated as he rocked slightly on his heels. "I don't know..."

"It doesn't matter," Jemima said, reaching for her handbag. "I should probably get home now anyway."

"No, don't go yet. The night is still young. Come on, we'll go to Mortons if you really want to." Gerald reached for Jemima's coat and held it out for her.

As Jemima's arms slid into her coat, she smiled. Step one was complete. Now came the difficult part.

***

Gerald had had far too much to drink. Jemima staggered under his weight as he leaned on her for support. Under normal circumstances, the walk to Mortons would have taken ten minutes, but thanks to Gerald's inebriation it took twice that long.

Jemima kept checking her watch anxiously. It was almost nine o'clock. Why did Gerald have to be so drunk? She glanced at her watch again. It had been an eighteenth birthday present from her father, and just looking at it made her imagine his reaction if he found out what she was doing. She shivered.

"Are you cold, sweetheart? Here, cuddle up to me. I'll keep you warm." Gerald was now slurring his words.

Jemima only just managed to resist rolling her eyes as they turned the corner and finally saw Mortons. She had never been so glad to see a nightclub in her life. Only a few more yards and they would be there.

Jemima nodded at the men on the door. They knew her father, red-haired Freddie, and Jemima often came to the club. She pulled on Gerald's arm, encouraging him to walk faster as they passed the queue outside the club.

Gerald looked bemused. "Do they know you here?"

Jemima nodded. "I live in the flat above the club," she lied smoothly.

Gerald was frowning, and Jemima tried to pull him into the club before he had a chance to change his mind.

"I thought Martin Morton owned the flat."

Jemima nodded again. "He does, but he doesn't have much use for it now he's inside, so the Mortons rent it to me."

"I'm not so sure this is a good idea," Gerald said as he looked around the dark club, which was packed.

"Why not?" Jemima shouted over the music.

"The Mortons aren't very happy with me at the moment."

"Oh, don't worry about that. The Mortons are never here. They own the club, but they don't drink here."

Gerald nodded but he still looked about the club warily.

Jemima leaned close until her lips were practically touching his ear. "It's ever so loud down here. I can hardly hear myself think. Why don't we go upstairs to my flat?"

They were the magic words. Gerald perked up and grinned at her. She took his hand and led him through the crowds beside the bar, heading towards the door to the living quarters.

At the bottom of the stairs, she turned back to smile reassuringly at Gerald and then let out a gasp of shock when she felt him squeeze her backside as he followed her up the steps.

Jemima couldn't get into the flat fast enough.

She opened the door, and once they were inside, Gerald pushed her up against the wall, pressing his lips down onto hers.

She pushed back hard on his shoulders, and he took a step back and blinked at her, surprised at her reaction.

She nodded down the hallway. "You go into the bedroom. I'll fix us a drink."

Babs had told her she and Henry would be waiting in the larger bedroom, ready to confront Gerald.

Gerald reached for Jemima again, holding her round the waist. "I don't need a drink," he said huskily.

Jemima gave him a hard shove. "Well, I do," she said firmly and then strode away from him along the hallway and into the open plan kitchen area.

"I like a feisty girl," Gerald said, moving like lightning and pushing himself up against Jemima's back.

Before Jemima could respond, the door to the bedroom burst open, and to Jemima's horror, she saw her father storming towards them.

Within seconds, red-haired Freddie had Gerald by the throat and pressed up against the kitchen wall. "That's my daughter, you bastard. If you have touched her–"

"Dad, don't!"

Freddie turned to face Jemima, but he didn't release his grip on Gerald's throat. "I'll deal with you later, Jemima."

Gerald's face was turning purple as Babs Morton calmly strolled out of the bedroom and through into the open plan kitchen.

"Have a seat, Jemima," Babs said and then turned to Freddie. "Let Gerald go. We have business to discuss."

Freddie reluctantly released his grip on Gerald, who slumped to the ground gasping for breath.

Freddie narrowed his eyes. "You didn't tell me Jemima was the girl you were using to lure Gerald here."

Babs also hadn't told Jemima that her father would be here to confront Gerald either.

"Never mind all that now," Babs said. "It's time to persuade Gerald to become a business partner of ours. Take him to the bathroom, Henry."

For the first time, Jemima noticed Henry the Hand hanging back by the door of the bedroom. He smiled broadly and walked forward to pick Gerald up off of the floor.

Jemima watched in horror as her father joined Henry and dragged a very reluctant Gerald into the bathroom. She then heard the sound of water running.

Jemima's eyes widened, and she turned to Babs and asked, "What are they going to do to him?"

Babs sat down on the settee and crossed her legs. "I hope they are going to persuade him." She leaned forward and her eyes gleamed as she asked, "Why? Would you like to watch?"

Jemima recoiled in horror. "No!"

As it turned out, the water wasn't needed. Gerald shouted out that he was perfectly willing to accept their business proposal.

Babs smiled at Jemima. "Well, that was a lot faster than I thought it would be."

She shouted over her shoulder, "Bring him in here."

The two men brought Gerald back into the living area, each one gripping an arm and keeping him upright.

"I'm very glad you have decided to reconsider, Gerald."

Gerald nodded anxiously. "Yes. I was stupid to turn you down. I'm sorry."

"I'm sure we can put that behind us and have a very happy business relationship from now on." Babs leaned forward in her seat and narrowed her eyes as she looked at Gerald. "So when can we expect our cut? I want fifteen percent."

Gerald's eyes widened, but he knew better than to argue. "That's fine. We've already moved the first shipment, but we are expecting another one in three weeks."

Babs nodded slowly and then said, "Never let it be said that the Mortons aren't reasonable people. I won't ask for a cut on the stuff you've already shifted, but I expect fifteen percent of your next delivery. Do we understand each other?"

Gerald looked like he might be sick. "Absolutely, Babs. I understand completely."

Babs smiled coldly. "Excellent. I'd like to be there when you get your next shipment. Just to check you're not trying to cheat us."

"That won't be a problem."

Babs waved a hand at Henry and Freddie. "Then we have a deal. Get him out of my sight."

The two women watched Freddie and Henry roughly handle Gerald out of the flat. Jemima wanted to ask what would happen to him, but then decided it was better if she didn't know.

31

A FEW WEEKS LATER, LINDA decided that no matter what Geoff said, she needed to visit the doctor. She sat in the waiting area at the doctor's surgery, nervously smoothing down her skirt and watching the seconds tick by on the large clock on the wall opposite.

She just knew there was something wrong with her. Hopefully, it was something the doctor would be able to fix, but she couldn't bear not knowing what the problem was.

If Geoff found out she'd been here today, there would be hell to pay. It was unlikely, though. As far as he was concerned, she was working at Bevels all day. And she knew for a fact that Geoff would be in the pub the moment the doors opened.

Despite the fact, he'd told her he was going to be working for Dave Carter, as it turned out, he'd only done a few jobs for him. As much as Linda wished Geoff could hold down a steady job, she was actually glad that he hadn't managed to get himself deeply integrated into Dave Carter's business. It was too dangerous. She had tried to talk to Geoff about it, but as usual, he had refused, telling her he couldn't bear her nagging.

Something would have to change soon, though. Mr. Bevel was already talking about cutting Linda's salary, and she didn't know what she would do if that happened. They barely managed to afford the rent and put food on the table as it was.

If Linda had fallen pregnant, then Geoff surely would have been forced to get a job. She sighed. Fate had a funny way of making sure things turned out for the best. Linda didn't want to bring a baby into this world if it had to live on the poverty line.

She thought she'd be able to accept it if the doctor told her she would never be able to have children. It wouldn't be easy, but at least she would know for certain and be able to get on with her life. She'd be able to tell her mother for one thing, and that would stop her nagging Linda about grandchildren every moment she got.

Linda was lost in her own thoughts, and when the doctor's secretary came out and called her name, it made her jump.

"The doctor will see you now," the secretary said kindly.

Linda smiled back at her and got to her feet, taking a deep breath before walking towards the doctor's office.

This was the first time Linda had been to see Dr. Morrison. When she was younger, her family used to see the doctor on Burdett Road, old Dr. Gill, but after getting married and moving in with Geoff, she had registered at this surgery because it was closer. Now, however, Linda felt nervous and wished she could see the friendly face of Dr. Gill rather than this new doctor. But Dr. Gill had retired years ago.

She opened the door and stepped inside feeling incredibly nervous. Dr. Morrison was sitting behind his desk. He didn't look very old at all for a doctor. Linda guessed he could only be about ten years older than her. He had a kindly face and smiled as she walked in, which made Linda feel a little better.

"Good morning. Come and sit down and tell me what's wrong."

When Linda sat down in the chair, she clasped her handbag on her lap and blinked up at the doctor. Now that she was here, she didn't know where to begin. She knew something was wrong, but it seemed such a delicate thing to discuss with somebody she didn't know.

"I hope you haven't caught the stomach bug that's been doing the rounds," Dr. Morrison prompted.

Linda shook her head. "No, doctor. It isn't that. It's rather more personal."

Dr. Morrison pushed his spectacles back on the bridge of his nose and nodded at Linda encouragingly. "I see. There's no need to be embarrassed, Linda. Tell me what's wrong."

Linda bit down on her lower lip and struggled for the right words. Finally, she said, "Geoff and I have been married a long time now, and I haven't been able to… fall pregnant."

The pleasant, relaxed expression on Dr. Morrison's face disappeared and was replaced with a frown. He looked at Linda intently.

"No, but we expected that, didn't we?"

Linda couldn't have been more surprised at Dr. Morrison's words. She'd expected him to look concerned, maybe a little shocked, but she never expected him to say that.

Seeing Linda's bafflement, Dr. Morrison continued. "Because Geoff contracted mumps about ten years ago, a rather bad case, and we did suspect it might leave him sterile."

Linda was unable to reply. She couldn't quite take in what the doctor was saying. If this was true, then why had Geoff never told her? Why had he gone on letting her believe that she was the one who had a problem?

Linda opened her mouth to reply to the doctor. "I…" But the words died in her mouth. How on earth was she supposed to respond to something like that?

"Geoff did explain things to you, didn't he? After you got married, I asked him to bring you along to the surgery so I could help explain, but he said he'd told you before you'd married."

Oh, he did, did he? Geoff had some serious explaining to

do.

He had never mentioned a word to Linda, going as far as banning her from ever coming to the doctors to discuss her trouble conceiving.

But Linda's pride prevented her from telling the doctor all that. Instead, she gave the doctor a false, bright smile and said, "Of course, he did tell me. I got confused."

Dr. Morrison's face relaxed once more. "Well, I'm happy to explain. It can be a rather unfortunate and uncommon side effect of mumps."

As the doctor continued to talk and tell Linda about the potential options open to her, such as adoption, Linda's mind wandered. She felt numb. How could Geoff have lied to her all this time?

He had been very cruel and callous during the years they had been married, but nothing compared to this.

***

In a daze, Linda left the doctor's surgery and began to walk back towards Bevels. She wasn't quite sure how she was going to be able to concentrate at work this afternoon, but she didn't have much choice. She had no idea what she was going to do. If she let Geoff know she had found out the secret he'd been keeping from her, there was no telling what he would do. He had gotten more and more violent just lately, and Linda found his behaviour very difficult to predict.

She was so caught up in her own problems that it took her a moment to realise the street she'd turned into was a hive of activity. People stood around in small groups, talking in hurried whispers.

Linda frowned. Something had clearly happened recently to set the gossips into action.

She'd barely taken another couple of steps when she was approached by Rita, a woman around Linda's mother's age, who was a good friend of Mary Diamond.

"Oh, Linda, it's terrible news, isn't it?"

Linda had no idea what she was talking about. "What's happened?"

"Haven't you heard?"

Linda shook her head impatiently.

"It was Mary Diamond. She was rushed out of her house on a stretcher less than an hour ago."

Linda put a hand to her mouth. "Mary? Oh, no. Is she going to be all right?"

Rita's face took on a grave expression. "I don't know, love. Mrs. Mackenzie, who lives just opposite, said Mary looked terrible when they put her into the ambulance. It's an awful thing. The poor woman has been through so much after her tragic daughter…"

"What about Jimmy?"

"The poor little lad was at home. I think he was the one who called for help."

"And where is he now?"

Rita shrugged. "I expect he's gone to the hospital to be with his nan. I'm going to visit this afternoon, but they're ever so strict with the visiting hours up at the London."

Linda didn't care about the visiting hours. All she knew was that she had to be there for Jimmy.

"I'd better get up there," she muttered under her breath.

"Suit yourself," Rita said. "But I'm warning you, the sister won't let you on the ward until visiting hours."

That didn't bother Linda. She just had to make sure that Jimmy was all right. He had no other close family, and Jimmy, although he liked to pretend to be grown-up, was still a little boy.

As she began to walk off, Rita called out behind her, "Aren't you supposed to be at work?"

Linda didn't bother to answer. Mr. Bevel would have to do without her for a couple more hours.

When she got to the hospital, she gave Mary Diamond's name to the lady at the reception desk, and it was some moments before someone came to talk to her.

A young nurse with bright, glowing skin and sparkling eyes approached her. "Hello, are you a relative of Mrs. Diamond?"

Linda had already been through all this with the lady at reception, so she answered quite snappily, "No, I'm a family friend. I've come to make sure that Jimmy's all right."

"Jimmy, her grandson."

Linda nodded. "That's right. He's too young to be going through all this on his own."

The nurse nodded. "If you would like to follow me."

As she began to lead Linda down the corridor, she explained Mary's condition. "We think it's her heart. She fainted at home this morning, and her grandson called for help. Do you know the family well?"

Linda nodded.

The nurse considered her next words carefully before saying, "I understand she drinks quite a bit."

Linda felt a little disloyal. But if it helped Mary's treatment, she had to tell the truth. "I think she has been struggling to give it up."

The nurse nodded and then pushed open a door, which led them through into yet another corridor. "I'm glad you came. We thought we may have to call someone and get Jimmy a temporary bed for the night."

Linda immediately said, "You don't need to do that. He can stay with me."

No one liked to get the social involved if they could help it. Once they stuck their sticky beak in, they were very hard to get rid of, and if they got wind of Mary's drinking problem and thought she was unable to handle a young boy like Jimmy, they could split the family up for good.

The nurse smiled. "That's very kind of you."

Linda followed the nurse up a flight of stairs, and they found themselves in a much wider corridor. Sitting on the left-hand side of the corridor, on a wooden chair, looking very sorry for himself, was Jimmy Diamond.

Linda rushed forward with her arms out. "Oh, Jimmy, I'm so sorry, sweetheart."

Jimmy stood up. He looked so lost that Linda's heart went out to him.

"They think she has a bad heart," Jimmy said. "It was horrible."

Linda put her arm around his shoulders. "She's in the best place now, Jimmy. Doctors can do marvellous things these days."

She sat down on one of the wooden chairs and listened to him tell her what happened this morning. It made Linda's heart ache to think of him going through all that on his own.

"They said I can see her for a couple of minutes once they've got her settled."

"Was she awake?"

Jimmy nodded, and Linda squeezed his hand. "Well, that's a good sign, isn't it?"

Jimmy tried to smile. "Will you wait with me?"

"Of course, I will," Linda said. She didn't give a damn what Mr. Bevel or anybody else said. There was no way she was going to leave Jimmy to face this situation alone.

32

AFTER A LONG AFTERNOON AND evening spent at the hospital, Linda brought Jimmy back to her house. Geoff was still at the pub, which was a relief. She could do without listening to him moaning today. She still hadn't worked out how she was going to confront him over his lies, but right now, she had more important things to worry about.

It was too late to prepare a proper evening meal, so Linda handed Jimmy an apple while she got to work making cheese sandwiches.

When they had left Mary, she'd been awake and talking and had a little more colour in her cheeks. The doctor was quite confident she would make a recovery, although she would need to spend another week in hospital, and even when she got home, she would have to take things easy.

Linda had only just started to butter the bread when she heard the front door open, and her stomach knotted. Christ, that was all she needed.

She ignored Geoff until he staggered into the kitchen. He was clearly worse the wear for drink again.

"This better be some kind of joke," Geoff growled as he looked at Linda standing beside the breadboard. "A sodding cheese sandwich is not dinner."

Linda did her best not to appear intimidated for Jimmy's sake. She didn't want him to be afraid.

As the boy sat at the table, half-hidden behind the kitchen door, Geoff hadn't noticed he was there.

Linda plastered a smile on her face and turned around to face her husband. "I've had a very difficult day, Geoff. Mary Diamond was taken into hospital and –"

"What the bloody hell has that got to do with my dinner?"

Linda tensed. If she didn't defuse this situation quickly, all hell would break loose. "I'm trying to explain, Geoff."

She pointed the butter knife at Jimmy, and Geoff turned slowly around and noticed the boy for the first time.

"What are you doing here?" he demanded.

Jimmy looked down at the table at his half-eaten apple and didn't reply.

"He's staying here for a few days until his nan gets out of hospital. She had a funny turn, something to do with her heart."

"And that means we get lumbered with the boy?"

"Geoff!" Linda said, shocked the man could be so cruel.

"It's all right," Jimmy said. "I'm not hungry anyway. I'll just go up to bed."

Linda had already made up the bed in the spare room for him, but she was furious at Geoff for making Jimmy feel so unwelcome. The man was heartless.

***

Linda continued to prepare the cheese sandwiches, even though Jimmy had gone to bed, and she was sure she wouldn't be able to stomach any food thanks to Geoff's outburst. After his temper tantrum, he had taken himself off into the front room and was now snoring in the armchair.

How had it all come to this? Geoff had changed beyond all recognition. There was no sign of the sweet, timid young man Linda had married, and it made her question the fact that perhaps Geoff had really been like this all along. He was just pretending.

It was bad enough Geoff acted that way to her, but to turn

on poor Jimmy after the day he'd had was unbelievably cruel.

Linda stabbed the knife in the butter and applied it to the bread in a mechanical fashion.

After she had made the sandwiches, she sat down at the kitchen table with a strong cup of tea, trying to see a way out of the mess. The resentment burned within her. How could Geoff have kept the fact he couldn't have children secret from her? If he had admitted the problem to start with, Linda would have accepted it. Perhaps they could have gone on to adopt and been a happy family, but Linda would never be able to forgive Geoff's betrayal. He had known Linda blamed herself, and he didn't care.

Linda wasn't usually a tempestuous person. She carefully thought through things that bothered her before she acted, but today her anger got the better of her. She pushed herself up from the table and marched into the front room. Geoff was sprawled out in the chair, drool hanging from the side of his mouth, and Linda felt her lip curl in disgust.

She prodded him in the chest. "I want a word with you."

Geoff woke up, startled. He blinked a couple of times as though he were surprised to see Linda in front of him, and then the blank look left his face, and his features tightened in anger. "You've got some nerve."

Linda laughed at him. "Me? Oh, I've got nothing on you."

"What the bleeding hell are you talking about, you daft mare?"

Linda put her hands on her hips. "I'm talking about the secret you've been keeping from me."

Geoff's expression changed from one of irritation to one of suspicion, but still he kept up his act. "You're talking nonsense."

Usually, Linda would sense the change in Geoff's mood and back down, but today she was having none of it.

"You're a nasty piece of work, Geoff Blum, and I'm on to you. I went to see Dr. Morrison today."

Geoff was out of the chair and towering above Linda in an instant. "I forbade you to go to him."

"It was just as well I ignored you then, wasn't it? Dr. Morrison was kind enough to point out that you are the one with the problem, not me."

Geoff's nostrils flared as he reached out to grip Linda's throat.

Linda gasped for air, and her hands came up ineffectually to try and push Geoff away, but he was too strong. As his grip tightened around her throat, Linda struggled desperately. She scratched at his face with her fingernails and tried to scream, but the noise came out more like a strangled sob.

Geoff was so much stronger than her. He practically lifted her off her feet. She kicked out at his shins, but he barely noticed.

As Geoff tried to throttle the life out of her, Linda didn't feel sad or even terrified. She felt absolutely furious. She swore to herself if she survived this, she would leave Geoff. She started to see spots as she stared up into Geoff's blazing eyes. She flung her limbs around wildly, making contact with a lamp and sending it crashing to the floor.

Just as Linda began to lose consciousness, she heard a voice scream.

Jimmy. She had to stop Geoff from hurting Jimmy.

As Jimmy hurtled into the room and Linda found a last burst of strength, Geoff was shocked enough to loosen his grip, and Linda slumped to the floor.

She stared in horror as she saw Jimmy Diamond brandishing the large serrated bread knife, slashing it towards Geoff.

"Leave her alone!" Jimmy warned.

Geoff managed to regain his wits and staggered towards Jimmy. "Oh yeah, and what are you going to do about it?"

Linda rubbed her hand to her bruised neck and croaked out, "No, Geoff. Leave him alone. He doesn't have anything to do with it."

"So why is he sticking his nose in then?"

Despite Geoff getting closer and standing menacingly over Jimmy, the boy didn't back down.

"I'm warning you. If you hurt Linda, I'll kill you."

An eerie moment of silence past when nobody uttered a word. Then Geoff suddenly burst out into laughter. Tears poured down his face as though Jimmy had just said the funniest thing he had ever heard.

As Geoff was incapacitated with giggles and fell down onto his armchair, Linda managed to pull herself to her feet and walk over to Jimmy.

"It's all right," she whispered, her throat raw and in agony. "Here, let me take that." She put her hand out for the knife.

For a moment, defiance shone in Jimmy's eyes, and she thought he might refuse, but then he held out the knife for her to take.

Linda put her hand on Jimmy's shoulder and led him from the front room up the stairs. "Let's get you back to bed. You should lock the door tonight."

As Linda and Jimmy made their way upstairs, Geoff's mocking laughter rang out through the house.

33

THE FOLLOWING DAY, JIMMY DIAMOND had gone to school, and his lessons had passed agonisingly slowly. He was going to visit his nan straight after school, and Jimmy couldn't concentrate on anything else.

As soon as the bell rang out to signal the end of the school day, Jimmy leapt up from his desk and bolted. He was the first pupil through the school gates, and he didn't stop running until he'd made it to the bus stop. Linda had given him his fare money so he could get to Whitechapel easily. The buses were on time, and he got to the hospital with plenty of time to spare before visiting hours started. He was scolded by a nurse as he ran along the hospital corridor.

"Hospitals are not the place for running, young man!"

"Sorry," Jimmy muttered, slowing his pace to a walk.

Rosy-cheeked, and breathless he arrived at Bartholomew's ward. There was nobody at the nurses station, so Jimmy pushed open the door and walked straight into the ward. At the far end, his nan was in the bed beside the window.

She had her eyes closed and looked pale. Jimmy raced over to her bedside. "Nan?"

Mary Diamond's eyes fluttered open, and when she saw her grandson, her face creased into a smile.

She reached out to grasp his hand. "Oh, Jimmy. You didn't have to come all this way. How did you get here?"

Jimmy perched on the side of his nan's bed. "By bus. Linda gave me the fare."

"Have you been all right staying at Linda's?"

Jimmy hesitated, considering telling his nan what had happened last night, but he quickly decided against it. The last thing she needed was more to worry about.

"Yes, Linda has been very nice."

His nan smiled with relief and then leaned back heavily on her pillows. "The doctor says I just need a bit more rest, and then I'll be able to come home."

Jimmy smiled happily. When his nan had collapsed, he had never been so scared. He was looking forward to her coming home.

They chatted away for an hour until the stern sister approached them to tell Jimmy it was time he left because visiting hours were over. Because many of the people on Bartholomew Ward were very ill, visiting times were restricted to only one hour a day.

Reluctantly, Jimmy kissed his nan goodbye and headed out for the bus stop.

When he got back to Poplar, he decided to go to the workshop. Usually, he went straight after school, but he was sure Georgie would have explained to his father the reason behind Jimmy's absence today. They wouldn't expect him to come in at all, but Jimmy didn't fancy going back to Linda's house yet. Linda would be at work, and Jimmy definitely didn't want to run into Geoff again.

He strolled across the yard, and as he approached the warehouse, he noticed something was different.

He was used to seeing different men hanging about. Dave Carter employed a lot of people, but usually it was only Charlie Williams, Brian Moore and Big Tim who worked at the workshop. The other men were based in Dave Carter's warehouse. Jimmy had never been there, and neither had little Georgie. Georgie said his father didn't even like to talk about the warehouse for some reason.

Today, the workshop was packed. There were lots of men he didn't recognise all standing in a huddle, arranged around Dave Carter. Jimmy slipped inside unnoticed and spotted Georgie sitting on a chair on the far side of the room. He walked over to join him and asked, "What's going on?"

Little Georgie's face lit up when he saw his friend. "I didn't think you'd be here today. My dad's having a meeting. There was a p...power cut at the warehouse, so they're having it here."

Jimmy nodded and turned with interest to watch the proceedings. The men were all silent as Dave talked.

It didn't sound very interesting to Jimmy, something about financial arrangements.

"Aren't there any motors to be washed today?" Jimmy asked Georgie.

Georgie shook his head. "No. Dad asked me to clean these for him." He pointed to the oil and grease covered set of spanners in front of him.

Jimmy picked up a clean piece of rag and set to work helping him while keeping one ear on what Dave Carter was saying.

Jimmy was focused on his work when he heard a very familiar laugh ring out inside the workshop. He froze and glanced at the men surrounding Dave Carter. He hadn't noticed him at first because Dave Carter was the sort of man who demanded people's full attention, but now Jimmy looked again, he saw him – Geoff Blum, Linda's horrible husband.

"What's he doing here?" Jimmy muttered, more to himself than to Georgie.

But Georgie looked up and said, "I'm not sure. I've seen him before. He works for my dad now and again, I think."

Jimmy picked up the rag again and began to vigorously polish off the grease.

When Dave had finished addressing his men, they began to file out of the workshop. Jimmy glared at Geoff as he walked past, but the man didn't even notice him.

The only men remaining were Dave Carter, his brother, Gary, and Charlie Williams when Dave called out, "Before you go I need to have a word about something else."

Both Charlie and Gary turned back, and Charlie asked, "What is it, boss?"

"I think we have a leak."

Jimmy stopped his polishing. This sounded much more interesting than the financial stuff Dave was talking about earlier.

"What do you mean?" Gary scratched his head and looked confused.

"I mean what I say, Gary. Someone has been leaking information," Dave said irritably.

Charlie waited patiently for Dave to continue, but Gary interrupted again, "Who?"

"I thought you might be able to help me with that." Dave's eyes bored into his brother.

"I hope you're not suggesting, I've leaked information," Gary said huffily.

Dave's eyes narrowed. "Perhaps not intentionally, Gary. But I wouldn't put it past you to go shooting your mouth off somewhere you shouldn't."

Gary's cheeks flooded with colour, and Jimmy couldn't tell whether it was because he was angry or ashamed.

"What information has been leaked?" Charlie asked as he hooked his thumbs in the pockets of his waistcoat.

"Information on our plans for Patterson's boxing club. Gerald Patterson has told me the Mortons have been trying to muscle in."

"So what? You're not going to let the Mortons intimidate you, are you? They're nothing without Martin Morton at the helm," Gary said.

Even from where he sat, Jimmy could see the anger radiating from Dave. "If I find out it was you who spilled that little tidbit of information to the Mortons, Gary, your life will not be worth living."

As young as he was, Jimmy could tell from the look on Gary's face that he was guilty. He held his breath wondering what Dave would do, but to his surprise, Dave just waved his hands at the pair of them. "I don't have time for this."

Jimmy wondered later what prompted him at that moment to speak up. He didn't really have a chance to think things through, but it was like he got a flash of inspiration as he walked towards Dave Carter.

"Excuse me, Mr. Carter," Jimmy said.

All three men turned to look at Jimmy, wondering if the stupid boy had a death wish, interrupting an argument between the two Carter brothers.

Dave Carter had a soft spot for Jimmy because he was a good friend to little Georgie, but Dave was unpredictable. Jimmy swallowed nervously.

Charlie Williams tried to guide Jimmy away, protecting the boy. "Come on, Jimmy. Show me how far you've got with cleaning those tools."

But Dave interrupted, holding a hand out to stop Charlie walking forward. "What is it, Jimmy?"

"I heard what you were talking about just now."

Charlie's grip tightened on Jimmy's shoulders in warning. "You shouldn't eavesdrop, Jimmy. But you're not going to say anything, are you?"

Jimmy knew Charlie was trying to protect him, but he didn't want his protection right now. He wanted to talk to Dave Carter.

Dave fixed him with a stare. "Go on."

"I know who leaked your information," Jimmy said.

For a moment, no one spoke, and then Gary rushed forward and said. "He's just a boy. You can't listen to him!"

Jimmy guessed Gary thought he was about to dob him in. Little did he know that Jimmy was about to save his skin.

Dave held up a finger in warning. "Shut your mouth, Gary. I'd like to hear what Jimmy has to say."

Jimmy took a breath. He knew there was no going back once these words left his mouth.

"It was Geoff Blum who leaked your information."

Charlie frowned, and Gary simply gaped at him in surprise.

Dave leaned forward, crouching down and putting his own face only inches from Jimmy's. "Are you sure about this, Jimmy? It's very important."

Jimmy nodded confidently. "Yes. I've been staying with him and his wife while my nan is in hospital, and I heard him boasting about it last night."

Dave's jaw tightened as he gritted his teeth, and then he stood up, put a hand on Jimmy's shoulder and said, "Good lad."

They all watched as Dave strode out of the workshop, and Jimmy stood there feeling a little stunned. He wasn't sure he'd done the right thing, but it was too late for doubts now.

***

Dave Carter couldn't have been more surprised at the words that had left Jimmy's mouth. He'd been expecting Jimmy to tell him he'd overheard Gary spilling the details. But Geoff Blum? Dave really hadn't been expecting that. Geoff had only been working with him for a couple of months, and Dave was surprised he even knew about Patterson's enterprise.

He turned to look at his brother Gary and wondered if he'd judged him too harshly. Dave was aware of his brother's shortcomings and had expected him to blab about the Patterson's side business. That had been all part of Dave's plan.

He wondered if Gary had turned over a new leaf.

But now Jimmy had told him about Geoff Blum, Dave had

a dilemma. If it had been his brother spreading Dave's business all over the East End, Dave would have made a fuss, but in the end, he would have let it slide. He was his brother, after all. But Dave didn't owe anything to Geoff Blum. He would have to make an example of him. When he invited someone to join his circle of men, he had to be able to trust them.

He thought about asking Tim to deal with it, but it was too soon. He would have to rely on Charlie and Brian to deal with this situation.

"What are we going to do about it?" Gary demanded.

Dave thought that was a bit fresh, considering how many times Gary had blabbed in the past. In Dave's opinion, he shouldn't be quite so eager to have someone punished for the same crime he had committed in the past.

"He will be dealt with," Dave said. "And the Mortons will try to muscle in and cut their own deal with the Pattersons."

Gary looked horrified. "They wouldn't dare! Tell me you won't let them get away with that."

"Things will work out," Dave said mildly as his brother's face flushed with anger and indignation.

He couldn't confide in Gary because his brother would never understand. He didn't know how to play the long game. If Gary had his way, he would storm in, kicking the Mortons when they were down and causing a great deal of resentment. Dave wasn't above a fight, but he liked to win. Timing was important. Martin Morton would soon be out of prison, and when he did get out, Dave wanted the Mortons to be decimated.

The truth was Dave couldn't wait for Babs Morton to cut this deal with Gerald Patterson. It was a crucial part of Dave's strategy.

Why should he get his hands dirty when he could get somebody else to obliterate the Mortons off the face of the East End?

***

Gary licked his lips nervously, and his eyes darted across to Dave. He had been convinced Jimmy was about to get him in trouble. He was still feeling on edge, as though he had just escaped by the skin of his teeth. He didn't really think Dave would harm him physically, but Gary had been cut off before, and he didn't like it at all. Everything he owned came through Dave. Without his brother, his life was worthless. He wouldn't get any respect, and he would lose his ability to make money.

He knew his brother was smart, but sometimes his actions confused Gary. Right now, the Mortons were low, and one final face-off would surely be enough to see them off for good, but Dave wasn't interested. He wanted to live and let live, and Gary thought that was a mistake.

Just then, Gary noticed that Jimmy Diamond's eyes were on him. There was something unusual about the boy. It was as though he had an old head on young shoulders, and something in the boy's dark blue eyes told him he wasn't quite the happy-go-lucky child Gary had always assumed he was.

Did Jimmy Diamond know he had really been the one to mouth off and spill the secrets about the Patterson deal? Surely not. Gary would never be so stupid when he was sober, and he wouldn't have run into the child in a pub.

That was another area where Gary thought Dave had it all wrong. In the old days, Morton's men would never have dared to show their face in the same boozer as the Carters. Nowadays, people drank wherever they liked, and Dave was happy enough to let them.

Gary tore his eyes away from Jimmy and wished the kid would stop looking at him like that. It gave him the creeps. It was almost as if the boy could tell what he was thinking.

Still, why should Gary care? He was in the clear now, and Geoff Blum would be held accountable.

34

LINDA TOOK A QUICK GLANCE at her watch and wondered how much longer she would have to stick around. She hadn't been able to attend Valerie's wedding because she had to work, and had just come along to the party afterwards. Valerie was a couple of months along now and already showing. She wore a pretty peach-coloured suit and couldn't stop smiling.

Linda was very glad it had worked out for her, but she wanted to get away as soon as possible to make sure Jimmy was okay after visiting Mary in the hospital.

This coming Saturday, she intended to look for a new place to live and put down a deposit. She knew her parents would be horrified, but there was no way Linda could continue to live with Geoff.

Valerie chucked her small bouquet into the air, and all the single girls from Bevels made a rush to grab for it. Linda thought they wouldn't be quite so eager if they knew what marriage was really like.

Valerie's mother and aunts had laid on a tea for the wedding guests, and Linda reached out for a ham sandwich.

As she walked along the table which was piled high with potato salad, sandwiches and home-made cakes, Linda felt very out of place. She didn't belong to the group of young, single women who were talking about going to a dance on

Saturday night, and she didn't feel she had anything in common with the group of young, happily-married mothers either, so she stood alone by the food table feeling very sorry for herself until Valerie approached her.

The girl had tears in her eyes as she thanked Linda. "I don't know what I would have done without your help, Linda," Valerie said earnestly. "I'm ever so grateful."

Linda forced herself to smile. "You don't need to thank me, Valerie. I'm glad everything has worked out well for you."

"You'll have to pop round for a cup of tea and see our new house," Valerie said with a hint of pride. "It's ever so modern."

Now that she was a married woman, with a baby on the way, Valerie wouldn't be returning to work at Bevels. As Linda watched her rush off and talk excitedly to her new husband, she felt a pang of envy and hated herself for it. She had no one else to blame but herself for the situation she was in.

She should have listened to her parents about Geoff. They had both warned her that he wasn't suitable. She doubted that either of her parents had had any idea just how awful Geoff would turn out to be, but they had known he wasn't good enough for Linda from the start.

Linda felt like she stood out like a sore thumb. She was wearing an old dress, which was a little tight on her hips. But there wasn't money for new dresses, especially not when there was only one wage coming in most of the time, and Geoff spent a large portion of their household income down the pub. All the other married women here today had their husbands with them, but Linda hadn't even bothered to invite Geoff. He would only show her up and humiliate her if he agreed to come along. He was probably at The Lamb and half cut already.

Linda glanced again at her watch and thought now was an appropriate time to leave. She had wished the happy couple well and done everything expected of her. Her shoes were pinching her feet after standing all day at Bevels, and she couldn't wait to get home and take them off.

She walked home slowly in the late evening, summer sun and thought about what she would do with Jimmy. With her wages, it was unlikely she would be able to afford a two-bedroom place, and so she might be forced to stay with Geoff until Jimmy was safely back at home with his nan. She wasn't sure how long Mary would be in hospital, but she guessed it would be at least another week. That meant another week putting up with Geoff, and Linda shuddered. Now that she had made her decision, she couldn't wait to get away from him.

She imagined the look on his face when she confronted him and told him she was leaving. She wasn't naive enough to think he would miss her, but he would certainly miss her wages coming in. He would be forced to get a job or else he'd be thrown out on the street for not paying the rent, and it would serve him right, Linda thought grimly.

***

Outside The Lamb, Charlie and Brian were waiting in a van. There were a couple of vehicles parked in the street, but not many.

"He'd better get a blooming move on. Someone's going to notice us sitting out here in broad daylight," Charlie Williams muttered and then took a drag on his cigarette.

Brian's meaty fingers drummed against the steering wheel impatiently. "The longer he is in there, the more drunk he'll be, and that means he won't be able to put up so much of a fight."

"I hope you're right," Charlie said. "He's a big bastard."

"Nah," Brian said dismissively. "He won't stand a chance."

That was all very well for Brian to say, Charlie thought. The man was built like a brick shithouse. Charlie, on the other hand, wasn't quite so brawny, and he didn't like doing jobs like this without a weapon. But Dave had specifically ordered them not to bring any guns or knives. He wanted this to look like an accident.

It wouldn't be so bad if they had Gary with them, but when they'd gone to pick him up earlier, the silly sod was high. There was no way Charlie was going to risk letting him come along and screw everything up. Years ago, Gary's coked-up reactions had got Charlie Williams sent down, and he had never forgotten it. Charlie had sworn never to work with Gary when he was high ever again.

The pub doors opened, and both men leaned forward eagerly, but it was just old Bob, looking the worse for wear as he began to stagger home.

"Are you sure he's in there?" Charlie asked.

"Relax," Brian said. "I saw him. He is definitely in there."

Charlie huffed and sat back in the passenger seat. It wasn't so much that he didn't like doing jobs like this, but he hated waiting around. His mother would have chucked his dinner in the bin by now, and he would have no end of nagging from her when he got home. No matter how old Charlie Williams got, his mother always read him the riot act if he wasn't home for dinner.

"There he is," Brian hissed and nodded at the pub entrance.

Charlie turned and saw Geoff Blum step out of the pub. He looked drunk and even larger than Charlie remembered. He sighed. They may as well get it over with.

This wasn't going to be easy. Geoff would recognise both Charlie and Brian and would put up a fight if he realised what was going on.

As Charlie and Brian walked across the street, Brian called out, "Geoff, wait up. Dave needs a word."

Geoff turned to face them, his forehead crinkling up as he struggled to focus on them. "What does he want?"

"Just get in the van," Charlie said irritably. "I'm not a mind reader. I don't know what he wants."

Geoff swayed a little as he stared at both of the men suspiciously. "It's not a good time. I'll speak to him tomorrow."

Brian chuckled. "That's not how it works, Geoff. If Dave asks you to jump, you ask how high. He wants to speak to you now."

Geoff's eyes darted up the street, and for one horrible moment, Charlie thought they might have a chase on their hands. But then he thought better of it and nodded as he followed Charlie and Brian to the van.

"You'll have to get in the back," Brian said. "There's not enough room upfront."

Geoff's eyes widened, and he seemed to sense the danger as Brian opened the large back doors on the van. "I can't get in there. I don't like enclosed spaces."

Charlie rolled his eyes. "Don't be daft. It's not that bad in there. Take a look."

As Geoff nervously peered into the back of the van, Charlie picked up a tyre iron and clobbered him over the head with it. Geoff flopped forward onto the floor of the van, unconscious.

"What are you doing?" Brian demanded. "We weren't supposed to use any weapons."

"He won't give us any trouble now," Charlie said as he reached down for Geoff's legs and pulled them up, trying to force the rest of Geoff's body into the van. "Give us a hand, won't you?"

With an impatient huff, Brian helped Charlie and then they locked the back doors of the van and walked around to the front.

***

With Brian Moore at the wheel, they drove out of Poplar and headed to North London. Geoff was quiet in the back, and Charlie thought he must still be unconscious. He had given him quite a whack with that tyre iron, but there was worse to come, and after they had finished with Geoff, he doubted anyone would notice the wound on the back of his head.

They drove in silence for a little while. Brian stared straight ahead at the road. The traffic was light as they travelled through London in the dusk. It would be dark by the time they got to their destination.

"What plans do you think the boss has in store for Big Tim?" Brian asked Charlie, turning away from the road momentarily with a scowl on his face.

Charlie hesitated before answering, he didn't like to talk about business when they could be overheard, but Geoff wasn't going to be spilling any of their secrets so he decided to reply, "No idea. I was surprised as you were when he told me Big Tim had started working for him."

Brian grunted. "Well, something is going on."

Charlie chuckled. "There's always something going on. That's what makes it exciting."

Brian gave another grunt. "Maybe for you. For me, it just makes it stressful."

Charlie grinned. He knew Brian thrived on this sort of thing just as much as he did. They stopped talking for a little while as Brian wasn't as familiar with the roads in North London and had to pay attention to the street signs.

When they got to their destination, Brian pulled up onto the pavement. Charlie looked around nervously as a stream of other cars went past them. He hadn't realised it would be so busy. They'd taken precautions such as swapping out the number plates, and as long as the Old Bill didn't come along, or a member of the public, they should be safe.

"How the bleeding hell are we going to get him over there," Brian said with an exasperated look on his face.

They were on Hornsey Lane Bridge, nicknamed suicide bridge. The plan was to tip Geoff over the edge and make it look like a suicide. That was why Dave had been so insistent on no weapons, and also why Charlie had thought the injury from the tyre iron wouldn't be a problem. When Geoff was lying crushed and broken under the bridge, no one would notice one extra head wound.

The trouble was Charlie hit him pretty hard, and when they opened the back doors, Geoff was still sprawled unconscious on the floor of the van.

"Oh, for Gawd's sake, Charlie. Why did you hit him so hard?"

"Stop complaining and help me pull him out."

Both men froze as a car went past, illuminating them with its headlights.

Charlie looked over his shoulder and saw that the car was gone, and the road was empty. "All right. The coast is clear. Let's get this over with quickly."

Between them, they struggled to pull Geoff from the van and then held him upright, walking him over to the edge of the bridge. "Jesus, he is heavier than he looks."

When they got him to the edge, they leaned on the railings, breathing heavily, and Brian muttered under his breath, "Don't look now, Charlie, but we've got a visitor."

Of course, Charlie ignored Brian and looked straight away. At the other end of the bridge, a woman was walking towards them. She was dressed in navy blue and wore a smart jacket with a long skirt and matching navy blue hat.

"What the hell do we do now?" Charlie said as the woman got closer and closer.

"Leave the talking to me," Brian grunted wrapping one of Geoff's floppy arms around his shoulders so he could prop him up.

"Good evening, gentlemen," the woman said and handed Charlie a leaflet, which he took with his free hand.

Charlie took a quick glance at it. It was full of religious stuff. Salvation Army. Bloody typical.

"Thanks," Charlie said stuffing the leaflet into his pocket and trying not to be crushed under Geoff's weight.

"Is he all right?" The nosy woman said, looking at Geoff.

"He's fine. Had a bit too much to drink and needed some air," Brian said quickly.

The woman nodded slowly, but she didn't move away. "It's probably not the best place to stop," she said. Her eyes flickered towards the van and then back to the three men. "What are you doing out here at this time of night?"

Charlie was really straining to keep Geoff from toppling over. Why didn't this annoying woman just go away? "What are you doing out here at this time of night? It's not really the place for a woman," Charlie snapped.

The woman seemed a little taken aback, but she answered Charlie's question, "There's a group of us at the Salvation Army who take it in turns to come here. Unfortunately, this bridge is a notorious suicide spot, and we come to offer help and guidance to those who are feeling desperate."

Charlie groaned. This was all they needed. A flipping do-gooder.

How long were they going to have to stand there with Geoff before the woman went away? He looked over his shoulder to the van. Perhaps they would have to rethink their plan and take Geoff somewhere else. Perhaps they could dump him in the Thames. They really hadn't thought this through. Another car rushed past them, and its headlights shone on the woman's face. She was older than Charlie had first thought and had a very serious expression.

"It's very kind of you to offer help to those in need," Brian said.

The woman smiled. "I was actually about to head home when I saw you. I thought you might be having difficulties, but when I saw that there were three of you, I realised you weren't likely to be suicide jumpers."

Brian laughed loudly, too loudly. "No, you're right about that. None of us are going to jump."

Charlie gave him a nudge. "Don't let us hold you up then. We'll be on our way soon."

Geoff's head lolled forward so his chin was resting on his chest. Charlie smiled at the woman as if it was perfectly normal and hoped she didn't see the blood on Geoff's collar.

"Very well. Goodnight."

As the woman walked away, both Charlie and Brian breathed out a sigh of relief. "That was a close one," Brian muttered as he gripped the railing.

They waited until the woman had disappeared before turning to each other and nodding. It was time. All they had to do was heave Geoff over the side of the bridge. It should have been easy.

They rested Geoff against the side of the railings, and then both men took hold of a leg to heave up. Geoff was halfway over the edge when all of a sudden his body jerked, and he kicked out, sending Charlie sprawling to the floor.

He had woken up.

Charlie scrambled to his feet and tried to help Brian restrain Geoff who was struggling as if his life depended on it, which of course, it did.

They pushed and shoved, Geoff's fingers were vice-like as they gripped the side of the railings.

"What are you doing?" Geoff screeched as Charlie tried to peel his fingers back.

"We're getting rid of you. You've been blabbing your mouth off about Dave's business, and he doesn't like that."

"I haven't. I swear!"

Charlie managed to release one of Geoff's hands, but then he gripped the railing tightly with his other hand. Charlie cursed in frustration.

As Charlie set to work again, pushing Geoff's fingers back, Geoff tried to clobber him around the head, and as his fist made contact, it made Charlie's ears ring.

"Ow," Charlie said rubbing his temple. He turned to Brian. "Why don't they ever go easily?"

But Brian had had enough of this. He punched Geoff hard,

full in the face, and that was enough to loosen Geoff's grip.

The scream Geoff made as he plummeted over the bridge made Charlie's stomach churn. He shuddered when he heard the dull thump.

Brian peered over the edge of the bridge to check the outcome and grimaced. "He's finished. Our work here is done."

Charlie felt a little bit sick as they returned to the van. Sometimes, this was a horrible job. He glanced over at Brian's stoic face as he drove away from the bridge and wondered if he felt the same way. It was true, you did get used to it to some extent, but Charlie would never enjoy this side of the job.

35

LINDA TIGHTENED THE CORD ON her dressing gown and frowned. Geoff still wasn't home, and she didn't like to go to bed until she had bolted the door. Jimmy was already tucked up in the spare room, and Linda had been drinking endless cups of tea as she waited for Geoff to come home. He usually kicked up a fuss if she went to bed first. She walked into the front room and glanced at the clock on the mantelpiece. The pubs had closed nearly an hour ago. She couldn't think where Geoff had got to. He was usually home hours before now, criticising Linda's choice of evening meal.

But Linda didn't feel unduly concerned. She thought perhaps one of the pubs might have a lock-in, which meant Geoff would be home in the early hours, even worse for wear than usual.

She reminded herself she wouldn't have to put up with this for much longer. Just as soon as Mary Diamond was out of hospital, Linda would make sure she had her own flat, and she would leave Geoff behind and start a new life.

She yawned, stretched and rubbed her tired eyes. It had been a long day.

Her thoughts briefly drifted to Valerie and hoped that the girl would have better luck than Linda herself had had in marriage.

She walked out into the kitchen to rinse up her teacup and

do a last tidy round of the kitchen before she went to bed. She had been keeping Geoff's dinner warm in the oven, but it was almost completely dried out now, and the mashed potato had turned hard. She scraped it into the bin and washed up the plate. There was bread and cheese in the larder. He would have to put up with that.

She switched off the kitchen light and was walking towards the stairs when there was a knock at the door. It made Linda jump before she guessed it must be Geoff. He had probably forgotten his key.

When she opened the door, Linda was shocked to see a policeman, who had removed his hat and tucked it under his arm.

"Mrs. Blum?" the policeman asked. He had light grey hair and a pair of kind brown eyes.

Despite the kindly expression on the policeman's face, Linda felt sick. Memories of the night she had been with Mary Diamond when a policeman had come to tell them that Kathleen's body had been found in the canal taunted Linda.

She knew that policemen didn't knock on the door in the middle of the night unless it was bad news.

Linda couldn't reply past the lump in her throat, but she managed to nod.

"Perhaps I could come in?"

Linda stood aside to let the policeman enter and shut the front door with a shaking hand. She pulled her dressing gown around her body tightly as she led the policeman into the front room.

"I think it's best if you take a seat, Mrs. Blum."

Linda couldn't take anymore. She had to know what had happened. Had Geoff got into a fight? Had he been arrested?

"Is it about my husband?" Linda asked anxiously.

"I'm afraid so," the policeman said gravely. "I'm very sorry to tell you that your husband's body was discovered on Hornsey Lane. We have reason to believe he took his own life."

Linda gasped, horrified. She stared at the policeman for a moment, unable to process what he was saying. "Are you sure it was Geoff?" she asked as she slumped down onto the settee.

The policeman sat down next to her. "He had some identification on him, and we asked his doctor to confirm his identity. I'm afraid he jumped from a bridge."

Linda didn't know why the stupid man kept saying he was afraid. What a stupid turn of phrase. She tried to massage her temples to get rid of the headache that was building around her eyes. "I don't understand."

"It must be a terrible shock," the policeman said. "Is there anyone who could come and stay with you, perhaps a neighbour or a family member?"

Linda shook her head. She didn't want anyone there right now. "My mother lives nearby. I don't want to bother her now, though."

"I'm sure she wouldn't mind given the circumstances."

Linda shook her head rapidly. "No," she snapped. "I'll tell her tomorrow. I'll be fine tonight."

The policeman looked at her doubtfully, but he nodded. "If you have any questions, you can speak to me tomorrow. My name is PC Smith. I won't be on duty in the morning, but you can speak to any of my colleagues, and they will help you."

Linda nodded numbly as she realised she would now have to arrange the funeral. She felt dizzy at the turn of events and very guilty. She didn't want anybody here, least of all her mother, who would certainly pick up on the fact that Linda wasn't upset that Geoff had gone. She felt ashamed that all she felt on hearing Geoff was dead was a sense of relief. She was quite sure nobody else would understand, and they would judge her.

"I'm not sure I should leave you alone," the policeman said.

"I'm not alone," Linda said, getting to her feet. "I have

someone staying with me at the moment. A friend's grandson. He is in the spare room."

The policeman's eyes flickered to the stairs, and then he said, "Well, if you are absolutely sure you are all right…"

Linda nodded firmly as she led the policeman to the front door. "Yes, thank you. It's been a shock obviously, but I would prefer to be alone now."

***

Linda spent the following day in a daze. She'd sat Jimmy down at breakfast time and explained to him as best she could what had happened to Geoff.

She didn't know how he would react to the news. Clearly his time with Geoff had been turbulent, to say the least, and although she wouldn't have been shocked to find Jimmy was relieved, she was surprised to see horror and what looked like guilt in the boy's dark blue eyes when she told him Geoff had died.

She told him Geoff had jumped off a bridge because she didn't see any point in lying. Rumours would soon spread around the East End, so there was no point in trying to keep it a secret.

She didn't read too much into Jimmy's reaction, though. After all, people reacted to death in all sorts of different ways.

Jimmy went to school as usual, and Linda spent the rest of the day feeling numb. After she told her family the news, her mother had accompanied her home and had spent the entire day watching Linda closely for signs of grief.

Of course, that just made Linda feel even more on edge because she wasn't really grieving for Geoff and had to try to stop her relief from showing. People were in and out all day, offering condolences and bringing food and flowers. By three o'clock, Linda couldn't wait to get the house back to herself.

Jimmy was due home from school at three thirty, and Linda was determined to take him to the hospital herself to see Mary. Unfortunately, Linda's mother thought this was a very bad idea.

"You don't need to worry about that now," she insisted. "The boy is old enough to get himself to the hospital alone."

Linda suppressed a sigh. "I know he's old enough, but I don't want him to go alone. I want to be there to support him."

Linda's mother's forehead wrinkled in a frown. "Surely somebody else can go with the child. I'll go if needs be."

"You don't understand," Linda said, beginning to lose her patience. "I want to go with him. It will take my mind off everything."

"I really don't think–"

"It isn't up to you. I've made my decision, and I'm going with Jimmy to the hospital," Linda snapped.

Her mother pursed her lips and folded her arms across her chest. "I know losing Geoff has been a terrible shock, but that doesn't excuse rudeness, Linda."

Linda got to her feet and went to the cupboard in the hallway to pull out her coat, so she was ready as soon as Jimmy got home.

With a loud sigh, her mother stood up also. "I can tell when I'm not wanted," she said, making Linda feel even more guilty.

"I'm sorry. I'll see you tomorrow."

Linda bid her mother goodbye and then waited for another five minutes until Jimmy arrived and they set off for the bus stop together. She found the boy's company relaxing. He didn't want to talk about Geoff or continually ask Linda how she was feeling. In fact, Linda welcomed the chance to worry about Jimmy rather than herself. It took her mind off her own problems.

It didn't take them long to get to The London, and as they walked along the hospital corridor, they discussed what would happen when Mary came out.

"I can prepare your meals and bring them round," Linda

said. "I know you're looking forward to having your nan back home."

Jimmy grinned happily, but as they turned the corner, they saw a group of men in white coats, standing by the entrance to the ward. Jimmy shot them a worried glance and then looked up at Linda.

"I'm sure it's nothing," she murmured reassuringly.

As they approached the doctors, Linda paused, and Jimmy went on ahead to talk to his nan.

"Excuse me, I've come to visit Mary Diamond. I'm looking after her grandson, and we were wondering when she might be let home."

The three men in white coats turned to face her, and the eldest one, with the bushiest eyebrows Linda had ever seen, said, "I'm afraid Mrs. Diamond has had a setback. We have had to increase the dose of her medication today because of the strain on her heart. I think she will be in hospital for at least another week."

"I see. Thank you." Linda turned away, knowing that Jimmy would be bitterly disappointed when he learned the news.

She walked into the ward and headed towards the window, where Jimmy was sitting beside Mary's bed. She could see the change in Mary immediately. She looked paler and very weak.

Mary smacked her lips together as though her mouth was too dry to talk.

Linda poured a glass of water from the jug on Mary's nightstand. She helped Mary to a sitting position and held the glass to the woman's lips.

After taking a couple of mouthfuls of water, she grasped Jimmy's hand and said, "The doctors won't tell me the truth, but I know I'm never getting out of here."

Jimmy looked horrified.

"Don't say that, Mary," Linda said. "You've just had a little setback. I've spoken to the doctors, and they say you'll only be in here for another week."

Mary shook her head. "Lies. All lies. I'm not getting out of here, Jimmy, and there are things you need to know. Things I should have told you before now."

Mary's voice sounded croaky, and Jimmy leaned forward so he could hear her better. Linda felt nervous. She didn't like the direction this was taking at all.

"It's about your father," Mary said. "His name is Martin Morton."

Linda gasped in surprise. She couldn't believe Mary was going to tell Jimmy this now. Her brain must be addled with all the medication the doctors had given her.

She had to stop Mary before she said anything more. "Mary, there's no need to talk about this now. You'll be out in a week or so, and you can tell Jimmy then."

Jimmy frowned. "No, I want to know now. Do you mean Martin Morton, the man who is in prison?"

Mary licked her lips and nodded. "That's right. But you should stay away from him, Jimmy. He's not a nice man."

Jimmy looked confused. And Linda was desperate to change the subject. She picked up the glass of water again and held it out towards Mary. "Would you like another drink?"

Mary shook her head and waved the drink away. "No, there's more I need to tell Jimmy about what happened to his mother..."

Mary's eyes looked wild, and her cheeks were flushed. Linda knew she wasn't in her right mind, and she had to stop this before it got any further.

"No, Mary don't. Not here. Not like this."

"What about my mother?" Jimmy asked.

Mary opened her mouth to speak but then her eyes rolled back in her head, and with a shudder, she collapsed back on her pillows.

"Nan!" Jimmy cried frantically.

Linda called for help and soon they were ushered back by the duty nurse, who closed the curtains around Mary and told them to wait outside.

Jimmy was trembling, and Linda did her best to comfort him as he gnawed on his fingernails.

It felt like they were waiting for hours, but it was probably only a period of a few minutes before the same doctor Linda had spoken to earlier approached them.

"That must've been very scary to witness," the doctor said, looking at Jimmy kindly and putting his hand on the boy's shoulder. "Your grandmother had a reaction to the medication we've given her. It looked worse than it was. She will be feeling a lot better tomorrow after a good night's sleep."

After Linda asked the doctor a few more questions, she took Jimmy by the hand, and they left the hospital.

Although Jimmy was quiet at the moment, Linda knew he would be full of questions about his father later on that evening. She didn't understand why Mary had done it. Did she really think she was about to die and want to pass on with a clear conscience?

Whatever the reason, the cat was now out of the bag. She was surprised Jimmy had got this far without finding out his father was Martin Morton. At least the horrible man was still locked up, Linda thought. That was one thing to be grateful for.

36

BABS MORTON SAT STIFFLY IN a hardback chair in the front room and glared at the welcome home tea Violet Morton had laid on for Martin. Babs was a hypocrite for even being there. She didn't want Martin to come home. She'd been praying that he wouldn't get the early release he'd been after.

The other two women in Martin's life were excited to see him again. Ruby couldn't sit still for a moment. She kept darting in and out of the kitchen, checking every sandwich and cake was perfectly arranged on the best china.

Violet Morton was her normal stuck-up self, but even she couldn't wipe the smile off her face at the thought of seeing her son again. If Babs hadn't already been in a bad mood at the thought of sharing a house with Martin again, Violet's presence would have put her in one anyway. The woman was unbearable.

"Are you not going to change, Babs?" Violet asked pointedly.

Babs scowled. She knew the horrible old bat was only trying to rile her. The trouble was, it was working. Babs could feel herself growing more and more tense as the minutes ticked past on the clock over the mantelpiece.

Martin should have been there already.

"No, Violet, I am not going to change," Babs said and smoothed down the smart red dress she was wearing.

She knew she looked good for her age. She had kept her figure well over the past decade, and although she couldn't do anything about the fine lines that had appeared around her eyes and mouth, she had made sure she looked her best today. She wore the sapphire earrings Martin had bought her years ago in happier times, and her hand reached up absent-mindedly to touch them. Things had changed so much over the years.

Babs had been so preoccupied she'd barely noticed Ruby at all, other than to be irritated with the girl for rushing about too much, but now she saw the length of her hemline. Babs pointed at Ruby's knees.

"What on earth do you think you are wearing, Ruby?"

Ruby looked up from the table, which was heavily laden with all sorts of good things to eat, and sighed heavily. "It's not even that short, Mum. It's nothing compared to what the other girls wear."

"I don't care what the other girls wear. I can see your knees. Next, you'll be walking around in a dress that shows your knickers, girl!"

"Mum, don't be ridiculous. It's hardly the same thing."

"I'll thank you not to call me ridiculous, young lady." Babs turned to face Violet. "Surely you can't approve of this either," Babs said and waved a hand in Ruby's direction.

Violet pursed her lips and shrugged. "It's the fashion, Babs. You need to move with the times."

Babs gaped at the woman. Violet was only saying that to contradict her. If Babs said something was white, Violet would insist it was black. Babs shook her head. What had she done to deserve such a family?

"Wait until your father sees what you're wearing. He won't be happy," Babs grumbled.

Ruby looked down at her outfit and hesitated. "All right. I'll go and change."

When Ruby left the two older women alone in the front

room, there was an uncomfortable silence. If Babs was honest, she preferred that to trying to make small talk with Violet. She just wasn't up to it today. She was dreading Martin turning up, but as she glanced at the clock, she started to worry. He should have been home by now. Freddie and Henry had gone to pick him up, and they were supposed to bring him straight home.

If Martin had taken himself off somewhere, rather than come home for his special tea, Babs would murder him. She hadn't even wanted to do the sodding tea anyway.

As if Violet sensed what Babs was thinking, she said, "He should have been home by now. What's keeping him?"

"I don't bleeding know," Babs snapped. She was sitting and waiting the same as Violet. How on earth would she know what had delayed Martin? Although, she could hazard a guess, and it probably involved women, booze or both.

Babs looked again at the table, which was groaning under a hundredweight of sandwiches, scones and Violet's famous Victoria Sponge. If he didn't turn up soon, Babs was going to dump the lot in the bin. She shouldn't be surprised by his behaviour. This was Martin all over. He liked the power of keeping people waiting.

"It's a shame Derek couldn't be here," Violet said with a malicious glint in her eye.

Babs stifled a groan. Violet had only been there an hour and already she'd mentioned Derek about ten times. "He's back at school. I didn't see the need to disrupt his schooling."

Violet arched an eyebrow and pursed her lips together in disapproval.

Babs was actually a little bit worried about Derek. After she had shipped him off to the boarding school, he hadn't returned home once. Instead of coming home for the summer holidays, he'd chosen to spend it with the new friends he had made at school. Perhaps Babs should have been happy he'd settled in so well, unlike Ruby. But she couldn't help worrying that her plan had backfired. It seemed that Derek liked his new posh friends a lot better than his own family, but she wasn't about to admit that to Violet.

"He's doing ever so well," Babs said. "He's made some friends whose fathers are very well connected. One of them is a Lord."

If Babs thought that might impress Violet Morton, she was sadly mistaken. The older woman grimaced.

"You're giving him ideas above his station, Babs, and it won't end well."

"What would you know about it? You've never been out of the East End."

"Of course, I have. I just know my place in this world, and I'm very content with what God has given me."

She must be very easily pleased, Babs thought, to be happy with the life she got, but Babs couldn't be bothered to point that out.

Ruby came back down, dressed in a longer, yellow dress.

"That's much better," Babs said, smiling at Ruby's dress which ended mid-shin.

"Is he still not here?" Ruby went to the window to peer through the net curtains.

Babs hated Martin for the disappointment she saw on the girl's face. No matter what Babs said, Ruby still thought her father was perfect. How was Babs supposed to break the news that her father had chosen to go to the knocking shop or the boozer rather than come home to see his only daughter?

Babs imagined how it would have been if young Emily had lived. She'd been barely a few months old when Martin had been incarcerated. If she hadn't had to deal with the grief of losing Emily after Martin got locked away, things would have been better. For one thing, Babs wouldn't be so bitter.

She tried to force the thoughts of Emily out of her mind and focused back on her older daughter, Ruby. For her daughter's sake, Babs lied. "You know what prisons are like. There's probably been a hold-up with the paperwork. He'll be back soon."

Violet wasn't so easy to placate. "It's all your fault," she said to Babs. "The poor man doesn't feel welcome in his own home. Imagine coming home to a face like that." She nodded at Babs. "You've got a face on you like a bulldog chewing a wasp."

Babs sprang to her feet. She didn't give a toss about Martin's welcome home tea anymore. She just wanted that horrible woman out of her house.

But before Babs could bark out an order at Violet to get her skinny backside out of the front room, Ruby put a hand on her mother's arm. "Don't, Mum. Not today, please."

God only knew how she did it, but Babs managed to bite her tongue as she whisked past Ruby out of the front room and into the kitchen.

She grabbed her packet of cigarettes then quickly lit one up.

This was typical Martin, Babs thought as she took a long drag on her cigarette. He caused trouble even when he wasn't here.

***

At the very moment Babs was struggling to contain her temper, Martin Morton sat in the back of Freddie's Jaguar. He sat in the middle, with his arms spread wide over the back of the seats, and grinned like a cat who'd got the cream.

He'd made Freddie and Henry wait outside his favourite whore house in Soho, and now as Freddie turned the car and headed back towards Poplar, Martin slapped the back of the passenger seat to get their attention.

"It feels good to be out, boys."

"Back where you belong, boss," Henry said.

Martin nodded and looked out at the London streets they passed eagerly. "We'll be back on top soon."

Red-haired Freddie looked in the rearview mirror at Martin. "Are we heading back to your place now?"

"God, no. I need a drink first. Take me to the pub."

Freddie and Henry exchanged a look. They both knew that Babs and Violet had laid on a tea for Martin and would be waiting at the house in Poplar. They told Martin this as soon as they picked him up outside the prison, but Martin didn't seem to care less.

"Babs and your mum will be waiting, and –"

"Let them wait. I've been waiting for ten years for a pint in a proper pub. I'm not going home for a bunch of poncy sandwiches and a couple of cups of tea."

"Right you are," Freddie said as they drove past the turning to Bread Street. "Is The Lamb all right?"

"That's fine," Martin said. "I can't wait to see the look on old Barney's face when I walk in. I need to show my face around here, and make sure everybody realises I'm back and things are going to change."

Freddie and Henry shifted uncomfortably in their seats. They were caught between a rock and a hard place. They dare not go against Martin's wishes, but they knew that Babs would lay into the pair of them when she realised they hadn't brought Martin straight back home.

Everybody knew that Babs did not get along with Martin's mother, and with the two women stuck in the same room, waiting for Martin... It was a disaster waiting to happen.

"Have you seen Big Tim around lately?" Martin asked as he wound down the window and whistled at a young woman they passed by.

Both Freddie and Henry hesitated before answering. They had kept Martin up-to-date, and Martin knew that Big Tim was now working for Dave Carter. But that didn't mean Martin had accepted it. He was unpredictable before he got sent down, and now he was looking for a way to stamp his authority back on the East End. What better way than teaching Big Tim a lesson?

Freddie ran a hand through his red hair and wondered how

best to tell Martin that Big Tim seemed to be thriving under Dave Carter's command.

But Henry spoke up first, "I've seen him around. He has not caused us any trouble, though, boss."

Both Henry and Freddie had got on reasonably well with Big Tim. They weren't exactly friends, Big Tim didn't encourage friendships, but they'd had a lot of respect for the big man and to see him lose his marbles and turned to drink had hit both Henry and Freddie hard.

Freddie would prefer it if Martin would let bygones be bygones, but that really wasn't in Martin's nature. He had a feeling that Martin would come down hard on Big Tim, and when he did, Freddie could only hope that Martin didn't decide to use him to dole out the punishment.

"Let's hope it stays that way," Martin said, and then he added quietly, "I never expected Big Tim to turn."

None of them had. Big Tim had been a stalwart member of Martin Morton's outfit from the early days, and he had never let him down, always going above and beyond the call of duty.

Neither Henry nor Freddie dared to ask the question they really wanted answered. They wanted to know what Martin was going to do about Tim's betrayal, but like everyone else, they would just have to wait and see.

***

Babs and Violet were only managing not to rip each other to shreds by staying in separate rooms. Babs kept to the kitchen, and Violet stayed in the front room. Babs was glad she was in the kitchen away from Ruby's unhappy face. She expected Martin to behave like this, but it was a big let-down for Ruby.

Babs stubbed out another cigarette when she heard the sound of the front door opening.

"About bleeding time," she muttered under her breath.

But when she got to the hallway, she saw it was Tony standing by the front door and not Martin.

"Where is he then?" Tony asked Babs with a charming smile.

"No sodding idea," Babs said.

Tony frowned as he hung up his coat and walked towards her. "What do you mean?"

"He hasn't shown up."

Violet and Ruby had also heard the door open and were now peering out of the front room, only to look in disappointment at Tony.

"Where is that useless brother of yours?" Violet said, glaring at Tony.

Tony shrugged, looking at the disappointed faces of his mother and Ruby. "Maybe there's been some sort of hold up at the prison."

Violet snorted out a very unladylike laugh. "Pull the other one. That boy has always been a disappointment to me."

Babs resisted rolling her eyes and going back into the kitchen. She ushered everybody into the front room, and they all sat down and looked at each other awkwardly. Babs wished she could throw everything away. She was sick of this. It was humiliating. Martin was going to waltz back in here and expect them all to toe the line. No doubt he would think he could come in and take over the business just like before. He'd probably claim the Patterson job, and in time, people would forget that Babs had ever played a role in forcing Gerald Patterson to cooperate.

Well, Freddie wouldn't forget. He was still angry with her for using Jemima.

Ruby hadn't said a word. She sat on the settee, staring down at her lap miserably. Babs felt sorry for the girl, but it was better she realised what her father was really like sooner rather than later.

No one spoke, and the only noise was the ticking of the clock over the mantelpiece.

Finally, Tony stood up. "I'll go and try and find him."

Ruby raised her head sharply. "I thought you said it was a hold-up at the prison? It isn't, is it? He's just gone to the pub rather than come home and see us."

Tony sighed, but he didn't try to deny it. He put a hand on Ruby's shoulder. "I'll find him. He'll be home soon."

Ruby stood up abruptly. "I don't care. I don't want to see him anyway."

As Ruby rushed from the room, Babs called after her, "You don't mean it. Don't be daft."

All these years, she had been frustrated that Ruby and Derek seemed to think their father was some sort of martyr, and she longed for the day when they woke up and realised exactly what he was really like, but now seeing her daughter so upset, Babs wanted to cry. Why did he have to be such a bastard?

As Tony opened the front door, he gave out a muffled curse and then there was a loud bang. Babs walked out into the hallway and saw Martin sprawled over the threshold.

He was wasted.

Babs leaned on the wall. "God give me strength," she muttered.

As Violet Morton pushed her way past Babs and clapped eyes on her son, she let out a horrified gasp. "Look at the state of him! He's drunk."

Babs wanted to give her a clap for stating the bleeding obvious, but instead she kept her mouth shut. She'd like to see how Violet was going to blame Babs for this one.

Violet stormed up to her eldest son, who raised his head and looked up at his mother through bleary eyes.

"Hello, Mum," Martin said, slurring his words.

"Don't you hello Mum me, my boy!" Violet leaned over and hit Martin round the back of the head. "Get up. You're a disgrace. All the neighbours can see you."

As Martin tried to struggle to his feet, Babs sensed movement and turned around. Ruby was at the top of the stairs looking down at her inebriated father. She didn't say a word, just turned and went back to her bedroom.

Babs didn't try to stop her. It was probably for the best.

Between them, Tony and Babs tried to pull Martin to his feet. It wasn't easy. And Violet smacking him and digging him in the ribs every few seconds didn't help either.

When they finally got Martin inside and propped up on the sofa, Violet announced she was leaving.

"I'm too old for this. I'm ashamed of you, Martin. Do you hear me?"

But in response, Martin let out a very large snore.

Violet pulled a face and stomped her foot. "That's it. I'm leaving!"

Babs didn't say anything. If Violet was expecting her to persuade her to stay, she was sadly mistaken. That wasn't going to happen. Babs couldn't wait to see the back of her.

"All right, Mum. Don't get upset. I'll walk you home," Tony said and took his mother's arm.

Tony gave Babs an apologetic look as he left her alone with Martin. As well he might. But Martin could sleep there all night as far as Babs was concerned.

She turned her back on the table of untouched food they'd all prepared for him and walked out of the room, shutting the door on her husband.

If this was a sign of things to come, God help them all.

37

THE FOLLOWING MORNING, BABS WAS still in a foul mood. She had roughly shaken Martin awake ten minutes ago, and he now sat at the kitchen table, rumpled and dressed in the same shirt and trousers he'd worn yesterday. He was clearly suffering and sat with his head in his hands.

Babs hit the kettle down on the stove with a large clang, giving a small smile of satisfaction when Martin winced.

"And another thing," Babs said. "Your daughter was devastated to see you in such a state last night. She'd worked ever so hard to prepare that tea for you."

Babs hadn't stopped nagging Martin from the minute he woke up. She wasn't planning on letting up anytime soon, either. He deserved everything he got.

"I've said I'm sorry," Martin said. "I'll apologise to Ruby."

Babs nodded firmly and collected some eggs from the larder. "I should think so, too. I don't know what Freddie and Henry were thinking, but I will certainly be having words with them."

"Give it a rest, woman," Martin growled, raising his head from his hands.

Babs opened her mouth to tell her husband exactly what she thought of his orders when Ruby walked into the kitchen, and Babs decided to hold her tongue.

Ruby stood beside the table, smiling shyly. "Hello, Dad."

"Hello, sweetheart. Sorry you had to see me in such a state last night. The boys insisted on buying me a drink, and I haven't so much as touched a drop all the time I've been inside. I was desperate to get home and see you."

Ruby smiled widely, falling for Martin's lies hook, line and sinker. Babs shook her head. She couldn't really blame Ruby, though. She'd fallen for enough of Martin's lies over the years herself.

She put the eggs in a saucepan of water and waited for them to come to the boil. Taking the bread from the bread bin, she listened to Ruby talk to her father. The incident last night had clearly had no effect on the adoration Ruby felt for him.

Feeling irritated and stressed, Babs continued to make the breakfast.

"What are your plans for your first whole day as a free man, Dad?" Ruby asked.

"I'm going to the club tonight to make sure everything is running well. Today I thought I'd do a bit of business, perhaps pop to Patterson's boxing club and talk about our new business arrangement."

Babs couldn't believe her ears. She slammed the butter knife down on the counter and turned around to look accusingly at Martin. "Oh, no, you don't! That's my deal. I arranged it, and I will see it through. Just because you're out doesn't mean you can take credit for all of my hard work."

Martin's eyes narrowed as he stared at his wife in disgust. "That's funny. I thought it was Henry who came up with the idea."

Babs' cheeks flushed. True, Henry had overheard Dave Carter's brother mouthing off in the pub over this new business opportunity with the Pattersons, but Henry hadn't done the hard work. That was all Babs, and she wasn't about to let anybody else take the credit.

"He just overheard something at the pub," Babs said snappily. "It was me who set it all up. I'm telling you, Martin,

I don't want you sticking your oar in."

Martin's lip curled as he snarled at his wife. "Suit yourself. If you think you can handle it alone, be my guest." He stood up from the table. "And I won't be back tonight. I'll stay at the club."

The look on Ruby's face was like a punch to Babs' stomach. She looked distraught. But Babs couldn't weaken. She shrugged and turned away to continue buttering the bread. And she didn't turn around until she heard the front door slam behind Martin.

***

After clearing away the breakfast things, Babs went to the shops. She got a few curious looks as she passed some of her neighbours on the street. She wanted to demand what they thought they were looking at and give them a piece of her mind, but she didn't. She couldn't really blame them for looking. Martin Morton getting out of prison was the biggest thing to happen around here for ages, and everyone was wondering what would happen next, including Babs.

She knew the next few weeks were vital in securing her place within the business. She'd seen what had happened after the war. While the men were fighting, the country relied on women to perform all the essential jobs, yet when the men came back, they wanted to shove the women back into the home and carry on as before.

The Pattersons' next shipment was due in soon, and Babs intended to be there when it arrived. She wanted to inspect the goods so she could make sure Gerald Patterson wasn't ripping them off. Henry hadn't mentioned anything other than the fact the goods were stolen from ships at the docks, and Babs wondered if she might be lucky enough to find some jewels in the shipment. Babs was rather partial to a little jewellery.

Whatever it was, the Mortons wouldn't play a role in selling it on, but by looking at the goods, Babs would have a good idea what their street value should be. Gerald had gone into this partnership quite unwillingly, and although he seemed too terrified of the Mortons to cheat them, Babs knew you could never be too careful.

She picked up a few things at the grocers and got another loaf of fresh bread at the bakers, ignoring the hushed whispers as she walked past the women gathered in the shop.

By the time she got back home, it had started to rain, and she was in an even worse mood than she had been when she set off.

She opened the front door, dumped her shopping bag on the floor and was about to hang her coat on the peg when the sound of male voices made her freeze. She didn't recognise Tony's voice, and as Martin had left in a huff that morning, she hadn't been expecting to see him for the rest of the day.

She heard the voices again and took a couple of steps closer to the front room. Then she heard Martin's voice, and she scowled. If he was conducting business in her front room, she would give him what for. He had the club for that.

Babs barged into the front room ready to chew Martin's ear off, but before she could, Martin stood up and grinned at her.

"Hello, Babs. I told you she wouldn't be long, gentlemen. Babs, this is Inspector Peel and Sergeant Cummings."

"You've only been out a day, Martin. How on earth have you had enough time to get in trouble already?"

Martin's smile only grew wider. "It's not me they're here to see, Babs. It's you."

Babs blinked at the two men. What on earth did they want with her?

"Me? Whatever for?"

"It's about Old Mo." Martin chuckled at the look on Babs' face.

She suddenly felt dizzy and sat down in an armchair. The mere mention of old Mo's name, made Babs' stomach churn. She could picture him now in the warehouse with the knife at his throat. She massaged her temples and tried to focus. She couldn't lose it in front of the coppers.

"Old Mo? He's in Spain, isn't he? Or was it Greece?" Babs tried to sound relaxed, but even she could hear the tremor in her voice.

As both the policemen turned to look at Babs, she swallowed hard.

"I'll leave you to it then, love," Martin said with a malicious grin. "I only popped back to get a change of clothes. I wouldn't know anything about Old Mo as I've been locked up, but I'm sure you'll be able to help the police with their enquiries, Babs."

Babs watched Martin leave with a rising sense of panic. The bastard. It had all been done according to his wishes anyway. His hands certainly were not clean.

After Martin left, Babs turned back to the policemen and tried to smile. She would have to put on the performance of her life to get out of this.

38

DAVE CARTER WAS A MAN on a mission. He walked up the Poplar High Street, nodding at various people he knew as he passed them. As he turned into Ming Street, he readied himself for a confrontation.

The Fang family had been in Poplar since the 1890s. They were originally from Shanghai but had adapted to life in the East End. They still held with the old traditions and stayed close to their roots, maintaining strong bonds with family in China.

After the Second World War, many of the Chinese immigrants had moved out to Chinatown, Soho. The Fangs had chosen to remain in Poplar.

Dave knew and respected the family, but that didn't mean he trusted them. He was here alone, and that meant he had to keep a lookout. Although his face and reputation earned him respect and perhaps a little fear, there was always the chance he'd come across a young upstart looking to make a name for himself by targeting a well-known face.

He'd already drawn some curious looks from families along the street. Dave smiled as he ducked beneath the washing line and saw two children splashing each other in a puddle. A Chinese woman appeared in one of the doorways and shouted at the children in Chinese, looking distrustfully at Dave.

He carried on his way as the street grew narrower and darker. The Fangs' laundry business was up ahead. There was a slight Chinese man on the door. Usually, a laundry wouldn't require someone to stand guard, but this was no ordinary laundry.

Dave nodded to the man as he passed inside and was immediately hit by the steamy, soapy smell of the laundry. As he passed through the public section, Dave smiled at the workers, but he just got blank looks in return.

There had been a great deal of prejudice against the Chinese when Dave was a boy, and it still hadn't completely gone away. The general public was scared about opium and illegal gambling dens. Most of the immigrants had been decent hard-working folk or sailors looking for honest work, but that didn't stop people panicking.

The Fangs, however, lived up to their reputation. There was nothing honest about them. Dave had a lot of respect for the way they ran their business, and wouldn't dream of interfering. If they stayed out of his way, he was more than happy to stay out of theirs.

Dave stepped into the back room, which was decorated with bright red and gold paper on the walls. The light was dim, and he didn't so much see the danger as sense it.

A man moved from the shadows and lunged at Dave. He saw the glint of light on a metal blade and stepped back quickly.

He grabbed the man's arm, forcing it back and twisting it savagely until his assailant was forced to drop his weapon. His Chinese attacker grunted with pain as the knife clattered to the floor.

Dave grabbed the man around the throat and slammed him against the wall.

The man kicked out and his face turned purple.

Before Dave could throttle the life out of him, a female voice sounded behind him.

"Please, put him down, Mr. Carter."

Dave turned, but he didn't release his hold on the man. He saw the beautiful, young granddaughter of old Mrs. Fang. She spoke perfect English with only the trace of an East End accent. Dave had spoken to her before and was furious at this treatment.

"What kind of welcome is this for an old friend?"

The young Chinese girl bowed her head and said apologetically, "I'm very sorry, Mr. Carter. Mr. Su Yin didn't recognise you."

Dave didn't believe that for a moment. It was a power play. Pure and simple. But he had to play along for now.

He released the man with a shove, and the young woman clicked her fingers, dismissing him.

"I hope you accept my sincere apologies, Mr. Carter. My grandmother would be very unhappy if she learned you had been mistreated on our premises."

Dave grunted. He wasn't in the mood for these games. "Where is she?" he demanded.

The young woman smiled. "My grandmother is very tired. She is advanced in years and doesn't like to see visitors."

Dave thrust his face in front of the girl and warned her, "I'm not playing your games. If you don't let me speak to her now, there's going to be hell to pay."

The girl smirked at his reaction. "Very well, please make yourself comfortable."

When she left him alone in the little red room, Dave didn't sit down. He hated being out of his comfort zone, so he stalked around the small room.

They kept him waiting long enough for Dave's temper to start to fray. He knew that was all part of their stupid game, and willed himself to relax.

A few more minutes passed before the door opened again, and the granddaughter entered, followed by old Mrs. Fang herself.

Her granddaughter hadn't been lying. Mrs. Fang was ancient. No one knew her real age, although people speculated she had to be over a hundred years old. Her face was as wrinkled as a raisin, and she had tiny, sharp, birdlike eyes. She walked towards Dave using her cane.

She was like a miniature doll of a woman, almost childlike, despite her wrinkles.

"Mr. Carter, you honour us with your presence. It has been a long time."

Dave nodded slowly. "It has. I've come here today with some information you'll be very interested in. Although after my reception here today, I'm not sure I should share what I know with you."

Mrs. Fang blinked up at him. "I am shocked at your treatment. Please be assured the man responsible will be punished."

He knew she was lying, but it was all for appearance's sake. Besides, he hadn't come all this way just to walk out now.

Dave paused for a moment as if he was considering what to do, even though he'd already made up his mind.

He enjoyed making them wait. "It's a little dark in here," he said. "Have you not thought of redecorating, perhaps in a lighter colour?"

A smile worked on the lips of the wizened old lady. She was no fool and knew exactly what Dave was doing. "I don't like change, Mr. Carter."

"You have a competitor importing into your area. That's not good for your business. I could tell you who, where and when," Dave said.

The old lady looked at him sharply, and Dave guessed they had already known that somebody else was importing their product. They just didn't know who yet.

"And what would you like in exchange for this information?" Mrs. Fang asked, and her granddaughter put a hand on her arm, whispering something in her ear.

Mrs. Fang waved her away and kept her gaze focused on Dave.

Dave shrugged. "Nothing. I just respect the old ways. The East End will be in chaos if everybody tries to muscle in. I think everybody benefits if you nip it in the bud early."

Mrs. Fang nodded slowly. "Very wise, Mr. Carter. You have my sincere thanks. Now, please take a seat. My granddaughter will prepare us tea, and we can get down to business."

***

Jimmy and little Georgie were sitting on the curb, watching the outside of Mortons' club. They were hidden by a parked car and had been sitting there for some time.

"What are we waiting for?" Georgie asked, hugging his knees to his chest.

After school, they'd gone to the workshop and washed the cars as usual. Normally they would go and have a game of football afterwards with some of Jimmy's other friends, or they would go straight to the sweetshop and spend the wages they received for washing the cars. Today, though, Jimmy didn't want to do anything other than stare at the building across the street, and Georgie was feeling quite confused.

"That's my father's club," Jimmy said unable to tear his eyes away from the front of Mortons.

Georgie's forehead wrinkled with confusion. "Your father? I thought you didn't have a dad."

"So did I," Jimmy muttered. "But my nan told me he was my father. She'd been keeping it from me."

"Why?"

Jimmy shrugged. "She said he wasn't a very nice man."

"Is he in there?"

Jimmy bit his lower lip. "I'm not sure. I know he owns the club. His name is Martin Morton."

Georgie blinked. "Are you sure?" Even Georgie had heard of Martin Morton.

Jimmy nodded. "Do you know him?"

"Not really. My Dad does. Didn't he just get out of prison?"

Jimmy nodded. "Yes, I bet he doesn't even know about me."

Georgie's eyes widened but before he could ask any more questions, the doors to the club opened, and two men stepped outside along with a young girl. She was a few years older than Jimmy and Georgie.

Neither boy spoke a word as they waited with bated breath to see if one of these men was Martin Morton. Jimmy had no idea how to find out unless he walked up to the man and asked him. But that wasn't really how you were supposed to handle things like this. He couldn't really just go up to the man and ask if he was his father.

Both the men who had exited the club were now in conversation. Jimmy stared hard at them, convinced one of them must be his father. They were of similar height and similar hair colour, although the man on the left looked more like a film star. The man on the right looked older and a little more haggard. He had a dimple in the middle of his chin, and Jimmy's fingers travelled up to his own chin, touching the small dimple he had in exactly the same place.

They were far enough away that he couldn't hear the conversation clearly, but Jimmy didn't dare creep any closer.

The girl with them was obviously bored. She kicked at a stray stone on the pavement and yawned. "Come on, Dad. The shops will be shut soon, and you promised to buy me that dress."

The man with the dimple in his chin turned to face his daughter and muttered something Jimmy couldn't quite hear. He then turned back to the man standing next to him, and they shook hands as if they were saying goodbye.

As they began to walk away from each other, the man with the film-star good looks turned back and said, "Oh, Martin, I forgot to tell you, Mum's on the warpath."

Jimmy felt like his heart had stopped beating. That was Martin Morton.

As Martin turned back to look at the other man, Jimmy got a good look at him. He hadn't really expected his father to look like that. In his mind, his father had looked like a handsome movie star, more like the other man Martin had been talking to.

He chewed on a fingernail as Georgie anxiously tugged on his sleeve. "Was that him?"

"I think so," Jimmy said, staring after them. If that had been Martin Morton, then was the girl with him, Jimmy's sister? He could have a whole family, relatives he didn't even know existed.

He'd promised his nan he would stay away from Martin Morton, but the idea of having a ready-made family with brothers and sisters was incredibly tempting for Jimmy, who had only ever really had his nan.

"What are you going to do? Are you going to speak to him?"

Jimmy shook his head. "Maybe, but not tonight. I'd better get home, or Linda will start to worry."

Jimmy wasn't very good company as the two boys walked back together. He couldn't get the thought of his father out of his head. He did trust his nan and knew that she only had his best interests at heart, but it had been a long time since she'd seen Martin Morton.

Perhaps he was a better man now. Maybe when he realised Jimmy was his son, he would welcome them both into his family with open arms.

39

BABS MORTON WAS ON HER way to the Pattersons' boxing club, and she was bubbling with excitement. The shipment had come in last night, and Babs couldn't wait to take a gander. Of course, it didn't really matter what the goods were because the Mortons would get their cut regardless.

Martin had been on at her to let him come along, but Babs had put him well and truly in his place. Tony had tried to smooth things over between them, but Babs was having none of it.

She was proud of the way she had handled both brothers, but if she was honest, she was very surprised that Martin had backed down so easily. That wasn't like him at all. It was probably because he was still adjusting to life on the outside, and Babs was more than happy to take advantage of that.

She turned up the collar of her fur coat. She looked the business today and was dolled up to the nines. She wanted to look the part when she met Gerald Patterson and inspected the goods.

She turned into Victoria Street and smiled to herself. Things were really starting to work out. She was feeling a lot more positive this morning. Last night, she'd had trouble sleeping. The idea that now Martin was out, it would be much easier for him to find out the role she had played in his incarceration. But as Dave Carter hadn't yet said anything to him, Babs thought surely she must be in the clear by now. It had been years since she'd spilled Martin's secrets to Dave. She wished she could put it behind her and hated the thought of anyone holding anything over her, especially Dave Carter.

She pushed through the double doors and entered Patterson's boxing club. As usual, the place smelled of sweaty old socks, and she could hear the sound of men sparring in the gym. She walked through the second set of double doors and stood there imperiously, waiting for someone to notice her.

Old Knuckles Bancroft was the first to spot her. He called out for Gerald, and as Babs waited, all the men in the gym turned to look at her. She didn't mind that, at all. It made her feel important.

She tapped her foot impatiently against the hard floor of the gym, waiting for Gerald. Luckily, she didn't have to wait long.

He rushed out of the small office at the back and walked briskly towards Babs with his hand outstretched.

"Mrs. Morton, I see you got my message."

Babs inclined her head, regally. "Call me Babs," she reminded him.

Gerald nodded. "Would you like to see the goods?"

Babs nodded impatiently. "That is why I am here. I didn't turn up to watch a bleeding boxing match, did I?"

There were a few muffled giggles from the men, who had paused in their workouts to watch the exchange between Babs and Gerald.

Gerald turned and glared over his shoulder, and the men soon got back to work.

"If you would like to follow me, Babs. We're storing the stuff upstairs."

Babs followed Gerald to the back of the gym and out through the door that led to a rickety old wooden staircase. The walls were scuffed and dirty, and Babs thought the whole place could do with a lick of paint.

At the top of the stairs, Gerald opened the door and gestured for Babs to enter the room first. She did so and stepped into a surprisingly bright, large space.

The floor was covered with wooden crates of varying sizes, all marked with lettering and codes. Probably something to do with the shipping, Babs thought, as she moved closer. The printed codes were funny symbols she didn't recognise. Babs couldn't help feeling slightly disappointed. There were probably only twenty boxes in total, and she had been expecting something a little more impressive.

She turned to Gerald, who was watching her closely.

"Are you going to show me what's inside, then?" Babs asked.

Gerald nodded and approached one of the crates that was already open. A crowbar lay on the floor beside it.

Babs walked closer so she could peer inside as Gerald lifted the lid. Inside the crate, packed in what looked like straw, was a blue and white vase. To Babs, it looked like a cheap bit of china. Feeling disappointed, she picked it up to study it and found that it was surprisingly heavy.

Gerald was studying her so closely that Babs was starting to feel a little self-conscious. She wasn't an antiques expert and didn't have a bleeding clue what a vase like this could be worth. Although her instincts told her its resale value wouldn't be very high. She had seen better quality stuff down the market. She put the vase back in the crate.

She was glad Martin hadn't come. He would be laughing his head off right now if he'd been here and would love to enjoy Babs' disappointment. All that fuss and the stand-off between the Mortons and the Carters over a few cheap vases, Babs thought. It was hardly worth it.

"Are they all the same?" Babs asked looking at the other crates. She thought maybe one of the others held something of more value.

Gerald nodded, and Babs' shoulders slumped. Well, that was that then. She'd have to report back to Martin and Tony and endure the humiliation.

"Fine. I'll expect payment of our cut when you manage to sell them. God knows who will be stupid enough to buy that tat, though."

Gerald started to laugh.

Babs looked up at him sharply. How dare he laugh at her? If there was some sort of joke going on, Babs didn't see it. It was almost as though he was amused by her disappointment, and Babs didn't appreciate that, at all.

"What the bleeding hell are you laughing at?" she demanded.

"You have no idea, do you? You pressured me into doing a deal with you instead of Dave Carter, and you didn't even know what we were importing."

Babs scowled. She knew what Henry had reported back to her — that he had overheard the Pattersons were fencing stolen goods. No one had said anything else. Babs stared back down at the crates and wondered whether these were some kind of Ming vases from some Chinese dynasty or something.

Babs nodded at the vase. "Is it valuable then?"

Her question just made Gerald laugh even harder, and she clenched her teeth together, only just holding back from slapping the cheeky sod around the face.

"I'm not finding this amusing, Gerald. And if you don't stop laughing, I'm going to smash that bloody vase right over your head."

Gerald struggled to regain his composure as he picked up the vase, and then to Babs' surprise, he smashed it down hard on the floor.

"What are you playing at?" Babs asked in disbelief, but as she looked down at the broken vase on the floor, she saw a carefully wrapped packet that had obviously been hidden in the vase.

She stared at it for a moment and then raised her head to look at Gerald. "What is that?" she asked although she already knew the answer. Drugs. It had to be.

Gerald's eyes shone with excitement. "It's opium, Babs." He gestured around at the other crates. "A lot of opium."

Babs looked around at the crates, feeling a mixture of excitement and trepidation. The Mortons had never been involved in drugs before. Sure, they handled black market booze and cigarettes, but drugs were a whole different story. It was a risky venture, but the rewards could be huge, and if they let Gerald take all the risks while they just took their cut as a silent partner, Babs couldn't really see the harm in it.

She licked her lips and looked at him eagerly. "How much is it worth?"

Gerald grinned. "Now, you are talking my language, Babs."

Before Gerald and Babs could have a conversation about how much money they would get from the sale of the drugs, there were shouts and a commotion downstairs. Gerald strolled across the large room towards the doorway at the top of the stairs.

Babs didn't pay too much attention. She was too busy calculating all the things she could buy when they got their cut. She was inspecting the crates when she heard the sound of footsteps on the stairs. She turned, and to her surprise, she saw a young Chinese man appear in the doorway.

Before Babs could ask Gerald who he was, the Chinese man produced a knife and plunged it into Gerald's stomach. Babs watched in horror as Gerald staggered backwards.

When the Chinese man's eyes focused on her, Babs let out a scream.

Then all hell broke loose as the place seemed to be overrun with more Chinese men. In the confusion, Gerald had fallen to the floor. The scarlet stain of his blood was slowly spreading across his white shirt. Babs rushed over to him and gripped his hand as he stared up at her, looking terrified.

The Chinese men seemed far more interested in the crates than they did in Babs, so she leaned down and whispered to Gerald, "I'll get help."

She made a dash for the stairs, and nobody tried to stop her. She moved so fast she nearly tripped twice, and she cursed the fact she'd worn her big fur coat. It was bulky and slowed her down.

She reached the bottom of the stairs and burst into the gym, intending to get out via the main entrance. She knew there was a public phone box just around the corner.

But before Babs could exit the gym, somebody grabbed her by the hair.

Babs screamed bloody blue murder and struggled until she saw the glint of a steel blade.

She froze and saw that the person holding her captive was a young, stunningly beautiful, Chinese woman. Babs wailed in terror. She couldn't understand a word they were saying, and she panicked.

"I don't know who you are. But you're making a mistake," she screamed.

The beautiful Chinese woman said, "Well, I know exactly who you are, Babs Morton, and you are the one who has made the mistake."

40

TONY MORTON BURST INTO THE flat above the Mortons' club. Gossip spread like wildfire around the East End, and Tony had just been told that it was all kicking off at Patterson's boxing club. He didn't have the full story yet, but he thought he'd better come straight to Martin.

"There's something going down at the boxing club, bruv," Tony said, breathless from running.

Martin was sitting on the settee, reading the paper with a cup of tea on the coffee table in front of him. "Really?"

Martin didn't seem worried, at all, and Tony thought he might have forgotten that Babs had gone there just an hour ago. He frowned. Perhaps the meeting had been called off, and nobody had told him. Maybe Babs was safe at home.

"Wasn't Babs supposed to be there? I legged it round here because I thought she might be in trouble."

Martin straightened the crease in his newspaper and appeared unaffected. "Yes, she did say she would be there this morning."

Tony shook his head. He couldn't understand why Martin wasn't more worried.

"Aren't you going to come and see if she needs our help?"

Martin lowered his paper and gave his brother a steely gaze. "Why would I do that?"

"Because she is your wife and she might be in danger,"

Tony said, starting to lose his temper.

Martin shrugged and picked up his cup of tea. "She wanted to handle it herself. Babs made that perfectly clear, and I intend to respect her wishes."

"This isn't a game, Martin. Babs could be in serious trouble."

Martin smirked. "I wouldn't dream of interfering. Babs has told me again and again how capable she is. I'm sure she can handle this on her own."

Martin raised his newspaper again, and Tony leaned forward to snatch it out of his hands. "Are you really that cold-hearted?"

Martin's eyes were full of rage as he stood up and glared at his brother. "If you're so worried about her, why don't you go and help, eh?"

Tony looked at his brother with disgust and then whirled around. "Fine. I'll go, and I'll make sure she knows you couldn't be bothered."

***

Babs whimpered with fear. That horrible bitch still held her by the hair, and Babs didn't dare try and escape, thanks to the knife pointed to her throat. Images of Old Mo having his throat cut kept flashing through Babs' mind. She hadn't prayed for years but now muttered the Lord's Prayer.

She wasn't ready to go yet, not like this. One reassuring thought in a tide of terror floated into her mind — if she were to die, she would be reunited with Emily and her mother and father. But with all the bad things Babs had done over the years, she'd be more likely to go to hell than heaven.

She squeezed her eyes tightly closed and willed herself not to cry.

She thought about poor Ruby and Derek. She hadn't done well by either of them, but she loved them to distraction. She swore to herself if she got out of this alive, she would be a better mother. After Emily had died, she had first neglected them and then gone overboard with affection, spoiling them. No wonder the poor kids had turned out like they had. It was all Babs' fault. She had messed everything up.

Babs had never been a quitter, though. She wasn't dead yet, and although she didn't have any weapons or anything with which to fight back, she could still use her wits.

"I don't have anything to do with this, so you had better let me go," Babs insisted.

The young Chinese woman smiled. "Mr. Carter is a very good friend of ours. He told us somebody was cheating us and told us where to find you."

Those words were like a punch in the gut to Babs. Dave Carter? That didn't make any sense. Dave Carter had wanted a cut of the Patterson's business, and it had taken Babs' skill in the art of persuasion to convince Gerald to work with the Mortons instead. Was this sour grapes? Had Dave punished them by telling this Chinese gang they were pushing drugs on their patch?

Or had it all been a ruse? Had he only tricked them into thinking he was interested in the Patterson's business?

Oh, Babs hated Dave Carter! Why had he done this to her? Surely it was Martin he really wanted to hurt? But then, maybe Dave had thought Martin would muscle in and take over when he got out.

Babs wished Martin was here, or Tony. Why had she come alone? She could have brought Freddie or Henry along and at least had some protection.

She twisted in the other woman's grip and through gritted teeth, said, "I'm warning you. I'm married to Martin Morton, and when he hears about this, he will be out for your blood."

To Babs' irritation, the woman simply smiled. "I'm sure Mr. Carter can handle Martin Morton."

***

Just when Babs began to accept it was all over, she heard the sound of sirens in the distance.

"You'd better get out of here," she warned. "That's the coppers."

Babs tried to come up with a plan quickly. She'd need a good story to tell the police when they turned up. Babs smiled. The best plan of action was to set the blame at somebody else's door. She planned to tell the police the drugs belong to the Chinese.

The young Chinese woman looked distracted and barked out orders to the men who had been carrying the crates down the stairs. Suddenly, it was pandemonium. The young Chinese woman released Babs with a shove and everyone tried to run to the exit.

Idiots, thought Babs. That was exactly where the police would be. Going that way, they would run straight into them.

Babs knew her best chance of escape was slipping out the back alleyway, so she rushed across to the changing rooms. There was no sign of any of the boxers. They had obviously done a runner at the first sign of trouble. Typical men, Babs thought.

At the back of the gym, Babs saw what she had been hoping to find— a small window. She climbed on top of the bench, which was scattered with discarded boxing gloves and men's shorts.

Luckily the window opened easily. Unfortunately, Babs wasn't as young as she once was and didn't have much strength in her upper arms. Four times she tried to leap up to the window, her feet scrabbling against the wall, only to collapse back down into a heap on the bench.

Sodding hell, thought Babs. Where was a ladder when you needed one?

With one last burst of strength, Babs jumped, gripping onto the windowsill and heaving herself up.

Holding on tightly to the window frame, she tried to manoeuvre her body carefully, swinging one leg over the window sill until she was sitting akimbo.

Nearly there, she thought with a grin.

She slid her other leg over, intending to slip down into the alleyway.

Sadly for Babs, her descent wasn't quite as graceful as she had planned. Her skirt caught on the window latch, and there was a loud ripping sound as Babs tumbled to the ground, leaving most of her skirt attached to the window.

But there was no time to worry about that now. Babs scrambled up onto her hands and knees, but before she could make her getaway, a deep voice behind her said, "Mrs. Morton, are you aware that your knickers are on show?"

Shocked and mortified, Babs turned around to give the pervert a piece of her mind. But before she did so, she realised the man standing next to her was Inspector Peel.

Of all the bleeding coppers in London, it had to be him.

Babs got to her feet and put her hands on her hips. "Had a good look, have you? You dirty old man."

She would have loved to smack the smirk off Inspector Peel's face, but instead she was manhandled along the alleyway and led back to the spot in front of the boxing club, where all the other policemen were handling the suspects they'd rounded up.

Babs could have died of humiliation. A crowd had already gathered on the opposite side of the street, and people were laughing at the fact she was standing there in her undergarments.

Finally, one of the young policemen handed Babs his jacket, and she quickly wrapped it around herself gratefully.

"You haven't got any right to hold me here," Babs shouted out at Inspector Peel. "I haven't done anything wrong. I just happened to be passing."

"Do you often go for a walk half naked, Mrs. Morton?" Inspector Peel enquired loudly, and there was laughter from the nosy parkers gathered on the other side of the street.

Babs scowled. "My skirt was ripped. It could have

happened to anyone."

But none of the policemen paid her any further attention until one of the officers escorted her to a police car.

***

Tony Morton drove like a maniac to get to Patterson's boxing club. It was only a few streets away, but he had to get there as fast as possible. What he had heard about the altercation at the club had made his blood run cold.

He couldn't believe Martin just didn't care. He had always been a cold bastard, but this defied belief. Babs could be difficult and bloody-minded, but she was still his wife and the mother of his children.

As Tony approached the boxing club, he realised he was too late. The police had beaten him to it. He didn't dare drive down the street and instead parked up just on the corner. Although he wanted to help Babs, there was no point in getting himself involved.

He quickly spotted Babs as she was being escorted to a police car. She was mouthing off and generally making life difficult for the officers, but the thing that really caught Tony's eye was the fact that Babs wasn't wearing anything other than her knickers on her lower half. He blinked in shock. What the bloody hell had gone on?

He held back, watching, even after the car containing Babs had driven away. Someone was taken out of the building on a stretcher, but Tony wasn't close enough to see who that was. The rest of the people being rounded up by the police were Chinese. He thought he might recognise a couple of them as belonging to the Fang family from Ming Street, but he couldn't say for sure.

After the last police car left, Tony approached the group of gossips on the opposite side of the road, who had been watching the show and enjoying the entertainment.

"What happened?" Tony asked addressing them all.

The smirks and whispers quickly died down when they

saw it was Tony Morton standing beside them.

Most of the men and women kept their heads down and rushed off, but big Martha, who liked to think of herself as a woman who spoke her mind, remained behind.

"They arrested your sister-in-law."

"I saw that. Do you know why?"

"Drugs," big Martha said bluntly, folding her arms under her ample bosom.

Tony shook his head. Drugs? Since when had the Mortons had anything to do with drugs?

"Are you sure?"

"I heard one of the police officers talking about it."

"Why wasn't Babs wearing a skirt?"

Big Martha broke out into a huge grin. "She ripped it, trying to escape."

Tony chatted to big Martha for a little longer, trying to find out as much as he could about what had gone down at the boxing club. He probably stayed longer than he needed to, but he was dreading what he had to do next.

He had to go back to the club and tell his brother that Babs had been arrested.

41

TONY WASN'T SURE HOW HE expected Martin to react when he gave him the news that Babs had been arrested, but he certainly hadn't expected him to laugh.

They were sitting down in the living area of the flat above the club. Ruby was downstairs, talking to Frieda Longbottom, who was cleaning the club.

It wasn't just a chuckle, either. It was a full on belly laugh, and as Martin wiped the tears from his eyes, Tony asked, "What the bloody hell is wrong with you? Has prison softened your head?"

Martin's laughter disappeared. "There's nothing soft about me."

"What are we going to do, Martin? She's been arrested, and they were talking about drugs."

"Drugs are a mug's game," Martin said with a sly smile.

Tony shook his head in exasperation. He just couldn't make his brother see sense. How was he supposed to drive the information through his thick skull?

"This is serious. She could go to prison."

Martin shrugged. "It serves the stupid cow right. She wanted to get involved, well now she is. I'm pleased the Old Bill are going to take the daft mare off my hands for a bit. They are doing me a favour."

Tony ran his hands through his hair. He and Babs had

certainly had run-ins during the time Martin was inside. But she didn't deserve this. At the end of the day, she was family.

"You can't just leave her to rot, Martin. She's done a lot for you. She stood by you while you were inside."

Martin snorted and looked unimpressed. "Don't think that was down to loyalty, bruv. She just knew which side her bread was buttered. Babs has only ever been interested in money. Clearly she got greedy, and that's why she went after the drugs."

Tony shook his head. He couldn't believe that. Surely even Babs wouldn't have taken a decision like that without informing him or Martin.

"I don't know, Martin. There's something fishy about the whole thing."

"You're reading too much into it. They'll probably just give her a slap on the wrist anyway."

"Tell me you are at least going to sort her out a brief."

"No, Tony. She wanted to do this alone so she can find out what alone really means."

Both men turned as Ruby entered the flat. She'd obviously overheard a little of their conversation.

"What's happened, Dad?" she asked as she walked towards them.

Martin got to his feet and stretched. "Nothing, sweetheart. It was just a bit of business. Now, are you ready to go to visit Grandma Violet?"

Tony couldn't believe it. Surely Martin wasn't going to try and hide something like this from his own daughter.

"So you are just going to leave her there?"

Martin gave him a scowl, warning him to shut up.

"Who?" Ruby asked.

"Nothing," Martin snapped. "Go and wait outside. I'll be there in a minute."

42

RUBY'S CHEEKS BURNED IN HUMILIATION as she left the room. Clearly, her father still considered her a child and didn't want to discuss matters in front of her. She was slowly coming to realise her father wasn't all she'd believed him to be. It was easy to look up to somebody and idolise them when you hardly ever saw them, but listening to how he talked to Ruby's mother and Grandma Violet, had opened Ruby's eyes. She still thought he was clever, and she was proud of him, but Ruby realised he wasn't the infallible man she had once thought.

Uncle Tony was really upset about something, and Ruby wanted to know what it was. She walked down the stairs and thought about eavesdropping at the bottom, but then she heard her father's voice, ordering her to wait outside.

Ruby huffed out a breath and stomped outside the club.

She thought about pressing her ear to the door, but that was pointless. There was no way she would hear anything from outside.

She leaned back on the wall beside the club and clutched her cardigan around her tightly. There was a chill in the air, and she wished she had brought her coat. Of course, her father didn't care that she was out there freezing to bits while he was toasty and warm in the flat.

Ruby gazed up at the grey clouds overhead and hoped it

wouldn't start to rain. If it did, she decided she would go back inside the club whether he liked it or not. If he wanted a private conversation why didn't he go outside?

She was supposed to be going to visit Grandma Violet with her father, but she wasn't looking forward to that much. They had seen less and less of Ruby's grandmother over the years because Ruby's mother really didn't get along with her. If it wasn't for Uncle Tony, they would have hardly ever seen Grandma Violet.

Not that Grandma Violet ever looked particularly happy to see Ruby or Derek when they turned up. She was a prickly so and so, and she made Ruby feel like she was a disappointment to her.

After everything that had happened recently, especially their father getting out of prison, Ruby couldn't believe that Derek hadn't come home. He'd spent the whole summer with friends and then had gone straight back to that horrible school. Ruby couldn't understand it. She had hated being away from the East End, but Derek seemed to have taken to the posh life like a duck to water. He hadn't even wanted to rush home to see their father.

When their mother had telephoned him, Derek had promised to return at half-term, which was still weeks away.

Ruby folded her arms and shifted position, so now she had her hip resting against the wall. She suppressed a shiver and sighed. She hoped whatever they were talking about up there wouldn't take much longer.

Lost in her thoughts, she didn't even notice the young boy approaching her until he spoke, "Excuse me, is Mr. Morton in there?"

Ruby turned around to see a young, dark-haired boy with a slight dimple in his chin. She narrowed her eyes and wondered why a young lad would want to talk to her father.

Ruby frowned. "Yes. What did you want to see him about?"

The lad looked down the street as if he was considering

running off.

"It's private," he eventually replied.

Ruby didn't bother to hide her scorn. What on earth could a little pipsqueak like that have to talk to her father about? "You can tell me," Ruby said. "He's my dad."

The boy nodded. "I know." He hesitated for a moment and then he added, "I'm Jimmy, Jimmy Diamond."

Ruby tensed and looked at Jimmy again, this time paying more attention. She had heard gossip while she was growing up. She remembered being tormented by a group of nasty children at school, who'd teased her and said her father had fathered a bastard.

Ruby had gone home in tears and asked her mother about it. Her mum had sat her down and told her it was a load of old bollocks. Her mother had always had a way with words. She reassured Ruby that it was just nasty gossip spread by people who were jealous of the Mortons' success. She said Ruby should just ignore the rumours and tell the children at her school it wasn't true.

Although children could be cruel, they also had short memories, because after those first couple of years at school, everyone seemed to forget about the matter, and nobody gossiped about the Morton bastard anymore.

"I think I might be your brother," Jimmy said, chewing on his lower lip nervously.

Ruby wasn't angry. The poor lad had probably just heard the same gossip she had. She actually felt sorry for him.

"You're not my brother," Ruby said kindly. "I don't know who told you that, but it isn't true."

Jimmy's face fell, and he looked down at the ground in disappointment as he shook his head.

"My nan told me, and she wouldn't lie."

Ruby shrugged. "Maybe that's because she heard the gossip, but it's not true, Jimmy."

Ruby turned her head when she heard raised voices in the

club. Uncle Tony and her father were obviously getting into quite a heated row.

"Look," Ruby said. "You seem like a nice boy, and I'm not saying this to be mean, but I heard some rumours years ago as well. I asked my mum about it, and she told me it was just silly gossip."

Jimmy looked disappointed at first, and then he tilted his chin in an obstinate fashion. "I still need to talk to him."

Ruby shook her head. She couldn't even imagine what her father's reaction would be today. He wasn't normally an easy man to talk to, and he barely had enough time for his own children, let alone some silly boy who'd been listening to gossip. And today he was going to be even worse than usual after his argument with Uncle Tony.

"I wouldn't do it if I were you," Ruby said.

But Jimmy's face took on an even more determined expression, and Ruby realised she was fighting a losing battle.

"Suit yourself, but don't say I didn't warn you."

Suddenly, a loud bang sounded from inside the club, and then her father and Uncle Tony exploded out of the swing doors, tumbling onto the street.

Her father had a cut lip, and blood was trickling down his chin.

"You're a heartless bastard, Martin!" Uncle Tony said furiously, pointing in her father's direction.

Ruby had never seen her uncle look so furious in all the years she'd known him. She gawped at the blood on her father's face. Had Uncle Tony hit him?

"Get out of my sight," her father roared, wiping the blood away with the back of his hand.

Ruby stared at the pair of them in disbelief. What on earth had they argued about?

Ruby noticed that Jimmy was trying to get her father's attention by tugging on his sleeve. She winced. Did the kid have no sense of danger?

Her father shook him off and began to walk away.

"I'm Jimmy," he called after Ruby's father.

Her father turned around and snarled, "So what?"

Jimmy looked vulnerable and scared, and Ruby really felt for him. She wanted to stop him and clamp her hand over his mouth to make him shut up because she knew he was only going to get hurt.

"I think you're my father," Jimmy said in a small voice.

Ruby's father paused, and his eyes scanned Jimmy's face. "You're a Diamond, aren't you?"

The relief was clear on Jimmy's face, and a smile tugged up the corners of his mouth. "Yes, that's right. My mother –" Jimmy began to say, but her father interrupted him.

"Your mother was a whore, who would open her legs to anyone. You ain't my son."

Her father turned on his heel and began to stalk up the street. "Ruby, get a sodding move on, girl!"

Ruby turned to rush after her father, but at the last moment, she sent an apologetic glance at Jimmy.

The poor kid didn't say anything. He just stood there, watching them walk away.

Ruby hadn't expected it to go well, but her father's reaction had been even worse than she'd anticipated.

She glanced back at Jimmy and couldn't help feeling sorry for the poor boy.

43

GARY CARTER CROSSED THE YARD and headed to the workshop. He had to update Dave on the latest news after the arrests at the Patterson's boxing club, and he wasn't looking forward to it.

When it had all kicked off, Gary hadn't been expecting it. If he had known he would have to have a meeting with his brother, he wouldn't have touched the coke. He'd only had a little sniff, just enough to get going, but Dave had some kind of obsession with Gary's use of drugs, and he was like a bloody bloodhound. It wasn't as if Gary was really an addict. He just did a little coke now and again to keep him alert.

His brother didn't understand that, though, and the last thing Gary needed was Dave threatening to cut him off again. He ran a hand over his face and tried to focus. He needed to keep calm and speak evenly so Dave wouldn't suspect he'd taken anything.

He should be all right. It had been over an hour since Gary had taken it, and the effects were already wearing off. They didn't seem to last very long these days at all, and he seemed to need more and more to have the same effect. Gary suspected the quality of the drugs must have gone downhill. He didn't even want to consider the fact that he could be building up a tolerance to the drug.

He'd managed to kick it for a little while, but it was so hard to stay away permanently.

Inside the workshop, the usual suspects were there along with Dave. Little Georgie was filling up the bucket ready to start washing the cars, and Gary noticed his usual sidekick, Jimmy Diamond, was missing.

Dave looked up sharply as Gary entered the workshop.

"What's the latest?" he asked.

Everyone in the garage turned to look at Gary. They had all heard the news about the drugs bust down at the docks, and they knew the Mortons were involved.

They also knew that Dave had somehow been behind it.

The trouble was, Dave wasn't going to be happy when he heard Martin had managed to escape scot-free, and unfortunately for Gary, he was the one who had to deliver the bad news.

"The police arrested Babs."

Dave cursed and sat down heavily on a metal stool, set back by one of the workbenches. "And Martin?"

Gary shook his head. "He's going about business as usual. He wasn't there apparently. It was just Babs on her own."

Dave shook his head. "Why would she have gone alone?" He clenched his teeth in frustration.

"Gerald is in hospital. He was stabbed, but luckily for him, it wasn't a life-threatening wound," Gary added.

Charlie stood close by but said nothing, and Brian returned to work on one of the motors. Big Tim loomed behind them as he watched the exchange between Dave and his brother.

"I don't understand why the police were involved, though, bruv," Gary said. "I mean you wouldn't have tipped them off would you?"

Dave looked up sharply. "What do you take me for? A grass? Of course, I didn't. I just let the Fang family know that the Pattersons were their new competitors. I figured the Fangs would come down on Martin Morton like a ton of bricks." Dave shook his head. "I was so sure he was going to be there. I can't believe he let Babs go on her own."

"Well, at least you got one Morton out of the way, I suppose," Gary said with a chuckle, trying to make light of it. "That's better than nothing."

Dave stood up and walked away, too angry to even talk to his brother any longer.

Gary shrugged and looked at Charlie. "It's not my fault. I'm just delivering the news."

Charlie nodded and then said quietly, "I think he had a bit of a soft spot for Babs. He'd been planning this for a while to coincide with Martin's release so he won't be happy."

"Well, I didn't expect him to hang out the bunting, but he doesn't have to take it out on me," Gary said moodily.

Charlie Williams narrowed his eyes and looked at Gary. "Are you all right? You seem a little on edge?"

Gary scowled. Charlie Williams still held a grudge against him after all these years. It hadn't really been Gary's fault, but Charlie had laid the blame on his door just because he'd taken a small amount of coke before doing a job, and Charlie had managed to get himself shot and then arrested.

Gary turned away from Charlie, feeling quite unwelcome. He wandered over to see where Big Tim was talking to young Georgie. Tim was asking Georgie where Jimmy had got to.

Gary was hardly listening. It didn't sound very interesting. He was considering knocking off work for the day and heading to the pub, after all, it didn't seem like any of them would miss him. His presence was obviously not required. But then he heard Tim say something that piqued his interest.

"What did you just say?" Gary asked loudly, attracting the attention of everybody in the workshop.

Little Georgie blinked up at his uncle. He didn't like it when people raised their voices. "Jimmy's father is Martin Morton. He just found out."

Gary did a double take and then turned around to look at Charlie, who was standing close to his shoulder. "Did you know about this?"

Charlie cocked his head to one side. "I suspected. I remember hearing gossip at the time. Surely you heard people talking about it, too. I was the one who got locked away, not you."

Gary scowled. Trust Charlie to bring that up again.

"Are you ever going to let sleeping dogs lie?" Gary asked.

Before they could continue their squabble further, Dave walked over and crouched down beside his son. "Is Jimmy all right?"

Little Georgie nodded. "I think so."

"Well, we can't have him hanging around here anymore, can we?" Gary said. "He's going to have divided loyalties that's for sure."

"I'll have a word with him," Dave said.

"What?" Gary now knew that Dave really had gone off his rocker. They couldn't have a little bastard like Jimmy Diamond hanging around, not now they knew that his father was their biggest rival.

But Dave turned away from him and looked over at the man who had just walked into the workshop. Knuckles Bancroft.

The grey-haired ex-boxer shuffled up to them, and Dave patted him on the shoulder and then took him off to the office, no doubt for payment.

Gary guessed that answered one question. Knuckles Bancroft must've been the snitch providing Dave with information about Patterson's business.

Brian was still at work on the motor, and Charlie had gone to help him. Tim was helping Georgie wash the motors, and Dave was dealing with Knuckles Bancroft.

Everybody had a job to do apart from Gary. He shrugged. He knew when he wasn't wanted. He shoved his hands in his pockets and strolled out of the workshop, heading for the pub.

***

Jimmy Diamond was absolutely devastated, and he turned to the only person he had always been able to rely on: his nan.

Visiting hours at the hospital were long over, but Jimmy didn't care. He snuck past the nursing station, creeping past a nurse, who was chatting with a porter in the corridor outside the ward.

The lights on the ward had already been dimmed for the night, and the blinds had been drawn.

The only sounds were the slight muffled snores and groans of the patients. Jimmy snuck past them all and headed to his nan's bed at the end of the ward.

She had her eyes closed. She wasn't lying flat but was propped up on her pillows.

There was a chair by the bed, and Jimmy kneeled on it and leaned over to grab hold of his nan's hand. He knew he shouldn't be bothering her because she was ill, but he felt so alone and hurt he needed her to put her arms around him and tell him everything was going to be okay.

***

Mary Diamond's eyes fluttered open, and she saw her grandson beside her.

She thought she was dreaming at first. They said your life flashes before your eyes before you go, and she thought perhaps this might be her time, but as her hands brushed through his hair, she realised he wasn't a figment of her imagination.

As poor little Jimmy's body was wracked with sobs, Mary pushed herself up in bed, horrified. "What on earth has happened, Jimmy?"

At first, the boy was too distraught to talk, then the story came out in spits and spurts as he described his run-in with Martin Morton.

Mary felt like cold ice had spread across her heart as she heard the way the nasty bastard had treated her grandson.

"I told you to stay away, Jimmy. Why didn't you listen to me?"

Jimmy shook his head and tearfully said, "I'm sorry. I just wanted to know who my dad was."

"He's a nasty piece of work, Jimmy. And you are not to let him upset you. He may be your father, but you've got none of the Morton in you, my boy. You're a Diamond, through and through."

As Jimmy's sobs returned, Mary could do nothing but hold the poor boy as he cried his heart out.

***

Jimmy had never felt so miserable in his life. Of course, Martin's reaction had been like a kick in the teeth, but it wasn't only that. Deep down, Jimmy knew there was something bad about him. But he couldn't confess that to his nan or to Linda.

They both thought Jimmy was a good boy, with none of Martin Morton's traits, but they didn't know the truth.

Jimmy was just as bad as Martin Morton. He'd told a terrible lie to Dave Carter because he wanted to get Linda's husband in trouble. He knew it was his fault. Geoff hadn't committed suicide, Jimmy had gotten him killed.

It had been a decision made in haste, and Linda would despise him if she knew. He wasn't even sure if his nan would be able to forgive him for such a terrible thing.

What would Linda say if she knew Geoff hadn't jumped from that bridge? He'd been pushed, and he'd been pushed because of what Jimmy had said.

He'd been so angry at Geoff's treatment of Linda that Jimmy had wanted to get him back. He knew his lie would get Geoff into terrible trouble, and yet he hadn't cared.

Jimmy tried to wipe away his tears because he knew he was upsetting his nan.

He was evil, and he didn't want his nan to know what he was really like. He wanted to be a Diamond through and through just like she said, but deep down, Jimmy was scared he had more of Martin Morton's characteristics buried inside him.

"Now, listen to me, Jimmy," his nan said. "You must stay away from Martin Morton, do you hear me? He is dangerous."

Before Jimmy could reply, he heard a startled exclamation from the entrance to the ward, and when he turned, he saw the nurse was rushing over towards them.

"What on earth do you think you're doing, young man? Visiting hours were over ages ago." She clapped her hands together until Jimmy stood up.

"Don't be too hard on him nurse," Mary said. "He's had a bit of an upset today."

The nurse's stern features softened for a moment. "That doesn't excuse him from entering the ward at this time of night. We have visiting hours for a reason. Our patients need their rest. Now, come along, young man."

Jimmy kissed his nan goodbye and then followed the nurse sheepishly out of the ward.

He was going to have to go back to Linda's now and hope she didn't notice how guilty he felt over Geoff's death. Linda had been so kind, allowing Jimmy to stay in her house, and she had no idea what he had done. If Jimmy had anything to do with it, she would never find out.

44

LINDA SAT ON THE BED looking down at Geoff's old shirts. She'd been trying to pack up his belongings. Her mother had told her it was a bad idea, and that she wasn't ready to do it yet, but she didn't know the real truth. Linda may have been a little shocked, but she wasn't sad Geoff had gone. She was relieved. Her love for Geoff had died a long time ago. How could anyone have loved a monster like that?

Deep down, she felt the stirring of guilt and tried to ignore it. She kept trying to tell herself that she had nothing to feel guilty for. She wasn't behind Geoff's decision to commit suicide. He'd obviously been a very troubled man and had taken that out on Linda.

Linda could dwell on it and try to work out what had made Geoff the way he had been, but there wasn't any point. The best thing she could do now was move on with her life and make a fresh start.

Of course, she would have to be careful not to be seen to be moving on too quickly as that would bring more gossip to her door, and she could do without that.

Linda began to fold a pair of Geoff's old trousers when she heard the door open.

That had to be Jimmy. She'd prepared a shepherd's pie for their supper, and it would be almost ready by now. She left the rest of Geoff's clothes discarded on the bed and went downstairs.

When she saw Jimmy, she immediately knew he was upset. His eyes were red as if he'd been crying very recently.

Linda immediately thought something terrible had happened to Mary.

"What's wrong, Jimmy?"

Jimmy shook his head. "Nothing."

But Linda knew that wasn't true. The boy looked thoroughly miserable.

She wondered whether he didn't want to burden her because of Geoff's suicide. Jimmy probably thought she had enough on her plate right now.

"Come and sit down," Linda said kindly, leading him to the kitchen table. "I'll just put the carrots on, and we can have dinner together in a few minutes."

She lit the gas under the pot of carrots and then moved across to the table and sat beside Jimmy.

"I know something has happened to upset you, and I want you to tell me what it was. If you don't tell me, I'm going to be up all night worrying, and that's not very fair, is it?"

Jimmy turned his dark blue eyes on Linda, and he looked so sad, Linda wished there was something she could do to make him feel better.

After a pause, Jimmy took a deep breath and said, "I went to see my father."

Linda put a hand to her throat. She had known that nothing good would come from Mary telling Jimmy about his father. There had been plenty of gossip at the time, so Jimmy would have found out eventually, but right now, with all the turmoil going on and Martin Morton getting early release from prison, this was the worst possible time for Jimmy to learn about his father.

Jimmy's eyes filled with tears as he told Linda he had spoken to Martin, and the man had said horrible things about his mother.

For a moment, Linda was too shocked to talk. She hadn't liked Martin Morton at the time, and after everything that happened to Kathleen, she thought the world would be a much better place without Martin Morton.

She reached out and held Jimmy's hand. "You mustn't listen to him, Jimmy. He's a very nasty man. Please, promise me you will never talk to him again or even go anywhere near him."

She wanted Jimmy to understand the importance of staying away from Martin Morton, but she couldn't say too much because she didn't want to put the fear of God into the boy.

"That's what Nan said, too. But it isn't fair. He is my father, and I should make him understand."

"No, you mustn't," Linda said urgently.

Jimmy continued as though he hadn't even heard Linda's comment, "I'll make him take back those horrible things he said. I just approached him at the wrong time. He was angry because he had just had an argument with somebody."

Linda's head was spinning. She had to make the boy see sense. He could not go anywhere near Martin Morton. "No! Jimmy, it's important. You mustn't go near him."

Linda's hand was gripping his so tightly, Jimmy flinched.

"Why? Why should I have to stay away from him? He's my father."

"Because your mother was murdered, Jimmy."

Jimmy paused and released his hand from Linda's tight grip. "Do you think Martin Morton murdered my mother?" Jimmy asked, his voice barely a whisper.

Linda swallowed hard. She hadn't meant to reveal so much to Jimmy, but she had to make sure he stayed away. Perhaps when Mary got out of hospital, she could persuade her to take the boy somewhere safer. She could feel Jimmy's eyes burning into her, and she knew he would see through any lies she told him.

Linda shook her head. "I don't know that for sure, Jimmy,

but I do know he is a very dangerous man, and I could never forgive myself if something happened to you. Promise me you'll stay away."

Jimmy's expression was strangely calm as he nodded. "I'll stay away from him. Don't get upset. You don't have to worry about me."

Linda had a feeling that Jimmy had given in too easily. Was Jimmy only trying to reassure her because she was getting upset?

"So you're going to stay away from him from now on?"

Jimmy nodded. "I'm sorry for making you worry about me. I know it's the last thing you need right now."

Linda smiled, feeling relieved. She was glad she'd managed to persuade the boy to stay away. No doubt he would be curious about his father, and the fact that he'd just been released from prison had come as a major shock.

Linda felt a responsibility towards the boy and wanted to keep him safe. She decided that when Mary got out of hospital, she would do her best to persuade her to take Jimmy back to Romford.

***

On Saturday, Ruby's father was heading to his mother's house again, and she decided to join him. Although she was enjoying having her father at home, she had recently become aware of some of his habits and noticed the odd way he treated people.

Ruby was old enough now to see that her father and her grandmother had a very strained relationship. Their last visit to Grandma Violet's house had been awkward, to say the least, and they were only returning so soon because Martin had promised to pop in and give his mother some money.

Ruby thought her grandmother really only wanted her son to sit and listen to her and show her a little respect, but Ruby's father didn't seem to be able to do that. On their last visit, he had lost his temper and ended up promising her money, thinking that that would solve everything. He was nothing like Uncle Tony, who would listen to Grandma Violet waffle on for hours.

Ruby wondered if her father knew what Grandma Violet really wanted from him was time and conversation, or whether he really didn't understand.

She had noticed he seemed completely oblivious to other people's feelings and didn't care if he upset anybody.

Like that boy, Jimmy Diamond. Ruby could still picture the look on the poor boy's face as her father had laid into him. There really hadn't been any reason to be quite as cruel or callous as her father had been. The boy had just made an honest mistake. He'd listened to the gossips just as Ruby had done herself when she'd been teased in the playground as a child.

Ruby couldn't help feeling sorry for Jimmy. Although her father hadn't been around much while she'd been growing up, at least she'd had a father.

Grandma Violet was all smiles when they turned up. She allowed Ruby to kiss her heavily-powdered cheek and ushered them into her front room.

Ruby always felt like she had to be on her best behaviour when she visited her grandma, and she always made sure to be polite and ask how her grandma was feeling, sometimes listening to her grandma moan on about her bunions for half an hour out of politeness, but her father just didn't do that sort of thing. He was blunt to the point of rudeness.

When Violet launched into one of her long-winded descriptions of her ailments, Martin fished out an envelope full of cash from his jacket and set it down on the coffee table. "Stop complaining, Mum. You're giving me a headache."

The change in Grandma Violet was instantaneous. Her face pinched and screwed up into a scowl, and her eyes narrowed. She actually looked more like her son than ever when she did that.

Ruby felt a shiver of apprehension. She had a feeling things were not going to end well today.

"Well, that's charming, that is. What a way to talk to your poor old mother! I've stuck by you through thick and thin, and when I tell you about my struggles, you act like I'm boring you. You ungrateful little sod."

Martin turned his cool gaze on his mother. "I'm busy, Mum. I've got a lot on today. We only popped round to give you a few quid."

That seemed to irritate Grandma Violet even more. She looked scandalised as she glared angrily down at the envelope on the table.

"It takes more than handouts to be a proper son, my boy. You could take a leaf out of your brother's book."

Ruby held her breath. It was really going to kick off now. Tony had always been his mother's favourite.

Martin stood up. "You always take Tony's side. But I don't see him handing you an envelope full of cash."

Her grandmother was really losing her temper now. Her mouth puckered up, and her cheeks flushed scarlet as she slapped her hand on the arm of the armchair.

"Get out! Get out! And take your blood money with you. I don't want it."

Ruby stood up and made a half-hearted attempt to smooth things over. "You don't mean that, Grandma. Dad wanted to come to see you. But he's very busy at the moment."

Ruby soon wished she hadn't spoken when her grandmother turned her furious glare on her. "That's the problem with your father, Ruby. He's always too busy for his family. And one day it will be his downfall. Mark my words."

Her father gave a grunt of disgust and then reached down, scooping up the envelope full of money. "You'd better stop harping on, or I'll cut you off without any money."

Violet reached down and picked up her teacup and then flung it at her son's head. "Get out!"

Her father ducked just in time as the cup smashed against the wall. Ruby could see there wasn't much chance of her smoothing things over when feelings were running so high, so she bolted for the front door. Her father followed with a swagger.

As she opened the door, she turned to her father and asked, "You're not really going to cut her off, are you, Dad?"

"She's a crazy old bat," Martin muttered. "I'll cut her off until she learns to talk to me with a bit of respect."

As they walked back to the club, Ruby gently tried to suggest how her father could smooth things over with Grandma Violet, but he didn't want to hear it.

"I'm not going crawling back to her, love. If she wants my money, then she'll have to apologise. I'm not putting up with her mouthing off all the time. I did enough of that before I got sent down."

No matter how hard Ruby tried to make him see sense, her father remained obstinately blind to the fact his mother wanted more attention from her son, not his money.

Ruby sighed.

"Come here," he said, wrapping his arm around Ruby's shoulder and giving her a squeeze. "Are you still upset about your mum?"

Of course, she was. She had no idea what was going on. Her father refused to talk about it, even though he'd obviously had a huge argument over whatever had happened with Uncle Tony. They wouldn't even let her go and see her mother, and Ruby had no idea how she was.

They'd always had a difficult relationship, but Ruby loved her and hated the thought of her mother locked away. She'd only just gotten her father back, and now it looked like she was going to lose her mother to prison.

"How long do you think they will give her, Dad?"

Martin smiled and looked far too cheerful considering the fact they were talking about his wife going to prison. "She won't be sent away for long. She'll be out before you know it. I'll tell you what, why don't I treat you to lunch? Just you and me. That should cheer you up a bit."

Ruby wanted to tell him what would really cheer her up was going to visit her mother, but she didn't want to put him in a bad mood again.

Her father had forbidden her from contacting Derek and telling him what had happened to their mother. Ruby was very tempted to disobey him. She'd spoken to her father and Uncle Tony, and they both told her that Babs wasn't allowed visitors yet. Ruby supposed she'd have to trust them. She didn't really have much choice.

She had a horrible feeling her father was secretly pleased her mother was in jail. So she wasn't one hundred percent sure she should believe what he told her, but Uncle Tony was a different story. She was sure that he had her mother's best interests at heart.

"Where shall we go for lunch?" Ruby said, thinking perhaps he meant to take her up West, or somewhere equally swanky.

"There's a little Italian cafe that has opened up just off Chrisp Street," Martin said cheerfully, and Ruby's heart sank.

It wasn't quite the fancy lunch she'd been hoping for, but still, it could have been worse. He could have taken her to Joe's greasy spoon for lunch.

45

BABS MORTON WAS NOT HAPPY. When the police had shown up at Patterson's boxing club, she'd assumed she was in the clear and thanked her lucky stars she'd managed to escape with her life. She thought it was only a matter of time before she was out, plotting revenge against Dave Carter.

She'd been sure the police were just going to ask a few questions and then release her. After all, what real evidence did they have that she was involved?

She definitely thought she would be out by dinnertime, but they'd held her all night, and it was at that point that Babs had started to really panic. Luckily, Tony had come through for her and organised a brief, but unfortunately by the time the solicitor arrived, the damage had already been done.

Babs had lost her temper and possibly let a few things slip she shouldn't have, causing the police to hold her and formally request to the court that she be detained without bail.

Even up until the court hearing, Babs was convinced it was all a load of old rubbish. She assumed the police were bluffing, so Babs had confidently walked into the court. Of course, she wasn't looking her best after a night spent in a police cell, but she tried to tidy her hair and wiped the smudged eye makeup from under her eyes, smiling pleasantly at the judge.

Her lawyer spoke for her, in some kind of legal gobbledygook Babs couldn't really understand, but she kept the smile on her face, expecting that at any moment she would be released.

At the end of the hearing when the judge pronounced that she would be detained until her trial without bail, Babs' calm veneer finally cracked.

"No, that's not right!" she had screamed out, trying to grab onto her solicitor's arm. "I'm innocent!" she had screamed as they carted her off.

Now she was in a temporary holding cell again until they could transport her to the main prison population. She supposed it wasn't Tony's fault. He'd done his best. At least, he'd bothered to get her a brief. Martin hadn't been in touch at all. The bastard had left her to rot.

After everything she'd done for him, Babs thought bitterly. She'd visited him every month without fail, and now the shoe was on the other foot, he'd dropped her like a hot coal.

Babs was still in shock. Her solicitor had told her it could be months before her trial, which meant she would be in prison all that time even though she hadn't really done anything. All right, so she'd been tempted by the drugs. The potential money they could have earned from the sale of so much opium would have tempted anyone, but Babs couldn't see how she'd actually done anything wrong. Let alone how the police could prove their case against her.

She'd been told she was going to be moved to a women's prison in a couple of days, and she was absolutely dreading it. All sorts of thoughts ran through her mind, mainly worrying about Ruby and Derek and how they would cope without her. They had to be beside themselves with worry, and Babs could do nothing to reassure them when she was stuck inside.

Now Martin was out, and his horrible mother, Violet, would be trying to dig her claws into Ruby and Derek and turn them against Babs. The old woman had always hated her, and she would be over the moon that Martin was moving on with his life without his wife.

Babs sniffed and tried to hold back the tears.

By the time anyone was allowed to visit her, she would look a state. She was quite sure her dark roots were already showing. Babs took a great deal of pride in her appearance and liked to touch up her roots with peroxide every two weeks.

She doubted they would be allowed bleach in prison, so Babs would have to go back to her normal hair colour of plain brown.

She stared at the wall of the cell and wished she had something she could throw against it. She wasn't even allowed her fags in there. It was awful.

When the peephole at the top of the door opened, and she saw the eyes of one of the screws peeking inside, Babs felt overwhelmingly tempted to stick a finger through the hole and poke his eye out.

They were all condescending bastards, looking down their nose at her when they had no idea of the real story behind what had happened.

But as it turned out, Babs was quite glad she didn't poke him in the eye because the screw had come with good news.

"Morton, chop, chop, you've got a visitor."

Babs eased herself off the bed and stood up. Visitor? She'd been told she wasn't allowed any visitors apart from her legal representative until after she was put in the main prison.

There was a clanging sound as the screw unlocked the door and then pushed it open quickly, beckoning Babs towards him. He looked up and down the corridor shiftily.

"Quickly," the screw said. "Unless you don't want to see your visitor."

Intrigued, Babs scurried out of the cell and followed the man up the corridor. They turned right and then came to a small door with a window. The screw pushed open the door, and as Babs stepped inside, she was surprised to see Tony sitting there, his elbows resting on the table.

He looked up as she walked in and smiled. "Babs, thank goodness. Are you all right?"

Babs was surprised to see him, and as the screw shut the door, giving them some privacy, Babs walked up to Tony to give him a kiss on the cheek.

"You're a sight for sore eyes. Where the bleeding hell is my husband?" Babs said, her mood going from pleased to angry in an instant.

Tony shook his head. "Don't get me started, Babs. I don't understand what Martin is playing at."

"He's abandoned me, hasn't he?" She shook her head. Obviously, she had realised this before now, but as it sunk in, Babs grew more and more furious.

As she began to rant and rave, Tony put his hands up. "I know, Babs. I feel the same way. But we haven't got long. I had to pay off the officer on the front desk to get in to see you. Apparently, they are moving you to a women's prison tomorrow. Probably Holloway."

Babs fell silent. Tomorrow. She hadn't really believed it before now, but when Tony said the word prison she realised with a jolt that she could be stuck inside for some time.

"How are the kids taking it?" Babs asked.

Tony licked his lips and looked a little bit shifty. "Ruby is very upset."

"And Derek?"

"Martin thought it best he wasn't told yet."

Babs' eyes widened in disbelief. The sodding bastard.

"Don't get upset, Babs. I will tell Derek. But I thought I would wait until you were settled in Holloway. He can't see you until then anyway, so there's no point upsetting the boy."

Babs thought about what he said and then nodded slowly. She supposed he had a point, but she was willing to bet that wasn't the reason Martin hadn't told her son. Martin just wanted to hurt her.

"And your mother? I bet she is in her bleeding element, isn't she? Has she moved into the house already?"

Tony looked wounded. "She's just as upset as me, Babs. She wanted me to let you know she would look after the children, and that you shouldn't worry about them."

Babs narrowed her eyes. She wasn't fooled for a moment. She bet Violet Morton was practically dancing when she heard the news Babs had been locked up.

"You will let Frieda know what's going on, won't you, Tony? She'll be ever so worried."

Tony covered Babs' hand with his own. "Of course, I will. I've spoken to your brief, and he reckons worst-case scenario you'll get two years."

Babs felt the blood drain from her face. Two years! Two years away from her children. "I didn't even do anything, Tony. I never got the chance! They can't have anything on me."

Tony shook his head. "Apparently Gerald Patterson is saying you were in on it from the start. Someone's gotten to him. Whether it's Dave Carter or the Fangs, I don't know."

"Well, you need to find out," Babs said urgently.

Tony nodded and was trying to reassure her when the door opened, and the screw poked his head in.

"All right. That is your lot. Time to go," he said, addressing Tony.

As Tony got to his feet, Babs felt distraught. Her eyes filled with tears as Tony gave her a weak smile, kissed her cheek and left the room.

The policeman jerked his chin, indicating Babs should follow him back to her cell.

And as Babs walked along the grim, narrow corridor, two words kept repeating on a loop in her head. Two years. Two years.

How on earth was she going to make it through two years in prison?

***

As was usual for a Saturday morning, Jimmy was hanging out with his friends. But he wasn't really in the mood. Since his run in with Martin Morton, Jimmy could think of little else. He knew that Linda and his nan both wanted him to stay away from the man, and Jimmy could understand why. He'd seen it in his eyes. His father was evil, and Jimmy was absolutely terrified that he had inherited the same evil nature.

He couldn't confide in any of his friends. They just wanted to talk about football and who could jump off the highest step outside the library without getting hurt. They'd already been there that morning, and had been chased off the steps of the Lansbury library by old Mrs. Toberton.

Bobby Green and a couple of the other kids wanted to go back, but Jimmy wasn't keen. Nothing seemed like much fun anymore.

"What's the matter with you, misery guts?" Bobby Green sneered.

Jimmy shrugged. He knew he was better off if he tried to act as if nothing was bothering him, but he just couldn't do it.

Finally, the other lads left him to it, and only little Georgie remained. The little boy had become like Jimmy's shadow. Jimmy didn't mind. They spent a lot of time together washing cars at the workshop, and he actually enjoyed Georgie's company.

There was nothing nasty about the boy, what you saw was what you got. He was a nice kid, far nicer than Jimmy.

"Are you still thinking about your father?" Georgie asked.

He could be perceptive when he wanted to be. Sometimes Jimmy thought Georgie wasn't as slow as everyone believed.

Jimmy nodded his head. He couldn't think of anything else other than how much he hated Martin Morton for what he'd said about his mother. It wasn't fair. His nan and Linda had told Jimmy how much of an angel his mother had been, and he certainly didn't believe Martin Morton's dirty lies about her.

He wanted to get the man back for what he'd said.

"I hate him," Jimmy said and looked down miserably at the floor.

Georgie nodded. "I don't think he's very popular. My dad doesn't like him either."

"I think he killed my mother," Jimmy whispered in a hoarse voice.

Little Georgie's head whipped around, and for a moment, he just stared at Jimmy, speechless with shock.

"You have to tell the p…p…police," Georgie said.

Jimmy shook his head. "I can't. I don't have any proof."

"But how do you know he did it?"

"Linda was my mother's best friend, and she thinks it was him. I looked in his eyes, Georgie. He's a bad man."

Georgie considered that for a moment and then nodded in agreement. "W…What are you going to do then?"

"I can't let him get away with it. My nan doesn't want me to go near him, and Linda made me promise to stay away, but I've got an idea. I'm going to get revenge." Jimmy smiled widely as he thought things through. "Do you want to come and watch?"

Georgie nodded eagerly and followed Jimmy down the street.

They went to the workshop first of all. It was shut as they didn't have any major work on, and they didn't open on a Saturday unless they had an important job or a breakdown.

But that suited Jimmy's purpose. The large roller doors at the front were locked, but that didn't bother him. The two boys walked around the back of the workshop and made their way through the yard.

At the back, Jimmy could see that the window was still open. It had been like that for a while. The catch was broken and nobody had fixed it yet, but you couldn't tell unless you looked very closely.

Jimmy scrambled through as Georgie kept watch.

He got through the window without much trouble, and once inside, he headed towards the back of the workshop and siphoned off some petrol into a small canister. He screwed the lid on tightly and then wiped his hands on a rag.

He breathed in deeply, loving the smell of the petrol as he thought about his plan for revenge.

He climbed out again through the window, and when Georgie saw the can of petrol his lower lip wobbled.

"I'm not sure you should do this, Jimmy."

"It's all right, Georgie. I know what I'm doing. Come on, let's go to the club."

They made their way back to Mortons' club, and Jimmy felt very exposed, walking along with a canister of petrol, but nobody seemed to notice, and they stuck to the back roads and alleyways as much as they could.

Jimmy was planning to dart behind the back of the club. He knew they kept the bins there, and it would be the perfect place to break-in because nobody could see them from the back and the club wasn't overlooked.

But just as they were about to cross the road they saw Martin Morton and his daughter, Ruby, leaving the club.

Jimmy froze. That wasn't in his plan. The club was never normally open until six pm.

The two boys sat down on the pavement hiding behind a parked car as they waited for the two Mortons to leave.

When Martin Morton and his daughter were far enough up the road, Jimmy turned to Georgie and grinned. "The coast is clear. I'm going in. You stay here and keep watch."

Georgie looked absolutely petrified, but Jimmy was too excited to notice. This was the best he had felt for ages. He loved knowing he had a purpose, and he could do something to hurt the man who'd hurt him.

He was sick of being a victim. He hated his nan being ill and not being able to do anything. He'd been so frustrated when Geoff had been tormenting Linda, and then the straw that broke the camel's back had come when Martin Morton turned to him in the street and called his mother a whore.

Jimmy gritted his teeth. All those things over the past few weeks had eaten away at him, but now he felt free. He was going to show Martin Morton that he couldn't say things like that about Jimmy's mother and get away with it. He was going to prove that he was no Morton. He was a Diamond through and through.

46

RUBY WAS STARTING TO FEEL irritated. She'd asked her father yet again when she would be allowed to go and visit her mother, and he just brushed off her questions. He really believed that Ruby could be bought with lunch.

When they'd arrived back at the club after the disastrous visit with Violet earlier that morning, Martin had put the money he was planning to give his mother back into the safe. Then he'd spent the next hour making phone calls until Ruby was bored out of her mind.

She'd had all kinds of plans for when her father got out of prison. She wanted to show both her parents that she could be trusted with a responsible position within the family firm. She thought perhaps they might give her a job in the club. But Martin didn't seem to see her as a grown-up. He still saw her as a little girl and was not prepared to give her any responsibility. He wouldn't even give her a straight answer about what was going on with her mother.

When Martin had finally finished his phone calls, he walked into the front room of the flat and smiled at Ruby. "All done, Princess. Are you ready to go?"

Ruby nodded sullenly. She'd been ready to leave an hour ago.

They walked downstairs to the club, and Ruby looked about at the plush velvet red seats and the gilt mirrors hung on the wall. The bar was well-stocked, and she could imagine herself as hostess of the club, overseeing everything. She could just picture it now. All she had to do was try to convince her father.

She might have had more luck if her mother was still around but goodness knows what was going on with her. She'd overheard snatches of conversation here and there between Tony and her grandmother. They had mentioned drugs, but Ruby knew her mother would never have anything to do with something like that, so it had to be a misunderstanding.

No doubt, she would be out soon, and things would get back to normal. Or would they? Ruby wasn't sure what normal was anymore.

The situation couldn't be too serious anyway because their father hadn't bothered to summon Derek from school. Surely he would have if it had been important, or if something terrible was going to happen to their mother.

Ruby stood to one side as Martin locked up.

He seemed happier now, and Ruby hoped he stayed in a better mood for the rest of the day. Just being at the club cheered him up. He really loved the place, and Ruby could understand why.

She slipped her arm through her father's, and they walked together along Bread Street. As people turned to look, Ruby felt proud of her father. She was pleased to be the daughter of someone well known and respected in the East End. It made her feel important.

They hadn't gone far when they saw red-haired Freddie's daughter, Jemima, just up ahead.

Jemima looked as gorgeous as ever. She had curves in all the right places, and whenever Ruby saw her, she always felt a little self-conscious of her own figure. Jemima's gorgeous red hair cascaded around her heart-shaped face and when she saw the Mortons, she broke into a broad smile.

"Hello, Jemima. Do you remember my dad?" Ruby asked proudly, beaming at Martin.

Jemima blushed. "Of course," she said with a husky voice.

A look passed between her father and Jemima that made Ruby suspect they'd seen each other not that long ago.

She frowned, looking at the pair of them and wondering what was going on.

Martin took Jemima's hand and pressed it to his lips, and it was all Ruby could do not to pull a face. That was disgusting. Jemima was only a couple of years older than Ruby.

She gave a little shudder.

"Where are you two off to?" Jemima asked, smiling, oblivious to Ruby's reaction.

"We're going to the new Italian restaurant just off Chrisp Street," Martin said, and he raised his eyebrows.

Jemima and her father laughed as if they were sharing a private joke, and all at once, Ruby started to think that perhaps this wasn't the first time her father had been to this new Italian restaurant, and she probably wasn't the first woman he had taken there either.

"You're lucky. I wish somebody would take me out to lunch," Jemima said to Ruby.

Ruby glared at her. She'd always quite looked up to Jemima, and admired the way the girl looked, but today, all Ruby noticed was the fact that her cheeks had too much rouge, and her lipstick was far too bright red for daytime wear.

Ruby pursed her lips, and as she did so, she remembered she'd forgotten her lipstick. She must have left it in her father's bathroom in the flat over the club.

She pulled her arm through Martin's and said. "I need to go back to the club. I left something behind."

But to Ruby's disappointment, her father didn't offer to come back with her. Instead, he said, "You go on. I'll wait for you here. I'm sure Jemima will keep me company."

Ruby didn't bother to dignify that with an answer. She turned with a nose in the air and stalked back up the street towards the club.

She had a mother who had been arrested, and now a father who was making a fool of himself with a girl half his age. Not for the first time since she'd been back in the East End, Ruby wondered whether she would be better off back at the bloody school run by nuns.

***

It was only her second day in Holloway, and Babs sat in the visitors room waiting for Frieda to get them a cup of tea. She had been so glad to see her. If there was one person she could rely on, it was her. As much as she loved her children, Babs couldn't tell them everything. Frieda was a different story. No matter what Babs did, Frieda would always be on her side.

She could also rely on Frieda to tell her the truth. She knew that Tony didn't tell her everything because he wanted to spare her feelings, especially when it came to Martin's actions. Frieda, on the other hand, had never really liked Martin Morton and was loyal to Babs and Babs alone.

As Frieda returned with two cups of tea, she smiled broadly at Babs.

"It's not as bad as I thought it would be in here," she said. "Look, they even let you have Garibaldi biscuits with your cup of tea."

Babs smiled. She had to admit they did make an effort with the visitors' room. Apparently the new Governor was keen to improve the prison's reputation. Sadly the same couldn't be said for the cell blocks. They were awful. They were overcrowded and dirty. The inmates had to bathe in communal areas, which Babs thought looked like they could do with a bloody good scrub. And the whole place had a lingering smell of boiled cabbage.

Still, she didn't want to worry Frieda, so she merely nodded and thanked her for the tea, pulling her cup towards her.

"It's all been a terrible mistake, Frieda. I was only passing the boxing club..." Babs began and then her words died in her mouth as she caught the look on Frieda's face.

"Now, you've never lied to me before, Babs. Don't start now, sweetheart. I'm on your side. No matter what happened, and no matter what you've done."

Babs' shoulders slumped, and she looked down at the table.

"It was all Martin's fault," she said bitterly.

"Why doesn't that surprise me?" Frieda said, sarcasm dripping from her words.

"We were supposed to be getting a cut from the Pattersons. I'd spoken to Gerald Patterson about it, and he never once mentioned anything about drugs. To be honest," Babs said, lowering her voice and leaning close to Frieda. "I think Dave Carter was behind the whole thing."

Frieda frowned. "But how is that possible?"

"I think he only pretended to be interested in the Pattersons, knowing full well his interest would spark ours. He's had history with the Fangs, and they go back years, so I wouldn't be surprised if he'd tipped them off."

Frieda folded her arms and leaned heavily on the table as she shook her head. "But why the police, Babs? It doesn't make sense. Dave Carter would never have done that."

Babs nodded. She thought the same way as Frieda. People in the East End didn't grass. They kept their mouths shut when it came to the police, and they sorted out their troubles between themselves.

Babs shook her head. "All I can think was that they were keeping tabs on Gerald Patterson already, and I just happened to get caught up in the middle of it."

Frieda sighed heavily and reached out to pat the back of Babs' hand. "Have they given you a date for your hearing yet?"

"It's still two months away. It's going to drive me crazy

being stuck in here for two months, but according to my brief, if it all goes badly, I could get two years. Two years, Frieda. I won't be able to stand it."

Frieda shook her head. "You won't have to. It won't come to that."

Babs took a deep breath and tried to calm herself. "I hope you're right. Have you seen the children?"

Frieda nodded. "I've seen Ruby, and she's a tough girl. She'll be all right. She is missing her mum of course."

Babs sniffed feeling even more sorry for herself. "And Derek?"

Frieda pursed her lips and then said. "No sign of him. He's still at school as far as I know, and Martin hasn't told him. Now, I'll follow your lead, but I was thinking… if he doesn't let the boy know soon, I will personally go down to Surrey and knock on the door of that school. No one will stop me telling Derek what's happened."

Babs smiled tearfully at the thought of Frieda going out of her way like that. She could picture the expression on that snooty headmaster's face if someone like Frieda Longbottom turned up at the gates of his school. The very idea made her smile.

"Thanks, Frieda. Tony has promised to let him know by the end of the week if Martin hasn't."

Frieda nodded, satisfied.

"Tony has been an absolute rock," Babs said. "I misjudged him. I don't mind saying so. I don't know what I would have done without him. He sorted me out a good brief while Martin has just left me to rot in here, Frieda. I swear, when I get out of here, that bastard is going to pay."

Frieda took a bite of her Garibaldi and grinned. "That's my girl."

47

AFTER JIMMY HAD SNEAKED AROUND the back of Martin Morton's club, he wrapped his jumper around his arm and crept up to the back door. There was a window just next to it, and Jimmy reckoned if he could break the window, he'd be able to reach in and unlock the door from the outside.

He looked over his shoulder, making sure nobody was watching. But the streets were empty, and the houses at the back weren't high enough to see over the fence.

He drew his arm back and thrust his elbow through the window pane. It felt good to smash the glass, and as it shattered, Jimmy felt a little thrill of excitement as he imagined Martin's reaction.

He carefully removed the last shards of the glass and then reached through to unbolt the door. It took a little while because although he turned the key in the lock, he hadn't at first realised it was also bolted. Eventually, his fumbling fingers found the bolt and pulled it across, and he was able to open the back door.

He stepped into Mortons' club and held his breath. Waiting. He'd never been inside, and he wondered if his mother had been. Jimmy was sure Martin deserved what he was about to do. The thought of his mother gave Jimmy confidence, and he walked straight into the main area of the club, holding his canister of petrol.

The inside looked ever so posh. There were red velvet seats and gilt-framed mirrors on the wall hung over fancy-patterned wallpaper.

Jimmy could tell that Martin Morton had a lot of money, and it made him feel even more bitter. His poor nan had struggled to bring Jimmy up alone. Money was always tight, and here Martin Morton was absolutely rolling in it and not once had he offered to help them out. Jimmy no longer believed Martin didn't know he was his son. He knew all right. He just didn't care.

Jimmy's hand shook as he reached down and picked up the canister of petrol. Then he took a deep breath and rushed over to one of the large red velvet sofas, pouring the petrol all over it so it soaked into the fabric.

Jimmy was quite fond of the smell of petrol. It reminded him of the cars he loved so much, but now the smell was overwhelming and tickled the back of his throat.

He caught sight of a movement outside, and for a moment, he froze.

Perhaps he was silly for doing this during the day. People were passing by the club all the time, but this was the only period where people wouldn't actually be inside the club. Jimmy didn't want to hurt anybody apart from his father. He wanted to punish Martin Morton by taking away one of the things he loved most in the world — his club.

He needed to get on with it. At any moment, somebody might see him inside or catch sight of little Georgie keeping watch on the other side of the road and wonder what was going on.

He rushed over to the bar and picked up a packet of matches. They had a large M on the front, and on the back, they had the address of Mortons' club. Jimmy smiled and opened up the box of matches as he walked back over to where he'd poured the petrol.

He lit one and held it between his fingers, hesitating.

This was it. There was no going back now.

Feeling a sense of euphoria, Jimmy dropped the match onto the sofa.

There was a fraction of a second when nothing happened, and then suddenly flames leapt up, and Jimmy had to take a step back.

He watched in fascination as the flames flickered along the sofa, consuming it.

The heat was intense, and he took another step backwards. The smoke was already making him cough. He had to get out of there. He rushed out of the back door, and in the yard, Jimmy stood to watch for a moment, mesmerised as he saw the grey smoke creeping along the window frame.

He imagined the look on Martin Morton's face when he saw his club had been destroyed.

Jimmy grinned. He'd found a way to get back at Martin Morton, but he had kept his promise to his nan and Linda by staying away from the horrible man.

Although the fire seemed to draw him in, and he longed to watch as the club burned to the ground, he realised he couldn't stay much longer. People would start to notice the fire soon, and they would definitely be suspicious of two boys loitering nearby.

Jimmy ran back around to the front of the club and then rushed across the street to Georgie.

"Come on," Jimmy said. "We'd better get out of here."

As Jimmy spoke, he wasn't looking at Georgie. He couldn't tear his eyes away from the club, but when Georgie didn't respond, he turned to his friend to see what was wrong.

Georgie was transfixed on the club, his mouth hanging open. Jimmy tugged on Georgie's arm. But he remained rooted to the spot.

"Come on, Georgie. We have to go." Jimmy spoke more urgently this time, continuing to pull on Georgie's arm.

Georgie shook his head. "Jimmy, the girl went back in."

Jimmy frowned. What was Georgie talking about? "The girl? Do you mean Ruby?"

Georgie nodded.

Jimmy felt his heart skip a beat. Georgie must've got it wrong.

"We saw them leave, Georgie. She left with her father."

"Yes, but… But she came back and went inside."

Jimmy couldn't breathe. His chest had suddenly grown tight. Suddenly the smell of petrol on his hands and shirt was overwhelming and felt like it was coating his throat.

"Are you sure she is inside Georgie?"

Georgie nodded.

Jimmy turned and said, "Go and get some help."

Then he ran back towards the club as Georgie ran in the opposite direction to the person he always went to when he was scared: his father.

Georgie ran so fast the soles of his feet stung as they slapped on the pavement, and his chest burned. He flew along Bread Street, bolted across the next road and was just about to head into the alleyway at the back of Narrow Street when he slammed into a wall of solid muscle, which sent him skidding to the floor.

***

Inside the bathroom in the flat above the club, Ruby picked up her lipstick. It was a light, shimmering pink, and in her opinion, much classier than Jemima's choice of bright red. She looked in the mirror and applied some lipstick, looking at herself critically. She couldn't help comparing herself to Jemima and wishing her nose was slightly smaller and her eyes were wider set.

She frowned as she thought she heard something break, it sounded like glass smashing. She paused and listened for a moment, but didn't hear anything else. She shrugged. It must have been something outside.

She slipped the cap back on the lipstick and strolled out

into the main living area of the flat. She peered out of the window, which looked out onto Bread Street, but she couldn't see her father or Jemima from there.

She wondered if she'd read too much into things. But she really hadn't liked the way Jemima had looked at her father. She couldn't imagine what her mother would say if she found out.

Thinking about her mum, Ruby's shoulders slumped. She felt so helpless. She wished there was something she could do. For all her moaning and complaining about her mother, Ruby knew that her mother had been the one person she'd been able to rely on for her entire life.

She loved her father, of course, but for most of her childhood, he hadn't been around. She felt like she had to pretend to be someone else around him, so he'd love her, whereas Ruby's mother knew every single one of her faults and loved her anyway.

From the corner of her eye, she noticed a boy standing on the opposite side of the road, staring up at the window.

Ruby frowned and then waved at him. He didn't respond. He just stood there staring. Weirdo.

She turned to leave. Her father would be waiting to take her to lunch, and she could only hope he hadn't invited Jemima to go with them. Ruby thought that would be more than she could stomach today.

As she walked past the kitchen area, she thought she smelled smoke. She sniffed the air and then walked into the kitchen, checking the oven. But it wasn't on. Then she realised the smell was coming from the front door of the flat.

She felt a stab of panic and quickly ran over to the door to open it. The smell was much stronger, and at the bottom of the staircase, she could see smoke curling up from under the door that led to the bar.

Oh, God. She gave a little cry of panic and then put her hand over her mouth and rushed downstairs. It couldn't be that bad. There had been no sign of fire just a moment ago when she'd entered the club. If it was a small fire, perhaps Ruby could put it out. She imagined how grateful her father would be.

But when she opened the door to the club, the heat was almost overwhelming, and the smoke surrounded her in an instant. It stung her nose and throat, and her eyes streamed.

It was impossible to see. She knew the layout of the club, so she fumbled forward, putting a hand against the wall to try and feel her way to the exit. The panic welled up in her chest.

Everything would be all right if she could just make it to the front door.

She began to cough then as the smoke invaded her lungs. She'd been trying to hold her breath, but it was no good her body needed air, and as she sucked the smoke-filled air down into her lungs, her body rebelled, coughing and choking.

She had to be nearly at the exit, surely. She felt the smooth wood of the bar beneath her fingers and followed it around, heading in the direction she thought would lead to the front door. But then she stumbled over something on the floor and went flying.

The coughing was overwhelming now. The smoke was choking her.

On her hands and knees, Ruby tried to make for the door, but she didn't know which direction she was moving in now, and as panic and adrenaline flooded her system, she screamed out for her father.

48

JIMMY DIDN'T BOTHER RETURNING TO the back door. He thought if Georgie was right, and Ruby really had returned, she would have entered through the front door and wouldn't have locked it behind her.

He couldn't help hoping that somehow Georgie had got it wrong, and Ruby hadn't returned, but when Jimmy was able to turn the handle easily, and the door opened, his stomach sank.

Georgie was right. She was inside.

Jimmy had seen Martin lock it when they'd left, so somebody had definitely come back and unlocked the door.

As he pushed the door open, smoke billowed out, and he had to turn away for a moment.

He took a deep breath of fresh air before running inside, trying to cover his mouth with his shirt. He couldn't believe the fire had consumed everything so fast. It was hot, but that wasn't the main problem. It was the smoke. It was everywhere. It has spread across the entire downstairs area of the club, filling it with thick grey smoke. A faint orange glow from the flames flickered on the walls, and the smoke was so dense Jimmy couldn't even see the bar.

As he staggered around in a circle, trying desperately to see Ruby, his eyes watered, and tears streamed down his face from the stinging smoke. He wanted to squeeze them shut but forced himself to keep them open, stumbling around with his arms out in front of him, desperately looking for Ruby.

Oh, God help him, what had he done?

***

Martin Morton looked at his watch and gave a grunt of impatience. Where the bleeding hell had that daughter of his got to? Jemima was pretty enough to look at, but Martin wasn't interested in her conversation.

He'd allowed her to spend the night at his flat last week, and now she kept giving him puppy dog eyes as if he owed her something.

She was a nice girl, but Martin wasn't keen. He had only just gotten rid of one moaning female from his life, and he didn't want to replace her with another. He wasn't looking for a woman to interfere in his life.

Plus, Jemima was red-haired Freddie's girl, and that opened up a whole other can of worms. Freddie had always been loyal to Martin, and Martin was sure he wouldn't be impressed if he learned that Martin had slept with his precious Jemima. Martin was hoping he wouldn't find out.

"Bloody child," he grumbled. "She gets more like her mother every day. Sorry, Jemima, love, I'd better go and see what's keeping her."

Jemima looked disappointed. "Of course, don't let me hold you up."

Martin walked away feeling irritated. He'd been right. Jemima was giving him the pout and sulky expression as if Martin owed her something. Bloody women. They were more trouble than they were worth. He hoped she would just drop it. Martin couldn't be bothered to deal with the fallout of red-haired Freddie's tantrum if he found out about Martin and his daughter.

Of course, Martin could understand where he was coming from. He had a daughter himself and would kill any bastard that tried it on with her.

Martin frowned as he considered the fact Ruby was only a couple of years younger than Jemima. The thought made him sick to the stomach, which surprised him. Martin didn't care about many people in his life. He did his duty by his mother, but truth be told, he couldn't stand the old bitch. His brother irritated him no end, but Martin supposed, in his own way, he was fond of Tony. He'd never really loved Babs. She was only a trophy. He'd wanted her because it proved he could have whatever woman he desired. All of the men in the East End had admired Babs Morton at one point, and look how she had turned out!

The only people Martin had ever really cared about were Ruby and Derek. He wasn't very good at showing it, and obviously being locked up for the last ten years hadn't really helped develop much of the father-child relationship, but there was a bond there that ran deep.

He tried to push away the thoughts of Ruby having any kind of relationship with boys. He'd castrate any bastard that came within a yard of his daughter.

He knew she was growing up. He'd watched as before his very eyes she appeared to look less and less like a little girl on each visit to the prison, but in his mind, he still saw her as a four-year-old with pigtails. He grinned to himself. Who would have thought it? Martin Morton was turning into a soppy sod.

As he walked, he looked up ahead and saw something odd. A crowd of people had gathered in front of the club. He frowned, and that was when he saw the smoke. The smell hit him in the same moment.

He screamed out his daughter's name, and with his heart in his mouth, he ran towards the club.

***

Breathless, Georgie looked up at the huge hulking figure of Big Tim, who frowned down at him and helped him back to his feet.

"Where are you off to in such a hurry?"

"Fire," Georgie managed to splutter out. "J... Jimmy is inside."

Big Tim gripped Georgie's arm tightly. "Where?" he demanded.

"The M...Morton's club."

Big Tim took off, heading back towards Bread Street, and Georgie followed him as fast as he could, but he couldn't keep up. By the time he turned the corner, Tim was out of sight.

***

Martin Morton looked in horror at the sight of his club up in flames. He scanned the crowd gathered nearby, desperately hoping to see Ruby among them.

She wasn't there.

That meant... He turned back to the club... She had to be in there.

He rushed straight towards the club, ignoring the shouts of people standing around watching.

"What are you doing? Stand back! The fire service is on the way," someone cried out, but Martin ignored them. He didn't have time to wait for the fire service to turn up, not if his daughter was inside.

He pushed through the front doors of the club and headed straight into the heart of the fire. The heat hit him immediately. His stomach flipped over when he saw how thick the smoke was inside. If she was in there, how on earth could she have survived?

He slammed into the bar, stumbling over a bar stool. He roared out his daughter's name as acrid smoke hit the back of his throat and made him cough.

Almost immediately, he bumped into something — someone – Ruby?

But he soon realised it wasn't her. Though his eyes were streaming from the stinging smoke, when he looked down, he recognised Jimmy Diamond.

How that stupid bitch, Mary Diamond, had ever thought it appropriate to bring the boy back to the East End, he would never know. But what on earth was the boy doing in here… Unless…

"Was this you?" Martin demanded. "Did you set my club on fire?"

The boy looked terrified. "I didn't mean it. I didn't think anyone was inside."

The door had remained open after Martin entered, and it had cleared a little of the smoke, but the breeze caused the flames inside to crackle even louder.

Martin stared down at the obnoxious little bastard. Fury flooded his veins. He raised his arm, and with a vicious swing, he gave Jimmy a backhander that sent him spinning to the floor.

Martin didn't have time to deal with the little sod now. He had to find Ruby and get her out before it was too late.

There was a tremendous crash and the sound of smashing glass behind him as the fire reached the bar.

Through the haze, he thought he saw somebody or something on the floor near to the bar.

"Ruby?"

It was her. He rubbed his eyes and kneeled down beside her motionless body. She didn't respond when he shook her.

Martin had never been so scared in his entire life. He scooped her up in his arms and quickly carried her outside, not sparing Jimmy Diamond, who was lying on the ground, a second glance.

49

JIMMY WAS DAZED, AND HE had a sharp pain throbbing in his jaw from where Martin had hit him. He whimpered in pain and fear as he tried to stumble to his feet. He didn't have the strength. A wave of coughing racked his body, and he felt like he was going to cough his guts up.

He could see the light ahead of him. The light had to be coming from the windows at the front of the club, he thought desperately, as he tried to crawl towards it on his hands and knees.

Before he got very far, he felt a pair of large hands on him hauling him to his feet. His first thought was that it was Martin Morton come back to finish him off.

Absolutely terrified, Jimmy tried to squirm out of the man's grip. He kicked out in panic, but he didn't stand a chance against a full-grown man.

Jimmy was lifted in the air and held so tightly, he couldn't even take a breath.

It wasn't until he was hoisted over a huge shoulder that Jimmy realised this wasn't Martin Morton. He tried to turn to see who it was, but he was held in an unyielding grip as he was carried outside.

It wasn't until they were outside, and Jimmy could suck in long lungfuls of fresh air between coughs that he noticed his saviour was Big Tim.

A safe distance away from the club, the big man set him down on his feet and looked at him solemnly.

Jimmy opened his mouth to thank him, but before he could speak, he was bent double with a coughing fit. Tim put his hand on the boy's shoulder as Jimmy's body was wracked with coughs.

As Jimmy gasped for breath, he looked over the other side of the street and could see Martin kneeling over Ruby's body.

Jimmy moved forward, desperate to see if Ruby was alive, but Tim pulled him back just in time.

"It's best if you stay away from the Mortons, lad," Tim said in a low rumble.

Jimmy felt giddy with relief when he saw Ruby sit up. She looked terrible and pale, and Jimmy winced as she vomited on the pavement, but at least she was alive.

His relief didn't last long, though.

Martin stood up and glared at Jimmy. He muttered something Jimmy couldn't hear because he was too far away, but he had no doubt those words were meant for him. Jimmy gulped and shrank back against Tim as Martin drew a finger across his neck and glared fiercely at Jimmy.

Big Tim squeezed his shoulder. "Don't be scared. I won't let him hurt you."

***

"I need to tell Ruby I'm sorry," Jimmy said as he tried to walk towards the Mortons. "I didn't know she was inside."

Tim looked at him sharply. "You did this." It was a statement more than a question, and Jimmy just looked at him miserably.

Tim stared at the boy for a long time and then he finally said, "It's not a good idea, Jimmy. Let's get you home."

"I can't go home. I'm staying at Linda Blums," Jimmy said miserably. "My nan is still in hospital."

Jimmy allowed Tim to pull him away from the Mortons and the crowd of onlookers. He escorted Jimmy all the way to

Linda's house and stood beside the boy as he rapped on the door.

It was only now beginning to sink in that there were going to be consequences of this action. Jimmy had been so caught up in the need to get back at Martin Morton over those horrible things he said about his mother he hadn't really considered what would happen next.

No doubt Tim would tell Linda what Jimmy had done, and she would be so disappointed in him. Maybe she would finally realise that Jimmy was cut from the same cloth as Martin Morton.

Both Linda and his nan thought Jimmy was something special. They thought he had none of Martin's evil in him, but they had been wrong, and Jimmy was sure they would never forgive him once they found out.

Jimmy gazed miserably down at the floor as he waited for Linda to answer.

When she opened the door and wiped her hands on her apron, she blinked in surprise. The sight of Big Tim was enough to give anyone a bit of a shock.

Linda immediately knew something was wrong. "What's happened?"

Jimmy was too ashamed to speak.

Big Tim said, "Mortons' club is on fire."

Jimmy dared to look up at Linda's face to see her reaction and then wished he hadn't. She looked so disappointed.

"Oh, no, Jimmy. What have you done?"

Jimmy opened his mouth to try and explain, but it was no good. He knew he had been stupid, and no matter what he said, he couldn't expect Linda to forgive him.

But then to his surprise, Tim spoke up, "Jimmy was very brave. He went into the club to try and save Ruby Morton."

Linda's gaze darted between Tim's face and Jimmy's as if she couldn't take in the information.

"He's a hero. It's probably best if nobody knows he was

there, though. It's not good for children to have police asking them questions."

Linda seemed to be shocked into complete silence and couldn't respond to Tim. She just stared at him.

"Well, I'll leave you to it. I think I need a bath to get rid of the smell of smoke."

As Tim turned and started to walk away, Jimmy finally found his voice.

"Thank you," he called after the big man, and when Tim turned around, he didn't smile or even look angry with Jimmy. He looked ashamed.

50

THE FOLLOWING DAY, MARTIN STOOD outside the burnt out shell of what used to be his club. He clenched his fists. He'd built the place up with hard graft, and it had thrived, even when he'd been inside. It signified everything Martin Morton was about — his attempt to bring a little class to the East End, and it had only taken one little boy to destroy everything.

He'd spent the previous evening at Ruby's bedside in the hospital, and fortunately, she hadn't suffered any long-lasting after-effects. They had kept her in overnight, but the doctor said she would be allowed out later today.

Last night, a tearful Ruby had begged Martin to get her mother, which of course he couldn't do because Babs had been banged up. Martin had almost felt guilty, but he quickly pushed that feeling away. Ruby had him now, and she didn't need her mother. Babs had had more than enough time to poison the girl against him. He was going to enjoy having his children under his care for once.

Tony still wasn't talking to him over his treatment of Babs. Tony's trouble was that he'd always been too soft. But Martin wasn't bothered. He had no doubt his brother would stop sulking eventually and come around.

His mother had been almost kind last night when Martin had told her what had happened. One of her neighbours had informed her about the fire and the fact that Ruby was in hospital, and she had rushed around as quickly as she could to find out how her granddaughter was faring. He hoped it was a sign of things to come and that his mother had changed her attitude.

Martin would need family he could trust around him as he rebuilt his empire brick by brick.

He knew Tony wouldn't be able to stay away for long either. He wouldn't be able to resist making sure Ruby was okay. He couldn't fault his brother for that. Tony had taken good care of the kids while Martin had been inside.

Martin peered through the window, which was coated with a layer of soot. He was sure there was no way anything inside could be salvaged. The fire brigade had ordered him not to go in the building as it was unsafe, but Martin was determined to see the damage for himself.

He stepped inside the club and turned in a slow circle, taking in the devastation. He looked at the charred and blackened furniture and could have wept.

"Mr. Morton?" A sharp voice cut through Martin's thoughts, and he turned to see Inspector Peel, standing on the threshold.

Bloody hell. Seeing the inspector's ugly mug was not what he needed right now. He didn't want the coppers sniffing around. But they were attracted to Martin. They couldn't seem to stay away. Particularly, Inspector Peel, who seemed to have made it his life's work to target the Mortons.

"What do you want?" Martin asked with a sneer, not bothering to show the man any respect.

Soon enough, he would have officers back on his payroll, and then he would personally target Inspector Peel. The man would soon see who was really the boss of the East End.

"I heard the news," Inspector Peel said with a smirk on his face. "Oh, dear. Look at the state of this place."

Martin pushed past the police inspector, sorely tempted to

teach him a lesson here and now.

"Do you have any idea who did it?" Inspector Peel asked.

"That's what you're paid for. It's your job to figure out who did it," Martin said coldly.

"I did wonder whether you'd done it yourself." Inspector Peel shrugged. "Maybe some kind of insurance scam."

Martin turned on him, absolutely furious. Blood rushed in his ears as he reached for the inspector's collar and shoved him back against the charred and blackened bar.

"My daughter is in hospital. It's not bleeding likely to be me behind the fire, is it?"

A smile stretched across Inspector Peel's face, and Martin realised he was playing straight into the policeman's hands. He'd intended to rile him. Inspector Peel wouldn't be happy until Martin was behind bars again.

With a shove, he pushed the inspector away from him.

"This is private property," Martin growled. "Unless you've got a warrant, I suggest you get the hell out of here before I throw you out."

***

Ruby Morton felt absolutely bloody terrible. Her chest was sore, and her stomach ached from all the coughing. Her throat felt like she'd swallowed shards of glass, and she hadn't been able to face the hospital breakfast they'd brought round early that morning. Despite feeling like she was on her last legs, the doctor told her he was happy for her to leave later that day, and Ruby wasn't about to contradict him. She hated being in the large, dreary ward. The starched white sheets were tucked around her so tightly she felt like she was suffocating.

From her bed, she couldn't even see the window, and she felt like she was in some sort of white prison.

She was impatiently waiting for her father to come back. Although he had spent yesterday evening at the hospital, just outside the ward, refusing to abandon his daughter and threatening violence against anyone who tried to make him leave, she hadn't seen him this morning.

Ruby was secretly pleased he'd insisted on staying last night. She didn't want to be left alone in a place like this. She had truly believed she was going to die, and she had wanted her mother beside her.

Her father must've left at some point in the early morning when Ruby was asleep because there was no sign of him now, and despite demanding that the nurse go and find him, there was still no sign of him.

The ward was full of other patients of varying ages. An old woman in the bed beside her had a huge great oxygen tank next to her to help her breathing.

She had no idea what they had done with her clothes, otherwise, she would have already gotten dressed and made her own way home.

She glanced over to the door, considering how she could make her escape when she saw someone she recognised.

How could he dare show his face in here? Her father told Ruby last night in no uncertain terms that Jimmy Diamond had been responsible for setting the fire in the club. The stupid little boy could have killed her, and now he had the gall to come to the hospital.

He was actually walking up to her bed right now. Ruby shook her head in disbelief.

When Jimmy reached the side of the bed, looking very sheepish indeed, Ruby said, "You've got some nerve showing your face around here."

Jimmy clasped his hands together and turned his dark blue eyes onto her beseechingly. "I'm sorry. I didn't know there was anyone inside. I thought it was empty."

Ruby shrugged. She hadn't thought he intentionally meant to kill her, but that didn't make it all right. "You still shouldn't have done it. You can't go around doing things like that just because someone upsets you."

Jimmy nodded slowly. "I know. I lost my temper."

"That's no excuse," Ruby snapped severely. "You're going to have to watch your back now. My father knows it was you, and he won't let you get away with it. And you shouldn't be hanging around here either. My dad is coming to collect me in a little while."

Jimmy nodded. "I know it was stupid. I just wanted to say how sorry I was and make sure you know that I would never have done it if I'd known you were inside."

She should be furious at him, calling him all sorts of names and possibly throwing things at him as well, but there was something about the boy that made Ruby pity him.

"I'm here because my nan is getting out of hospital today," Jimmy said.

"How interesting," Ruby snapped and then she felt bad when she saw the hurt look on Jimmy's face.

Honestly, what was the matter with her? This boy had almost killed her, and she was feeling sorry for him.

There was something about the boy that Ruby thought was interesting. She wanted to continue the conversation because she was so bored, and it was nice to have someone to talk to, but she couldn't risk it because she knew her dad would be there soon. And that meant a run in between Jimmy and her father, and for some reason, Ruby wasn't keen to witness that.

Perhaps it was because she'd always felt a little bit on the outside of her own family, so she understood how Jimmy's feelings had been hurt.

Ruby nodded. "Look, I'm not going to hold a grudge, but my father will. My advice is to keep out of his way as much as you can."

"But I'm only a boy. You don't think he'd hurt a child, do you?"

Ruby shrugged. That was a hard question. To be honest, she didn't know. Her father had been away for so long she felt like she didn't really know him all that well. She would like to think he would never harm a child, but she wasn't convinced and didn't believe Jimmy should take the risk.

Out of the corner of her eye, Ruby saw somebody else entering the ward. She turned and gasped at the sight of Grandma Violet striding towards them.

"That's my grandma. You'd better get out of here," Ruby warned.

Jimmy didn't need telling twice. He turned on his heel and quickly brushed past the stern-looking woman who gave him the evil eye.

Ruby let out a sigh of relief when Grandma Violet didn't accost him. Perhaps she didn't realise who he was.

"Come on, Ruby. I've come to collect you. Get your things together. Where are your clothes?"

Ruby shrugged, "I don't know. I think one of the nurses must've taken them."

Violet clicked her fingers, and one of the nurses at the station looked up and narrowed her eyes at being beckoned in such a fashion. But she got to her feet and listened politely to Violet's demands for her granddaughter's clothes. Within two minutes, Ruby's clothes had been returned, and she was dressed and ready to go.

"I thought Dad was coming to pick me up," Ruby said not bothering to hide her disappointment.

Violet pursed her lips and nodded. She was a small woman and at least six inches shorter than Ruby.

"He had a bit of business to attend to," Violet said. "Besides, I wanted to have a word with you."

Ruby frowned as her grandmother handed her coat to her.

"What did you want to talk to me about?" Ruby asked suspiciously.

"Your mother."

Ruby turned to her eagerly. She'd been anxious for news about her mother, but nobody had wanted to tell her what had happened. "How is she? Is she coming home?"

"She won't be home for the foreseeable," Grandma Violet

said in her usual blunt fashion. She linked her arm through Ruby's and pulled her along briskly.

Ruby felt a little dizzy as she did her best to keep up with Violet's fast pace. She walked very fast for someone with such short legs, Ruby thought.

"You're not a baby, Ruby. I know that your father would like to keep all of this from you because he thinks you're too young to understand. But I think he's wrong. You have every right to understand what's going on in your family."

Ruby nodded. She couldn't agree more.

"So I will tell you everything you want to know, but in exchange, you are to behave like a Morton. There are to be no tears, no tantrums and no shouting the odds. Do we understand each other?"

Ruby's chest was hurting as she marched along the hospital corridor with Violet, but she nodded her head, eager to hear what her grandmother was going to say.

"I've never believed in secrets. I think they do a family more harm than good. So fire away. Ask your first question."

They came to the hospital's main entrance, and beside the reception desk, Ruby had to pause to catch her breath. She turned to her grandmother. "Tell me what's happening with my mother."

"She made a mistake. A silly one. It looks like she's been fitted up, and she is going to go away for a little while. The hearing is in a months' time, and it's looking like she'll be sent down for at least two years."

Ruby's legs trembled, and she thought for a moment she might faint. Two years? For a moment, she couldn't say anything, and then when her mind slowly processed what her grandmother was saying, she asked, "When can I see her?"

"As soon as she has been moved to the main prison. Probably next week."

Ruby nodded. She was shocked to the core, but she was

grateful her grandmother was telling the truth.

"Does Derek know?" Ruby asked.

Her grandmother shook her head. "Your father thought it best not to worry him while he is at school."

Ruby wasn't so sure how she felt about that. If she were Derek, she would want to know.

Even though Derek had shown he preferred his school to family these days, Ruby knew he would want to know what had happened to his mother, and he would be very angry when he found out it had been kept from him. But as Ruby had promised, she didn't lose her temper or even say how unfair she thought it was. She liked the new improved Grandma Violet, who was so honest and open with the truth.

"Are you ready to carry on, Ruby?" Grandma Violet asked, offering her arm again. "Freddie's waiting in the motor, just outside. He is going to drive us home."

Ruby nodded and slid her arm through Grandma Violet's as a thought occurred to her. It was something that had been bothering her for a little while: Her father's strong reaction towards Jimmy.

Her mother had always been fond of saying there's no smoke without fire, and if that was true, was there some truth in the rumours suggesting Jimmy was her father's son.

"What about Jimmy Diamond?" Ruby asked, hardly daring to look her grandmother in the eye.

She was so convinced her grandmother would laugh and tell her she had a fanciful imagination, so the old woman's response came as a complete surprise.

Grandma Violet sniffed. "You're not a naive little girl anymore, Ruby. The boy is obviously Martin's son. He's even got the same dimple in his chin, for goodness sake."

Ruby's eyes widened, and she felt like she was going to pass out as a coughing fit suddenly engulfed her.

Grandma Violet waited patiently and then smoothed Ruby's hair back from her face. "It's probably quite a lot to take in, but your father is certainly not a saint."

Ruby's mind was reeling. That meant Jimmy Diamond was her half-brother. So why had her father been so nasty to him?

"Are you really telling me that Jimmy is my brother?"

"I'm telling you he's a bastard," Grandma Violet said haughtily. "Now, I'll treat you like a grown-up so long as you act like one. I'm going to take good care of you while your mother is inside."

Ruby shook her head. "I thought you just had a big argument with Dad? And didn't want anything else to do with us."

"We've come to an understanding," Violet Morton said. "Things are going to change around here, Ruby. You can either help us or make life difficult. But I would highly recommend you don't choose the latter option."

Ruby was too shocked to respond. She couldn't believe that all the time she'd been growing up, she had a little brother living just around the corner, and nobody had bothered to tell her.

She looked at her grandmother's pinched expression and began to wonder whether Derek was right to stay away from the East End. She had a feeling things were going to get a lot worse around here before they got better.

51

JIMMY HELPED HIS NAN ON with her coat. "Are you sure you'll be all right getting the bus, Nan?"

Jimmy's nan nodded, but he had his doubts. She seemed very shaky on her feet.

"I'll be all right," she said. "We'll just have to take it slow."

"The nurse did say that there was a hospital transport on this afternoon if we didn't mind waiting."

Mary Diamond shook her head firmly. "I'm not staying in this place any longer than I have to. The bus suits me just fine."

His nan waved and called goodbye to a couple of the other patients as Jimmy helped her out of the ward. She stopped beside the nurses' station to thank them for taking such good care of her, and then with Jimmy holding her small bag of belongings, they hobbled out into the corridor.

Jimmy looked up in surprise. Leaning against the wall of the corridor, dressed in a long overcoat, was Dave Carter.

When he saw Jimmy and his nan, Dave smiled and walked towards them.

He took the bag from Jimmy and held out his arm for Mary Diamond.

"I hoped you might permit me to give you a lift home," Dave said. "Your grandson has been a very good friend to my son, and it would be an honour if I could drive you home today."

Jimmy's nan smiled. "That is ever so kind of you. Jimmy and I were just wondering how we would manage with the bus."

Dave returned her smile, and as Mary slid her arm through his, he helped them down the corridor, supporting Mary's weight.

Jimmy couldn't utter a word. He wondered how much Georgie or Big Tim had told Dave about what happened at Mortons' club. For the most part, Jimmy was trying to keep his head down and avoiding everyone.

Although Linda thought he was some kind of hero after trying to save Ruby, she still didn't know the whole story. Jimmy felt anxious about the whole thing. He was convinced that soon everybody would find out exactly what he had done, and they would hate him for it.

Dave chatted away amiably with Jimmy's nan. When Jimmy first started washing the cars at Dave's workshop, Mary hadn't been very keen on the idea at all, but to hear her talk to Dave Carter now, anyone would think they were old friends.

Jimmy shook his head. He didn't think he would ever understand grown-ups.

Dave had a brand-new Ford waiting for them. He'd parked just up around the corner from the hospital. He told Jimmy and Mary to wait at the front entrance and brought the car round to them.

It was a smashing motor. Jimmy liked the Ford Zodiacs, and this one was really something special, with its gleaming two tone paintwork in red and cream.

"Oh, my," his nan exclaimed as she sunk into the comfortable back seat. "This is lovely, isn't it, Jimmy?"

Jimmy grinned at her enthusiastic reaction, and after she was safely settled in the back, he joined Dave in the front, slipping into the passenger's seat.

Jimmy was determined that he would have a motor just like this when he was older. He wanted money and power. He didn't want to be like Martin Morton, but he wouldn't mind growing up to be just like Dave Carter.

It didn't take them long to get from The London Hospital back to their home in Poplar. And to Jimmy's surprise, Dave didn't simply drop them at the door and leave them to it. Instead, he helped Jimmy get Mary inside and settled.

"Linda made us a stew, nan," Jimmy said. "She left it in the kitchen for us to heat through later."

His nan sank back into her favourite armchair with a sigh of contentment. "That was very kind of Linda. I'll pop round when I'm feeling a bit better and say thank you. She did right by us when I was ill. You don't forget things like that."

Jimmy told Dave and his nan he would make the tea and headed off to the kitchen.

He could hear Dave and his nan talking in the front room, and it felt nice. It warmed his heart to see his nan sitting in her armchair again. He had missed her so much when she'd been in hospital. It seemed like everything in Jimmy's life had spiralled out of control starting from the moment his nan had been taken ill.

He hoped things could get back to normal now. No doubt, Martin was still out for his blood, but Big Tim was on Jimmy's side, and Jimmy hoped that if he was good from now on, and didn't get into any more trouble, then maybe things could go back to how they used to be.

As Jimmy poured boiling water into the teapot, he heard Dave enter the kitchen behind him.

He replaced the lid on the teapot and then turned to look at Dave, who wore a serious expression.

Dave pulled out a chair from the kitchen table and sat down. "I hear you've done something stupid, Jimmy. Do you want to tell me about it?"

Jimmy shook his head urgently. No. He didn't want to talk

about it ever again.

Dave tilted his head to one side, studying Jimmy. "Have you ever heard the saying that only fools rush in?"

Jimmy wasn't sure where this was heading, but he nodded slowly.

"You won't get anywhere in this world if you're always acting with a hothead," Dave told him. "You've got a lot to learn, son."

Jimmy wondered whether he could confide in Dave. Could he trust him? Or had Big Tim and Georgie already told him everything?

If Dave knew he had started the fire, then Jimmy wanted him to know his reasons behind it. He didn't want him to think that he was just a young hooligan.

"I think Martin Morton killed my mother," Jimmy blurted out.

Dave didn't contradict him or even try to reassure him, which is what Jimmy had expected him to do.

Instead, he reached over and patted Jimmy on the shoulder. "You've got a lot to learn, Jimmy. The first lesson is that revenge is a dish best served cold. You can't rush things like this. But if you stick with me, son. I'll see you get your revenge."

Jimmy blinked in surprise. He knew, from the chatter around the workshop and from what little Georgie had said, that Dave Carter did not like Martin Morton. He might be young, but even Jimmy understood that Dave Carter would be a powerful friend to have in his corner.

Jimmy nodded his agreement, and Dave smiled. "Good lad. If you feel the temptation to take matters into your own hands again, you come to me first. Deal?"

Jimmy considered it for a moment and then nodded. "Deal."

52

BABS MORTON SAT ON THE narrow bed in her cell. She'd been in Holloway for a few weeks now. At first, they'd put her in one of the shared cells, and that hadn't worked out too well. Babs had kicked up such a stink eventually they'd moved her to one of the single cells.

But now she was regretting being so hasty. Although they had time in the communal areas and were allowed to have some time outside in the yard, most of her days were spent staring at the dreary, blue walls with nobody to talk to.

The only thing that kept Babs going was thinking up ideas for her revenge.

Two years was a bloody long time, but Babs knew she could get through it.

It had broken her heart when Ruby had come to visit her. She could tell the girl was confused, and she knew that behind-the-scenes Martin and his horrible mother were pulling the strings.

The night after Ruby's first visit, Babs cried herself to sleep. Tony swore blind he'd told Derek his mother was in prison, but she hadn't seen Derek yet, or even received a letter. It was almost as if her son had fallen off the face of the earth.

When she talked the matter over with Frieda, the older woman had nodded and said perhaps Derek was rather taken with his new posh way of life and suggested he was ashamed of his old East End family.

But Babs couldn't believe Derek had turned his back on her for good. She just needed to get out of this place, and she knew everything could be made right again between her and her children. But for now, it was a waiting game. A matter of counting down the time until she could get out.

She bit down hard on her thumbnail.

If any of her old neighbours or friends could have seen her now, they wouldn't recognise her. She had almost an inch of dark roots on show and couldn't be bothered to use any makeup. Some of the other women smuggled certain cosmetic items in, but Babs didn't see the point.

Her once beautifully painted nails, which used to be her pride and joy, were now bitten down to the quick as she chewed on them constantly, thinking over how she could payback her treacherous husband and that bastard, Dave Carter.

When Babs got out of there, she was going to teach them a lesson they wouldn't forget in a hurry. The pair of them had better watch out because they wouldn't know what had hit them.

She crossed her arms over her chest and smiled. Oh yes, Babs Morton would be back, and then the whole of the East End better watch out.

Thank you for reading East End Diamond! If you enjoyed this book, don't forget to sign up to the mailing list : http://www.danioakleybooks.com/newsletter/ so you are first to know when the next book is out.

It would really help me if you left a review, telling me what characters you would enjoy to read about in the next book. Reviews help the book's visibility and help me see what my readers would like to read next. So if you have the time to leave a review that would be fantastic!

I really do appreciate each and every review. Thank you so much for reading.

I also write under the name D.S Butler and you can find a list of those books on the next page.

Dani x

Dani Oakley also writes police procedurals under the name D. S. Butler. You can find all the books on Amazon.

Here is the series reading order:

- Deadly Obsession
- Deadly Motive
- Deadly Revenge
- Deadly Justice
- Deadly Ritual
- Deadly Payback

If you would like to be informed when the new Dani Oakley book is released, sign up for the newsletter: http://www.danioakleybooks.com/newsletter/

Printed in Great Britain
by Amazon

57915617R00215